Max Barry is an Australian who pretended to sell high-end computer systems for Hewlett-Packard while secretly writing his first novel. He has lectured in marketing at two universities, but came to his senses. Born March 18, 1973, he now lives in Melbourne, Australia, with his wife and three million other people. Although only his wife lives in the same house. He writes full-time, the advantage of which being that he can do it wearing only boxer shorts.

JENNIFER GOVERNMENT

MAX BARRY

An *Abacus* Book

First published in Great Britain by Abacus 2003
Reprinted 2003 (twice)

Copyright © 2003 by Max Barry

The moral right of the author has been asserted.

A CIP catalogue record for this book
is available from the British Library.

ISBN: 0 349 11598 2

Typeset in Baskerville by M Rules
Printed and bound in Great Britain
by Clays Ltd, St Ives plc

Abacus
An imprint of
Time Warner Books UK
Brettenham House
Lancaster Place
London WC2E 7EN

www.TimeWarnerBooks.co.uk

For Charles Thiesen
Who really, really wanted me to call it 'Capitalizm'

With money we will get men, Caesar said, and with men
we will get money.

THOMAS JEFFERSON, 1784

. . . a wise and frugal government, which shall restrain
men from injuring one another, which shall leave them
otherwise free to regulate their own pursuits of industry
and improvement, and shall not take from the mouth of
labor the bread it has earned. This is the sum of good
government.

THOMAS JEFFERSON, 1801

PUBLISHER'S NOTE

There are a lot of real company names and trademarks in this book, most in situations that you will not see on the covers of any annual reports. That's because this is a novel, and the things that happen in it aren't true. It is set in the future, in an imaginary world. In the novel, for example, Australia is part of the USA, and this is clearly not true. The names and products mentioned are used simply to illustrate the increasingly important role played by large corporations in the future and not to denigrate them in any way. However, some people (whom we shall call 'lawyers') get very uptight when you describe large corporations masterminding murders. So let's be clear: this is a work of fiction set in the future. The actions depicted are not real or based on real events. It is not suggested that anyone involved with any of the companies referred to would behave as described in these futuristic, imaginary scenes. Any resemblance to actual people is coincidental and wholly unintentional and the use of real company and product names is for literary effect only and definitely without permission.

PART ONE

1 NIKE

Hack first heard about Jennifer Government at the watercooler. He was only there because the one on his floor was out; Legal was going to come down on Nature's Springs like a ton of shit, you could bet on that. Hack was a Merchandise Distribution Officer. This meant when Nike made up a bunch of posters, or caps, or beach towels, Hack had to send them to the right place. Also, if someone called up complaining about missing posters, or caps, or beach towels, Hack had to take the call. It wasn't as exciting as it used to be.

'It's a *calamity*,' a man at the watercooler said. 'Four days away from launch and Jennifer Government's all over my ass.'

'Jee-sus,' his companion said. 'That's gotta suck.'

'It means we have to move fast.' He looked at Hack, who was filling his cup. 'Hi there.'

Hack looked up. They were smiling at him as if he was an equal – but of course, Hack was on the wrong floor. They didn't know he was just a Merc Officer. 'Hi.'

'Haven't seen you around before,' the *calamity* guy said. 'You new?'

'No. I work in Merc.'

'Oh.' His nose wrinkled.

'Our cooler's out,' Hack said. He turned away quickly.

'Hey, wait up,' the suit said. 'You ever do any marketing work?'

'Uh,' he said, not sure if this was a joke. 'No.'

The suits looked at each other. The *calamity* guy shrugged. Then they stuck out their hands. 'I'm John Nike, Guerrilla Marketing Operative, New Products.'

'And I'm John Nike, Guerrilla Marketing Vice-President, New Products,' the other suit said.

'Hack Nike,' Hack said, shaking.

'Hack, I'm empowered to make midrange labor-contracting decisions,' Vice-President John said. 'You interested in some work?'

'Some . . .' He felt his throat thicken. 'Marketing work?'

'On a case-by-case basis, of course,' the other John said.

Hack started to cry.

'There,' a John said, handing him a handkerchief. 'You feel better?'

Hack nodded, shamed. 'I'm sorry.'

'Hey, don't worry about it,' Vice-President John said. 'Career change can be very stressful. I read that somewhere.'

'Here's the paperwork.' The other John handed him a pen and a sheaf of papers. The first page said CONTRACT TO PERFORM SERVICE, and the others were in type too small to read.

Hack hesitated. 'You want me to sign this now?'

'It's nothing to worry about. Just the usual noncompetes and nondisclosure agreements.'

'Yeah, but . . .' Companies were getting a lot tougher on labor contracts these days; Hack had heard stories. At Adidas, if you quit your job and your replacement wasn't as competent, they sued you for lost profits.

4

'Hack, we need someone who can make snap decisions. A fast mover.'

'Someone who can get things done. With a minimum of fucking around.'

'If that's not your style, well . . . let's forget we spoke. No harm done. You stick to Merchandising.' Vice-President John reached for the contract.

'I can sign it now,' Hack said, tightening his grip.

'It's totally up to you,' the other John said. He took the chair beside Hack, crossed his legs, and rested his hands at the juncture, smiling. Both Johns had good smiles, Hack noticed. He guessed everyone in marketing did. They had pretty similar faces, too. 'Just at the bottom there.'

Hack signed.

'Also there,' the other John said. 'And on the next page . . . and one there. And there.'

'Glad to have you on board, Hack.' Vice-President John took the contract, opened a drawer, and dropped it inside. 'Now. What do you know about Nike Mercurys?'

Hack blinked. 'They're our latest product. I haven't actually seen a pair, but . . . I heard they're great.'

The Johns smiled. 'We started selling Mercurys six months ago. You know how many pairs we've shifted since then?'

Hack shook his head. They cost thousands of dollars a pair, but that wouldn't stop people from buying them. They were the hottest sneakers in the world. 'A million?'

'Two hundred.'

'Two hundred million?'

'No. Two hundred pairs.'

'John here,' the other John said, 'pioneered the concept of marketing by refusing to sell any products. It drives the market *insane*.'

'And now it's time to cash in. On Friday we're gonna dump

four hundred thousand pairs on the market at two and a half grand each.'

'Which, since they cost us – what was it?'

'Eighty-five.'

'Since they cost us eighty-five cents to manufacture, gives us a gross margin of around one billion dollars.' He looked at Vice-President John. 'It's a brilliant campaign.'

'It's really just common sense,' John said. 'But here's the thing, Hack: if people realize every mall in the country's got Mercurys, we'll lose all that prestige we've worked so hard to build. Am I right?'

'Yeah.' Hack hoped he sounded confident. He didn't really understand marketing.

'So you know what we're going to do?'

He shook his head.

'We're going to shoot them,' Vice-President John said. 'We're going to kill anyone who buys a pair.'

Silence. 'What?' Hack said.

The other John said, 'Well, not everyone, obviously. We figure we only have to plug . . . what did we decide? Five?'

'Ten,' Vice-President John said. 'To be safe.'

'Right. We take out ten customers, make it look like ghetto kids, and we've got street cred coming out our asses. I bet we shift our inventory within twenty-four hours.'

'I remember when you could always rely on those little street kids to pop a few people for the latest Nikes,' Vice-President John said. 'Now people get mugged for Reeboks, for Adidas – for *generics*, for Christ's sake.'

'The ghettos have no fashion sense anymore,' the other John said. 'I swear, they'll wear anything.'

'It's a disgrace. Anyway, Hack, I think you get the point. This is a groundbreaking campaign.'

'Talk about edgy,' the other John said. 'This *defines* edgy.'

'Um . . .' Hack said. He swallowed. 'Isn't this kind of . . . illegal?'

'He wants to know if it's illegal,' the other John said, amused. 'You're a funny guy, Hack. Yes, it's illegal, killing people without their consent, that's very illegal.'

Vice-President John said, 'But the question is: what does it cost? Even if we get found out, we burn a few million on legal fees, we get fined a few million more . . . bottom-line, we're still way out in front.'

Hack had a question he very much didn't want to ask. 'So . . . this contract . . . what does it say I'll do?'

The John beside him folded his hands. 'Well, Hack, we've explained our business plan. What we want you to do is . . .'

'Execute it,' Vice-President John said.

2 McDONALD'S

Until she stood in front of them, Hayley didn't realize how many of her classmates were blond. It was like a beach out there. She'd missed the trend. Hayley would have to hotfoot it to a hairdresser after school.

'When you're ready,' the teacher said.

She looked at her note cards and took a breath. 'Why I Love America, by Hayley McDonald's. America is the greatest group of countries in the world because we have freedom. In countries like France, where the Government isn't privatized, they still have to pay tax and do whatever the Government says, which would really suck. In USA countries, we respect individual rights and let people do whatever they want.'

The teacher jotted something in his folder. McDonald's-sponsored schools were cheap like that: at Pepsi schools, everyone had notebook computers. Also their uniforms were much better. It was so hard to be cool with the Golden Arches on your back.

'Before USA countries abolished tax, if you didn't have a job, the Government took money from working people and gave it to you. So, like, the more useless you were, the more money you got.' No response from her classmates. Even the teacher didn't smile. Hayley was surprised: she'd thought that one was a crack-up.

'But now America has all the best companies and all the money because everyone works and the Government can't spend money on stupid things like advertising and elections and making new laws. They just stop people stealing or hurting each other and everything else is taken care of by the private sector, which everyone knows is more efficient.' She looked at her notes: yep, that was it. 'Finally I would like to say that America is the greatest group of countries in the world and I am proud to live in the Australian Territories of the USA!'

A smattering of applause. It was the eighth talk this period: she guessed it was getting harder to work up enthusiasm for capitalizm. Hayley headed for her seat.

'Hold it,' the teacher said. 'I have questions.'

'Oh,' Hayley said.

'Are there any positive aspects to tax?'

She relaxed: a gimme question. 'Some people say tax is good because it gives money to people who don't have any. But those people must be lazy or stupid, so why should they get other people's money? Obviously the answer is no.'

The teacher blinked. He made a note. That must have been an impressive answer, Hayley thought. 'What about social justice?'

'What?'

'Is it fair that some people should be rich while others have nothing?'

She shifted from one foot to the other. She was just remembering: this teacher had a thing about poor people. He was always bringing them up. 'Um, yeah, it's fair. Because if I study really hard for a test and get an A and Emily doesn't and fails' – renewed interest from the class; Emily raised blond eyebrows – 'then it's not fair to take some of my marks and give them to her, is it?'

The teacher frowned. Hayley felt a flash of panic. 'Another thing, in non-USA countries they want everyone to be the same, so if your sister is born blind, then they blind you, too, to make it even. But how unfair is that? I would much rather be an American than a European Union . . . person.' She gave the class a big smile. They clapped, much more enthusiastically than before. She added hopefully, 'Is that all?'

'Yes. Thank you.'

Relief! She started walking. A cute boy in the third row winked at her.

The teacher said, 'Although, Hayley, they don't really blind people in non-USA countries.'

Hayley stopped. 'Well, that's kind of hypocritical, isn't it?'

The class cheered. The teacher opened his mouth, then shut it. Hayley took her seat. *Kick ass,* she thought. She had aced this test.

3 THE POLICE

Jack sat in traffic, biting his nails. This had not been a good day. He was beginning to think that visiting the marketing floor for a cup of water was the worst mistake he'd ever made.

He turned into a side street and parked his Toyota. It rattled angrily and let loose a puff of black smoke. Hack really needed a new car. Maybe if this job paid off, he could move out of St. Kilda. He could get an apartment with some space, maybe some natural light—

He shook his head angrily. What was he thinking? He wasn't going to *shoot* anyone. Not even for a better apartment.

He climbed the stairs to the second floor and let himself in. Violet was sitting cross-legged on the living-room floor with her notebook computer in her lap. Violet was his girlfriend. She was the only unemployed person he had ever met, not counting homeless people who asked him for money. She was an entrepreneur. Violet was probably going to be rich one day: she was smart and determined. Sometimes Hack wasn't sure why they were together.

He dropped his briefcase and shrugged off his jacket. The table was littered with bills. Hack hadn't bargained very well in his last performance evaluation and it was really biting him now. 'Violet?'

'Mmm?'

'Can we talk?'

'Is it important?'

'Yes.'

She frowned. Hack waited. Violet didn't like being disturbed during her work. She didn't like being disturbed at all. She was short and thin and had long brown hair, which made her look much more fragile than she was. 'What's up?'

He sat on the sofa. 'I did something stupid.'

'Oh, Hack, not again.'

Hack had missed a couple of turnoffs on the way home lately: last Tuesday he'd gotten himself onto a premium road and eaten through eleven dollars in tolls before he found an exit. 'No, something really stupid.'

'What happened?'

'Well, I got offered some work . . . some marketing work—'

'That's great! We could really use the extra money.'

'—and I signed a contract without reading it.'

Pause. 'Oh,' Violet said. 'Well, it might be okay—'

'It says I have to kill people. It's some kind of promotional campaign. I have to, um, kill ten people.'

For a moment she said nothing. He hoped she wasn't going to shout at him. 'I'd better look at that contract.'

He dropped his head.

'You don't have a copy?'

'No.'

'Oh, *Hack*.'

'I'm sorry.'

Violet chewed her lip. 'Well, you can't go through with it. The Government's not as pussy as people think. They'd get you for sure. But then, you don't know what the penalties in that contract are . . . I think you should go to the Police.'

'Really?'

'There's a station on Chapel Street. When are you meant to . . . do it?'

'Friday.'

'You should go. Right now.'

'Okay. You're right.' He picked up his jacket. 'Thanks, Violet.'

'Why does this kind of thing always happen to you, Hack?'

'I don't know,' he said. He felt emotional. He shut the door carefully behind him.

The station was only a few blocks away, and as it came into view he began to feel hopeful. The building was lit up in blue neon, with THE POLICE in enormous letters and a swirling light above that. If anyone could help him out of this situation, it would be someone who worked in a place like this.

The doors slid open and he walked up to the reception desk. A woman in uniform – either a real cop or a receptionist dressed in theme, Hack didn't know which – smiled. Playing over the PA system was the song from their TV ads, 'Every Breath You Take.'

'Good evening, how can I help you?'

'I have a matter I'd like to discuss with an officer, please.'

'May I ask the nature of your problem?'

'Um,' he said. 'I've been contracted to kill someone. Some people, actually.'

The receptionist's eyebrows rose a fraction, then settled. Hack felt relieved. He didn't want to be chastised by the receptionist. 'Take a seat, sir. An officer will be right with you.'

Hack dropped into a soft blue chair and waited. A few minutes later, a cop came out and stopped in front of him. Hack rose.

'I'm Senior Sergeant Pearson Police,' the man said. He shook Hack's hand firmly. He had a small, trim mustache but otherwise looked pretty capable. 'Please accompany me.'

Hack followed him down a plushly carpeted hallway to a small, professional-looking meeting room. On the wall were pictures of cops escorting crims out of buildings, in front of courthouses, and busting protestor heads outside some corporate building. As Pearson took a seat, Hack caught a glimpse of handcuffs and a pistol.

'So what's your problem?' He flipped open a notebook.

Hack told him the whole story. When he was done, Pearson was silent for a long time. Finally Hack couldn't take it anymore. 'What do you think?'

Pearson pressed his fingers together. 'Well, I appreciate you coming forward with this. You did the right thing. Now let me take you through your options.' He closed the notebook and put it to one side. 'First, you can go ahead with this Nike contract. Shoot some people. In that case, what we'd do, if we were retained by the Government or one of the victims' representatives, is attempt to apprehend you.'

'Yes.'

'And we *would* apprehend you, Hack. We have an eighty-six percent success rate. With someone like you, inexperienced, no backing, we'd have you within hours. So I strongly recommend you do not carry out this contract.'

'I know,' Hack said. 'I should have it read it, but—'

'Second, you can refuse to go through with it. That would expose you to whatever penalties are in that contract. And I'm sure I don't need to tell you they could be harsh. Very harsh indeed.'

Hack nodded. He hoped Pearson wasn't finished.

'Here's your alternative.' Pearson leaned forward. 'You subcontract the slayings to us. We fulfill your contract, at a very competitive rate. As you probably know from our advertisements, your identity is totally protected. If the Government comes after us, it's not your problem.'

Hack said, 'That's my only alternative?'

'Well, if you had a copy of the contract, I'd tell you to go talk to our Legal branch. But you don't, do you?'

'Um, no.' He hesitated. 'How much would it be to . . .'

Pearson blew out his cheeks. 'Depends. You don't need specific individuals done, right? Just people who buy these Mercury shoes.'

'Yes.'

'Well, that's cheaper. We can make sure we don't take out anyone with means. For, you know, retribution. And you need ten capped, so there's a bulk discount. We could do this for, say, one-fifty.'

'One-fifty what?'

'Grand,' Pearson said. 'One-fifty grand, Hack, what do you think?'

He felt despair. 'I'm a Merc Officer, I earn thirty-three a year—'

'Come on, now,' Pearson said, looking pained. 'Don't start that.'

'I'm sorry.' His vision blurred. Twice in one day! He was falling apart.

'Look, final offer: one-thirty. You can go talk to the NRA but you won't get better than that, I promise. Now do we have a deal?'

'Yes,' Hack said. He wiped angrily at his face as Pearson began to draw up the contract.

4 MITSUI

The alarm clock said: '—*and rumors of strong profits. Microsoft tumbled to twenty-two after the company announced shipping delays would . . .*'

Buy couldn't breathe. His chest ached. He thought: *I'm having a heart attack!* Then he remembered. No. Not a heart attack.

He staggered into the bathroom and looked in the mirror. His face stared back at him. It didn't look impressed. He said, 'I am a great person. Today is a great day.'

Taped to a corner of the mirror was a piece of paper. It said:

I AM A GREAT PERSON

TODAY IS A GREAT DAY

EVERY OBSTACLE IS AN OPPORTUNITY

It was Monday, October 27, and therefore the fifth-last working day of Mitsui Corporation's financial year. Buy was an Account Manager, Competitive Accounts Group, Southern Region, which meant he was a stockbroker, which meant he was a salesman. He had a $4.2 million quota. That hadn't looked like a problem after an outstanding first quarter and a solid Q2, but in Q3 they'd reorganized some accounts away from him, and Q4 had been *terrible*, a catastrophe. Buy had five days to find half a million dollars.

He showered and padded out to the living room. His apartment looked over the ExxonMobil Botanical Gardens and beyond that the city of Melbourne, USA (Australia). It was a little after six, and the office towers were flaring orange in the dawn sun. The sky was a solid blue expanse. Buy had stopped seeing it in Q3.

He ate toast and washed it down with juice. He dressed and caught the elevator to the parking lot, where his Jeep was waiting for him. Jeeps were one of the safest vehicles on the road, Buy had read; safe for people in the Jeep, anyway. He roared out onto the street.

The cheap roads were clogged, even at six-thirty, but he was only four blocks from a premium Bechtel freeway and that was eight lanes, two dollars a mile, and no speed limit. He sped past office buildings and factories with the needle on 95 mph.

He pulled into the Mitsui parking lot and caught the elevator to the sixth-floor cube farm. Brokers didn't get proper offices, or even walls above shoulder height, at least not in Competitive Accounts. In his first year here, Buy had been grateful for that, because it was so easy to turn to a coworker for help. Now it annoyed him, for the same reason.

Hamish, who ran the night shift from Buy's desk, was pulling off his headphones. 'Hey, Buy.'

'Hey.' Hamish looked relaxed and happy. Buy felt a flash of jealousy. 'How's the market?'

'Even jumpier than you. Take it easy, buddy. You'll get there.'

'Yeah, I know.' He tried to sound sincere. Hamish patted him on the back and left for what was no doubt a day of lying on the sofa watching football, or activities equally casual and stress-free. Hamish had made quota six weeks ago, and Buy was finding it harder and harder to not hate him.

Buy slid into the seat, plugged in his telephone headset, and dialed. Taped to his cubicle wall was a note he'd written in Q1:

SUCCESS = 500 CALLS PER DAY

He stared at it while his client's phone rang. Buy was starting to think that success was a big crapshoot.

In France, he wouldn't be in a position like this. Of course, in France he wouldn't have received last year's paycheck of $347,000, either. That was why he'd left: the EU was a socialist morass, with taxes and unemployment and public everything. Until recently, Buy had thought that moving to a USA country was the best move he'd ever made, with the possible exception of changing his name from Jean-Paul.

'You've reached Michael Microsoft, Project Manager Business Solutions Division. Leave a message and I'll get back to you.'

Buy started rambling about market indicators pointing to increasing volatility, clicking through his e-mail at the same time. There was a message from a friend who now worked for US Alliance, one of the big customer loyalty programs:

> Buy—
>
> A priest and a stockbroker meet at the Pearly Gates. Saint Peter gives the broker a golden harp and silk robes and lets him into Heaven. Then he gives the priest a rusty trumpet and some old rags. The priest says, 'Hey, how come the stockbroker gets the harp and robes?' And Saint Peter says, 'Because while you preached, people slept – but his clients, now, they prayed.'
>
> —Sami.
>
> P.S. We just passed 200 million subscribers at US Alliance

and are about to sign on the NRA (still hush-hush). But I guess
that's not as exciting as making monkey trades for Mitsui, huh?

Buy looked at his watch. It was noon in L.A. He hung up on
Michael Microsoft's voice mail and dialed.

'Sami UA.'

'Are you serious about NRA?'

'Buy! How you doing?'

'You don't want to know.'

'Yeah, I'm very serious. You have no idea how fast things are
moving here.'

'You know what will happen to NRA's stock price if they sign
with US Alliance?'

'Gee, I don't know, Buy. I'm not a stockbroker anymore.'

He felt a rush of gratitude. 'Thank you, Sami.'

'Wait. You can't use this information. It's company confidential.'

Buy paused. 'Are you—'

'Come on,' Sami said. 'You know I have to say that. You've had
a rough year, right? Maybe things will turn around for you.' He
hung up.

For a second, Buy felt paralyzed. There were too many things he
needed to do at once. Fifteen years ago, this would have been
insider trading, but that quaint concept had disappeared a decade
or two ago when so many brokers were doing it that it was impossible to jail them all. Now it was called smart trading.

He tucked the phone under his ear, hit SPEED DIAL 1, and
started tapping out an e-mail.

'Jason Mutual Unity.'

Buy said, 'I'm calling because you're my best client. I have some
information that's going to make a lot of people a lot of money and
I want you to be one of them.' At the same time, he tapped out:

17

He dragged his entire client list into the address field and hit SEND.

'Buy, I just stepped out of the shower.'

'Tell me you've got liquid.'

'What am I, a day-trader? Which company?'

'National Rifle Association.'

'The NRA? Are they even listed?'

'Jason,' Buy said, 'everyone's listed.'

'I don't know . . . I'd have to sell out of another position. Look, tell you what, leave it with me—'

'There's no time. You know how this works. The first fish to take a bite will stir up the sharks.'

'I'm sorry, Buy. We don't operate like this.'

He heard himself say: 'I'll forfeit the commission.'

'What?'

'If the stock doesn't rise, I'll eat the commission.' He swallowed. He was pretty sure he wasn't allowed to do that. He was pretty sure that if the NRA ticker price fell, Mitsui would both fire and sue him. 'Give me at least twenty million and I'll take no commission unless you make money.'

'Are you serious?'

The commission on twenty million dollars was four hundred thousand. He thought, *October 27, October 27.* 'Very serious.'

'Well, fuck,' Jason said. 'You've got yourself a deal, buddy.'

'Thank you,' Buy said. He closed his eyes. His chest still hurt.

5 WAL-MART

'I found your presentations to be uniformly disappointing,' the teacher said. He was leaning against his desk, arms folded. Every time he turned his head, his glasses reflected sunlight at Hayley, as if he was shooting rays of disapproval. 'I recommend that you all improve the level of your critical thinking.'

He began walking between aisles, dropping papers onto desks. Hayley saw a *D,* and an *F;* a little guy with glasses got a *C-.* She exhaled. This was not going to be good.

She heard whispering behind her and turned. Three girls were huddled together. When they saw Hayley looking, they closed tighter.

A paper landed on her desk. There was a lot of red pen, with words like *superficial.* At the bottom: *F.*

Hayley raised her hand. 'Why do I get an *F* for saying capitalizm is good when that's what everyone else says too? It's not fair.'

'Hayley, what's not fair is that our society rewards selfishness. *That's* not fair.'

So move to China, Hayley thought. 'You should know I'll be challenging this grade.' The McDonald's curriculum panel wouldn't let this crap stand, you could bet your ass.

'I don't think it's fair, either,' a boy to Hayley's left said. 'My parents say you have to understand how capitalizm works to get ahead. That self-interest is a *good* thing. Shouldn't you be preparing us for the real world?'

'*Mercurys,*' one of the whispering girls said.

Hayley turned around again. 'What did you say about Mercurys?'

They looked at her, their faces guarded. 'The Nike Town at the mall is getting in some Mercurys.'

Hayley's jaw dropped. 'Are you *serious*?'

'Thanks to *self-interest*,' the teacher said, 'it's legal to let a person starve to death in the street while you drive past in your Mercedes. Is that fair?'

'We heard five pairs.'

'No *way*! When?' Hayley gripped the desk. 'When are they getting the Mercurys?'

'Tonight. Six-thirty.' The girl glanced at her friends. 'Want to meet us there?'

'Oh, yeah!' She felt faint and sick all at once. Mercurys were two and a half thousand dollars, and Hayley didn't have that much, but she could borrow: there were ATMs at the mall. It would be totally worth it; Mercurys weren't just cool shoes; they were an investment. She could sell them tomorrow for twice what she bought them for, maybe more. What if – what if she could get *two* pairs?

'It's very disappointing,' the teacher said, 'that none of you can see past simple consumerism. Very disappointing.'

Mercurys, Hayley thought. *Oh my God.*

6 NRA

Billy Bechtel built tanks. Big ones. They had caterpillar treads and cannons on the front and swiveling machine guns; they were fucking impressive, was what they were. When anyone asked what Billy did for a living, he said, 'You know the Bechtel military yards, outside Abilene? I work there,' and watched their eyebrows jump. It got so Billy started wishing his job was as cool as it sounded.

Billy's job was to check steel plates to make sure they weren't buckled. How it worked was a forklift came and dumped a load of plates in his area, then Billy checked them with a metal ruler, then another forklift came and carted them away. If he found any warped ones, they went in a separate pile, and when Billy showed up for work the next day, they were gone. Most of the guys on the Bechtel site worked in teams, but Billy was stuck on his own. It was driving him nuts.

After he'd been there a few months, he let a plate with a pucker at the edge go through, just to see what would happen, but nothing did. Someone was now driving around a tank that leaked when it rained, he guessed. After that he let a plate go through that was almost bent in half, and a guy from welding came and yelled at him.

He took up smoking so he could hang around with some of the other workers, and that's where he met the shooters. There were ten or twelve of them, and they met after day shift three times a week. 'You should come along,' one of them told Billy, looking him up and down. Billy was young and blond and worked out a lot. 'You'll have fun.'

So Billy went, and it *was* fun. He also discovered he was a good shot. He had done some hunting as a kid growing up on a farm, but then his dad died and his mom moved them to Dallas and there hadn't been much call for shooting after that. Until now, where on the back blocks of the Bechtel Military Abilene site, Billy earned the respect and admiration of his coworkers by clocking torso-shaped targets from farther out than anyone else. Things were good then. Sometimes even the forklift drivers stopped to talk to him.

Then came the bad news. The foreman gathered them all in Hangar One, among the scaffolding and half-assembled tanks, and a guy from Head Office, some guy in a suit, said, 'Unfortunately, due to cost pressures . . .' Then there was a lot of stuff about com-petition and efficiencies and how painful it was for management to

21

make tough decisions. But what it came down to, the workers agreed afterward, was: *You can all fuck off now*. Billy was out of a job.

They gathered out front and stood around uncertainly. They bitched about management and wondered what they would do now; some of them talked bitterly about the days when there were unions, when shit like this wasn't tolerated. One of the shooters clapped Billy on the shoulder and said, 'What about you, champ? What are you going to do?'

'I think I'm gonna go away somewhere,' Billy said, surprising himself. True, he had enough saved up for a working holiday, and he had always wanted to travel outside of Texas, but that was a long-term goal, of the sort he'd never expected to actually accomplish. This shooting thing had really developed his self-confidence. 'I always wanted to go skiing, you know? Maybe I'll go somewhere and learn how to ski.'

The man roared with laughter. 'Hey, get this! Billy the Kid is going skiing!'

The men around him erupted. Hands clapped him on the back. 'Good on ya, Billy!' someone said, and someone else said, 'We should all go fuckin' skiing!' They thought it was terrific, Billy realized: they thought he was sticking it to Bechtel management. For a construction worker in Abilene, Texas, skiing was about as exotic as you could get. It was like going to Disneyland.

'That's the way, Billy the Kid,' the man said. 'You learn to ski.'

He thought he'd go to Sweden, because of the ski bunnies. He imagined days of riding steep white slopes by day, and gentle white curves at night. But the travel agent told him it was impossible to work there: Sweden was a non-USA country. Billy couldn't believe it. He didn't even think countries like that existed anymore. 'Oh, sure,' the agent said, who was a girl Billy had dated in high school.

She still chewed gum. 'There are plenty. Mostly places you don't wanna go, of course.'

'So where can I go?'

'How about Singapore? Singapore's real nice. I can get you a great price on—'

'Not Singapore,' Billy said. He was pretty sure this travel agency had some kind of deal with Singapore; they tried to talk everyone into visiting. 'I need somewhere with mountains. I want to go skiing.'

'Skiing?' Her eyes widened.

'Yeah.'

'Wow. Okay, then.' She poked at her computer. 'Well, there's Alaska, that's right up north. And Canada, of course.'

Billy was hoping for something more exotic. 'Anything farther away?'

'Okay, lemme see here.' Billy waited while she flicked through screens. 'You wanna go to New Zealand?'

'Where?' Billy said.

But he liked New Zealand, he really did. At first he was apprehensive: it was so far away, tucked down in the bottom of the world like something Australia coughed up. But he landed in Auckland Airport and the people spoke American and there were McDonald's and Coca-Cola machines everywhere and he felt relieved: it was a USA country, after all. He was feeling good when he asked the hotel concierge about the best places to ski, and then the guy laughed so hard he had to sit down. '*Ski* season?' he said. 'Buddy, you're too late. It's *spring.*'

'What are you talking about?'

'Come on,' the concierge said. 'You know the Southern Hemisphere has backward seasons, right?'

'You're shitting me,' Billy said, but the concierge wasn't: the concierge was telling the truth. He couldn't believe it. Spring in October! Who would have thought?

Hoping to catch the last vestiges of snow, he caught a ferry to New Zealand's South Island and a bus down to Invercargill, where it was freezing all year round. On the bus he met some backpackers from Massachusetts. They wanted to go somewhere exotic, they told Billy; they wanted something different. 'We've done Laos, Thailand, everything,' one of the girls said. 'You know the first thing we saw when we got off the boat at Ko Phangan? A Starbucks.' She looked disgusted. 'Everything's Americanized. We should have stayed home.'

'Yeah, right,' Billy said, although he didn't see what was wrong with being able to get good coffee in Thailand. The girl was pretty cute. 'I'm here for the skiing. We could get a package together, maybe—'

'Skiing, uh-uh,' the other girl said. 'No sanitized experiences, thank you.' She wasn't so cute.

He disembarked alone in Invercargill and walked the main street looking for a cheap hotel. But first he came across an NRA office: a squat, professional-looking building with *National Rifle Association Ltd* embossed in black letters on gray. He looked at it for a while. Then he went in. He was browsing the bulletin board for local shooting ranges when the receptionist said, 'Would you like to join the local chapter, sir?'

Billy looked at her. She was young and blond, wearing a blue sweater. It fitted her very nicely.

'If you're going to be staying in town.' She smiled. Crumpled on the desk beside her was a ski parka.

'I'm staying,' Billy said.

He was on an NRA shooting range east of Invercargill when they approached him. There were two of them, both wearing blue suits. Neither of them seemed to be carrying guns. Billy nodded at them as he reloaded his rifle. He'd bought it at member discount prices: a Colt M4A1 carbine, sleek and heavy, thirty rounds to a clip.

'Nice shooting,' one of the men said, smiling. He had a detectable accent, which was rare: most New Zealanders just sounded as if they were from California. His hair was slicked back. Both men were wearing sunglasses.

'Thanks.' He slotted the next clip in. 'You guys shooters?'

The man glanced at his companion. 'Yeah, you could say that. You're Billy Bechtel, right? You're new here?'

'Yep.' He fired. A stuffed dummy a hundred meters away spat a puff of feathers from its head.

'Funny, I didn't know Bechtel had anything going on down here.'

Billy looked at him. The truth was he wasn't Billy Bechtel anymore, of course: he was just Billy, unemployed wanderer. But it was too embarrassing to announce yourself without a surname. People thought you were a bum. 'I'm on vacation.'

'Right. Seeing the sights, eh? Getting to know a few of the locals?'

He wondered if they knew he'd dated the NRA receptionist. They'd gotten a little hot and heavy last night in her car. Maybe one of these guys was her father. He tightened his grip on the rifle.

'Well, Billy, we'd like you to work for us.'

'Uh-huh. And who are you?'

'The NRA,' the man said, and smiled broadly. He was creeping Billy out a little. 'You'd be surprised what we're doing these days, Billy, you really would. The NRA isn't just about pamphlets and gun shows anymore.'

'We need men like you,' the second guy said. 'Men just like you. And we pay well.'

'Yeah? For what?'

The man turned and looked out at the target. Billy could see the dummy reflected in his sunglasses. 'That's some nice shooting, all right. That's really nice shooting.'

7 MERCEDES-BENZ

'Woo!' a broker said, sloshing champagne on his arm. 'Shit! Sorry, Buy.'

'That's okay.'

'Come on, loosen up.' She took his arm. 'They'll approve your trades. I'm sure they will.'

Buy was sitting on one of the desks, his tie slung. He had averaged four hours' sleep for the last five days. Around him, brokers drank and laughed and shook hands. It was 6:15 P.M., Friday, October 31. The financial year was officially over. 'I am loose.'

'Leave him alone,' Cameron said, putting a hand on Buy's shoulder. Cameron was the floor manager, and he would be sacking Buy in a few minutes, Buy suspected. 'The guy's put in a heroic week.'

'Well, the suspense is fucking killing me,' the woman said. 'When do we find out if they're canning him?'

'I'm expecting—'

'Don't say you're expecting the call any minute.'

'Lisa,' Cameron said. 'As soon as I know, I'll announce it.'

'Well, I think you did the right thing, Buy. That was a gutsy move, promising to eat the commission if the stock fell. Really gutsy.' She looped her arm through his. 'A few of us are hitting the bars tonight. Want to come? I think you should.'

'I just want to go to bed. But thanks.'

'Okay.' She took her arm back. 'See you Monday, I hope.'

When she left, Buy said, 'Am I fired?'

Cameron considered. 'Depends whether they want to make an example out of you more than they want to book your trades.'

'Maybe they'll only disallow Mutual Unity,' Buy said. 'Just enough to push me under quota.'

'Buy, we don't fire everyone who misses quota.'

'Who missed quota but wasn't fired?'

'I'm saying theoretically,' Cameron said. 'It's not automatic, is what I mean.'

'Oh,' Buy said.

'Cameron? Call from Head Office.'

Everyone stopped talking. 'Thank you,' Cameron said. His office was up some stairs and glass-encased, so he could look over the trading floor. Everyone watched him ascend.

'Well,' Buy said. 'It's been fun working with you.' He felt giddy.

There was a knock on glass. He looked up. Cameron had his phone tucked under his ear. He gave Buy a thumbs-up.

He felt himself go faint. People surrounded him, slapping him on the back and shouting. Relief rushed through him like a physical thing and then he couldn't stop laughing.

All he wanted to do was sleep, but halfway home the Chadstone Wal-Mart mall called out to him. He deserved something to celebrate after today, didn't he? He deserved something really expensive. Buy turned the wheel.

Inside the mall, he found a bank of ATMs installed at the base of a series of mezzanine floors, like peons gathered to stare up at a glass sky. A Mercedes-Benz dealer was conducting a raffle in the center, and Buy looked at the cars with interest. He had two cars

27

already, but his Saab was no longer current-year. Maybe he deserved a new car.

A dark-haired schoolgirl was taking forever at the terminal. He peered over her shoulder. She was getting out a loan. He sighed.

The girl glanced at him. 'I can't get it to work.' With alarm, Buy saw tears forming in her eyes. 'I've been trying – I really need—'

'Maybe you should try a different machine.'

'None of them will loan to me!'

'How much do you need?'

'Five thousand dollars.'

'Oh.' He smiled sympathetically.

She stood there a moment. Buy thought she might be about to scream. Then she walked away.

He stepped up to the machine and inserted his card. His current balance was a little over a hundred thousand. On impulse, he looked after the girl. She was pushing through shoppers, heading for the exit.

He pulled out five thousand: fifty hundred-dollar bills. Then he hurried after the girl. 'Hey!' She didn't turn until he put a hand on her shoulder. 'Hey. Here.'

'What?'

'It's a present.' Her eyes widened, staring at the cash. Buy felt elated, better than he had in months. 'Go on, take it. Get yourself something nice.'

Her hand crept up and wrapped around the notes. 'Why – why would you do that?'

'I'm celebrating.'

'Thank you so much! Oh my God, thank you *so* much!'

'What's your name?'

'Hayley! I'm Hayley McDonald's!'

'I'm Buy,' he said. 'Have fun.'

8 VIOLET ENTERPRISES

Hack was jumpy as hell tonight, and he was driving Violet nuts. She was working sixteen-hour days to finish her software, and with two days to deadline she didn't have time to talk him out of his tree again. There was a lot riding on this: it was her big chance. Three months of coding based on a year's worth of research and an idea so brilliant it had stopped her dead in the street one day; she couldn't throw that away to deal with Hack's latest drama.

Hack started tapping his foot, jiggling her laptop. 'Hack. *Please.*'

'I'm sorry.' He looked at her plaintively.

'It's not your problem, Hack.'

'I'm killing somebody,' he whispered.

'You're not. You just passed on a job. It's got nothing to do with you.'

He started jiggling his foot again.

'Have a drink,' Violet said. 'Go down to the supermarket, buy some drugs.'

'I don't want to.'

'Then do something else! I don't have time for this!'

He looked at her screen. She resisted the urge to snap the lid shut. 'You working on your program?'

'Yes. The security software.' This wasn't strictly accurate, but it was less complicated than the truth, which was: *the virus.* Nontechnical people had trouble appreciating Violet's vision.

'Need any help?'

'No.' She forced herself to say: 'Thanks.'

'Okay.' He walked over to the window and looked up at the sky.

Violet went back to her code. She was almost lost in it when he said, 'I hope it's no one nice.'

'I'm sure it's not, Hack,' she said, not really paying attention.

9 GOVERNMENT

She was wearing a long coat, to hide what was underneath. Her hair was tucked into a shawl. She wore dark sunglasses, although they couldn't conceal the barcode tattoo beneath her left eye. But she didn't mind that. It made it harder for people to tell what she was.

The Chadstone Wal-Mart mall was six stories in places, and mezzanine-style all the way down. The Nike Town was on the fourth level. She glanced down as she stepped off the escalator. On the ground floor, shoppers flowed around two gleaming Mercedes automobiles.

There was already a crush around the Nike Town, made up of maybe four dozen teenagers, most in school uniforms. The store had its shutter down, but a bald man in a suit was talking through it. He waved his arms excitedly. The kids rattled the shutter in response. The doors to the Nike Town had long, metal swooshes as handles, she saw, tapering to a point: they looked pretty dangerous. She hoped none of these teenagers were going to impale themselves.

There was a Barnes & Noble a few stores down with a nice reflective window, so she stood in front of it. For twenty minutes, she saw no one likely to be her target. At one point she caught herself reading the jackets of the books in the window, and jerked her eyes away. *Possibly the book of the year,* the jacket had said, which she found unlikely. This was Barnes & Noble's Non-Best-Selling Authors floor.

After thirty-five minutes, she saw a young man in camouflage pants. He was on the side opposite to the Nike Town, across the gap, leaning on the guardrail. He lit a cigarette. From the bulge in his jacket, he was carrying a gun in a shoulder holster. There was thirty feet of air between him and the Nike Town, which would protect him from the crowd, and an emergency exit directly behind him. There was no doubt. This was her target.

The kids had been chanting for five minutes – *O-PEN, O-PEN, O-PEN* – but now they started shrieking, almost screaming. Girls waved rolls of money, jumping in excitement. Then the Nike Town shutter clattered upward and the noise turned into a cacophony. The teenagers stampeded: she saw a boy go down, crying out. She turned and began walking quietly toward the store, glancing at the target. He was straightening, tossing aside his cigarette.

'*Sold!*' a man shouted. In the Nike Town, four girls wearing McDonald's school uniforms were screaming with delight, holding a box of Mercurys – no, *four* boxes. And there were more: the shelves were lined with them. Her information had been wrong. This store had more than five pairs. It had dozens.

The girls forced their way out of the store, talking excitedly. The target slipped a hand in his jacket.

'I can't *believe* it! I can't believe we each got a pair!'

'We should get more – we should go back in—'

The girls squeezed past her. She kept still, unable to move until the target did. The last girl, the one with dark hair, moved directly in front of her. She could smell the girl's perfume.

A man in the crowd pressed a gun to the back of the girl's neck.

Her instinctive reaction – the emotion that burst across her brain first – was disappointment. *Wrong one, I targeted the wrong one.* Then the gun fired, sharp and loud. The girl went down. The crowd screamed and flinched like a single animal. The assassin was a muscular young man in a black T-shirt. He was five feet away from her, and their eyes met.

'They're killing people for their Mercurys!' someone shouted, and the crowd surged. The assassin broke for the Barnes & Noble.

She threw off her coat and hefted the machine gun concealed inside it. It was a Vektor SS77: heavy and awkward, but capable of nine hundred rounds a minute. Four steps to her right took her out of the crowd. She dropped to her knee and squeezed the trigger.

He zagged as if he'd known it was coming, and she blew out the Barnes & Noble window, disintegrating novels. She tracked him as quickly as she was able to with the Vektor shuddering against her shoulder, and tore up the floor in thick plaster chunks. The assassin dived through the Toys 'R' Us window.

She dropped the Vektor and broke out her two .45s. He was scrambling for his footing among the display of life-sized Barbie dolls; she wasn't fortunate enough for him to have cut his throat on the plate glass, it seemed. She squeezed the triggers, letting the pistols go fully automatic. The arm of a Doctor Barbie exploded; she tore a Prom Queen Barbie in half. The assassin rolled and vanished into the store.

She pulled off her glasses and shawl and ran. This was not good: she was not going to be able to chase down muscular young men in T-shirts, not with the amount of body armor she was wearing. She ran anyway.

The assassin had reached the in-store escalators. There were shoppers everywhere, staring at her. '*Out of the way!*' she shouted. 'Get down!'

They scattered, and she dived for the escalator, landing on her stomach and sliding, leading with her .45s. There was a man at the bottom, looking up, and she almost put him down before recognizing he wasn't the target. She regained her feet and looked around. Toys 'R' Us was like a bowling alley, nothing but endless aisles. 'Which way? Where'd he go?'

He pointed at the nearest aisle. She ran, but it was empty. Fluorescent-lit racks of Star Wars characters stood mutely. She moved to the next aisle, then the next.

It was quiet. No panting, no running, no shrieking shoppers. This meant the assassin had gone native, trying to blend in with the crowd. She ran for the exit.

A checkout boy saw her guns and hollered. She jumped the turnstile and kept running. A crowd had gathered at the railing to stare up at the Nike Town on level four. And a man was walking briskly toward the central escalators, a well-built young man in a black T-shirt.

She pushed through the crowd to the edge of the mezzanine and clambered up onto the railing. When she could see him clearly, she balanced herself with her legs and shouted: 'Freeze!' Her voice echoed. 'This is the Government!'

He turned. It was the assassin. Less than two feet in front of him, the escalator churned. He looked at it, then at her.

'Don't move!'

He raised his hands.

Thank Christ, she thought. She gestured with a pistol, and he stepped away from the escalator. She glanced down to see if it was clear for her to jump down from the railing.

The thing was: she should have seen it coming. She had identified him from the beginning, when she saw his reflection in the window of Barnes & Noble. She should have realized there were two of them.

He was maybe twenty feet away. He had a pistol pointed at her. There was nothing she could do.

He fired, and it was like being hit by a car. Her feet went out from under her. As she fell, the fluorescent lights twisted and swirled above her. She had time to think: *The lights look like angels.* Then she landed on the roof of a Mercedes, catching the car with her spine. Its windshield blew out. The car rocked wildly. She blinked. She could still blink.

After a while, some faces appeared above her. 'Get her down,' someone said, and someone else said, 'No, don't move her.'

'Honey?' a woman said. 'I'll call help for you. What's your name?'

'Government.' Her tongue felt like a bloated, broken sausage. All she could taste was blood. 'Jennifer Government.'

10 AMERICAN EXPRESS

Buy hadn't meant to hang around. He was happy with himself; now he was going to go home and sleep. But he hesitated at one of the Mercedes, attracting the attention of the dealer and becoming ensnared in a sales pitch, and so was still there to hear the shots.

He dropped to a crouch, aware that everyone around him was doing the same, and craned his neck upward. Gunfire broke out again: an automatic weapon. He heard screaming, glass breaking.

Buy and the dealer crawled toward the cars, seeking cover. The mall fell silent. It was eerie, so many people being so quiet. Then after a minute they started to emerge. Buy got to his feet.

The dealer wrung his hands. 'Excitement.'

'I think I'm going to take a look,' Buy said.

'You should leave it to mall security,' the dealer said.

'I know first aid.' Not many people did; there was too much risk of being sued. Buy caught the escalator up. On the fourth floor, there were a lot of teenagers standing around, dazed; some were cowering inside shops. Glass sparkled outside the Barnes & Noble and a line of jagged holes in the floor marked a path toward Toys 'R' Us. On the ground outside the Nike Town, a girl was bleeding to death. He said, 'Hayley?'

Her neck was exposed. He ran to her, tore off his jacket, and tried to staunch the flow of blood. Her eyes rolled. 'Someone call an ambulance!' he roared. 'Does someone have—'

'I have a cellphone,' a kid said, handing it to him. Buy dialed 911 and tucked it under his ear. Hayley was looking at him; he realized she wanted him to take her hand. He squeezed it tightly.

'Nine-eleven Emergency, how can I help you?'

'I need an ambulance. Quickly, a girl has been shot at the Chadstone Wal-Mart mall.'

'Certainly, sir. Can you tell me the girl's name?'

'Hayley. Hayley something. Please, come straight away.'

'Sir, I need to know if the victim is part of our register,' the operator said. 'If she's one of our clients, we'll be there within a few minutes. Otherwise I'm happy to recommend—'

'I need an ambulance!' he shouted, and it was only when water splashed on his hand that he realized he had started to cry. 'I'll pay for it, I don't care, just *come*!'

'Do you have a credit card, sir?'

'*Yes!* Send someone now!'

'As soon as I confirm your ability to pay, sir. This will only take a few seconds.'

He looked at the faces around him. 'Someone help her. *Help* her!' The kid who had loaned Buy his cellular knelt down and held the jacket over the wound. A girl began stroking Hayley's hair. Buy dragged his wallet out from his back pocket and retrieved his credit card. Hayley's eyes were fixed on him. *I promise*, he told her. *I promise*. 'I have American Express—'

'That's fine, sir. Could you read your card number to me, please?'

'Nine seven one four, oh three—'

Two shots rang out from somewhere below them, close. The people around him shrieked and fled; only the kid stayed, crouching lower.

'—six six—'

People were screaming. Something hit the ground – or one of the Mercedes? – with a deafening *boom*.

'Sir? Are you there? I didn't catch the number, sir.'

'*Nine seven—*'

The kid put his hand over Buy's. 'Mister . . . I don't think it matters.'

Hayley was no longer looking at him. Her eyes were turned upward, at the Nike Town sign, at the fluorescent lights. Her face was white.

'Oh, no,' Buy said. 'No, please.'

'Sir?' the operator said. 'Can you please repeat your credit card number for me, sir? Sir? Are you there? Sir? Sir?'

PART TWO

11 HACK

They came for him at eleven o'clock the following night. Hack was in front of the television. He had AOL Time Warner, 182 channels, and four including CNN-A were running nonstop on the Mercury killings. He sat on the floor, wrapped in a blanket, and flicked from one channel to another. He'd been doing it for thirty hours.

That's one theory, Mary. But one thing's for sure: there are fourteen confirmed dead, and nobody's—

Some Nike Town stores are now closed, but many remain open, despite the obvious risk. With demand for Mercurys running at fever pitch—

The words flowed around him. He couldn't hear anything except the number *fourteen*.

The security buzzer sounded, startling him. He got up and walked to the kitchen. 'Hello?'

'It's John. Can I come up?'

'Who?'

He heard laughter. 'He said, "Who?"' John said. 'Come on, Hack, don't mess with us. This is a shitty neighborhood.'

Hack froze. 'John Nike?'

'You subcontracted, didn't you, Hack? You passed on the job. I guess we didn't make ourselves clear. And that's really our fault. I blame myself, and John here, he feels terrible. Don't you, John?'

A second voice. 'Let's talk about it, Hack. Open the door.'

'This isn't a good time.'

There was a pause. Then, much clearer: 'Hack, you little shit, *open the door.*'

He pushed the security button and heard it sound downstairs. He took a step away from the intercom and stared at it. He hoped he wasn't making another big mistake.

When the Johns knocked on his front door, he unlocked it with trembling fingers. The door swung open. The sudden light from the hallway dazzled him. He shielded his eyes and lost his grip on the blanket.

'Oh, God,' Vice-President John said, stepping past him. 'What are they, Disney boxer shorts? And you a Merchandising Officer.'

'You look like crap,' the other John said. They were both wearing dark suits. They had gleaming black shoes. 'Hack, your *breath.*'

John was already in the living room. The bedroom door was ajar, Hack saw. Violet was asleep in there. 'Come here, Hack. We've got something to show you.'

As he passed by the bedroom door, he pulled it closed. The Johns didn't seem to notice. Hack sat on the sofa and tugged the blanket around himself.

The other John found Hack's remote and zapped the TV. An image of Vice-President John jumped onto the screen. 'Aw, we missed the start. You kept us waiting too long, Hack.'

On the screen, John said, '*None of that takes away from the fact that this is a real tragedy. We understand that people value our products very highly — the Nike Air range, the very successful Nike Jordan label, and of course the amazing new Nike Mercurys. But to kill for a pair is wrong, and Nike will not tolerate it.*'

'I still think you should have thumped the podium,' the other John said. 'For effect.'

'Understatement,' John said. 'That's the key.'

'We will hunt down the killers, and we will see justice done. That's a promise from Nike. That's a money-back guarantee.'

'Killer close,' John said. 'Pardon the pun.' He looked at Hack. 'What do you think?'

'You're going to turn me in to the Government.' There was no point going for the door. Maybe the window? Hack's hands tightened into fists.

The Johns burst out laughing. 'Hack,' the other John said, 'you are one crazy kid.'

'You're a Merc Officer,' Vice-President John said, putting a hand on his shoulder. 'Sometimes we forget that not everyone understands marketing like we do. Hack, what you just saw was a press release. We have no intention of hunting down the people responsible, because the people responsible are us. All right?'

Hack nodded.

'But the thing is, that was meant to be our little secret. And it's not anymore, is it? You couldn't keep your mouth shut.'

'I mean, Hack, if we wanted to use someone outside the company, we would have picked up the fucking phone, you know?'

'I didn't know that,' Hack said. 'You never said anything about—'

'Look, there's no point wasting time over whose fault it is,' Vice-President John said. 'Although frankly, Hack, it's yours. All we can do now is control it. So first question: who'd you subcontract to?'

'I – the Police.'

John nodded. 'Okay. A professional organization, at least. You seen their ads, John?'

'Sure. Eighty-six percent success rate.'

41

'Yeah,' John said. 'That's a really amazing figure.' He looked at Hack. 'I'm assuming you told them this was Nike's job.'

'Ah . . .'

'Don't be coy, Hack. We know these agencies insist on knowing where the job is coming from.'

'Um, okay. Yeah, I told them.'

'Fuck!' the other John said. 'Hack, you dumb shit!'

'Shh,' Vice-President John said. 'It's okay, Hack. Now we're getting somewhere. I mean, obviously none of this is good, from a big-picture point of view. Overall, it's very fucked, a commercial-in-confidence arrangement getting spread all over the place. But on the individual level, as far as our relationship goes, Hack, I'm very pleased you're being straight with me.' He leaned forward, so his face was almost touching Hack's. His skin seemed uncomfortably tight, his cheekbones artificially prominent. 'And since we're sharing, I'm going to let you in on a secret. The Police didn't do these shootings. You want to know who did?'

'Uh,' Hack said.

'The NRA. We've got data on six incidents, and it smells like those National Rifle clowns all the way. They think undercover is guys in black T-shirts and camouflage pants. So what does that suggest to you, Hack?'

Hack shook his head.

'It means the Police subcontracted, too.' John sighed. 'Everyone wants to outsource these days. No one has any respect for core competencies. But Nike is friendly with the NRA, Hack, with us both being in the US Alliance program; if we'd wanted to subcontract, we would have chosen them ourselves. So if the job went from you to the Police to the NRA, that's only one unsecure link in the chain, which, again, is not fantastic, but isn't a catastrophe. What *would* be a catastrophe is if there are other links in the chain. Links we don't know about. You follow me?'

42

'You want to . . . find out if the Police went straight to the NRA?'

'Brilliant, Einstein,' the other John said. He was watching the TV, which was replaying a scene at a Sydney Nike Town. About two hundred teenagers were storming it, clawing at each other for position. The plate-glass window shattered. The John snickered.

'That's exactly what I want you to do,' Vice-President John said, smiling. 'Now.'

'Now?'

'I'll accompany you. John will wait here.'

'Got any snacks?' the other John said.

'Um . . .' Hack said, thinking about Violet. 'You – why don't you both come with me? Or, how about I'll go talk to the Police and afterward I'll call you—'

The other John looked up. 'Don't tell us what to do, Hack. Don't even think about doing that.'

'I think we should go,' Vice-President John said. He wasn't smiling anymore. 'Now. I really do.'

12 JENNIFER

'Hey,' somebody said. 'Jen. Hey.'

She opened her eyes. Then she shut them. *Lights like angels,* she thought. *God is fluorescent.*

'Come on. Open up.'

'Ahh,' she said.

'That's my girl. Come on.'

She forced open her eyes. Calvin, her partner, was sitting by a bed. She was in the bed. The bed seemed to be in a hospital.

'The Mercedes dealer is suing us for the cost of the car you landed on, can you believe that? Forty-eight thousand bucks.'

'Did – did they get away?'

He sighed. ' 'Fraid so. We got screwed at the downtown Nike Town, too. And in Sydney . . .' Calvin scratched his nose. 'Well, Ben's fine. There were no bad guys at Ben's Nike Town, he spent the night watching thirteen-year-olds buy sneakers. But Taylor . . . Taylor tagged a bad guy. Then we figure his accomplice got her.'

'Oh, no.' She tried to cover her face. Pain shot through her shoulder. 'Ahh!'

'Don't move that arm,' Calvin said. 'You're getting a sling or something. Anyway, we're all happy that you made it back in one piece, okay? Clearly we went into this operation with bad information.'

'My source is reliable. I know she is.'

'Um,' he said. 'Not that I want to press the issue, but those stores all had more than five pairs of Mercurys.'

'I trust my source,' she said. She felt thirsty. Her whole body ached. She needed to go to the bathroom, and from the tubes coming out of her arm, it looked like she'd have to take a stand full of bags and drips with her.

'Well, we can debate that later. She called last night, by the way. Left a name, too. Hack Nike.'

'Who?'

'Beats the hell out of me. You didn't hear about anyone called Hack when you were sniffing around Nike?'

'No.'

'Well, maybe he's nobody,' Calvin said. 'Like I say, the quality of our information to this point has not been spectacular.'

She screwed shut her eyes, trying to think.

'You know, I should come back later.' Calvin rose from his chair. 'You need some rest. I'll take care of—'

'Wait. How . . . how many . . .'

He sat again. 'Fourteen dead. At least eight were contract killings, all from families of limited means. At this stage it looks like the victims were selected for low incomes. I hate to say it, but it's going to be tough to get budget on this one.'

'What about leads?'

'We've got two. First, a dead bad guy, courtesy of Taylor. We're running background on him now. Second, some stockbroker who was on the scene with a victim. He says he didn't see anything, but we haven't pushed him yet.'

'What about this Hack Nike?'

'Well,' Calvin said, 'since your source didn't turn out to be so reliable, I haven't followed it up yet.'

'Get him.'

'If we get funding, sure, I'll—'

'Now,' Jennifer said. 'Get him.'

'Before budget approval? Are you sure?'

'Do I look sure?'

'You look awful,' Calvin said, and laughed.

13 BILLY

Billy had been involved in some weird shit before, but this was right up there. The NRA had given them animal code names, so now he couldn't even say howdy to someone without feeling like a dick. Some guys took straight to it, all, 'Evening, Horse,' and, 'Jackal, can that shit,' but Billy thought it was stupid. Billy was Mouse.

He'd been out in the bush for three days, sleeping in ditches. He was wearing camouflage pants and a heavy jacket over a black T-shirt and carrying a slicker. He'd used that as a pillow last night, even when it started raining. This morning his smokes were too wet to light and his arms were so stiff he could hardly lift them.

The NRA called it a war game, and it was meant to test his skills. So far it had only tested Billy's patience. This was not skiing.

'The flag's gotta be close now,' Grizzly said. 'Gotta be *real* close.'

'We need that flag,' said Calf. She was the scariest-looking woman Billy had ever met. 'I really want this job.'

'What do you mean?' Billy said. 'We're already hired, right? I thought this was just training.'

'Yeah,' Calf said. 'The kind of training that costs you your job if you mess up.'

'Oh,' Billy said. 'Wow.'

'Can the chatter!' Finch said, walking backward. 'And stay tight!'

Billy scowled. He'd had enough of Finch, the squad leader, too. If Finch said 'chain of command' again, Billy was ready to pay out.

They walked. The bush was much thicker now, almost a forest. There were weird-ass animals out here, Billy knew. Types of animals he'd never seen before. The idea spooked him.

Something moved in the scrub to their left. The squad dropped to the ground. Billy raised his paintgun. It might not stop a charging bear, or rhino, or whatever the hell they had here, but if he aimed for the eyes—

'Naw, lemme do it. You load it like *this*.'

Voices. Finch gestured, *Fan out*. Billy didn't think that was such a great idea; if they snapped twigs, they'd give themselves away. He looked at Finch questioningly.

'*Move*,' Finch hissed.

He sighed. He and Drake took one flank, Grizzly and Calf the other. They made ten yards before either Grizzly or Calf snapped a branch and said, 'Ahh, shit!'

'*Go! Go!*' Finch shouted. '*Attack!*'

Billy ran, thinking this was really generous of Finch, yelling out to let the enemy know they were coming. He leapt over a fallen tree. Drake pounded behind him.

They burst into a clearing, which had a red flag and a lot of NRA guys with red bands around their arms, and suddenly everyone was shooting paintballs. Drake caught a glob on his chest and sat down. Billy dived, rolled, and took up a position behind a tree. He globbed four enemies, fluidly shooting and reloading. Then Grizzly and Calf entered the clearing from the other side.

'Take that, asshole!' Grizzly shouted, and pumped a paint round into a man who was already sitting down.

'Behind you!' Billy yelled, but it was too late. Grizzly took one in the buttocks.

'Son of a bitch,' said Grizzly.

'Sit down, you moron,' the dead enemy said.

Calf ran for a clutch of trees that was sheltering the remaining red soldier. He fired at her once, then ran. Calf was pretty scary. Billy globbed the soldier, then walked out into the clearing.

Calf met him in the middle. 'Hey, good work, Mouse. You got a good eye on you.'

'Thanks.' He eyed her pants. 'Hey, Calf . . . I think they got you.'

'What? Aw, shit!'

'Well, well!' Finch said, arriving. 'A good day for the blue team!' He walked to the flagpole and began tugging at the ropes. 'I think the blue team will all find secure NRA positions.'

'You got everyone *shot*,' Billy said. 'Everyone except me.'

Finch looked around. 'Well, perhaps not all of us, then.'

'You asshole!' Calf said. 'You let them know we were coming!'

'I did not,' Finch said. 'That was your own fault, snapping branches and so forth.'

47

'You did, man,' one of the enemies said. 'I heard someone say, "Go, attack!"'

'Thanks a lot, Finch! You probably cost me a job!'

'Your ineptitude in combat isn't my fault,' Finch said. He began folding the flag, tucking one end under his chin.

Billy said, 'You think you're a real squad commander? This is a *game*! You think they'd ever put you in charge for real?'

Everyone fell silent. Finch raised his paintgun. 'Shut your mouth, Mouse.'

Billy laughed. 'What are you going to do? Shoot me?'

'I said stand down!'

'Give me the flag. You don't deserve it.' He reached for it.

Finch pulled the trigger. Billy felt something sharp strike his chest. He looked down and saw a mess of blue paint on his jacket. He raised his head. Finch said nervously, 'Now, Mouse—' and Billy punched him in the face.

Finch fell to the ground. Arms grabbed at Billy. He flailed wildly and connected with something soft. Someone yelled, 'Ahh, my nose!' Then Billy was on the ground and a lot of angry people were holding him down.

'What's the matter with you?'

'Get out of here,' a man said. 'The NRA doesn't need thugs like you.'

'The NRA will hear about this, Mouse,' Finch said, his voice shrill. 'You can forget about your job!'

Billy looked at Calf, hoping for support. She looked at the ground. 'You'd better scoot, Mouse.'

'Fine!' He scrambled to his feet. He tore off his blue armband and threw it to the ground, but no one seemed very impressed. He almost shouted, *Screw you all,* but strangled the impulse. He turned on his heel and walked away.

Twenty minutes later, he realized he didn't have a solid grip on his bearings. The bushland looked the same in every direction. In places it was so thick he had to scramble over fallen trees and hack through bushes. The blue paint on his jacket dried to form a hard layer that chafed against his skin, and he pulled it off and hurled it at a tree. Ten minutes later his arms were attacked so violently by mosquitoes that he headed back for it.

But this was harder than it sounded, and Billy realized he was well and truly lost. He spent half an hour smashing through the bush, getting increasingly irate at himself, the NRA, and misleading blue birds. He wished he'd never met those NRA suits at the firing range. When he got out of this, the first thing Billy was going to do was cancel his membership.

About three hours later, he stumbled across a dirt road. He was so relieved he fell to his knees. He was dirty and tired and his throat made clicking sounds when he swallowed. He was also dying for a cigarette, but scared of how much worse his thirst would get if he smoked one. He peered down the road, first one way, then the other. Neither looked especially promising.

He walked forever. Not a single car passed him. The sun began to fall below the tree line and a chill settled in the air. Billy was now really regretting pitching that jacket. He was thinking he might be in real trouble. He was beginning to think he might die.

Then he glanced to his right and saw the Jeep. There was a tiny track off the road, just a gap in the trees, really, and a few hundred yards down it, a red glow of brake lights. Billy stopped and stared. Then he ran toward it.

It was an NRA vehicle, he could tell even in the gloom, with a few NRA uniforms sitting in it. One of the men was looking in his direction. 'Hoy!' Billy yelled, waving his arms. 'Hello, hello!'

The man raised a rifle. Billy stopped running. A spotlight snapped on, blinding him. He raised an arm to shield his eyes.

'Identify yourself.'

'I'm Billy! Billy NRA!'

Silence. His legs started to tremble. He had a terrible feeling he was somewhere he shouldn't be. He heard someone jump down from the Jeep and walk toward him, boots crunching through the undergrowth. A man entered the light. He was short and maybe fifty and wearing a uniform with a lot of shiny bits and pieces. None of this made Billy feel any better.

'You're Bill NRA?'

'Yes.'

The man exhaled. 'Jesus. We thought you weren't going to show. I'm Yallam.'

'I'm – pleased to meet you, sir.' His legs wouldn't quit shaking.

'You all right?'

'I'm fine, sir.'

'We heard about the trouble in Sydney. Sorry about Damon.'

'I—' Billy said, then realized there was only one correct response here. 'Yes, sir.'

Yallam turned around. 'Frank! Turn off that light.'

The light died. Billy blinked in the sudden darkness.

'We'd better get moving. You disposed of your vehicle?'

'My – yes, sir.'

'Good man.' Yallam clapped him on the back and began steering him toward the Jeep. Billy very much didn't want to get into that Jeep. 'You're a credit to the NRA, son. Don't think your work this last week won't go unrewarded.'

'Thank you, sir,' Billy said. A soldier opened the door for him and he climbed in. He had never been so scared in his life.

14 JENNIFER

The shrink said, 'Now you're going to tell me you don't need to be here.'

'Wow, you're good,' Jennifer said. The plastic chair was uncomfortable. The office was small, dark, and had no view. She had been discharged, or so she'd thought. The Government was insisting on an outgoing psych evaluation. Jennifer just wanted to go home.

'Danger is part of your job, right? You're wasting time here when you could be out pursuing the perpetrators.'

'Amazing,' she said. 'It's like I don't even have to be here.'

The shrink rested his elbows on his desk. She could see an open file, which she guessed was hers. 'Jennifer, I'm not going to ask you about your childhood, or your sex life, or what an ink blot looks like. I'm only here to help you deal with the trauma. Prevent it from dominating your life.'

'The only trauma was my stupidity. I was there to do a job; I screwed up. I practically deserved to get shot.'

'Do you really think that?'

'No,' she said. 'I deserved to save that girl, and those two gun-toting assholes deserved to die instead of her. But you can't win them all.'

The shrink paused. It was a meaningful pause, Jennifer suspected: it was to give her time to consider her response and revise it. She kept her mouth shut.

'You know,' the shrink said, 'some people, as they recover from trauma, obsess on the perpetrators. Their lives come to revolve around the enemy. They constantly think about obtaining justice.'

'These people sound sensible.'

51

'They withdraw from loved ones. Only the trauma is important to them. They can feel desensitized to violence; they can become aggressive. Does any of this sound familiar?'

'Well, we could discuss these people all day,' she said, standing. 'But since I have work to do—'

'Sit.'

She sat. 'You know, this isn't even about me. This is about some asshole at Nike thinking he can build a career out of dead teenagers. You don't know what these people are like. They don't stop until you make them stop.'

'Yes, I'm aware of your corporate past,' the shrink said. His eyes slid to her barcode tattoo. 'You have scores to settle, yes?'

'Hey,' she said. 'That has nothing to do with this. It's not me who can't forget that, it's you people.'

'Are you working for the Government to atone for your past?'

'Yeah,' she said. 'I'm a real idealist.'

'"From the single-minded idealist to the fanatic is but a step." F. A. Hayek wrote that. "There is only one step from fanaticism to barbarism." That's Denis Diderot.'

'Someone should shoot you and drop you three floors,' she said. 'You could write an article.'

He sighed and made a note in the file. She didn't think it was a good note.

'You're recommending I be suspended? Is that it?'

'Jennifer, clearly you could benefit from a rest before returning to active duty.'

'I don't need a rest!'

He looked up. 'I'm told you don't date. Is that true?'

'I thought we weren't discussing my sex life.'

'It's relevant to your loss of perspective.'

'I'm leaving.' She stood up, too quickly. Her chair toppled backward and hit the floor.

'Wait! Jennifer!'

She slammed the door behind her. People in the corridor turned. She stared back at them. Outside the hospital it was dark and there were no cabs, so she stood by the road and waited. It wasn't until her jaw began to ache that she realized she was clench-ing it.

The cab dropped her on Peckville Street and she struggled up to the front door. Jennifer was discovering how difficult it was to do anything with one arm in a sling, even to get into her own house. In the end she rang the bell.

She owned a single-fronted house in North Melbourne, a small, innercity suburb that had so far mostly resisted the apartment block invasion. Jennifer had moved to Melbourne from Los Angeles nine years ago: she had needed an escape, Australia was completing its absorption into the United States, and the TV advertisements were calling it the new California. 'Melbourne is L.A. without the smog,' a real estate man told her, which she guessed was true, but it was also L.A. without the amenities. She had been shocked by how small the place was. That had changed, of course. There had been so much construction since then that she hardly recognized the city anymore.

The porch light flicked on. An eye appeared at the peephole. 'Oh!' a girl said. She unlocked and swung open the door. 'I won-dered if you were coming home tonight.'

'I – sorry. I should have called.'

'No, it's fine,' the girl said. 'I'm just studying.' She hefted her bag. 'I'll hit the road, unless there's anything you need.'

'Um,' she said. 'No, thanks.'

'Give me a call if you need me again.' The girl banged her way out the front door.

Jennifer went in and dropped her bag on the sofa. The hallway light was on, but Kate's room was dark, so she snuck inside and stood there for a moment, letting her eyes adjust.

'Mommy?'

'Hi, sweetie.' She knelt beside the bed.

'Your hair looks funny.'

'They had to cut it. Look, I have stitches.'

Kate touched Jennifer's skull, feeling her hair. 'I liked it better before.'

'Well, I think it looks snappy,' she said. 'Were you good for the baby-sitter?'

'Yes.'

'Good girl.' She stroked Kate's face. 'You want to have a glass of milk with me?'

'It's very late, Mommy.'

'I know.'

'All right.' She pulled back the covers. Jennifer took her hand as they walked to the kitchen. 'Did you hurt your arm?'

'A little, yeah.'

'Is it going to be all right?'

'Of course,' Jennifer said. 'Everything always works out all right.'

15 VIOLET

Violet woke and a man was sitting on her bed. 'Hi,' he said.

She scrambled away, pulling the blankets with her. 'Who are you?'

'I'm a friend of Hack's. But he didn't say anything about you. Are you his girlfriend?' He sat down on the bed. 'You have nice shoulders.'

'Where's Hack?'

'He went for a walk.' The man's face was smooth. His suit was dark and anonymous. 'He won't be back for a while.'

'Please leave.'

'But Hack invited me in. What's your name?'

'I want you to go.'

'I'm John Nike.' He smiled, his teeth gleaming faintly in the gloom. 'Who are you?'

'Violet.'

'Violet who?' He shifted closer. 'Are you unemployed? It's all right. It happens, sometimes. I tell you what, unemployed Violet. I'll give you a hundred dollars for a kiss.'

She tightened her grip on the blankets. 'Get out. Now.'

He raised his eyebrows. 'That's pretty generous. Considering you're in no position to negotiate.' His hand touched her thigh.

'Let go of me!'

'You need to be enterprising to get ahead, Violet. You need to take advantage of opportunities.' He squeezed.

She reached for his hand. He grabbed her wrists and pinned them to the wall. The blanket dropped.

'Hoo,' he said, looking down. 'Those are nice puppies.'

She bit his ear as hard as she could.

'*Ahhh!* God*damn!*'

She rolled off the bed, landing on her hands and knees. She scrambled to her feet and ran. She had the front door half-unlocked before she realized just how bad an idea that was, running naked at night through this neighborhood. She ran into the kitchen and began pulling open drawers.

'You little bitch,' John said, entering. 'If I need cosmetic surgery, you're going to pay for it.'

She found a knife, a long one. 'Stay away from me.'

'I don't think so, unemployed Violet.' He edged closer, watching the knife. 'I don't think you want to get in any more trouble than you already are.'

'*You* attacked *me*—' she said, and he grabbed her wrist and slammed it onto the kitchen bench. She cried out. The knife clattered to the floor.

There was a crumpet toaster on the bench, a shiny, heavy thing Hack had bought her for her last birthday. It had variable-sized slots for different bread and an auto-sensor so it never burnt. Violet grabbed it with both hands and swung it at John's face. It rang like a bell. John dropped to the floor.

He didn't move. Violet peered at him. He didn't seem to be breathing. After a moment, she prodded him with her foot. 'Are you—'

He grabbed her ankle. She fell backward and banged her head against the stove. His hands clutched at her legs. She shrieked and flailed at him with the crumpet toaster. She cracked his knuckles, then hit her own knee. She slammed the toaster on his hands, his head, his face, until she realized he'd stopped moving again. He hadn't been moving for a while.

She pulled herself out from under him, breathing heavily. John was limp. She looked at the toaster. There were spots of blood on it.

She dropped the toaster and circled around his body. She shut the kitchen door and went into the bedroom, pulled on a T-shirt and pants, and sat on the bed. After a while she started to bite her nails. She thought she may have just done something terrible.

16 HACK

'You sure we shouldn't drive?' John said. There were some teenagers across the road, listening to loud music.

'It's just up here,' Hack said.

'Why do you even live here? How much are you earning at Nike?'

'Um . . . about thirty-three.'

'Jesus!' John said. 'What's the matter with you?'

'I . . . guess I'm not very good in pay negotiations,' Hack said. Hack sucked in pay negotiations. Every year his boss sat him down and talked about competitive pressures and budget cuts; at the end he named a figure and Hack took it, grateful to be still employed.

'There are courses you can do. Assertiveness training. You should look into it. Is this it?'

Hack looked up. The Police, the swirling blue light. 'Yes.'

John straightened his tie. 'Now, this is what you're going to do. You go in, you ask for whoever you talked to last time. You establish *exactly* how many other links in the chain there are. Then you leave. Nothing else.'

'Okay,' Hack said. They went in. The same music, 'Every Breath You Take,' was playing. That must get pretty annoying, Hack thought. 'Can I speak to Sergeant Pearson, please?'

'Certainly, sir.' It was the same receptionist. She smiled at him. 'Your name?'

'Hack Nike.'

She looked at John. 'And?'

'A friend,' John said.

The receptionist eyeballed him. She was friendly so long as you didn't mess with her, Hack realized. 'Take a seat.'

They sat. 'You gave your real name?' John whispered.

Hack said nothing. He was thinking about Violet at home with the other John.

Pearson didn't keep them waiting: within a minute he strode into the lobby. He was a real presence, Pearson, Hack thought. Pearson commanded respect. 'Hack, glad to see you. Right this way.' He led them into the same meeting room. 'What can I do for you?'

Hack said, 'I'm here to talk about the job.'

'Uh-huh.' Pearson raised his eyebrows at John.

'I know about it,' John said.

'Uh, yeah, he does,' Hack said. 'I just wanted to ask who you, um, gave the job to.'

Pearson was silent. 'Are you happy with the results, Hack?'

'Happy?' he said, and almost laughed. 'I – sure, I guess.'

'This was a significant enterprise. I'm not sure if you appreciate the complexity of the assignment. The pricing we offered was extremely generous.'

'Um, sure. I just want to know about subcontracting.'

'I see,' Pearson said. 'You knew we reserved the right to do that, right?'

'Well . . . I guess. I mean, it doesn't matter if the NRA actually did it. I just want to know—'

Pearson's eyebrows shot up. 'What makes you think it was NRA work?'

'Oh!' Hack glanced at John, who looked disgusted. 'I just . . . thought.'

'Did you?' Pearson said. 'Well, that's a very interesting guess, Hack. Because, as we discussed, we treat our business associations with the utmost confidence. The *utmost* confidence.'

'That's what I want to talk about. I want to know if there were any other, um, business associates, besides the NRA.'

Pearson folded his hands neatly. 'In our line of work, Hack, discretion is critical. I'm surprised you don't know this already. Did I give you a brochure?'

'Ah—'

'I'll give you a brochure. We have safeguards in place to protect your confidentiality. They are incontrovertible.'

'Okay,' Hack said.

'But I see you want additional assurance,' Pearson said. 'Which, given the nature of the job, I can understand. Very well. I can inform you that the directive passed directly from us to a third party, who carried out the work. No intermediaries were involved.'

'Right,' Hack said, relieved. 'Okay, well, thanks—'

'I hope you appreciate the magnitude of what we've accomplished here, Hack. You will remember that when you make your monthly payments.'

'Yes, Sergeant Pearson,' Hack said.

'Senior Sergeant Pearson,' Pearson said.

John was upbeat on the walk home from the Police. 'They're a very focused organization, all right. John was one hundred percent right about that.'

'Uh-huh,' Hack said. He was thinking about Violet again.

John peered at the brochure. 'Each case has a single contact. Everything's encrypted, so employees can't tell what their colleagues are working on. Even management can only access job numbers, not names. And it's the largest Australian-based company in the world! Did you know that?'

'No.'

'You want to know why Americans took over the world, Hack? Because they respect achievement. Before this was a USA country, our ideal was the working-class battler, for Christ's sake. If

Australians ruled the world, everyone would work one day a week and bitch about the pay.' He shook his head. 'Then there's the British, who thought there was something wrong with making money. No surprise they ended up kissing the colony's ass. The Japanese, they think the pinnacle of achievement is a Government job. The Chinese are Communist, the Germans are Socialists, the Russians are broke . . . who does that leave?'

'Canada?'

'America,' John said. 'The United fucking States of America, the country founded on free-market capitalizm. I tell you, those Founding Fathers knew their shit.'

Hack was silent.

'So here's this Australian company,' John said, waving the brochure, 'doing the only thing Australians still have a competitive advantage in: keeping their traps shut. Still, it makes our job easier.'

'Does it?'

'Sure. It means we only have to kill Pearson.'

'Oh.'

'Although, when I say "we" . . .'

Hack dropped his head.

'It's in your contract,' John said. 'Page eight. A clause called "logical extensions."'

Hack shook his head wildly. 'No, I can't do this again. Please. I can't.'

John sighed. 'Jesus, Hack, you are the worst goddamn assassin I ever heard of. We wanted a nice little rampage, something we could write off as an employee gone postal if the Government caught up with us. Neat and tidy. But no, you had to go and outsource.' He sighed. 'Good people get the job done, Hack, no matter what. Remember that. Is this your apartment?'

'Yes,' Hack said. When they reached the top of the stairs, he fumbled for his keys.

John reached out and stopped him. 'Knock first. We don't want John getting jumpy.'

'Okay.' He hoped John wasn't the sort to get jumpy. He hoped he hadn't explored the apartment.

An eye appeared at the peephole. 'Hack?' It was Violet's voice. He heard her unlocking. 'Hack, there's a man in here—'

'Violet! It's okay, there's a guy with me, too. It's all right.'

Silence.

'Hello?'

'Who's that?' John said. He tried the handle. 'That's not John.'

'It's my girlfriend. Violet.'

'Give me the keys,' John said. He wrestled with the door. Finally the door swung open. It was dark inside. 'John? You there, buddy?'

'Violet?'

'You go first,' John said. He pushed Hack forward.

Hack moved blindly, his hands out before him. He couldn't think why the lights would be out. And why Violet had answered the—

John said, 'Ag!'

He turned. John was two steps behind him and Violet had a long knife to his throat. She must have hidden behind the door. 'Violet! He's John Nike! Let him go!'

'Girl,' John said, 'you want to let go of me, right now. You really do.'

'Hack,' Violet said, 'pack some clothes. We're leaving.' She looked at him. 'Do it!'

Hack jolted into motion. He went into the bedroom and started pulling open drawers. He threw clothes into a bag and showed it to her.

'What about shoes? Hack! And get my computer.'

He grabbed some shoes from the bedroom closet and collected her notebook. When he emerged, she was patting down John's pockets.

'Violet,' Hack said, 'I really think you're making a mistake.'

'Go,' she said. 'Outside.' She pulled a pistol from John's jacket and looked at him.

'That has sentimental value,' John said. Violet pushed him into the living room. He regarded them from the darkness. 'Violet – is that your name? This is your last chance. If you do this, you'll regret it. I guarantee it.' He held out his hand. 'Give me back my gun.'

She slammed the door. Hack followed her down the stairs and into the car park. 'What's going on? Where are we going?'

'I think I killed a man,' she said.

'Oh.' Hack left a respectful silence.

'Now *drive*,' she said, and he got in.

17 BUY

Buy couldn't tell what color the walls were. The sounds of the crowd were dulled and thick, and he kept realizing that his head was heading for the bar just before he reached it. Buy was very drunk. He was going down in flames.

Buy hadn't been in to work for almost a week. He'd arranged the leave a month ago, knowing that the last week of the financial year would leave him drained; of course, he hadn't known just how true that would turn out to be. It was Wednesday night, and tomorrow Buy was meant to front up to Mitsui with the stain of a dead girl on his soul, and he absolutely, definitely was not ready for that.

A woman at the bar was looking at him. He squinted at her and she rose and came toward him. He tried to sit straighter on the stool.

'Hi.'

'Hi,' Buy said. When she didn't say anything else, he added, 'Can I buy you a drink?'

'A Manhattan, please.'

He ordered the drink. 'I'm Buy Mitsui.'

'Sandy John Hancock. You got life insurance?' She laughed. 'I'm kidding. Are you a stockbroker?'

'Yes,' Buy said. He managed to discern a black skirt and a tight green top.

'I wanted to be a stockbroker, once. But I didn't like the math. Do you have to know math?'

'Sometimes,' he said, even though the answer was no, not really.

'Thanks.' He realized she wasn't talking to him. The barman was looking at him expectantly. He dug out a card from his wallet and fumbled it onto the bar.

'Points card?'

'No.' Buy had one, but didn't think he could find it.

'You should get one of those,' Sandy said. 'I got one last year, after they formed US Alliance. I got a Team Advantage card, too. You earn so much free stuff.'

'I don't need free stuff.'

'You must be rich. Are you?' She laughed. 'I'm just kidding.'

'I have an unlimited AmEx. But you have to be able to . . . recite the numbers . . . to use it.' He felt his head dipping toward the bar again.

'Unlimited? Wow. So you could, like, buy a whole apartment on plastic.'

Buy said nothing. He tried to drain his glass, but nothing came out. He set it down on the bar as carefully as he could. 'Life insurance,' he said. 'It doesn't actually protect your life, does it? It just gives you money for it.'

'Well, life insurance is for your dependents,' Sandy said. 'If you have any.'

63

Buy realized she was waiting for an answer. 'I don't.'

'I find that hard to believe.' He saw teeth.

'Mmm,' Buy said. The bar was swaying. 'Do you want to see my apartment?'

'Does it have a view?'

'Um,' he said. 'Yes, it—'

'I'm just kidding,' she said. 'Let's go.'

On the street, he asked, 'Have you ever done something generous for no reason?'

'Sure. Everybody has.'

'Once I gave a girl five thousand dollars.'

'For no reason?'

'Because she wanted it.'

'You know, *I* want five thousand dollars.' Sandy laughed. Buy said nothing. 'What did she do?'

'She died.'

'She *died*? What, because you gave her money?'

'I think so.'

'You mean the one time you did something nice for no reason, the person *died*?'

Buy swayed, and she caught his arm.

'Let me help you,' Sandy said.

'No,' he said, but she did anyway.

18 JENNIFER

It was hard to believe how far Kate could strew the contents of one schoolbag. 'Kate!' Jennifer yelled. 'Where have you put your drink bottle?'

'It's on the TV.'

'Why is it on the TV?' She didn't really want to know. She'd spent twenty minutes trying to make sandwiches with one arm in a sling and when she picked them up all the cheese fell out. It was her first day back at work and Jennifer was being thwarted by slippery condiments.

Kate entered the kitchen, carrying her schoolbag. 'It makes the reception better.'

'Well – go get it, please. We're both late.'

Kate left. Jennifer wrapped the sandwiches and tucked them into the schoolbag. There were some papers crammed in there, and Jennifer pulled them out. Papers usually meant things she had to sign to avoid getting scammed by a school fund-raising drive. Last year she'd ended up with a crate of Barbie dolls to sell; they were still under the house. Mattel ran good schools, but the merchandising was killing her.

The papers weren't about fund-raising. It looked like Kate's schoolwork, a paper on penguins. There were drawings and writing and printouts of pictures from the internet. It looked pretty impressive to Jennifer. 'Kate?'

Kate reentered. 'I've got it.'

'What's this?'

'What? Oh. A project. It's due in today.'

'It looks great. *Really* great.'

'Well, I like penguins.'

'Do you want a folder for it? It's going to get crushed if you take it in like this.'

'Do we have folders?'

She looked at her watch. 'For you, I have folders.' She led Kate into the study and rooted through her desk drawer. There was a Government report on inner-city crime rates in a smart, gray folder, and she tipped it out. 'How about this?'

'Yeah!'

'You know, we should put the pages behind plastic sheets,' Jennifer said. 'They'll look snazzy.'

'Mommy, you said we were late.'

'A project this nice,' Jennifer said, 'should be behind plastic sheets.'

'Okay!' Kate said, excited. She ran to get it.

She was so late to work she missed her own Welcome Back party, which she was grateful for. Since she'd been injured her answering machine had fielded fourteen well wishes from colleagues. It wasn't totally about her, she knew: it was about Taylor, who had gone to work Friday morning and died in a shopping mall. Jennifer hadn't done anything except stay alive. But this was a big deal to agents, who had the highest death rate of any occupation except machine operators.

There was an e-mail waiting for her from Legal, about the suit from the Mercedes-Benz dealer whose car she'd fallen on. It said:

> Dear Field Agent Jennifer,
>
> Please justify why damage to the property in question (1 × MERCEDES-BENZ E420 SEDAN) was unavoidable in the course of carrying out your duties. In particular, please specify:
>
> (1) whether you considered any alternative plans of action that would not have led to the destruction of this property;
>
> (2) if so, why you did not pursue these alternative plans;
>
> (3) a statement about your mental state at the time.

She had a lot of experience with allowing memos from Legal to grow old and die in her In Box, but this one, she decided, deserved a response. She tapped out:

> The alternatives I considered were:
>
> (1) jumping under a passing bus;
> (2) shooting myself in both legs;
> (3) dragging some sorry asses out of the Legal Department and throwing them off the third floor.
>
> I did not pursue the first two strategies because they did not guarantee me as much personal injury as landing on a Mercedes. I did not pursue the third strategy because my mental state at the time must have been severely impaired.

'My God,' Calvin said, entering. 'You're really back. How's the shoulder?'

'Hi,' she said, turning. 'Did you get Hack Nike?'

He dropped into a chair. 'Come on, Jen, this isn't Europe. I can't just get someone. We have no evidence. We have no *budget.*'

'I *asked* you to.'

'I assumed you were delirious,' Calvin said. 'Look, anyway, I've been busy interviewing families, trying to scrounge up funding. So far, zip. And I'm down to the last couple.'

'Who?'

'Ummm . . .' He slid his chair over to the desk and shuffled some papers. 'Jim GE and Mary Shell. Parents of Hayley McDonald's. Killed at . . .' He looked up.

'Chadstone?'

'Maybe you should sit this out.'

'Don't coddle me,' she said. 'I can run an interview.'

There was a knock on the door. A man stood in the doorway. His suit was so cheap it shone. 'Jennifer Government,' he said. 'Maybe you think you're a comedian. Maybe you think this whole situation is funny.'

'Who are you?' Calvin said.

'Lemme guess,' Jennifer said. 'Legal?'

'My department has a job to do, Jennifer. We're trying to defend *your* budget. We can do without you sending us insulting replies.'

She said, 'Don't ask me why I chose to fall onto a car and talk about being insulted, you shit. I'm wearing a sling here.'

He reddened. 'Well, we still need that information. It may not seem important to you, but this is a serious suit.'

She couldn't help it: she looked at his suit.

'I see,' the lawyer said. 'It's all very, very amusing.'

'Ah, look,' Calvin said. 'We'll get you the info you want. We have interviews to conduct now. Okay?'

'Fine,' the lawyer said, and left.

'What did you do to him?'

'Nothing,' she said. 'Go get Hayley's parents.'

He left. She tried to push back her hair before remembering there wasn't anything left to push: just a crude, dark shock. She missed her hair.

Calvin led Hayley's parents in and offered them seats. They were shy, clutching coffees in polystyrene cups. She stared at them. It was hard to forget she'd seen their daughter shot. Calvin cleared his throat.

She blinked. 'Jim, Mary, I'm Field Agent Jennifer Government. I'm very sorry for your loss. I'm not sure how familiar you are with Government procedure in these circumstances.'

Mary looked lost. Jim said, 'You want money.'

Jennifer folded her hands on the desk. 'In order to pursue the perpetrators, we need funding, yes. The Government's budget only extends to preventing crime, not punishing it. For a retributive investigation, we can only proceed if we can obtain funding.' She gave them a moment. 'I apologize for the question. Can you contribute?'

Mary shifted. Jim said, 'I . . . I've had a very bad three months. I lost my job . . .'

Silence. Calvin folded his arms.

'She played hockey,' Mary said, then bit her lip.

'There were Government agents at the mall,' Jim said. His ears were red. 'If you had stopped these people then, Hayley would – we wouldn't be here.'

'We did our best with the information we had,' Calvin said. 'We're sorry, Jim. We lost an agent in this mess.'

Jennifer leaned forward. 'I was there. At Chadstone. If anyone should have stopped them, it was me.'

His eyes darted to her sling. 'And now you want money.'

'Yes.'

Silence. 'This wasn't some street shooting.'

'No. We think it was planned.'

'Then they'll be hard to catch.'

'Yes.'

He nodded. He looked at Mary, then his hands. Then he looked at Jennifer. 'Will you try?'

'If I have the budget, I will get them. I promise you that.'

'All right,' he said. 'Then I'll sell my house.'

Her relief was frightening. 'Thank you, Jim.'

'Jen, that was really bad form,' Calvin said, closing the door. 'You know you're not meant to promise results. No investigation is a slam dunk.'

'We have funding.' She couldn't stop jiggling her leg.

'And don't smile like that,' he said. 'What's the matter with you? You're freaking me out.'

'Let's go pick up Hack,' she said.

19 BILLY

Someone was shaking him. 'Nnn,' Billy said. 'Quit it.'

'Get up,' the someone said. 'We're leaving.'

He sat up. It was an NRA clone. Black T-shirt, camouflage pants, buzzcut haircut, too much time in the gym: Billy was having trouble telling them apart. 'Leaving where?'

'There's a briefing in the mess. Get dressed and assemble there in fifteen.'

'Yes, sir!' Billy said. He had discovered that everyone was much more relaxed if you called them sir.

He showered, standing under the water for too long. When he was done, he went back to his bunk and dressed in the crisp pants and T-shirt laid out for him. The T-shirt was black with a big NRA logo on the chest: an AK-47 crossed with a burly arm. Underneath, it said: FREEDOM IS AN ASSAULT RIFLE. That was kind of catchy, Billy thought. The NRA was getting hip.

There was a kid standing guard outside the barracks, and he snapped to attention. Billy attempted a salute, squinting in the sun.

'Good morning, sir!' the kid said. His head was shaved so brutally it looked like someone had gouged his skull. 'I am informed that you may wish to visit briefing tent 4A, sir!'

'Sure, okay.'

'If you will accompany me, sir!'

Billy followed. The compound was like a mutant Boy Scout camp: all green tents and vehicles and barrels, smack in the middle of nowhere. He saw a troop of soldiers drilling in a field. They reminded him of high school football players with guns. Then a tank rolled past.

'Shit! What's that?'

'That is an Abrams M1A battle tank, sir!'

Billy looked around with new respect. Now he understood why the NRA membership fees were so high.

The kid led him to a tent at the front of the camp, set back from a dusty road. He held open the flap for Billy. Inside, a dozen men looked up.

'Close the fucking door,' the man at the front said. He was the older man Billy had met in the bush: his name was Yallam. 'Mosquitoes like birds in this place.'

'Yes, sir!' Billy said. He squeezed onto the end of a bench.

'Now we're all here,' Yallam said. 'We depart camp in exactly six minutes. Our destination is Melbourne, our target is an employee of the Police, one Senior Sergeant Pearson. We will eliminate the target quickly and quietly, and return to base. Questions?'

A man at the front raised his hand. 'Weapons?'

'Issued in-flight. Anyone else?'

In-flight? Billy thought.

'Yeah,' a soldier said. 'What's with the FNG?'

'Bill's a good man,' Yallam said. 'He's been reassigned here after completing some classified action.'

'All right,' the guy said, nodding at Billy. Billy raised his eyebrows in return.

'Other questions?'

Billy became aware of a drone outside the tent. He looked around.

'All right. Good luck, God speed, straight shooting.'

The men began filing outside. Billy wondered if now was a good time to cut and run. The past few days he'd kept a low profile, but now it was sounding as if the NRA expected him to *fight*, and he definitely wasn't—

A hand fell on his shoulder. 'You're probably wondering why you're being sent back into action so soon,' Yallam said. 'The truth is, we were only assigned this action this morning. Command feels that moving you again might arouse suspicion.' He held Billy's gaze. 'Maybe it's for the best. Get back on the horse.'

The drone had turned into a roar. 'Uh, I see.'

'It's important that you integrate into the team like any other NRA soldier, Bill. Our enemies are looking for you. Now go join your squad.'

'Yes, sir!' Billy said. He pushed his way out through the tent flap, thinking: *I am surrounded by maniacs.* Then he stopped.

There was a green military transport aircraft straddling the road. Fat NRA logos adorned its sides. The noise from its engines was tremendous. The NRA squad was marching up a ramp into its belly.

'Bill!' one of the soldiers shouted. 'Come on, move your ass!'

This is not skiing, Billy thought. He jogged toward the transport.

20 HACK

Hack woke to Violet moving about the bedroom, gathering clothes. He sat up, rubbing his face. 'What . . .'

'I have to do my software demo.' She was pulling on a short black skirt; already wearing a cream shirt. 'You knew this, Hack.'

Hack did know that. 'But . . . aren't we going to the Police? Or the Government?'

She blew air through her teeth. 'You packed me *one* pair of underpants. And—' She shook her head. 'I don't have time to go to the Government. You go.'

He bit his lip. 'You sure you don't want to come? Since, I mean, you killed that guy . . .'

'You want me to defend myself against a murder charge with two hundred dollars?'

'But it was self-defense. It doesn't matter how much money—'

'Don't be naïve,' Violet said. 'Look, if my demo goes well, I'll have money. Then I can talk to the Government.'

'I guess,' Hack said. 'Okay.'

She hefted her laptop. 'Wish me luck.'

'Good luck. And – be careful, okay?'

'I will,' she said. 'Don't wake my sister.'

Hack padded out to the kitchen in his dressing gown and made a bowl of cereal. He couldn't find the sugar, so added some strange, unbranded honey. He sat at the dining table and tried to eat quietly.

Violet's sister had a lot of books. They filled three bookcases, with bizarre titles like *An Equal Society* and *Socialist Thought*. Hack wondered what they were about.

At ten o'clock he caught a cab downtown to the Government office, which was a couple of floors in a dingy building that looked as if it hadn't been cleaned since 1980. The lobby was huge, though, and crawling with people in scruffy-looking suits who Hack could only assume were Government agents. He felt them looking at him as he walked up to reception, and started sweating. This wasn't like the Police, with magazines and nice-looking women dressed in cop uniforms.

The agent behind the desk was doing something to his computer. Hack waited patiently. After a while, he cleared his throat.

'Just a second,' the agent said.

'Sorry.' He waited.

'All right.' The agent looked him up and down. 'Who are you here to see?'

'Um, I don't know. I'm here because I – I mean my girlfriend – might have killed someone.'

'You don't have an appointment?'

'No,' Hack said. 'See, there's this body in my kitchen—'

'You're meant to call first,' the agent said. 'To set up an appointment. We can't drop everything just because you walk in.'

'Oh. Sorry.'

The agent poked at his computer a bit more. Hack wondered if he should clear his throat again. The agent said, 'You sure this guy's dead?'

'My girlfriend said she thought he was.'

'Your girlfriend?'

'Yep. She wasn't sure but—'

'Why didn't *she* make an appointment?'

'Uh,' Hack said, 'I don't know. I just wanted to report—'

'Yeah, okay, look,' the agent said. 'Take a seat. I'll try to find someone to talk to you about your alleged dead body.'

'Maybe I should come back later,' Hack said.

'Just sit down,' the agent said.

He sat on a hard wooden bench for fifty minutes. Then an agent came out and spoke to the desk guy. The desk guy gestured at Hack, and the other agent came over, scratching his stubble. 'Hack Nike?'

'Yes.'

'You found a dead body somewhere?'

'Um, not exactly,' Hack said. 'What happened was—'

'Yeah, okay. Come with me.' The agent led Hack down a lot of corridors and into a room that had a table and two chairs and that was it. The walls were glass, and Hack could see agents in other offices moving around, glancing in at him. 'You want a coffee?'

'No thanks.'

'Well, I need one. Hold tight.' He left. Hack jiggled his leg, nervous. There were two agents in an office across the corridor, and one of them had a weird smudge underneath her left eye, like a rectangular bruise. No: a tattoo, a barcode tattoo. That was strange, Hack thought. The Government was meant to be against all that consumer stuff.

'Okay,' the agent said, entering. 'So about this body.' He yawned.

'Well, he attacked my girlfriend,' Hack said. 'I was out and he . . . he tried to assault my girlfriend. She defended herself and hit him with a crumpet toaster. She thinks she killed him.'

'A crumpet toaster?'

'Yep.'

'What is that?'

'It's . . . you know, like an electric toaster. You cook crumpets in it. It's better than broiling them.'

'Huh,' the agent said. 'Can you do bagels in that?'

'Um, no,' Hack said. 'Bagels don't fit in the slots. But you can get bagel toasters, I think.'

'How about that,' the agent said. 'I had no idea.'

'So, anyway,' Hack said. The barcode agent and her partner were in the corridor, now, speaking to someone. The woman looked up and met Hack's eyes. He looked away quickly. 'It was self-defense and everything, but I thought I should report it . . . just in case.'

The agent rubbed his face. 'Hack, this is something your girlfriend will have to sort out with the deceased's lawyers. Contact them, negotiate some sort of compensation. It's not a Government matter unless you can't come to an agreement.'

'Oh,' Hack said, relieved. 'Okay, sure, I can do that.'

The door opened. The woman with the barcode tattoo and her partner were in the doorway. 'Hack Nike?' the woman said.

He started. 'Yes.'

'What's up, Jen?' the agent said.

'Out,' she said. 'Now.' Her eyes were fixed on Hack. Hack realized: it had happened. He had made another big mistake.

The first agent left and then nobody spoke. The woman sat across the table from him and her partner stood against the wall, his arms folded. Finally, Hack said, 'I just came in to report—'

'Hack Nike, I'm Jennifer Government, Field Agent. This is Calvin Government, Field Agent. We have information that you're responsible for the illegal initiation of deadly force against up to fourteen persons at various Nike Town stores. Do you understand?'

'Ag,' Hack said. He felt his throat closing. 'No, no—'

'Yes, yes,' Jennifer said. 'You arranged for the NRA to shoot a bunch of kids who'd bought Nike Mercurys. Some kind of promotion, right? Get out with your shoes alive and win a trip for two?'

He felt faint. 'Wait, I . . . I want to call my girlfriend.'

'She a lawyer, Hack?' Calvin said.

'No, she's . . .' He couldn't make himself say *unemployed*. 'She'll know what to do.'

'Sorry,' Calvin said. 'No girlfriends.'

'Oh, and we're recording you,' Jennifer said. 'The first guy told you that, right?'

'Let me save you some time,' Calvin said. 'We know you're a Merchandising Officer. We know you're eager for promotion.'

'It sounded like a great idea at the time, right?' Jennifer said. 'Kill a few kids, make a few bucks, back slaps all round at the office.'

'And a bonus in your next paycheck – maybe tied to sales growth? Ten thousand, fifty thousand dollars? More?'

'Plus a promotion, of course. You get out of Merc work, into the creative stuff. White-collar gutter jobs are so repetitive, aren't they, Hack? After a while you go *nuts*—'

'Stop! It wasn't my idea! I just did what they told me!'

'Who?' she said, leaning forward. 'Who, Hack?'

'There were two of them – they made me—'

'*Who?*'

He swallowed. 'I don't think I should tell you.'

Jennifer leaned back. She looked at Calvin.

'They could kill me,' Hack whispered. 'If I tell you.'

'Aw, we'll take care of you,' Calvin said. 'Don't worry about that.'

'You're going to have to tell us who they are, Hack,' Jennifer said.

'I can't! They – they made me sign a contract without reading it.'

'Made you? They used force?'

Hack was silent.

'No,' she said. 'No force. So you voluntarily signed a contract without reading it.'

'I know that was a mistake—'

'A mistake,' Jennifer said, disgusted. 'You dumb shit, why do you think anybody wants you to sign a contract without reading it? Because it's *bad*, Hack, it's a bad contract.'

'We're going to need a copy of that,' Calvin said.

Hack dropped his eyes. 'I don't have one.'

Silence. When he looked up, they were staring at him.

'You don't *understand*. They offered me a *job*, a job in Marketing.' He stopped, choked up.

'Hack,' Jennifer said, leaning forward. 'It's time for you to make a decision. You can either help us go after the people responsible for the Nike slayings—'

77

'Which will expose you to whatever penalties are in that contract,' Calvin said. 'And I'm guessing they're not that you have to bring the cups to the next company picnic, if you know what I mean.'

'Or you can keep your mouth shut,' Jennifer said. 'Which will expose you to *us.*'

'I'd hate to land fourteen counts of deadly force against someone who didn't deserve it, I really would. That's—' He looked at Jennifer. 'Pretty much life, right?'

'For sure. And the financial penalties – well, maybe you can negotiate to pay them off at ten cents on the dollar, something like that. Plenty of crims do that. If you work hard, you can clear your debt in twenty, thirty years.'

'I don't know, Jen,' Calvin said. 'Prison housing prices have really jumped lately. Some of these places, you do fifteen years' labor and come out owing them for food and board.'

'I guess in your case it would be academic anyway,' Jennifer said to Hack. 'Since you wouldn't ever get out.' She leaned forward. 'Think about it, Hack. A guy like you, reasonable skills, employable – suddenly you're laying tar in Utah for the rest of your life. And you know the safety record of prison workers. Only last month, those eight guys in – where was it?'

'Wichita Falls,' Calvin said. 'Texas. Although I think one of them made it. I mean, obviously he's all messed up from the scalding, but I think he's still alive.'

'You can take freedom for granted, Hack,' Jennifer said, 'until you're living in a cell and you have to ask permission every time you want to take a shit. Don't you think?'

'Marketing guys,' Hack whispered. 'It was John and John, from Guerrilla Marketing.'

Jennifer leaned forward. '*John Nike?* Vice-President?'

He nodded dumbly.

'Brown eyes, brown hair, flat face, John Nike?'

'Yes.'

'Good boy, Hack,' Calvin said. 'You won't regret this.'

Jennifer dragged her chair closer to him. 'Let's start from the beginning.' She smiled. It was the first time Hack had seen her do that. She looked almost tender. 'Tell me everything.'

21 VIOLET

When Violet arrived at the ExxonMobil building, they gave her a CONTRACTOR badge, which she pinned to her jacket lapel. Her escort was a kid in a white short-sleeved shirt and pants so cheap his knees reflected. Violet was disappointed. Geeks didn't dress that way anymore, or rather, successful geeks didn't. Even Violet knew it was worth investing in impressive threads.

'I heard about what you're doing,' the kid said in the elevator. 'It sounds pretty cool. But it won't work. Eight months ago, maybe. We had a whole bunch of attacks, denial of service, e-bombs, phreaking, the works. Then management gave us a ton of money to upgrade everything.' He led her down a corridor and opened a door.

Violet went in. There were computers and wires and crap everywhere. Four men sat around the boardroom-sized table, all in front of keyboards except one, who was therefore in charge. He was very large and didn't smile.

'Violet.' He extended his hand. 'I'm Rendell ExxonMobil. This is my team: James, Peter, Saqlain, Hunter.' She nodded at them. 'If you don't mind, let's get started. We have fifteen minutes before our next applicant.'

She took a seat at the thick table and snapped open her laptop case. The geeks slid their chairs inward, preparing to do battle.

She powered on her laptop, snapped in an RJ45 connector. 'Do you want to give me a login, or should I do it the hard way?'

Rendell looked at Hunter, who was so thin it was like Rendell had been stealing his food. 'An ordinary employee password?'

'Yes.'

'I'll spot you that.'

'I can crack it if you want me to.'

'It's trivial.'

'That's why I'm asking.'

Hunter managed to sound gracious. 'I'll ghost your machine. User is "applicant8," pass is the same.'

Applications began streaming into Violet's laptop, transforming it into a standardized, centrally managed ExxonMobil PC. While she waited, she glanced at the beige box humming behind her. It had the dimensions and aesthetics of a refrigerator: a Hewlett-Packard Unix machine. 'This is your server here?'

'That's it.'

'And we're isolated from the company network?'

'We're safe enough.'

'I strongly suggest you physically isolate this room from the rest of the network.'

They locked eyes for a while. She had to resist a sigh. Violet wasn't interested in comparing dick size with skinny geeks.

'Unplug it,' Rendell said.

The kid, James, crawled under the desk. 'Okay, got it.'

'Buckle up,' Violet said, and logged in. There was a little icon on her desktop called Fizz, in the shape of a soda can. She clicked it.

Her machine said: *bing!* A window appeared: *McAfee Anti-Virus: WARNING! McAfee has detected a possible virus on your computer. Virus Type: unknown. File(s) infected: Fizz.exe. Delete–Fix–Ignore.*

'Game over,' Hunter said across the table, pushing back his chair. 'Sorry, you're dead, Violet. Thanks for playing.'

'You shouldn't have let him ghost your machine,' James said. He was looking over her shoulder. 'He installed our virus checker.'

She looked at her screen a while longer. When the network activity stopped, she closed the lid and rested her elbows on the table.

'And not only did we bust your virus,' Hunter said, 'but we got a copy of its signature, so we can spot it if it shows up anywhere else. You're history.'

Violet glanced at the hub, a squat, plastic box routing traffic between the server and PCs. Its green lights were flashing. 'So my virus is getting transmitted to the server.'

'No, not your virus. Its signature. Big difference.'

The hub's lights were increasingly active. The geeks eyed it. *Flash-flash-flash-flash.* Violet said, 'Then your server transmits my virus to the checkers on every PC. Right?'

'No, no, no.' Hunter's eyes flicked to the hub. 'Virus checkers don't store actual viruses. They store *patterns.*'

'My virus checker is updating,' one of the other geeks said.

'Mine, too.'

'It's meant to!' Hunter said. 'Be cool, guys. It's inoculating us.'

'You have a lot of faith in your checker,' Violet said, 'for a product with buffer-overrun issues.'

Hunter stared.

'Last chance,' she said.

It was a small noise, and to anyone but tech-heads, hardly noticeable. From each PC: *chik-chik-chik-chik-chik*—

'Shit!' Saqlain said. 'Disk activity—'

'Me too—'

The machines crashed together. The geeks stared at dark screens. Each computer beeped simultaneously, rebooting. Violet knew what they were looking at now, a screen that said: *BOOT DISK FAILURE: INSERT SYSTEM DISK.* This meant that either someone had unscrewed each computer and removed the hard drive, or the disks had been trashed so thoroughly the computers couldn't tell if they were still there.

'Jesus, she wiped the master boot record!'

'Did you go through the virus checker?' Saqlain asked, astounded. 'Did you send a worm through the *virus checker?*'

She swiveled her chair to see the lights on the HP server lock up. When that was done, she turned to Rendell. 'Interested?'

Rendell looked from his server to his dead PCs.

'It could have been your whole company,' Violet said. 'Not just this room. You tell me: how vulnerable do you want to be?'

'Whoa, whoa,' Hunter said. 'You know, I hate to ruin the party, but we don't need to buy anything from you. I can recover this thing. Two seconds of disk activity, it'll be *somewhere.*'

'Whatever you can recover from those drives,' she said, 'you're welcome to.'

Silence. Rendell lifted his chin. 'James? Cancel our other applicants, please.'

22 BUY

Buy woke up feeling like someone had rearranged his intestines. He staggered into the bathroom. On the mirror in red lipstick was:

HOPE YOU'RE FEELING BETTER,

SLEEPYHEAD! CALL ME!

♥SANDY

He sank to the cool tiles. Buy didn't think he'd be calling Sandy John Hancock. He crawled into the shower instead. This was not going to be a good day.

He arrived at Mitsui very late, which for a stockbroker was not just improper but obscene. The stock markets had been twenty-four-hour for several years now, and Hamish would be angrily waiting for Buy to relieve him.

The elevator doors opened and he walked between the cubicles. Hamish jumped to his feet, snapping closed his briefcase. 'Sorry, Hamish, I—'

'That's all right.' He was looking at Buy oddly. His whole reaction was odd. 'They told me what happened. You don't even have to be here, we can get a temp—'

'No, I'm fine.'

'You sure?'

'Yeah.'

'Okay. Well, good luck.'

Buy watched Hamish leave, then sat down. He felt eyes watching him and turned. Suddenly a lot of brokers were frowning at their screens and flicking lint off their pants. He turned back to his screen.

He looked at it for a long time. Something was wrong, but he didn't know what. He clicked through a few pages of overnight financial summaries, but kept losing focus on the screen. His attention was drifting back to Friday night. His phone rang, and he looked at it, abruptly frightened. He didn't want to answer it.

He felt sweat on his forehead. Brokers burned out sometimes; everyone knew somebody who had derailed. It was a terrifying idea, that you could lose the motivation to keep going. That everything that used to define and sustain you could collapse into meaninglessness.

An hour later, Buy felt a hand on his shoulder. He was staring into space.

It was Cameron. 'Want to talk?'

*

He'd only been inside Cameron's fishbowl office a couple of times. Everyone outside could see you, so you knew they were speculating about you. Not the office for a paranoid, Buy decided.

'You don't have to be here today,' Cameron said. 'You know that, right?'

'I don't get paid if I'm not.'

Cameron shrugged. 'Even so.'

Buy said, 'I'm fine.'

'How many trades have you made this morning?'

Buy was pretty sure the computer on Cameron's desk could answer that question. He was pretty sure it already had. 'None.'

'I'm going to help you, now,' Cameron said. 'All right? I've heard a whisper that ExxonMobil could be the target of a takeover.'

'ExMo?'

'The word is that Shell likes the idea of ExMo at up to forty-seven.'

He thought. 'Shell is . . . half ExMo's size. It can't be true.'

'I think it is.'

Buy considered. This was a huge tip, even more valuable than the NRA information Sami had given him. If he remembered right, ExMo was trading around thirty-one. Cameron was offering him sixteen dollars a share. 'Then thanks.'

'Thank me by making trades. You're a good broker, Buy. Don't let yourself get thrown.'

'I won't.'

'Good. Now get out there and trade.'

Buy left the office and walked down the staircase, trying to ignore the eyes on him. He sat down and clicked for the latest ExMo price. It was even lower than he'd thought: just above thirty.

He picked up the phone handset. The dial tone hummed in his ear. His hand shook. He felt sweat on his forehead. He tried to force

himself to focus on what was important. *Seventeen dollars a share.*
Seventeen dollars a share.

After a while, he put the phone down. His fingers felt like ice.
He could feel it in his gut: it had happened. He had burned out.
Buy had lost it.

23 JENNIFER

She requested an arrest warrant right away, but that was wishful
thinking. She was in the car with Calvin when Elise, her boss,
radioed. 'What's this application? Are you trying to create paperwork?'

'No, Elise,' Jennifer said. 'We have reason to believe John
Nike—'

'Because one suspect says so? You need more than that.'

'Right, but we're going to interview this Police officer and we'll
get him to confirm meeting with John Nike. Then we—'

'So talk to me after that. Right?'

'Right,' Jennifer said, and hung up the radio. 'Shit.'

'Well, it was worth a shot,' Calvin said. 'Hey, you know who
works around here? That Mitsui stockbroker. Want to interview
him?'

'Yeah. Sure.'

He changed lanes. 'So where do you know John Nike from?'

She blinked. 'What?'

'The way you reacted in the interview room, it seemed like you
knew him.'

'Oh,' she said. 'I just – you know, I've dealt with him before.'

'When?'

'Hey,' she said. 'Here's a question for you. Apparently someone told the hospital shrink I'm not interested in dating anymore. Any idea who that was?'

'Uh,' Calvin said. 'I might have said . . . you hadn't dated in a while . . .' He glanced at her. 'I was just trying to help.'

'I date plenty,' she said.

'Okay, okay. Fine.'

'I do,' she said.

'I wasn't arguing.'

'I've been busy, that's all.'

The radio said, 'Unit three-three-nine, come back.'

Jennifer picked up. 'Three-three-nine.'

'It's Gary. We're at that apartment you wanted us to check out, Hack Nike's? There's no dead body here.'

She looked at Calvin. He shrugged. 'You sure?'

'You want us to start cutting up furniture?'

'No.' She didn't have the budget to replace furniture. 'Any sign of a struggle?'

'The bed's unmade.'

'In the *kitchen*. There's meant to be a dead man in the kitchen.'

'The kitchen's spotless. It's the cleanest room in the apartment.'

'Okay. Thanks.' She hung up the radio.

Calvin said, 'You think Hack lied to us?'

'He never said he saw the body. He said his girlfriend told him it was there. This Violet.'

'So either Hack's lying, or Violet's lying—'

'Or John Nike cleaned up the scene.'

'Hmm,' Calvin said. 'I'll take door number three.'

'Shit!' she said. 'That asshole!'

Calvin looked at her.

'What?'

'So where did you say you knew John Nike from?'

'Why does it matter?'

86

'I'm trying to work out why this case is so important to you. Why you won't take time off, even though—'

'He killed fourteen people. Isn't that enough?'

'To explain the look you get? No.'

'I don't have a *look*.'

'Now you're getting irritable,' Calvin said. '*I* think you used to work with him. Before you joined the Government. And I think your mysterious source is someone you used to work with, too.'

Jennifer pressed her fingers to her temples. 'I've never worked for Nike. Okay? Now drop it.'

'Hmm,' Calvin said. 'Well, you sure didn't get that tattoo in the Government.'

Buy Mitsui took a long time to come down. Jennifer amused herself by reading the wall hangings. There were case studies up there, with pictures of suits shaking hands under headlines like *Mitsui & Reebok: Float Debuts Up 118%!* It reminded her of the photos they had in casinos: elderly couples in front of slot machines with improbable readouts. *JACKPOT!*

'I'm Buy,' a man said, and she turned.

He was tall and good-looking, which surprised her. It *had* been a while since she'd dated. 'Jennifer Government. Thanks for your time.'

'I thought I'd been through this. At the mall. I don't see why—'

Calvin said, 'Somewhere we can talk?'

His shoulders dropped. 'There's a room through here.'

They followed him. The meeting room was big and tastefully lit, the chairs heavy and wooden. There was nothing like this in the Government. 'Nice digs.'

'Our business sells intangibles,' Buy said. He took a seat opposite her. 'Nothing you can touch. So we like to appear very . . .' He knocked on the table.

'Rich?'

'Solid.' He smiled, but it was a strange, disconnected smile; it worried Jennifer a little. Buy Mitsui was not running on all cylinders.

Calvin flipped open his notepad. 'You were at the Chadstone Wal-Mart mall last Friday?'

'Yes.'

'But you didn't see anything.'

'I got there too late. The girl . . . she . . .'

'Take your time,' Jennifer said.

'I'm sorry. I'm not . . . The girl died. I couldn't help her. I tried.'

'You didn't see who shot her?'

'I didn't see anything. I told the Government people this last Friday.'

'Right,' Calvin said, flipping some more. 'You gave the girl some money? Why was that?'

'I wanted to.'

'But you'd never met her before?'

'No.'

Calvin paused. He was waiting for her to come in, Jennifer knew: to run a flanking formation, to squeeze from the other side. Instead, she said, 'I was there that night.'

Buy's eyebrows rose. 'At Chadstone?'

'They peeled me off the top of a Mercedes.'

His eyes widened. Then he laughed. 'I'm sorry. I didn't recognize you. You are . . . much improved.'

She looked down, a little flustered. 'It's a pretty fucking strange coincidence, you giving Hayley money to buy the shoes she was killed for, don't you think?'

She regretted the words immediately. Buy's face fell. 'I wish more than anything I had never met her.'

Calvin said, 'Did you see any of the assailants that night?'

'No.'

'Anyone who looked suspicious? At all?'

'No.'

Silence.

'So, the only suspicious thing you saw that night was yourself. Is that right?'

'I suppose so.'

Calvin looked at her. She nodded. 'All right,' he said. 'Then we're done. For now.'

Jennifer stood. Buy was staring at the tabletop. On impulse, she sat again. 'Hey,' she said.

He looked up.

'I understand how you feel.' He said nothing. She slid her card across the table to him. 'If there's anything else, call me. All right?'

He nodded wordlessly, looking at the card.

She touched his hand across the table. Then they left, passing through the lobby and exiting to bright sunshine. The door wheezed pneumatically behind them.

'Goddamn, Jennifer Government,' Calvin said finally. 'There may be hope for you yet.'

'Oh, shut up,' she said. 'Let's go talk to Pearson.'

24 BILLY

Billy NRA's plan was very simple: the second he could, he was going to run like hell. The longer this charade continued, the more fucked-up things were getting.

The inside of the plane had not seats but benches and straps, and when they were in the air, instead of getting peanuts and Cokes with too much ice they were given Vektor R4 assault rifles. It was the heaviest gun Billy had ever held. That somebody thought he might need it scared the crap out of him.

They landed somewhere rural and piled out of the plane and into the back of two Ryder rental trucks. More benches and straps. There was some chatter, none of it making much sense, and Billy stared at his black boots. He was starting to think he'd be better off if he was still lost in the bush.

The truck idled for two hours, then took off with such a start that Billy fell into the guy next to him. 'Sorry,' Billy said, and the guy said, 'You're right, buddy.' But Billy was not right. He was not right at all.

The squad leader pulled himself to his feet. 'We are now at T minus two minutes! Our primary objective when we reach the target is to maintain a safe operating perimeter, inside of which Team B will operate! Is this clear?'

'Yes, sir!' the men shouted. Billy didn't shout anything, but the word 'perimeter' was the most interesting thing he had heard all day.

The truck slowed, then stopped. The leader cracked open the doors and peered out while everybody else sat tight, fingering their Vektors. It was becoming clear to Billy there was going to be some fairly serious law-breaking going on here.

'Go, go, go!' the leader said, and threw open the doors.

Billy immediately saw two things: first, they were on a leafy, reasonably urban street, and second, someone was about to have a very bad traffic accident. The car was a late-model Ford, and the second Ryder truck plowed into it, catching its rear. The Ford made two full, smoking-tire revolutions, then bent itself around a telephone pole.

'Move!' someone yelled, and Billy realized he was gaping like an idiot. Some of the NRA soldiers were running toward the wrecked car, keeping low, as if they expected the guy inside to jump out with guns blazing. Two others were carrying something from the second

Ryder truck, something like the jaws of life. The largest group of soldiers were dragging metal barriers across the south side of the road. Billy started jogging north.

'Hey, you! South side, south side!'

'I'll cover the north!' he yelled back. 'Just gonna check it out!'

He heard footsteps behind him. He put on a burst of speed, but with the Vektor it was like trying to run with a motorcycle around his neck. A soldier grabbed his arm. He was a young guy, like Billy, but without the terror. 'What's the matter? South side, man!'

'Dude, I really have to go,' Billy said. 'No offense, but—'

Behind him, the jaws of life screeched. Billy jumped. NRA guys were tearing into the Ford, or what was left of it. For the first time, Billy noticed a Police insignia on its side. He saw someone moving inside it.

'Yallam's going to hear about this. Now get your ass back to the perimeter!'

'Look, this is all a big mistake,' he said, and then there were shots and Billy hit the deck. He raised his head. The young soldier was looking down at him contemptuously. The NRA soldiers were jogging away from the smashed Ford, holstering weapons. Billy realized they'd just accomplished their mission. He felt sick.

'Hostiles from the south! Hostiles inbound!'

'Come on! They need us!' The young soldier ran back toward the line of soldiers.

'No thanks,' Billy said. He got to his feet. 'See you later, man.'

Three dark blue cars crested the hill. They were fast and low and had some kind of rotary cannon set into their hoods: he vaguely recollected seeing them in the Police TV advertisements. The NRA soldiers opened fire. Then the Police car cannons clamored and suddenly there were bullets everywhere, bouncing off the cars, chewing up the road, and passing much too close to Billy's body.

'Fuck, fuck!' one of the jaws-of-life guys yelled. He was running to the second Ryder, which struck Billy as a good idea, too. He jumped into the back of it with the jaws guy and two other sweaty NRA soldiers. Inside, bullets like a hailstorm beat against the truck's side, creating alarming indentations. Someone up front revved the engine and the vehicle lunged forward.

'Team A, come back, come back,' the jaws guy said into his radio.

'Team A's gone, man,' a soldier said. 'Those cop cars! They annihilated us!'

'They can't get past the blockade,' the jaws guy said. 'They'll have to go around, do a full block. We've got maybe ninety seconds to lose them.'

Billy decided he was going to stick close the jaws guy. This dude knew what he was doing. The truck bounced and lurched. Billy clutched at the strap. Then he felt them slowing.

The jaws guy said, 'What's going on?'

'Don't ask me,' Billy said, but the man was talking to his radio. The radio said something like: *Crrsshuvfss ssahvunt.*

'Right,' the jaws guy said. He looked at the rest of them. 'Okay. Now we have a problem.'

25 JENNIFER

'It's a good deal,' Calvin said, overtaking a Chrysler. 'It's not like I actually spend more. I buy what I would have anyway, but from US Alliance companies.'

'Mmm,' Jennifer said.

'You buy your computer from IBM, your gas from Shell, use

AT&T for calls . . . soon you're getting gift vouchers, for like, fifty bucks. And if you buy a car—'

'I don't like loyalty programs.'

'Well, you could go with Team Advantage,' Calvin said. 'But US Alliance has twice as many companies that are number one in their industry.'

'What is that, from their brochure?'

The car radio said: 'Field Agents Jennifer and Calvin, please identify your position.'

She picked up. 'Downtown, King and Flinders.'

'Proceed to corner Chapel and Inkerman streets, St. Kilda. Crime in progress, extreme caution advised.'

'That's where we're going. What's the situation?'

'Distress call from the Police. One Senior Sergeant Pearson Police is under attack. Instigators may be NRA.'

'Fuck!' She dropped the radio. 'Go!'

Calvin gunned the engine, weaving through traffic. She flicked on the siren and they roared down St. Kilda Road. 'We shouldn't have stopped to talk to that stockbroker.'

'Inkerman Street is, what, the—'

'Two more blocks,' she said. 'See where that Ryder truck came from?'

'Yep.' He slowed and killed the siren.

The truck passed them, heading in the opposite direction. Its front had sustained some damage, she saw: the grille was smashed in. She frowned. 'Turn around.'

'What?'

'Let's pull over that truck.'

'For what, being in an accident?'

'Just do it.' He swung the wheel. She chewed her lip. The truck had been through more than a traffic accident: its side looked speckled and pocked. 'Are our lights working?'

'Yep.'

'So why aren't they stopping?'

'Don't know. I'll go around front, cut them off.'

'Yeah, okay,' she said, and the truck's rear door opened.

'Oh, shit,' Calvin said.

She saw men in camouflage pants and black T-shirts. Calvin dragged the wheel left. Bullets thudded into the car. She heard a tire blow. The steering wheel jumped through Calvin's hands. White palings from a picket fence bounced off the windshield and then she caught a glimpse of a thick tree.

After a while, she realized that Calvin was talking on the radio. She fumbled at her belt.

'Jen. You okay?'

She found the latch and tumbled out of the car. Her head felt thick and heavy. She looked around and saw a tree in the middle of their car's hood. She walked unsteadily toward the road.

'Backup's on the way, Jen! We wait here!'

She stopped in the middle of the road.

Calvin came after her. 'Jen, come sit down. You're bleeding.'

She touched her forehead. Her fingers came away red and sticky. That meant clotting. 'You think they got Pearson?'

'I guess so.'

A white Taurus crested the rise. Jennifer held out her ID until it stopped. The driver was a young man, unshaven. His eyes flicked nervously. 'Yeah?'

'I want to commandeer your vehicle for Government business. We pay three hundred dollars per hour of use, plus any necessary repairs. Also, you have the satisfaction of knowing you've helped prevent crime in your community.'

'Three hundred up front?'

'No,' Jennifer said. 'Sorry, I don't carry large amounts of cash with me on the off chance I'll need to commandeer somebody's car.'

'Jen,' Calvin said. 'Please, let's not blow our budget on this.'

'No, wait,' the kid said, getting out. 'Okay, sure. Three hundred an hour?'

'Right,' she said. 'Calvin, will you take this person's details?'

'Jen! You can't even drive!'

He was almost right: she could hardly drive. But the car was an automatic, and she could use her bad arm to hold the wheel, if not turn it. Jennifer stomped on the accelerator.

She figured the NRA would be putting as much distance between themselves and the scene as possible, but they'd avoid the freeways, which had choke points. That pretty much left Dandenong Road, and she felt confident guessing they'd head out of the city, not into it. She accelerated through the traffic.

Within a minute, she spotted the truck. She moved up behind it and waited until they got onto a straight stretch of road. Then she wound down the window, held the steering wheel with her knees, and leaned out with her .45.

The driver must have seen her: he swerved before she'd squeezed off a shot. If he'd braked, she would have been screwed, would have slammed right into him. But he tried to zigzag, and since Ryder rental trucks weren't the most maneuverable vehicles in the world, she was able to take out three tires, one after the other. The truck ran up the sidewalk and burst through a storefront.

Jennifer sailed past and started a U-turn. Her bad shoulder made it harder than she'd anticipated, and by the time she'd swung around, NRA guys were spilling out of the truck.

She hit the brakes and ducked, and the windshield imploded. Bullets chewed through the driver's seat, filling the car with a snow-storm of yellow foam. She squeezed down among the pedals, then poked her pistol over the dash and fired randomly. The gunfire stopped. She grabbed at the rearview mirror, popping it free, and clutched it to her chest, breathing hard.

It was still quiet. She raised the mirror and swung it around. There were three NRA guys by the truck . . . and one running low, toward the car. She dropped the mirror, picked up the pistol, and fired three shots. A man yelled out. She raised her eyebrows. Back to mirror: one NRA guy, crawling away and clutching his leg. 'Hot damn,' she said.

The gunfire started again, peppering her car. Jennifer found the radio and got Government agents en route, then settled into a regular exchange of fire that she hoped would keep everybody entertained. The important thing was to fire often enough so they could all feel comfortable that they were engaged in a pitched gun battle and not feel the need to do anything overly tactical, like advance on her.

When she heard cars, she raised the mirror again. A line of black Cadillac SUVs was stopping by the wrecked Ryder truck. Doors opened and closed. 'Where's my backup?' she yelled at the radio. 'They're getting away!'

'ETA four minutes, Field Agent.' Jennifer dropped it in disgust. When she heard the cars start to move away, she yanked open the door and fell out onto the road.

It was already too late. She lined up the wheels of the last car and fired again and again. She hit the road twice, blew in its rear windshield, and popped open its trunk, which would have been an amazing shot if that's what she was trying to accomplish. But it wasn't. '*Shit!*'

Something moved to her right. She turned. A man was sprinting down an alley: she saw camouflage pants and a heavy rifle.

'Freeze! This is the Government!'

He kept running. She aimed above his head and fired.

He dove into the asphalt so hard that she thought she'd accidentally clocked him. But she jogged over and he was alive. He was covering his head with his hands.

'Please, don't shoot!'

She executed an academy-approved arm twist that finished up with her knees in his back and her gun against his head. 'You kill any girls last Friday? Visit any Nike Town stores? You good friends with John Nike?'

'I'm not with them! I swear, I'm not with them!'

'We'll see about that,' she said.

PART THREE

26 EGRESS

Hack took deep breaths, gulping air. It felt so good to be out! What that Jennifer Government had said was true: you didn't appreciate freedom until it was too late. It really put things in perspective, an experience like this. It made you realize what was important.

He couldn't feel depressed, even though he knew there was a good chance he'd lose his job, and that debt to the Police wasn't going anywhere. Hack was happy to be alive.

He caught a cab to take him to Violet's sister's house, then changed his mind halfway and got out at Sears in Fitzroy. He wanted to buy Violet a present: something to show her how he felt. This experience had brought them closer together, he thought.

He stopped. Sears had a jewelry section. Rows of glass-encased stones and rings gleamed at him. He hesitated, then entered.

'Help you?' a salesgirl said. She had curly red hair.

'Um . . .' Hack said. 'Do you have any . . .'

'Lemme guess,' she said. 'Engagement rings?'

'How did you know?'

'You look nervous,' the girl said, and smiled.

*

He clutched the package, lining up at the register behind a large woman who was buying a tricycle. '*Surely* you can wrap it,' the woman said to the checkout boy. 'You have a *wrapping service*; I want this *wrapped.*'

'I can only wrap smaller items here,' the boy said patiently. 'Something this size you have to take to the wrappers on level three.'

'It didn't say that on the advertisement.'

'I'm really sorry,' the boy said.

The woman pushed past Hack, poking him in the arm with one of the tricycle's handlebars. Hack protected his package. He had been to the wrapping desk first, even though his item was small.

The boy scanned Hack's box. The price materialized on the orange readout: *$649.95.* 'You got a US Alliance card?'

'Yes.' He handed it over.

'Do you have a Team Advantage card, too?'

'What?'

The boy pointed to a bright blue badge on his chest. It said: THROW AWAY YOUR T.A. CARD AND SAVE! ASK ME HOW. 'If you quit the Team Advantage program, you get fifteen percent off from all US Alliance-affiliated stores for the next two months. Got a T.A. card?'

'No. I work for Nike.'

'That's okay. If you stick with US Alliance and don't get a T.A. card, you can accrue points too.'

Hack blinked. That sounded all right. 'How do I register?'

'Like this,' the boy said, and pushed a button. The register chatted out a couple of extra lines onto Hack's receipt. 'Thanks for shopping at Sears. Have a nice day.'

'Thanks,' Hack said. He took his package and walked out of the store. On impulse, he turned to look back at the registers. There were thirty or forty stations, lined up like battlements. Each was staffed by a clean-cut girl or boy in Sears uniform. Their blue badges winked at him.

Violet's sister, Claire, was watching TV when he arrived home. Hack had actually known Claire first: he had met Violet through her. Claire was tall and had long hair and brown eyes and a nice smile. She was shier than Violet; more like him. For a while Hack had thought he was in love with her. But then Violet came along. Violet was pretty determined.

'Hi.'

'Oh! Hi, Hack. Where have you been?'

'I had to see the Government.'

Claire's eyes widened. 'Are you in trouble?'

'No. Not really. Is Violet home?'

She shook her head. 'I thought she was with you.'

'She had a business meeting today. If she's not back . . . maybe it went well.' He looked at his watch. It was pretty late.

'Have you eaten? I can cook something, if you want.'

'Oh – no, thanks.' He felt embarrassed. Claire was always offering to do stuff for him. 'Can I call my apartment? Maybe she's there.'

'Of course.'

'Thanks.' He went into the kitchen and dialed. The phone rang and rang.

27 DISLOCATION

Violet had never flown before, and Rendell, the fat ExxonMobil manager, thought that was hilarious. 'Not even interstate?' he asked, and shook his head, amazed. Rendell had two million frequent flier miles.

She wished she could fly without Rendell, who took up the full girth of his extra-wide business-class seat and leaned into her when he wanted to talk, which was all the time. She had a paperback novel, selected from a range the flight attendant had brought around, but Rendell wouldn't leave her alone with it. After fourteen hours, all she wanted was for Rendell to choke to death on an airline-issue peanut.

He leaned across. 'You can plug into the web from here, you know. There's a jack in the armrest.'

Violet looked. There was, too.

'Although, with your virus – I mean, you've got that thing under lock and key, right? Maybe you shouldn't plug in.'

'I really doubt the customer network is connected to the flight controls,' Violet said.

'Even so.' Rendell smiled nervously.

'Fine.' She didn't want to e-mail with him looking over her shoulder anyway. She raised her novel.

His arm pressed against hers. 'There are phones, though. If you want.'

She looked at him.

'If there's anyone you need to tell you're en route to Texas. Don't worry about the cost, it's taken care of.'

'There's no one I need to call,' Violet said. She didn't want to call home with him there, either.

She was surprised by Dallas's ugliness. Even with the sun rising behind it, the city looked as if it had been built to withstand bombardment. She'd never seen so much concrete in one place.

'What do you think?' Rendell said in the cab. 'Nice, huh?'

'Where are the trees?'

'There are some parks.' He craned his neck. 'I think you can see one . . .' A heavy truck roared alongside them. The cab darkened like it was descending into the earth. Violet put her fingers in her ears. 'Past that traffic accident.'

She looked. There was a snarl of turnpike ahead, and tow trucks were extracting cars and pickups from one another. The cab driver slowed to avoid a shredded tire that had rolled onto the road. Violet didn't see any park.

'See it?'

'Yes,' she said. 'Which is the ExxonMobil building?'

'ExMo's out of town, in Irving. It's about a thirty-minute drive.'

'Oh.'

'You're going to be sick of me by the end of all this,' he said, smiling. She tried to smile back. 'I thought you'd want to see Dallas. This is where the President was assassinated, you know.'

She looked at him in surprise. 'The President of ExxonMobil?'

'No. The Government President. Kennedy.'

'Oh,' she said, turning back to the window.

'You're probably too young to have heard of him,' Rendell said, and Violet bit her lip until it hurt.

The ExxonMobil man was tall, with bright blue eyes. He stood, smiling, and extended his hand. His mouth showed teeth, but his eyes never changed. 'Violet. Please, sit.'

She took an ornate chair across the table from him. Rendell took a seat beside her. She couldn't escape him anywhere.

'I'm Nathaniel ExxonMobil, CEO.' Behind him was a door with a snarling tiger, the ExMo logo, engraved in frosted glass. 'I appreciate you coming on such short notice.'

'No problem.' She felt thirsty.

'We're going to have a conversation now. But first, I want you to understand some ground rules.'

'I'm happy to sign a nondisclosure agreement.'

'I don't want you to sign an NDA.' He smiled. 'I prefer to do this by word of agreement.'

'Oh.' Violet felt her heart sink. This was already deviating from the little she knew about how business worked.

'Contracts force people to do things, Violet, and nothing good comes from force. People achieve great things by voluntarily working together for mutual gain. Does that sound all right to you?'

'Sure,' she said, but she could feel the bridge creaking beneath her feet, the boards splintering. An NDA was standard; everybody used them. She didn't think Nathaniel would talk to her without one unless he had a better way of ensuring her silence.

He folded his hands on the table. 'I understand you have some software that can take down a company-wide computer network. Is that right?'

'Yes.'

'Any company's network?'

'Pretty much.'

'If you wanted to attack my network at a particular time, on a particular day, could you do that?'

'Um, no. The software can only spread when the clients request an update from the server. That could be immediately; it could be next week.'

Rendell leaned forward. 'But in Melbourne, it happened so fast—'

'You guys were ultra-paranoid, you had your virus checkers all geared up. The more active the checker is, the faster my software spreads.'

'Ah,' Nathaniel said.

'I didn't realize that,' Rendell said. 'Sorry, Nathaniel, I just assumed—'

Nathaniel ignored him. 'Violet, for this software to be useful to me, I need to be able to control the time at which it activates.'

'But if you want to simulate an attack, you can—'

'Let's just agree I need to control the timing,' Nathaniel said. 'Shall we?'

And Violet realized Nathaniel ExxonMobil wasn't interested in simulating anything. He didn't want her software for defensive purposes. He didn't want to shore up his I.T. security. She felt a tinge of fear.

'What if we could gain access to a key server?' Nathaniel said. 'Could you control the timing then?'

'Then – yes, you could load it and tell the server to push an update. But if you can access a server, why would you go to the trouble of—'

'We could gain temporary access. If we have to.'

She took a breath. 'Well, if you can do that, you can control the timing.'

Silence.

Rendell said, 'How would you like to become an employee of ExxonMobil, Violet?'

She jumped. 'I'm not here to become anyone's employee. I just want to license my software.'

'We'll license it,' Nathaniel said. 'And pay you well for it. But I want your services to implement it, too.'

Her gut tightened. 'Implement how?'

'We gain access to the server, you load your software and spread it through the network.'

'You mean remotely?' Violet said, although she didn't think he did.

Nathaniel said, 'I won't risk doing anything remotely. It'll have to be on-site.'

'But – on-site – how will—'

'A small group of our security personnel will enter the target building,' he said, 'and take steps to allow you passage to the server.'

She gripped the seat. 'I thought you didn't believe you could accomplish anything by force.'

'A-ha-ha,' Nathaniel said, amused. 'You've seen right through me, Violet ExxonMobil.'

28 ESPIAL

Billy NRA was giving Jennifer a headache. She rubbed her forehead. 'You're saying these NRA guys just *assumed*?'

'They had guns. I wasn't going to tell them they'd made a mistake. And then they put me on the plane – I had no chance to get away.' He looked from Jennifer to Calvin. 'You gotta believe me.'

She said, 'This is the biggest horseshit story I ever heard in my life.'

'You say the NRA approached you because of your shooting,' Calvin said. 'Are we talking sniper shooting? Who'd they want you to assassinate?'

'Pearson Police, obviously,' Jennifer said.

'No!' Billy said. 'That was some *other* NRA guys. These guys thought I was someone else, they thought I was someone called Bill!'

'So where's the real Bill?' Calvin said. 'Who is he?'

'How should I know?'

'And you never heard anybody mention the name John Nike?'

'For the fifth fucking time, I've never heard of John Nike! I just got put in a plane and sent here and then people are getting chopped up by cars with machine guns on the front and—'

'Quiet!' Jennifer said. 'Calvin?'

He dragged his chair over. Billy rubbed his face. 'Look, can I get a smoke? I'm—'

'Shut your pie-hole.' She leaned close to Calvin. 'What about the NRA guy Taylor tagged?'

'He wasn't called Bill.'

'Any of the victims?'

'There are no dead Bills.'

'So this guy's story is full of shit. He's covering.'

Calvin shrugged. 'Maybe the real Bill decided to split once he capped a Government agent.'

'Or maybe this guy is the real Bill, and he killed Taylor.'

They looked at him.

'I could really use a cigarette,' Billy said. 'Really.'

'You know what the Police will do to you?' Jennifer said. 'Do you have any idea? They run their own prisons, you know.'

'Whoa, whoa—'

There was a knock at the door. She turned. It was Elise Government. 'Hi, boss,' Jennifer said.

'A word?'

'Sure.' She closed the door behind her.

'Guess what I just got?' Elise said. 'A psych evaluation.'

She supposed she'd known it was coming. 'Oh, hey, Elise, I was joking around with that shrink. I didn't think he'd take me so seriously. Between you and me, that guy needs a vacation.'

'You're taking a vacation,' Elise said. 'As of right now. Go home.'

'No, wait, no. Elise, I'm making a major breakthrough here. I've caught a murderer red-handed; we can roll him over on John—'

'This isn't a breakthrough. The labs finished checking your suspect's weapon. It hasn't been fired.'

Jennifer blinked. 'Not once?'

'Listen to me. You need a break. This case will be solved without you. You're not my only competent agent.'

She hesitated. 'Give me an arrest warrant for John Nike and I'll go home.'

'No.'

'Elise! Today John killed one of the few people who could link him with the Nike Town killings. If we don't pick him up, Hack is next. John is *cleaning up.*'

'I can't give you a warrant on one person's say-so.'

Jennifer said, 'I – have more evidence coming in.'

'Something substantial?'

'Yes.' She bit her tongue.

'Soon?'

'Yes.'

'You wouldn't lie to me, would you, Jen?'

'Elise!' she said.

Elise eyed her. 'Here's the deal: I'll approve an arrest warrant on condition that somebody else serves it. You go home, you watch TV, you resist the urge to call in every five minutes. We'll take care of John Nike. All right?'

'Okay,' Jennifer said, thinking she could ride along on John's arrest without Elise finding out. 'Deal.'

'And get yourself a decent haircut,' Elise said. 'What did they use on you, garden shears?'

'Ha-ha,' she said, and went back inside. Calvin had given the NRA guy a cigarette. She sat down and watched him a while.

'What?' Billy said.

'You never fired your gun. Not once.'

'That's what I'm trying to tell you,' he said. 'That's what I'm *saying.*'

*

Jennifer stayed late at the office, formulating a plan. By the time she left, she had a good idea what she was going to do with Billy NRA. She thought he would turn out to be useful after all. It meant she'd have to come back to work tomorrow, but that was okay. Elise's direction to go home was probably more of a suggestion than an order anyway.

When she arrived home, Kate was scribbling on some drawing paper on the coffee table. 'Heya!' Jennifer said.

'Hi, Mom! How was your day?'

'Great! I caught a bad guy.'

'Yay!'

'I know,' she said. 'It was very satisfying. How about you?'

'I had a good day, too.' Kate rummaged in her schoolbag and emerged with a gray folder.

'What are you doing with an internal Government report?' Jennifer said. She took it and flipped open the front. It said: PENGUINS! In the corner, Kate's teacher had written: *Excellent work, Kate! You obviously put a lot of time and effort into this one. 10/10.* 'Kate! This is fantastic!'

'Yeah.'

'Wow! Come here!' She knelt and opened her arms and Kate fell into them. Jennifer kissed her. 'You are *very* clever.'

'Next I'm going to do one on Dalmatians. They're a type of dog.'

'I had heard that,' she said. 'You're really into animals, huh?'

'I like them, Mommy. When I grow up I want to be a vet.'

'I know you do,' Jennifer said. 'I love you. You'll be the world's best vet.' Kate hugged her back. 'You know, it's a pity that . . .'

'What?'

'Well,' Jennifer said, 'if you're going to be this famous vet, it's a shame you have nothing to practice on.'

'What do you mean?'

'I'm reconsidering my no-pet policy,' she said. 'In light of this excellent penguin project.'

'Mom! Are you serious?'

'How about a dog? We could rescue one from the shelter.'

'Yes! Yes! Can we get a dog? Can we go this weekend?'

'Yes,' she said. 'This weekend.'

Kate squealed and threw her arms around Jennifer's neck. 'I love you, I love you!'

'I love you, too,' Jennifer said. She hugged her tightly.

29 CLEMENCY

The man in bed 18C was buzzing her again, and Georgia had run out of patience. She ignored the sound as best she could and helped a teenage girl vomit into a bucket.

The girl spat and moaned. Georgia stroked her hair. 'Shhhh.'

'I don't know if I can—' She doubled over again, launched a stream of yellow bile into the bucket. 'I want out!'

'No you don't,' Georgia said. 'There's a waiting list for your bed.'

'I hate this . . .'

'I'll get you another blanket.' Georgia drew the curtain around the girl's bed – it didn't provide much privacy, but it was much better than last year, when they hadn't even had curtains – and headed into room 18. 'So you're awake.'

'Where the fuck am I?' the man said.

'The Church of Latter Day Saints Charity Hospital, King's Cross.'

'*What?*'

'It's a Sydney hospital. Do you know what year it is?'

'Of course I know—' He pawed at the tubes coming out of him. 'What's all this shit?'

'You were found unconscious on the streets with gunshot wounds. You had no identification, so we took you in. The surgeons operated on you two days ago, and—'

'*Surgeons!*'

'Sir, please calm down.'

'I will not calm down! I have insurance, I don't need your dumb-fuck religious doctors cutting me!'

'The administrators will be glad to hear you have insurance,' Georgia said patiently. She'd worked here almost three years. 'We can bill them for the cost of saving your life.'

The man tried to pull himself out of bed. 'I'm leaving.' His face whitened.

'You're not strong enough to go anywhere. Sit back and I'll tell the doctors you're awake.'

'No! Wait. If I tell you who I am, will you contact my employer for me?'

'If your insurance is handled through your employer, yes.'

'And my details are confidential, right?'

'Sure,' she said, not wanting to debate it. The truth was he would be getting a lot of junk mail from the Church from now on.

'All right. All right. My name is Bill NRA. Now tell them to get me out of this hole.'

30 ASCENDANCY

The hospital walls were light blue, which John liked. The only reason hospitals had white walls was because people associated white with cleanliness: it was marketing, effectively, and there was no point in marketing to a marketer. John would paint a hospital for marketers black.

The door to 412 was open. It was a nice room, with a view of the city skyline. He sat in the chair beside the bed and checked if John was awake.

It was hard to tell, with all the bandages. That girl Violet had really let him have it: the doctors still weren't sure if there was brain damage. Personally, John thought the bigger problem was his face. He hoped a lot of the swelling was temporary. There was no place in marketing for a man who looked like that.

Mercurys had sold as if they were religious artifacts, but for John the whole campaign had taken on a sour taste, thanks to Hack's inability to be a proper fall guy. Now he and his psychotic girlfriend had vanished, and it was only a matter of time, John was sure, before Jennifer Government came calling. She'd been sniffing around before the campaign; now she'd almost intercepted the NRA team sent to eliminate that Police officer. John was in trouble.

He decided to scribble a note for John – *Looking good, big guy! Everyone at Nike's rooting for you* – when his cellphone rang. He tugged it out of his jacket pocket and walked over to the window, in case the signals interfered with John's equipment. John didn't need any more aggravation. 'Go.'

'John Nike,' a voice said. 'What makes you think you can organize a campaign like this from fucking Australia?'

'Who's this?'

'Gregory Nike, VP Global Sales.'

John stiffened. He checked the phone display, in case someone thought he was being funny. The number suggested otherwise. 'Sir! I can't tell you what a pleasure it is to speak with you.'

'Did you think you were handing out baseball caps? You'd better have a seriously good reason for exposing the company like this.'

From the bed, John groaned and muttered. 'Well, I don't want to preempt my report, sir, but I think the sales results speak for themselves. We've sold four hundred thousand pairs in three days, and in dollar terms that's—'

'I'm going to explain something to you now, and you're going to shut up and listen. All right?'

'Yes, sir.'

'I don't give a flying fuck about your sales. We have strategic initiatives in place that make four hundred thousand pairs look like dick. And it pisses me off, John, when those initiatives are jeopardized by a dumb fuck like yourself in Melbourne, Australia, who thinks he can lead worldwide corporate policy.'

'It was radical, I admit,' John said. 'And perhaps I should have consulted—'

'I assume that even the Australian office is aware of the importance of the US Alliance program. Yet you go and involve a Team Advantage company in a – a highly risky campaign.'

He suddenly realized what Gregory was talking about. 'The Police – yes, that was beyond my control, sir. It—' He bit his tongue. What was he doing? 'I won't make excuses. I made an error. However, you'll be pleased to hear I've taken steps to address that. The non-US Alliance link is being dealt with.'

'How?'

'I probably shouldn't answer that on an unsecured line.'

Heavy breathing, originating in Portland, Oregon. Transmitted via satellite to Melbourne, the Australian Territories, re-created by AT&T in John's left ear. 'If you've fucked this up for us, John, you're out of a job. You better realize that.'

'Sir, perhaps we should meet. We can discuss the initiatives I've taken and you can brief me more fully on the US Alliance situation. I think I've demonstrated my ability to take decisive action and provide outside-the-dots thinking, and you might make better use of my abilities by keeping me inside a higher-level loop.'

115

'Jesus,' Gregory said. 'You've got some nerve.'

John waited.

'Get on a plane. I'll be in L.A. tomorrow. Meet me there.'

'Yes, sir!' Gregory hung up. John stood in front of the window, elated. What a phone call! Talk about decisive action!

He picked up his briefcase and dialed his P.A. On the way out, he glanced at John. He hadn't written that message yet.

'Sorry, buddy,' he said, straightening his tie. 'Strategic initiatives are in place.' He closed the door on his way out.

31 DECLIVITY

Buy was a corpse. He sat in his Mitsui cubicle and stunk up the place. Brokers circumscribed wary arcs as they passed, as if what he had was contagious. He was a dead man in a suit.

On Tuesday, Cameron said, 'Buy. That's enough.'

Buy looked up. He'd known he was going to be fired for a while now. He'd thought it would be more exciting.

'My office.' Buy followed him up to the fishbowl. Cameron waited until they were seated, and even then threw in a pause. Buy waited patiently. 'I offered you time off. You remember that.'

'Yes.' His voice cracked. He wasn't using it much these days.

'I'm going to suggest it again. This time, I want you to think about it very carefully. It could save you.'

Buy felt like laughing. The idea that a week of daytime TV could make him happy again was very funny. 'No. Thank you.'

Cameron sighed. 'You want me to fire you? Is that it? Your termination package isn't so hot, you know.'

'I know.'

'All right. Here's your last chance. A transfer.'

'What?'

'You're finished in brokerage. But there's a lifeline, if you want it. The Mitsui Liaison to US Alliance wants an Australian assistant. That could be you.'

'The Mitsui what?'

'Mitsui is part of US Alliance, the customer loyalty program. We have a person to represent our interests there, he's called a Liaison. You could be his assistant.'

'Oh,' Buy said. 'Okay.'

'It's not such a bad job,' Cameron said. 'Could be a real growth area, you never know.'

'Thank you.' He wanted to feel more grateful, but he just felt tired. He stuck out his hand.

Cameron blinked, then shook it. 'You're in a new office, on level eight. Maintenance will get you everything you need. You should clear out your desk.'

'When?'

'No time like the present.'

'Right,' Buy said. He supposed they wanted to get the smell out.

He went to level eight and was shown his new office. It was small but had a big window with a view of the rest of the city. He wasn't sure that was good. He had been thinking about the city a lot, lately. About how the city ate people.

Buy caught the elevator back to brokerage and began collecting his personal items: a coffee mug, a photo of a dog he'd owned once, and a few pens. That was it.

'Hey, I heard about your big move,' Lisa said. Buy looked up. She was smiling, but her eyes were sharp and vigilant, as if she wasn't ruling out the possibility that he would lunge at her. 'Sounds like your thing, Buy. Congratulations.'

'Thanks.'

Her eyes softened. 'We're all rooting for you, Buy. Remember that.'

'Thank you, Lisa,' he said. He was now pretty sure he was going to kill himself.

32 AGENCY

The man in the cell was Jesus Christ, or so he kept telling Billy. This hadn't been very amusing when he'd first arrived, and had become less so over the next three hours. He sat on the bunk in the cell's corner and pulled his knees up to his chest.

'Righteous fire!' shouted Jesus. 'Damnation for – all you cock-suckers!'

Billy closed his eyes. He wondered if he could bang Jesus' head into the cell wall and claim self-defense.

Someone rattled keys in the lock. Billy sat up quickly. The door opened. It was the woman from earlier, Jennifer. She was alone.

'Hi,' she said. 'Had time to think?'

'I am the Lamb of God!' Jesus said. 'The Lamb, the Lamb!'

'Not you. Billy, you thought about my offer?'

'You can't keep me here.' Billy tried to say it as calmly as he could, but he felt his hands shaking. He really needed another cig-arette. 'I'm a US citizen. New Zealand can't lock me up because I was in the wrong place at the wrong time. I want to speak to some-one from the American Government or the NRA.'

Jennifer stared at him.

'What?'

'You're in the Australian Territories, Billy, not New Zealand. Don't you even know which country you're in?'

'I . . . they flew me – right, Australia.'

'And I *am* the American Government. This is a USA country. I leave you here overnight, that's the best you can do?'

'Uh . . .'

'I'll come back later.'

'No! Wait! Okay, let's talk!'

'No more talking. I've offered you a deal, you say yes or no.'

'Fuckers!' Jesus shouted. 'The fucking nnnnn-nnnnn—'

'Quiet!' Jennifer said.

'All right,' Billy said, feeling hope drain away. 'Get me out of here.'

She held open the door. He left the cell, feeling like he was sinking deeper and deeper.

'I'm glad you made the right choice, Billy,' Jennifer said. 'I think we're going to work well together.'

'You're going to carry this with you at all times,' she said. 'Don't leave it where anyone can see it. Don't let anyone pick it up.'

'A pack of smokes?'

'There's a bug inside. I can talk back, if you plug headphones into the little jack down at the bottom. When it vibrates, that's me telling you I want to talk. Do you smoke Marlboro?'

'Yeah, sure.'

'Don't smoke these.'

He stared at them. 'Are they drugged?'

'No, Billy, they're cigarettes. But if you finish the pack, there's no reason for you to hold on to the box. If you leave this thing in a trash can somewhere, I will not be happy.'

'Right,' he said, and licked his lips. He wondered if he could have one of those cigarettes now.

Jennifer eyed him. 'Maybe you're not cut out for this.'

'I am, really! It's just . . .' He reached for the pack.

She looked disgusted. 'What are you, on one of those high-nic brands?'

'I'm cutting back.' He lit one with shaking fingers. The taste was incredible.

'Feel better?'

'Ohhh . . .' Things were so much better with the smoke. Even Jennifer Government looked cute, in a hard-ass sort of way.

'Now let's get this clear. You get in, you get me some people on tape talking about John Nike and NRA jobs, you get out, and you're in the clear. But if you ditch this device and run back to Mississippi or wherever the hell you're from, I'll come after you. I'm the Government, Billy. You can't escape me. Understand?'

'Yes.'

She was silent for a moment. Billy sucked on his cigarette.

'He killed fourteen kids. Thought about it, planned it, made it happen. I'm not going to tolerate that. Do you believe me?'

'Yes.'

She nodded. 'You're booked on a flight to Invercargill, New Zealand, in two hours. Don't mess up.'

'You can count on me.' His whole body was tingling. In this moment, he really meant it.

33 CECITY

She moved quickly, but even so they caught her outside her office. 'Jennifer!'

She looked up. Elise and Calvin were by the watercooler. 'Oh, hey, Elise.'

'Explain to me why you're in this building.'

'I'm just collecting some things to take home—'

'Two weeks ago they were stitching your head back together. Now get out of my station.'

'You know, I feel really recuperated,' Jennifer said. 'And I saw the shrink again and he said I'd made real progress toward processing the negative experience and resolving my role within it.'

Elise looked at Calvin. 'Has she seen the shrink again?'

'Uh,' Calvin said.

'Get out,' Elise said. 'I swear, Jennifer, don't you so much as call in.'

'I'm touched by your concern, but—'

'Did it sound like I was giving you an option?'

She resisted a sigh. 'No.'

'Then go home.'

'Fine,' she said, and turned.

'What do you need to go to your office for?'

'I'm getting my *jacket*!' she shouted. 'Is that all right?'

'I'll drive you home,' Calvin said.

'So,' she said in the car, 'now we've got this arrest warrant—'

'Don't even ask.'

'What?'

'You're not coming along, Jen.'

'That's not what I'm saying,' she said, nettled. 'That's not even what I meant.'

'Oh,' Calvin said. 'Good.'

There was silence.

'So how many agents are you going in with?'

'Depends who's available.'

'You'll let me know how it goes?'

He stopped at a light and turned to her. 'I will keep you informed, Jen.'

'Good. Thanks.'

'You know, the break could be good for you. Take some time to step back, cool down, get some perspective. Hang out with Kate.'

'I *have* perspective,' she said. 'I have shitloads of perspective. That's why I don't want to sit at home while John Nike is still out there. I want him in jail. I want to know that when Kate goes to the shops, nobody's going to *shoot* her. That's my perspective.'

'Okay, okay,' Calvin said. 'I get it.'

'If you let him get away, I'll be really pissed.'

'Jen, I am a competent human being.'

'I know. I'm sorry.' She rubbed her face. She felt frustrated. 'Don't take Church Street.'

Kate was waiting for the bus at the school gate. 'Mommy!'

'Hiya,' Jennifer said. 'What's that on your face?'

'A sticker. See, it has a star on it.'

'Oh yeah.'

'How come you're here so early?'

'I'm on vacation.'

'Oh, yay!'

'I thought maybe we could go to the park and play soccer. Do you want to do that?'

'And, after, can we go to the dog shelter?'

'It's a bit late tonight, honey. Come on, Calvin's driving us home.' She took Kate's hand.

'Alex's dog rolls on its back every time you go near it,' Kate said. 'It's weird.'

'Our dog will be much cooler,' Jennifer said.

'Can we go to the shelter tomorrow?'

'Tomorrow or the weekend,' Jennifer promised. The codes to Billy's bug were in her pocket. 'I have a couple of important things I need to do first, honey.'

34 COMPETITION

John Nike was reading a novel called *The Space Merchants*; it had been reissued and he'd seen a review in *Fast Company*. They called it 'prescient and hilarious,' which John was having a hard time agreeing with. All these old science-fiction books were the same: they thought the future would be dominated by some hard-ass, oppressive Government. Maybe that was plausible back in the 1950s, when the world looked as if it might turn Commie. It sure wasn't now.

In *The Space Merchants*, the world was dominated by two advertising companies, which was closer to the truth. But still, there were so many laws the companies had to follow! If these guys had all the money, John wondered, who could stop them doing whatever they wanted?

'We're about to commence our descent, sir,' a flight attendant told him. John looked at her cleavage. 'Is there anything else I can get you?'

Manual relief, John thought, but didn't say; this was United Airlines, not American. 'No.'

He started to put his novel into his briefcase, then tucked it into the seat pocket instead. It was turning into a sly, anti–free market statement, and irony irritated him. There was no place for irony in marketing: it made people want to look for deeper meaning. There was no place in marketing for that, either.

He was in a cab less than ten minutes after touchdown. He'd visited the States a couple of times before the last barriers to free trade had come down and there had been hassles with taxes, with what you had in your suitcase, with changing money – it was ridiculous. And when you made it through, the culture was so different you didn't even know how to order a beer properly. Now things were much better: the only sign you were in Los Angeles instead of Sydney was that the air was lousier.

Nike's L.A. office was a single floor in an anonymous building on Santa Monica Boulevard. Los Angeles was not a big deal for Nike: Nike was born in Portland, Oregon, and had never left home. He wondered why Gregory was meeting him here.

He paid the cabdriver and bounded into the building. The receptionist sent him to the eighth floor, where a woman told him Gregory would be a few minutes. This was a good sign: 'a few minutes' meant Gregory still intended to see him. John had been braced for 'unexpectedly called away.'

He wished he'd held on to that novel now. It would have been good to be seen reading it: relevant yet left-field, demonstrating initiative and a creative approach to problem solving. He sifted through the magazines on offer. The best available was *Sports Illustrated*. He sighed.

Twenty minutes later, Gregory appeared from a side door. 'John, VP Guerrilla Marketing, Australian Territories?'

John rose. 'Gregory, it's a pleasure to—'

'Sorry I'm late.'

'You're not late at all,' John lied. 'I just got here.'

Gregory looked at him in annoyance. Maybe that had been too much. 'Come through.'

He followed Gregory past a small, shabby cube farm of what had to be low-level managers – possibly even Merchandising Officers. Maybe Gregory was trying to humiliate him.

'You'll forgive the surroundings,' Gregory said, holding open the door to his office. 'I'm only in town to meet with US Alliance.'

John sat. No coffee was on offer, apparently. 'US Alliance is based in L.A.?'

'Yes.' Gregory planted himself behind the desk and leaned forward. It was a cheap desk, but Gregory made up for it, John decided: he was ominous even with bad props. 'This is a critical time for us. Which is why your antics aren't appreciated.'

John wondered if now was a good time to produce his sales report. 'I apologize again, sir. I'm looking forward to being brought up to speed on Nike's vision.'

Gregory folded his hands. 'What I'm about to tell you is strictly confidential. It's covered under trade secrets in your employment contract.'

'I understand.'

'You better. We don't screw around with breaches of trade secrets.'

John had ruined a few ex-employees in his time. 'I understand, sir.'

'All right. You're aware of Nike's participation in the US Alliance customer loyalty program. What do you think of it?'

John considered. He thought loyalty programs were useless, especially to an image-centric consumer goods company like Nike. But obviously that wasn't the answer Gregory was looking for. 'I believe they can be very valuable, in the correct application.'

'Loyalty programs aren't worth dick to us,' Gregory said. John cursed silently. Tricked! 'You think anybody buys Nike because they get frequent flier miles? Give me a break.'

John rowed hard. 'Sir, I feel the same way. Our brand is weakened by discounting and giveaway promotions. If anything, the higher our price, the more we sell.'

'And yet Nike considers the US Alliance loyalty program to be the most important strategic initiative it has taken in twenty years. Why?'

John kept his mouth shut.

'You know how US Alliance got started, John?'

'Some kind of . . . airline miles?'

'That's it. You bought a tank of gas on American Express,

125

you got flier miles for American Airlines. If you didn't have an AmEx, well, you thought about getting yourself one pretty quick. And right there, the competitive environment changed forever. Because suddenly credit card companies were in competition with airlines.'

'Right.'

'So Visa goes out and gets itself a frequent flier miles deal. They think, "Hey, what can we do to make our program more attractive?" And they realize—'

'More ways to earn points. More services. More companies.'

'And ten years later we have US Alliance and Team Advantage, and there aren't more than five major companies in the world that haven't signed up with one of them. The more companies joined in, the more customers signed up, and so the more companies want in. At the end of last month, US Alliance had five hundred million subscribers. T.A. has two-ninety million.'

'Five hundred million . . . I didn't realize.'

'Believe it. US Alliance only accepts one company from each industry, but we've got the biggest and best. General Motors, IBM, AT&T, Boeing – they're all here.'

John hesitated. 'But Boeing only has industrial customers. What does it gain?'

'The battle lines have been drawn. Every Alliance company is in competition with every Team Advantage company. Every customer who flies on a T.A. airline will buy a computer from Compaq instead of IBM. Boeing is with us because otherwise United Airlines won't buy from it.'

'And the Police is . . .'

'Not with us,' Gregory said. 'It's in Team Advantage.'

'Ah,' John said. 'You know, I want to stress that that situation is now resolved—'

'Good. Because we have bigger concerns. A week ago, the US

Alliance member companies, including us, began offering rewards for customers who throw away their Team Advantage cards. We're forcing everyone who signed up with both programs to make a choice.'

John sat back. 'This is very impressive. I had no idea that initiatives of such . . . scope . . . were in motion.'

'It's a war,' Gregory said. 'I'm not exaggerating when I say that. We've only seen skirmishes so far, but the war has started. And you don't want to be doing business with the enemy. You understand me?'

'Completely.'

'I'm glad we had this talk,' Gregory said. 'I'm impressed by your quick grasp of the situation.'

'Tell me what to do,' John said.

'Exactly,' Gregory said. 'That's exactly what I mean.'

35 SERENDIPITY

A bunch of college students got it into their heads to protest at a downtown Starbucks, so Calvin got no backup for Nike. Starbucks was a big Government client: when they had trouble, agents scrambled. 'You can wait, if you want,' Elise said. 'We'll free up Johan and Emma by three—'

'Don't worry about it,' he said, knowing Jen would blow an artery if she found out. He drove to Nike and parked in a visitor's bay. The front doors parted, enveloping him in air-conditioning. The receptionist was attractive and looked like she ran track in her spare time.

'Welcome to Nike. How may I help you?'

'I have an appointment with John, Vice-President, Guerrilla Marketing.'

'Your name, sir?'

'Calvin McDonald's.' He smiled. Trespass was an assault against property and therefore a crime, but fraud was fine: fraud was practically a constitutional right, like free speech.

'Just a moment, sir.' She murmured into a microphone. 'I'm sorry, John's P.A. has no record of your appointment. Are you sure you have the right time?'

'I'm very sure. Goddammit, what's going on here?'

'I don't know, sir, you'll have to ask her.'

'I think I will.' He grabbed the visitors' book. 'I sign in here? What floor is she on?'

'Ah – the fourteenth.'

'What's her name?'

'Georgia.'

He took an ID tag from the box. The elevator boomed pop music at him. Calvin hummed along with it. On the fourteenth floor, he pushed through glass doors to enter a large, tasteful reception lined with wall-sized pictures of sportspeople Calvin recognized from soda commercials. A woman in her late twenties rose. 'Calvin McDonald's?'

'Where the hell is John Nike? I've got an appointment.'

'Vice-President John is on an overseas business trip. He has no appointments.'

'Overseas!' Calvin said. Jennifer was not going to be happy. 'Where?'

'Sir, I don't believe you ever made an appointment for John to see you.'

'Maybe I'm getting confused. Is there another John in Guerilla Marketing?'

'There is Operative John, but he's in a hospital. If you had an appointment with him, we would have called you.'

'A hospital! I hope he's all right. What happened?'

'Sir, I'm afraid I have to ask you to leave.'

Fraud, Calvin thought, will only get you so far. He flipped open his Government ID. 'Okay, I'm not really from McDonald's.'

She gasped. Calvin blinked. The plastic didn't usually have such an effect. 'You're not meant to come here! You're not meant to — put that away!'

'Oh, crap,' he said, realizing. 'You're Jen's source.'

'I—' She froze as someone passed in the corridor. She hissed, 'This is not the deal!'

He made the ID disappear. 'I'm Jennifer Government's partner. Where's John Nike?'

'Los Angeles. He left this morning.'

'Where's he staying?'

She lowered her voice even further, so he could hardly hear her. 'I can't talk here. Call me later, from a pay phone.'

'Okay. I will.' Calvin turned to leave, then stopped. 'By the way, where do you know Jennifer from?'

'I worked for her at Maher. Please, you have to go.'

'Maher?'

Georgia stared at him. 'The advertising firm. She's Jennifer Maher. Didn't you know that?'

'Jennifer Maher . . .' It sounded vaguely familiar.

'She was one of the best at the biggest ad company in the world. She ran campaigns for Coke, Apple, Mattel . . . she could sell anything. Why do you think she got the tattoo?'

'Well,' he said, 'I've wondered about that.'

'If you'd been part of corporate America ten years ago, you'd already know. People still talk about her.'

'So what happened? Why'd she quit?'

'John Nike happened,' Georgia said. 'Look, you have to go. If anyone knows you're here—'

'What do you mean, John happened?'

'Please. You have to leave. *Please.*'

'Okay. Thanks for your help, Georgia Nike.'

'Saints-Nike,' she said. 'I work part-time for the Church of Latter Day Saints.'

'What do you do?'

'Whatever's needed.'

'And they pay you?'

'No. But it's still Saints-Nike.'

'Okay,' Calvin said. 'Then thank you, Georgia Saints-Nike.'

36 TRANSPOSITION

Hack was sure of it: Violet was dead. She hadn't come home after her business meeting, and there was only one plausible explanation: some NRA heavies had found her and taken her out. Maybe John Nike had tracked her down himself. Either way, Hack had made one big mistake too many, and it had killed Violet.

He still had the ring. How poignant! His eyes watered every time he thought of it. He had tucked it in his bedroom drawer, but now he got it out and turned it over in his hands. That was how Claire found him: sitting on the bed, a blubbering mess. She hesitated in the doorway, wearing her Sears uniform. 'You okay?'

Hack held out the ring. 'She's *gone.*'

'Violet?'

'I killed her!' *That made fifteen,* Hack realized. He had murdered fifteen people. He was a serial killer.

'Did you hear something?'

He shook his head.

Claire sat beside him on the bed. 'Hack . . . until we know for sure, you should try not to worry so much. Violet is . . . Violet doesn't always think of other people. She might just be busy.'

'No, no!' He didn't want to hear of Violet's faults. Violet had been kind and thoughtful.

'Hey, come on . . .' Claire put her arms around him. She hugged him tightly. For a second Hack was lost in the scent of her hair – but that, no doubt, was because Claire reminded him of *her*. 'I'm sure she'll be okay. You're a sweet guy, Hack. You care too much.'

He accepted this silently. His nose touched her nametag. It said: CLAIRE SEARS. She began stroking his hair. Hack closed his eyes. He might have drifted off, because then she was saying, 'I have to go,' and he realized time had passed. He sat up. 'I'm sorry,' Claire said. 'If I'm thirty minutes late for work, I drop a pay grade.'

'That's okay.'

'I'd stay if I could.' She took her arm back.

'I know.'

'Stay cool,' she said, and poked his nose. He watched her leave. Claire was so good to him. He didn't know why she didn't have a boyfriend. *Any guy in their right mind would grab on to Claire and not let go,* Hack thought.

He looked down. He was still holding the ring. He felt himself tearing up again. 'Oh, Violet,' he said to the empty room, and no one answered.

He spent an hour and a half wallowing around the house. Then he got hungry and made himself breakfast. As he ate, he wondered what people at Nike would be saying about him not showing up for work again. There were a bunch of posters that were meant to go to a store in Sydney, and Hack wondered if anyone had taken care of them.

Then it struck him that if he did go in to Nike, he would be safe. His employment contract required Nike to provide a safe workplace, and surely John wouldn't risk messing with that. Which meant Hack could confront John with total impunity. He could demand justice. Hack bit his lip. That was a daring idea. He began to get dressed.

By the time the cab dropped him at Nike, his legs were shaking. His throat was parched. He decided to go to his desk first and get a drink of water. Then he could confront John.

His boss, the Manager of Local Merchandising, caught him at the watercooler. It had been refilled since the day it had sent Hack off to the marketing floor: it had been refilled by the time he'd come back. 'Hack! You take a sick day yesterday?'

'Um . . . yes.'

'Hack, you have to phone those in. You can't just not show up for work. To qualify for sick pay, you need to phone in.'

'Right. Sorry.'

'I can't approve pay for that day. I'm sorry, but it's in your contract. Maybe next time you'll remember.'

Hack sat down at his desk. There was a stack of messages there, but he ignored them. He sipped at his water, then dialed reception and asked for John's P.A.

'Georgia Saints-Nike, good morning?'

He took a breath. 'I need to speak to John. It's Hack from Merchandising.'

There was a pause. 'Oh, Hack . . . I'm sorry, John is overseas.'

'Oh.' That was a surprise. 'When's he coming back?'

'I don't know. Not for a while.'

'Oh. Thanks.'

Hack hung up and stared at his desk. So much for a confrontation. So much for publicly denouncing John. He felt relieved, and was ashamed of himself.

'Hey, Hack,' his boss said, stopping at his desk. 'You know something about posters for a Nike Town in Sydney? They've been calling and calling.'

'Yeah,' he said. 'I'll take care of it.'

'Good man,' his boss said.

There were a bunch of cars parked outside Claire's house, and Hack felt a stab of fear. Maybe John had people watching him. Maybe the NRA had tracked him here! But even in the streetlights he could see the cars were tiny and rusting and had bumper stickers that said things like THE WORLD IS NOT FOR SALE. Hack didn't think the NRA would get around like that.

He entered the house. Claire was in the hallway, carrying a bunch of coffee cups. There were voices coming from the living room: loud and strident. Claire said, 'Oh, Hack! How are you?'

'Fine. Did Violet—'

'She hasn't called.'

'Oh.' Someone in the living room said, 'That kind of mentality is what allowed the corporate sector to dominate society in the first place!'

Claire hesitated. 'I have some people over. You might want to stay out of the living room.'

'What people?'

'Just a group . . . we talk about capitalizm and society and things.'

'Oh,' Hack said. He thought he would keep out of the living room.

'I mean, you're welcome to join us, if you want.'

He almost agreed. He didn't want to say no to Claire. But he said, 'No, that's okay. Thanks.'

'No problem. Come in later, if you want.'

133

He went into the kitchen and got some juice from the fridge. The door to the living room was ajar, and the conversation from Claire's friends spilled through.

'That's what they *rely* on,' a girl said. 'They know no one wants to get involved. But until you stand up to them, they'll push you as far as they can. Nike's a prime example.'

Hack started. For a second he thought they were talking about him. Then he realized they weren't. Then he realized they were.

He stood up and walked to the doorway with his juice. There were five of them. 'Hi,' he said. 'Sorry, do you . . . mind if I join you?'

'Here,' Claire said. She patted the sofa beside her. Hack thought her smile was very beautiful.

37 INADVERTENCY

Billy nearly lost the bug even before he made it to the plane. Those Marlboros weren't as satisfying as his regular brand, and he smoked one after another until they were all gone. He carefully stowed the empty pack in his jacket pocket, then, when the cab dropped him at the airport, fished it out and tossed it on the ground. He was inside the terminal before he realized what he'd done and sprinted back outside. It was lying on the concrete. He snatched it up and put it back in his pocket, where his restless fingers tried to crush it when he wasn't concentrating.

There was a ticket for Billy NRA at the counter, just like Jennifer had promised. He looked at the Departures board. Beneath his flight to Invercargill was one bound for Dallas, Texas.

'Everything all right with your ticket, sir?'

Billy hesitated. 'How much to change my ticket to Dallas?'

The girl behind the counter tapped at her keyboard. 'I can get you on that flight for an additional three hundred and twelve dollars, sir.'

'Oh,' he said, deflated. 'Never mind.'

He dragged his bag to the waiting lounge and stared at the TV. It was maybe ten minutes later when it occurred to him that Jennifer Government would have heard every word he said.

He wandered through Invercargill Airport until he found a bus station that advertised services to Bluff, the small town the NRA was more or less running these days. There was only one other person there, an unshaven, rough-looking man guarding a canvas bag. Billy leaned against the wall and lit up a Camel from a pack he'd purchased on the plane.

'Dude,' the man said. Billy turned, on guard. 'Got a spare?'

'Sure.' He dug out a cigarette and lit it for him.

'Thanks, man.' He stuck out his hand. 'I'm Bill NRA.'

Billy blinked. 'You're kidding me.'

'What?'

'I'm *Billy* NRA!' He laughed.

'Hey, brother! Geez, it's good to meet another grunt. You stationed in Bluff?'

'Yeah, I am!'

'Just got back from Sydney myself.' He leaned closer. 'You been on business or pleasure?'

'Business,' Billy said.

The man grinned. 'I know about that. I know about that all right.'

'You seen some action?'

'Man, look at this.' He pulled up his shirt. There was a red, ugly scar line across his side; it looked pretty recent. '*That's* action.'

'Whoa, yeah.' He thought: *That might have happened to me.* If one

135

of those Police cars had lined him up . . . 'You didn't do the Police job, did you? I don't think I saw—'

Bill shook his head. 'No, dude. Something else.' He winked.

'Cool.' He wondered if Jennifer Government was getting all this. It sounded like the kind of thing she would be interested in.

'Hey, you wanna share a cab to base? We can report in together.'

'Yeah, great idea!'

'Maybe we'll end up working together. That'd be shit-hot, eh?'

'That'd be unreal,' Billy said. 'Shit, it's so funny, us having the same name.'

'Oh yeah,' Bill said. 'They're gonna go nuts trying to tell us apart.'

Billy laughed. The Marlboro packet was in his shirt pocket, and he felt it abruptly begin to vibrate. He slid it to one side. Jennifer probably wanted to bawl him out for thinking about skipping out to L.A.; well, she could fucking wait. 'That's so true,' he said to Bill. 'Man, that's so funny.'

38 DISCONTINUANCE

From his new office window, Buy Mitsui could see a gun store. It was NRA-affiliated, which was appropriate, or ironic, or something. Buy had decided that at the end of the day, he would visit this gun store, purchase a firearm, and shoot himself.

People were going to say he'd cracked, that he'd been grief-stricken. But that wasn't it. The truth was simpler: nothing Buy could ever do would be as important as saving that girl Hayley's life. He couldn't watch a girl bleed to death and then go make 3 percent off stock trades. The idea was monstrous. So Buy was finished as a productive member of society, unless he managed to lose so much perspective that margin calls began to seem important again. Either way, Buy was prepared to put a gun in his mouth and pull the trigger.

He was debating which was the biggest waste, buying lunch or saving the money, when his phone rang. He was so surprised he picked it up. 'Uh – hello?'

'Konitchiwa-hello,' the phone said. 'Stand by please for Kato Mitsui, Liaison.'

'For who?' Buy said.

'Buy, hello!' a new voice said. 'How are you? I hear the weather is lovely.'

'Who is this?'

'It is Kato Mitsui, Liaison. You are working for me, is that right?'

'Oh, right,' Buy said. 'Yes.'

'Excellent! It is most good to speak with you. I hope you are excited about this new position, Buy. Are you excited?'

'Uh,' he said. 'Well—'

'Good!' Kato laughed heartily. Buy had to hold the phone away from his ear. 'We have much to do. Our consumer-marketer friends are launching programs of most excellent potential. If we do not wish Mitsui to be relegated to any sidelines, we too must devise some cunning marketing strategies. I am hoping you are well equipped in this department.'

'Marketing strategies? I don't know anything about—'

'Ah, you are modest,' Kato said. 'To begin, I shall tell you of a program belonging to our friends at IBM. They are rewarding customers who bring in a competitive product and submit it to their in-house crushing machine. It smashes it in-store, you see?'

'Yes, I see—'

'A most brilliant strategy, to relegate the competition to the status of junk and garbage. You must understand, it is difficult for we Japanese to think along these lines of head-to-head competition. This is why we are now finding ourselves running behind our energetic American friends. But the times they are a-changing, are they not?'

'They are,' Buy said.

'Very good! Now, you try one.'

'What?'

'I am needing all your esteemed ideas, Buy, to improve and establish our role in US Alliance.'

'Uh . . .' he said. 'Can I think about it and get back to you?'

'Of course! I am trusting on your support, Buy. We will talk again when you have had some thoughts.'

'I'm on it,' Buy said. He put down the phone. Then he stared at it. *I'm on it.* That was the sort of thing Buy used to say. *I'm on it, I'm all over it, let me find out what the story is and get back to you.* Why had he said that? Because what Kato was talking about was interesting?

I'm on it, he thought. It was happening already. He felt disgusted with himself.

It was almost two. Close enough. Buy packed his briefcase and closed his office door behind him.

There were so many guns, and Buy couldn't be bothered looking through the racks. 'I want a pistol,' he told the man behind the desk. 'Something suitable for putting in my mouth and pulling the trigger.'

The man raised his eyebrows. 'You want to cap someone?'

'Myself.'

'Right, right,' the man said, smiling. It took Buy a moment to catch the insinuation. 'Something powerful but disposable. Right?'

'In the sense I only need it once, yes.'

He unlocked a cabinet between them and hoisted a pistol. 'This is a Vektor Z88, nine millimeter. Powerful at close range, simple to operate, doesn't make a lot of noise, and on the cheap side. This what you're after?'

'I don't care about the cost.'

The man made the Vektor disappear. 'Then you should take a look at this baby right here.' He slapped a gun on the desk. It was sleeker and looked more powerful than the Vektor. Buy picked it up and weighed it in his hand. 'A Colt .45, fully automatic. Extremely reliable, American-made, can make a man's head disappear from two hundred feet.'

'I don't need—'

'I know, you don't need long-range. But if you want power and reliability, this baby has it in spades. The accuracy is a bonus.'

'How much?'

'For you, three thousand,' the man said. 'And I'll throw in a case of bullets and some cleaning solution.'

Buy handed over his AmEx. 'Keep the solution.'

The man wrapped the Colt in white paper, then put it in a box. 'And, in case you were wondering, this model has no serial number.' He winked.

'Just give me the gun,' Buy said.

He parked his Saab in the apartment block's underground area and got out. Without thinking, he locked it; it only occurred to him in the elevator how pointless that was. He should have left it on the street with the motor running.

The apartment was neat and quiet: his cleaning service had been in. Buy dragged a huge leather armchair over to the floor-to-ceiling windows and looked out at the city lights. They stared back at him. He began unwrapping his gun.

He was struck with the thought that the assassin – whoever had killed the girl, Hayley – must have done this, must have acquired a gun and loaded it with bullets. It didn't seem right to Buy that it was so easy. He looked at the Colt, feeling disgusted. Then he put the barrel in his mouth.

There was a plane descending from the north, its red and white lights winking at him. Buy watched it until it disappeared behind the AT&T building, then pulled the trigger.

39 PERTINACITY

Jennifer's finger was getting sore from holding down **V**, the key that told Billy NRA's bug to vibrate. The signal went from her keyboard to her modem, through the telephone line to the Government Communications Center in Sydney, to a geosyncronous satellite, to the fake cigarette packet in Billy's pocket. It was a lot of technology the Government was still paying off, and it was all useless thanks to the astounding stupidity of Billy NRA.

She had a plan: Billy would overpower Bill and get him to a Government station. This was clearly the man the NRA had confused Billy for. Why he was only now returning to New Zealand, Jennifer didn't know, but that was just details. The important thing was that she'd been given this opportunity to arrest him and replace him with Billy, who could then gather evidence to link the whole mess back to John Nike. But Billy wasn't picking up, Billy was en route to the NRA in blissful, moronic ignorance, and if he reported in alongside the man he was pretending to be, it was all over for Jennifer's clever plan and probably all over for Billy, too.

'Mommy?' Kate said, coming into the study. 'Can we go to the dog shelter now?'

'In a little while.' She picked up the phone, but it hissed and squealed at her. She'd forgotten about the modem. 'Can you get my cellphone from the kitchen table, honey?'

'I thought we were going to *go*.'

'Kate, Mommy's very busy.'

'Then when can we—'

'*After*,' she said. 'When I'm done, all right? Please get my phone. It's very important.'

Kate left. Jennifer waited, holding down the **V** key. Her head hurt.

'Is this it?'

'Thank you. I won't be much longer, sweetie, maybe twenty minutes, okay?'

'That's what you said an *hour* ago.'

'It was not an hour,' she said, but she looked at her watch and maybe it was. 'Kate, please go and – find something to do.'

Kate left wordlessly. Jennifer swapped hands on the keyboard – she was about ready to dump this sling – and dialed with her free hand.

'Government Comms Center.'

'It's Jennifer, Field Agent. I'm using that Marlboro bug and I need to get a message to the user.'

'You know that vibrate feature I told you about? If you go into the Transmit screen and press **V**—'

'I'm pressing the **V** right now. How else can I get a message to him?'

'Um . . . you could just try transmitting a message anyway.'

'He'll hear that?'

'No, not unless he's got the headphones in.'

'Why would he have the headphones in?'

'I dunno, I'm just saying—'

'Fuck!' she said.

'It's designed to be unobtrusive,' he said, wounded. 'An undercover agent doesn't want his bug to start broadcasting, "Come back, Agent Grimes." Maybe your operative has a good reason for not responding.'

'My operative's reason for not responding is that he's an idiot. You're telling me there's no way—' Her cellphone beeped. She looked at it. It said: INCOMING CALL.

'Apart from vibrate? No, there's not.'

'I'm going to put you on hold, and I want you to think of a way for me to contact my operative. All right?'

'I'm sorry, there's no—'

She switched lines. 'Hello?'

'Jen!' Calvin said. 'How's home life? I didn't interrupt you in the middle of baking cookies, did I?'

'No,' she said. 'Did you get John Nike?'

'Ah . . . no, not exactly.'

'*No?*'

'Before you get upset—'

'I'm upset!'

'He jumped a plane for Los Angeles.'

'Son of a bitch!'

'I've already contacted the L.A. office. They're going to assign a couple of agents. They'll take care of it.'

'No. They won't. John isn't going to be caught by a couple of agents looking for him in their spare time. Jesus!'

'Well, I guess you'll just have to trust in their abilities,' Calvin said. 'By the way, the other John is in a coma.'

'What?'

'There are two Johns, right? Vice-President John is in L.A. The other one is in a coma. They don't know if he'll ever recover.'

'Oh,' she said. 'Right.' That was kind of good news.

'Aren't you going to ask me how I know this?'

'How do—'

142

'It's a funny story,' Calvin said. 'At Nike, I ran into this Georgia Saints-Nike. Nice woman. She told me all about working with you and John in your halcyon advertising days at Maher. At first I had trouble picturing you in a power skirt and heels, but now I think about it—'

'I have someone on hold,' she said. 'Does this story have a point?'

'You lied to me. You said you never worked with him.'

'I said I never worked for Nike.'

'That's sneaky, Jen. Very sneaky. What happened? John stole a juicy account from you? Pinched your ass at the office Christmas party?'

'I really hope you found some time to work on the case in between snooping into my past.'

'I'm starting to wonder if there's any difference.'

'Look,' she said. 'I'm Government. He's a criminal. Does it matter if I used to know him?' In the living room, she heard the TV go on. 'Kate!' she called. 'Too loud!'

'If you've got a prior interest in John Nike, you're not helping the Government by keeping it a secret. He could use that in his defense.'

'Calvin, please.' Her phone beeped, reminding her about the call on hold. 'Nobody else knows what John is capable of. I'm the *best* person to track him down. Because I used to work with him, I can't be on this case? No. That's stupid.'

'Jen—'

Her phone beeped again. 'Hang on, I've got someone on the other line.' She put Calvin on hold, yelled, 'Kate, turn the TV down!' and switched calls. 'You still there?'

'Hello? Is . . . is that Jennifer Government?'

Jennifer blinked. This wasn't her guy on hold: it was a new call. 'Who is this?'

'It's Buy Mitsui. You interviewed me on Tuesday?'

'Oh. Buy, sure. Look, can I call you back? I'm kind of—'

'I have a question.'

'Is it quick?'

'I think so. I have a . . . a Colt pistol, and I can't get it to fire. There's . . . some kind of lock, I guess.'

'There's a safety just in front of the trigger,' she said. 'Have you loaded the magazine?'

'Yes, I put some bullets in.'

'If the magazine's not full, you have to chamber the first round. Did you do that?'

'Oh,' he said, and laughed. 'No. Thank you.'

'No problem.' She was reaching for the button to cut him off when she realized what he was saying. 'Wait a minute. What's this for?'

'Um . . . I'd rather not say.'

'Please. Say.'

'Well,' Buy said. 'Okay. I'm going to kill myself.'

'Bad day at the stock exchange?' He was silent, and Jennifer regretted the words. 'Buy, I'm sorry. Give me one second. Okay?'

'Okay.'

She clicked her phone. 'Any ideas?'

'You could try sending the vibrations in Morse code,' the Communications Center guy said. 'Does your operative know Morse?'

She laughed before she could stop herself.

'Is that a no?'

'Thanks for your help.' She killed the call. 'Calvin, I'm coming in tomorrow. See you at the office.'

'Jen! No!'

'Buy?'

'I'm here.'

'Where do you live?'

'That's – really not necessary.' He sounded embarrassed. 'Please—'

'This is about the girl. Hayley. Right? Tell me where you live.'

He told her. Jennifer took her finger off the **V** key to write down the address.

'I'll be there in ten minutes.'

'I – okay. Okay.'

'Do you have wine?'

'Wine? Yes.'

'Good,' she said, and hung up. She looked at her computer screen, at the collection of technology that left her unable to speak to Billy NRA. Then she turned it off.

Kate was watching a television show about giant pandas. Jennifer squatted down in front of her. She looked up.

'That last baby-sitter, she was nice, wasn't she?'

'*No!* You said we'd go to the dog shelter!'

'Kate, I'm really sorry.' She sat down and put her arms around her. Kate was upset and resistant; it was like hugging a cat. 'I know I said we could go today. But we can go tomorrow, and that's still earlier than the weekend, right?' Kate didn't respond. 'Honey, I'm sorry. But sometimes you have to be brave and put your own needs on hold, to help someone else. Do you understand?'

'I don't want you to go!'

'I know you don't, sweetie. Look, you're the most important person in the world to me. I've told you it's important for me to go. But if you really don't want me to, I'll stay. Okay? What do you say?'

'Stay!'

'Kate!' she said, exasperated. 'I have to go!'

'I don't want you to!'

'You didn't mind me going out when you had those new videos to watch! You hardly noticed I was gone!'

'I *did* notice!'

'All right!' she shouted. 'All right, all right! I'm a terrible mother! I've ruined your life! I'm sorry, but *I have to go*!' She ground the heel of her hand into her forehead. When she removed it, Kate was looking at her. 'What?'

'You're not a terrible mother, Mommy.'

'You . . .' she said. 'Well, that's nice of you to say.'

'Are you sure we can go to the dog shelter tomorrow?'

'Yes,' Jennifer said. 'Honey, I promise. I'll pick you up from school and we'll go straight there. We'll pick out the perfect dog.'

'Okay,' Kate said. 'And . . . soon you won't be so busy, right? When you've caught the bad guys.'

'That's – that's right. I wish I could spend all my time with you. I love you, Kate. Mommy is just under a lot of pressure right now.'

Kate nodded. 'She was nice. The last baby-sitter.'

'Good girl.' Jennifer kissed her. She felt proud and tired.

40 ACCULTURATION

The easier your job, the more you got paid. John had suspected this for many years, but here was the proof: pulling down five hundred bucks an hour to sit in the afternoon sun on top of an L.A. office tower. He was wearing a suit and shades, reclining on a deck chair while a light breeze blew in from the bay. John thought he might have found the perfect job.

'Hey,' he said to the foreman. 'I've got an inventory sheet. None of this stuff had better go missing.'

The foreman looked at him. He was not so relaxed: he was getting paid much less than John and doing much harder work. 'Nothing's going to go missing.'

'It better not.' He closed his eyes, enjoying the sun. He was building a nice tan out here.

'Nothing's going missing,' the foreman repeated. He hesitated. 'I don't know your business, but – you want these things pointing north, right?'

'So?'

'Well, north is downtown. You're going to end up with a bunch of missiles pointing at other office towers. If you're worried about security—'

'You're right,' John said. 'You don't know my business.'

After a while, the foreman went away. John folded his hands on his chest and closed his eyes. Tomorrow, he thought, he would bring a couple of beers.

His new title was US Alliance Liaison. He didn't know exactly what that meant; it was something to do with making sure Nike was doing its part for the team and the team was doing its part for Nike. Last night he'd met Liaisons from General Motors, Microsoft, and Johnson & Johnson. It was amazing to think they were all on the same side. What they could do with all those marketing budgets working together!

He and Gregory met in a bar on Sunset every night, or almost every night. When Gregory didn't show, John downed scotches and picked up women. But mostly Gregory showed. John was into his third drink and eyeing a girl with curly brown hair when Gregory sat down. 'John.'

'Hey, buddy.'

'You get the installation done?'

John drained his glass. 'Half of it. We're putting the rest in tomorrow.'

'Get someone else to do it. You're going to London.'

'What's there?'

'Our interests. You'll get more information when you arrive.'

'All right,' John said, but he was annoyed. London would not be eighty degrees with a light breeze; London would not provide opportunities to network with the type of people he wanted to meet.

'You'll be working with the Shell Liaison. You do what he tells you. Understood?'

'We're taking orders from Shell now?'

'It's called teamwork.'

'O–kay,' John said.

'I have to go. Collect your ticket from the office and call me from London.' He studied John. 'Also, it may be a good idea for you to keep a low profile. I'm told the Government is looking for you. The little matter of fourteen dead teenagers.'

'Hey,' John said. 'You know I only ordered ten.'

'You can explain that to the Government,' Gregory said, looking at his watch, 'if they ever catch up with you.'

'It's not the whole Government,' he said, disgusted. 'It's just Jennifer. The bitch never quits.'

Gregory raised his eyebrows. 'Jennifer?'

'Long story,' John said. 'Don't worry, I'll take care of it.'

Gregory considered. 'Don't expect the company to help you, John, if the Government gets you for this. It won't accept responsibility for a criminal act.'

'Then maybe the company should hand over the billion dollars my criminal act just made it.'

Gregory was silent.

'Uh-huh,' John said. He smiled at the girl with curly hair.

'Does it bother you, John? That you're responsible for those kids?'

John looked at him. 'How do you mean?'

'Forget it,' Gregory said.

'Hey,' John said, nettled. 'It's my job to increase sales. Is it my fault that was the best way to do it? If the Government had the

148

muscle to enforce the law, it wouldn't have made economic sense, but they don't, and it did. This is the world we live in. If you don't take advantage of the rules, you're a sucker.'

'I see,' Gregory said. He was disappointed, John realized. You could never do enough for some people. No matter how much you delivered, they always wanted more. 'For now, deal with your Government problem. And call me from London.'

'Sure.' He tried to end on a positive note. 'You can count on me.'

He watched Gregory's back until he disappeared onto the street. He had overstepped his mark there. He had mouthed off. The talk about Jennifer Government had thrown him. The idea she was still tailing him gave him the creeps.

'Another?' the bartender said.

'Sure,' John said. He looked around the bar. The girl with curly hair was still there, talking with her friend. She looked at him, smiled, and looked away. She was maybe sixteen. John smiled back at her. He could end L.A. on a positive note, too.

Georgia picked up on the first ring. John was pleased: it was eight A.M. in Melbourne, and most P.A.s would be taking advantage of his absence. John liked Georgia Saints-Nike; he'd used her since Maher. The only thing she lacked was a knockout body and a penchant for skimpy outfits, but John had been down that road before and it never worked out. Other managers got jealous, your diary never got organized, and after you'd been fucking them a few months they turned whiny and disobedient.

'Georgia, good girl, in early. I've got some work for you.'

'Hi, John. How's L.A.?'

'Great.' He was calling from the airport gate; he had his finger plugged into his other ear. 'I'm going to London today. Has the Government been around?'

'The Government?'

'You know: cheap suits, dour expressions, always asking for money.'

'No, John.'

'You haven't heard from Jennifer?'

'Jennifer Maher? No, John.'

'Okay.' Superficially, that was good; fundamentally, it meant Jennifer was chasing him but being sneaky about it, which was bad. 'If they come knocking, I'm in Cuba.'

'Cuba?'

'Or some country I might actually visit, I don't know. Make something up.'

'All right, John. Can I get a number for you in London? An address?'

'I don't know where I'll be. Just use my cellphone.' The flight had started to board: attractive women in short skirts were processing business-class tickets. 'I have to go. If anything's not clear, get John to sort it out.'

'He's still in a coma.'

John blinked. 'Still? How long is that guy going to take to get back to work?'

'The hospital said it's hard to tell.'

'Jesus,' he said. 'Those places have no accountability. Look, I'll call you from London.'

'With an address?'

'Sure, yeah. You clear on my instructions?'

'Yes, John.'

'Good girl,' he said. 'I can always rely on you.'

'Business class?' one of the women called. 'Business class?'

'Right here,' John said, handing her his ticket. He looked into her eyes and smiled.

*

Ten hours later he was wandering around the Heathrow lounge looking for anyone with a JOHN NIKE sign. He did two vague laps, then settled into a plastic bench seat with his briefcase on his lap.

After a long time, a kid wearing baggy pants and a puffy jacket wandered into the lounge. 'You John?'

'Yes.'

'Sorry I'm late, man. The airport is, like, two hours out of this city.'

'Really?' John said. 'Well, how about you turn around and go back there.'

'Say what?' said the kid.

'You see those things on your feet? That's my company. There are some people you can leave waiting for thirty minutes, and I'm not one of them. I don't get met by trainees, especially when they're an hour late. So go back to London and tell your boss that when a real person wants to talk to me, I'll be at the Hilton.' He stood.

'Dude,' the kid said, 'no need for hostilities. I'm a Liaison, too.'

John started. 'You're the Shell Liaison?'

'PepsiCo. We'll be working together with Shell.'

'Pepsi.'

'So are we cool?'

'You're the Pepsi Liaison.'

'Straight up.'

John sighed. Consumer marketing could be so tiresome.

'So can we move?' the kid said. 'My Ferrari's double-parked.'

'I've never been to England before,' the Pepsi kid said. He had mentioned his name, but John hadn't bothered to remember it. 'I gotta say, I'm disappointed. I thought it would be all cottages and meadows and shit. But it's just another city.'

'Mmm,' John said. He looked out the window as they roared past a Mini.

'I mean, I'm glad it's not all, you know, European Union and police. But I thought there'd be *some* differences.'

'Where'd you get the car?'

'I just asked my P.A. to get me something hot.' He glanced at John. 'It's a 550 Barchetta. You like?'

'It's all right.' He decided to get Georgia to rent him a Porsche.

'You wanna drive?'

'No.'

'Twelve cylinders, dude, it's like wrestling a crocodile.'

'How old are you?'

'Twenty-four. But trust me, I'm competent.' The kid swerved through lanes. 'Hey, I saw this old British movie, all the people spoke so different, you could hardly understand them. But everyone here speaks American as good as you and me. What's with that?'

'It's a smaller world these days,' John said. 'Where are we going?'

'Oh, sorry, man. We're going straight to the stock exchange. Didn't they tell you? Shell's buying out ExxonMobil. They launch a hostile takeover bid in . . .' He looked at his watch. 'Thirty minutes.'

'That's why we're here? To watch a bunch of bankers?'

'Brokers, dude. It's a serious event. If this one comes off, US Alliance controls two-thirds of the world's heavy fuels.'

'And what are we meant to do?'

'Crowd control.' The kid grinned.

John said, 'I'd really like to speak to the Shell Liaison.'

'We're meeting him there.'

John said nothing. This was very screwed up. He wondered if he should call Gregory.

'And what's with these road signs?' the kid said. '"Motorway?" What's wrong with "interstate?"'

'They don't have states. They call them shires.'

'Why?'

'They just do.'

'Huh,' the kid said. He was silent for a while. 'Well, I guess that's different.'

41 INTERSECTION

Buy was halfway into a new shirt when the buzzer went. He buttoned and hurried into the kitchen. He could see Jennifer in the fuzzy screen of his intercom, wearing a long coat.

He suddenly decided not to answer. He shouldn't have called her in the first place: that had been pathetic. He might as well have said, 'Hi, Jennifer, this is Buy with a cry for help.' He felt embarrassed at his failure to competently kill himself.

The buzzer rang again. On the intercom screen, Jennifer shifted impatiently. He pushed the button. 'Hi.'

'Oh, good. You're still here.'

'Uh,' he said. 'Yes. Come on up.'

He buzzed her in. His apartment looked plain and embarrassingly bachelorlike. Buy wished he had some flowers, or knickknacks, or something.

She knocked. Buy took a breath and answered the door.

'Hiya,' she said.

'Hi! Come in, let me take your coat.'

'Thanks.' Jennifer wandered in and looked around, almost professionally. 'Nice view. How much does a place like this cost?'

'You don't want to know. Would you like a drink?' He had wine chilling in the fridge and two glasses on the sideboard.

'Yeah, that'd be great.' She dropped onto the sofa.

'I'll be right back.' He went into the kitchen, collected the wine and glasses, tried to calm down, and went back in. Jennifer was flipping through a magazine he'd left on the coffee table: *Investor.*

'Does this stuff really interest you?' she said. 'All these numbers and graphs?'

Buy sat down in the chair next to the sofa. It was hard to not look at her barcode tattoo. He kept wondering what would come up if you scanned it. 'Not anymore.'

'Ah.' She smiled wryly. Buy suspected that Jennifer Government had quite a repertoire of wry smiles; they might, in fact, be the only kind she had. 'Hence the Colt.'

'Uh, right.'

'Can I see it?'

'Okay.' He fetched it from his bedroom desk drawer and brought it back. She turned it over, then put it in her bag. 'What are you doing?'

'I don't want you to do anything you won't be able to regret later.'

He felt himself redden. 'You must think I'm pathetic.'

'No.'

'I shouldn't have called you.'

She touched his hand. 'Buy, I was at that Nike Town. I know what it feels like to fail. I do.'

He looked at her for a while.

Jennifer said, 'At least you got out of it with a decent haircut.'

He laughed.

'Come on,' she said. 'I'm starving. Let's get some food.'

They ordered Chinese and spread it across the carpet in front of the window. Jennifer kept staring out at the city, and when she did Buy snuck looks at her. She caught him once, and he looked away, embarrassed.

'I can hardly hold these damn chopsticks,' she said. 'You know, my shoulder.'

'Does it hurt much?'

'It's not so bad anymore. My hair is worse.'

'No, no. It's very . . . noticeable.'

'Hey,' she said.

'I like it. It's French. Short and messy is hip.'

'Yeah, well,' she said. 'You're too generous.' She drained her glass. 'So what's France like?'

'Different. People pay tax, and the Government is . . . much stronger.'

'My kind of place,' Jennifer said.

'There isn't the poverty of here. Or the wealth. There is unemployment. But France is very beautiful. The great buildings of Paris, and the villages like paintings . . .' He saw her smile, and it looked like a real one. 'It is a truly romantic place.'

'Mmm,' she said. 'I could do with some of that.'

'Unfortunately, it didn't seem to help when I lived there.'

'No?'

'If anything,' Buy said, 'it only seemed to make the breakups more poignant. One time I broke up with a girl outside the Notre Dame. She slapped me and ran away crying. I felt like the bad guy in a movie.' Jennifer snickered. 'Oh, and you've never had a bad breakup?'

'No, I guess I have.'

'Don't just sit there,' he said, topping up her glass. 'Let's have it.'

She frowned. 'It was in the board room of an L.A. office tower. This enormous room, with glass walls and views over the city, and we'd both just finished the most important meeting of our lives. I asked him to hang up a minute.'

'Uh-oh.'

'He had no idea it was coming. He thought we were going great. I told him I was pregnant.'

Buy said nothing. Jennifer's dark eyes watched him.

'He flipped. I mean, really flipped. He didn't want a kid. He didn't want me to have a kid. I can understand it, in a way. We were young and trying to establish careers. But when he said that, I hated him.' She shook her head. 'As soon as I discovered I was pregnant, I knew I wasn't giving up my baby. It sounds stupid, but it changes your life. It makes you realize who you are.

'So he and I . . . went to war. It was insane. In the end I quit my job and moved out here. He thought that meant he won. But I have a beautiful daughter, and she's everything I want. She's everything.'

They held each other's eyes. Buy thought wildly: *Should I kiss her? Should I?*

Jennifer looked down. 'You mind if I make a phone call?'

'Of course,' he said, trying to recover. 'I'll clean up.'

She produced a cellphone and Buy carried the remnants of their meal to the garbage. When he returned, she was on the sofa. He carefully sat beside her.

'. . . you, Billy. You have to get rid of him, any way you can. You'd better understand what I mean.' She paused. 'You get all that? Okay. Thanks.' She beeped off her phone.

Buy raised an eyebrow.

'Work,' Jennifer said.

'Right,' Buy said, and, like an idiot, kissed her.

She tensed. For a second he thought she was going to flip him and dig her knee into his back. But then she kissed him back. It was strange and tentative. Then he felt her hand on his shoulder, pulling him closer. Her lips curved beneath his.

She pulled away. 'This is why you called me, right?'

'Yes,' Buy confessed.

'Good.' She smiled again, almost shyly. 'That's what I was hoping.'

42 REVELATION

The NRA camp had grown a lot since Billy was last here. There were more tents, more soldiers, and spotlights sweeping the grounds. It didn't look so temporary anymore.

'Wow,' he said. 'What's going on?'

'Expedition,' Bill said. 'They're bringing more of the regular NRA membership into the fold.'

Billy didn't know what that meant. 'Wow.'

The cabdriver was nervous. He slowed to a halt twenty feet from the gates, where NRA guards eyed them from behind metal fortifications. 'You get out here. Okay? No further.'

'They won't hurt you,' Bill said, but he reached for his wallet. He grinned at Billy.

As soon as they closed the doors, the driver spun the cab around and bounced down the dirt-packed road. Billy and Bill walked up to the gate.

'Name and business!'

'Bill NRA, Strike Team Operative, Operation Instigate.'

'Billy NRA,' Billy said. 'Uh, Strike Team Operative, Operation . . . Police.'

The guards were kids, not even Billy's age. 'You got some ID?'

'Son,' Bill said, 'the work we do, we don't carry identification.'

'Um . . .' the guard said. 'I'm gonna have to check this out.'

'Look,' Bill said, 'the only person in this camp who's going to know me is Corporal Yallam. Now, you can either wake him up, or let me and my buddy in so we can get some goddamn sleep.'

The guards huddled together, conferring. Billy frowned. That was another coincidence: Bill worked for Yallam, too! But that didn't make any sense. Why wasn't Bill with Yallam's squad for the Police job, then?

'I can put you in a secured area for the night,' the guard said finally. 'Lock you in until Yallam can verify you in the morning. All right?'

'Some homecoming,' Bill said, but he hoisted his pack and Billy did the same. The guards showed them to a secured barracks, a squat, wooden building with no windows and a metal door, and locked them in.

Billy found the light switch. There were six bunks and a door to the bathroom. He dropped his pack on a bed. 'Man, I'm beat.'

'Me too. Let's hit the sack.'

In bed, Billy kept thinking about Yallam. Something was bugging him about that. Then he wondered if he'd be able to get away and see that NRA receptionist again, the one with the great body. That would be nice. That would be real nice.

He woke sometime just before dawn with a full bladder. It was just light enough to see Bill asleep in the bunk across the room. Billy got out of bed and went to the bathroom.

As he was pissing, he thought about Jennifer Government. She'd been pretty keen to talk to him yesterday, with all that buzzing. Maybe he should check in.

He zipped and went back to his bunk. Bill was still asleep. He fished through his pack until he found his jacket and the Marlboros in the pocket. He needed that little headphone jack, too, but it was way down in the bottom of his pack. He tried to keep quiet. Bill didn't stir.

He went back to the bathroom and sat in a stall, pushing the door closed with his foot. That funky packet was still vibrating, although now only in little bursts. Maybe the batteries were running low. He plugged in the headphones, and was surprised to hear Jennifer Government's voice.

'—you check in together, it's going to take them about ten seconds to realize what's going on. Then they'll kill you, Billy. You have to get rid of him, any way you can. You'd better understand what I mean.'

'Hello?' he whispered.

There was a click and then she started again. It was a recording.

'Billy, this is Jennifer. You dumb shit, the guy you're with *is the guy you're pretending to be.* You said the NRA were expecting someone called Bill NRA. *This is the guy.* If you check in together, it's going to take them about ten seconds—'

Billy felt his body freeze over. 'Oh, shit!'

He heard the bathroom door squeak open. 'Hey, buddy,' Bill said. 'What you doing in there?'

'I'm—' The words hardly made a sound. 'Just taking a dump, dude.'

He heard Bill's footsteps. He looked at the door. No lock! There was no lock on the door! 'What, another one?'

His throat tightened until he could hardly breathe. 'What?'

'You get up, come in here, go back to your bunk, come back in here. What's that about?' His voice lowered. 'You got some girly mags or something?'

'Yeah!' Billy said. 'Yeah, I've—'

'What are you, talking to them?'

'Um,' Billy said. 'Yes . . . sometimes I like to . . . um . . .'

'Well don't be selfish, dude,' Bill said, and pushed open the door. They looked at each other for a while.

'What the fuck is that?' Bill said.

'It's . . .'

'Some kind of radio? Can you get the baseball on that?'

'What?' Billy said. 'I – yeah! Yeah, I'm listening to a game now.'

'Man, that is awesome! Who's playing?'

Billy coughed to give himself enough time to think. 'The Yankees and the White Sox.'

'You're shitting me! The Sox are my team! Mind if I have a listen?'

'Uh . . . sure.' He unplugged the headphones and handed the packet to Bill.

Bill turned it over. 'I've never seen anything like this. They look just like regular smokes! Where'd you get it?' He put the headphones into his ears and listened.

Maybe the recording stopped, Billy thought. *Maybe Jennifer heard us and turned it off.*

'Hey,' Bill said. 'This ain't baseball.'

Billy kicked the stall door as hard as he could. It hit Bill in the face and rebounded. The door blocked Billy's view for a second, then he saw Bill lying against the opposite wall underneath the sink, looking surprised and hurt. Bill spat blood onto his chest. 'You're *Government.*'

'Sorry,' Billy said. He stood and walked over, looking for something to knock Bill out with.

'Infiltrator!' Bill shouted, and kicked out Billy's legs. Suddenly Bill's thick arm was wrapped around his neck. Billy coughed and struggled. 'Help me!' Bill yelled. His voice bounced off the tiled walls. 'Security! I need help!'

Billy got an elbow free and rammed Bill's head up into the bottom of the sink. The porcelain shattered, raining down onto him.

'Uh!' Bill said. 'You . . . nnnn . . .'

'Sorry,' Billy said again. Then he felt something hot and wet on his stomach.

'Take that, asshole,' Bill said.

Billy looked down. There was a long, thin shard of porcelain sticking out of his side. He was so horrified at the blood that he forgot about Bill, so didn't see his knuckles coming. His head rocked back and hit the wall. Then Billy stopped thinking about anything for a while.

He must have slumped over and knocked the porcelain shard against the floor: that regained his attention. He screamed. He was alone in the bathroom. He felt dizzy. His hands and feet were numb.

He knew he should probably leave the shard in his side, but he couldn't stand it hanging there. He yanked; his vision flared; he felt blood stream down his side. He tried to cover the wound with his hand.

'Infiltrator!' Bill's voice echoed from the sleeping quarters. 'Will you guys hurry up, there's a goddamn Government infiltrator in here trying to kill me!'

Billy heard keys rattling. Someone, or more likely some people, were unlocking the front door. He got to his feet, fell over, then stood up again. The bathroom door was a long way away. He staggered forward and grabbed hold of the doorway.

Bill was assembling a gun on one of the bunks. It was an FN M249 automatic, if Billy wasn't mistaken: not very accurate over long range, but pretty much guaranteed to chop him into pieces from ten feet away. Bill raised it. Billy took the only evasive action he could and dropped to the floor. The woodwork exploded above his head.

The front door popped open. Four men in combat fatigues stormed in. They were carrying submachine guns.

'Infiltrator,' Billy croaked, and pointed at Bill.

They opened fire, and Bill backflipped across the room. For a second, Billy thought Bill must be incredibly acrobatic. Then he realized, and turned away.

'Are you all right?' an NRA man said to him, and another shouted, 'Medic! We need a medic in here!'

'Ag,' Billy said, and slept for a while.

43 APOSTASY

Hack felt her touch his hair. He felt her hand on his face. 'Violet? Violet!'

'Shh,' Claire said. 'It's just me.'

He struggled awake. 'What time—'

'It's just after six. There's a phone call for you. It's Violet.'

Hack threw back the covers. Relief washed through him. Violet was alive! He ran to the kitchen and grabbed the receiver. 'Hello? Violet?'

'Hi.' She sounded small and far away. There was a lot of background noise, as if she was in a car on a busy freeway. 'I can't talk long. I'm calling from an airplane.'

'A what?'

'I just wanted to tell you I'll be away a while. I got a job.'

'What airplane?'

'I'm going to London.'

'London?' He felt confused.

'Yes.'

'But . . . how come . . . when are you coming back?'

'I don't know. Maybe a couple of weeks.'

'*Weeks?*'

'I sold my software. To ExxonMobil.'

'Oh, Violet, that's great! How did—'

'I have to go. I'll call again later.'

'Wait! How come you didn't call before?'

'I've been busy. I had to go to Dallas.'

'Dallas?'

'Hack, I have to go.'

'Why didn't you call me from Dallas?'

162

'I'm calling you now, aren't I? Come on, don't dick me around.'

'I'm not dicking you around.' Hack heard the whine in his voice. He turned his back on Claire, who was waiting in the doorway. 'I just think you could have called so I didn't have to worry you'd been killed.'

'You know, forget I called. I thought you might be happy for me.'

'I am, Violet, but—'

'You're like a rope around my legs, you know? Everything I do, you try to hold me back. It's too much.'

'Violet, I've never held you back! We've lived on my income for a year!'

The phone clicked in his ear.

'Violet? Violet?'

Hack couldn't move. After a while he felt Claire's arms encircle his waist, hugging him from behind. 'You okay?'

'She's . . .' He couldn't speak.

'She doesn't deserve you, Hack,' Claire said softly. 'She never did.'

Hack went in to work, but he couldn't concentrate. He spent most of the day staring out the window and chewing on his pen. So many things had turned out lately to not be what Hack thought. First there was Violet, who was neither as affectionate nor as dead as he'd believed. Then there were the things Claire's hippie friends had said, things that made more sense than he really wanted them to. Like how he was being exploited by Nike. That was truer than any of them knew.

But most confusing was Claire. It was possible she was just being nice to him, Hack knew. Claire was sweet. But it was also possible she still cared for him. It was possible she'd never stopped caring for him, the whole time he'd been with Violet. That thought kept running around and around in his head.

'Hey, Hack,' a woman across the aisle said. 'You still with us?'

'What?'

'You're staring at nothing.'

'Oh,' he said. 'Yes, I'm fine.'

She rolled her eyes. Hack felt annoyed. He was sitting right here, did she think he couldn't see her? No one respected Hack at Nike. No one respected him anywhere.

He stood up. 'I'm going to get going.'

She looked startled. 'It's only five o'clock.'

'Yeah, well,' Hack said. 'I'm still going.' He had things to do.

The cabdriver thought it was pretty funny, Hack not knowing where his own car was. Hack was having trouble seeing the humor in the situation, but that might have been because it was costing him a buck a minute to uselessly circle the airport parking lot. Then it occurred to him that Violet might not have driven herself here at all: she sure hadn't paid for her own plane ticket. He had the cab take him to the ExxonMobil building and walked up to reception. 'Excuse me, where's your visitor's parking?'

'To use visitor's parking, you need to book ahead, sir.' The receptionist smiled sympathetically.

'I don't want to use it,' Hack said. 'I just want to know where it is.'

'But, sir, there's no point in me telling you where it is unless you've booked.'

'But I – oh, fine,' Hack said. He would wander around until he found it. He started to walk away. The receptionist said: 'Oh – are you the owner of a red Toyota?'

He stopped. 'Yes.'

'We had that towed.'

'Towed where?'

'I'm not sure . . . there's a firm we use, you'll need to call them.' She slipped a card across the desk.

'Can I use your phone?'

She looked at him doubtfully. Hack resisted the urge to drop his eyes. Instead he met her gaze with what he hoped was force and natural authority. 'Um . . . sure,' the receptionist said. She slid the phone across the desk. 'I really shouldn't let you, though.' She smiled.

'Thanks.' He tried not to show his surprise. What a reaction! Hack had never gained such results in his life. There was something to this assertiveness stuff. 'I won't be long.'

'Take as long as you need,' the receptionist said.

The tow truck company would give Hack's car back only if he came out to their lot, showed them some ID, and paid them five hundred dollars. That wasn't such a great development. Hack didn't have five hundred dollars, not even close. The man from the towing company wouldn't budge no matter how much force and natural authority Hack used.

Still, he felt upbeat on the cab trip back to Claire's. He felt like he'd discovered something important. People like John Nike hadn't been pushing him around for no reason, Hack realized: he had let them do it. He'd *expected* them to do it. Well, all that was going to change. Hack was going to take control.

Claire wasn't home yet. Hack sat on the sofa and jiggled his leg. He couldn't wait to talk to her. He wanted to ask about that group of hers. He wanted to know if they did more than just talk.

44 COLLABORATION

Violet pushed END CALL on the airphone. It had a long cord that was meant to retract into her seat, but she couldn't get it to work. She caught Nathaniel ExxonMobil looking at her across the aisle. 'Trouble at home?'

'It's fine,' Violet said. She didn't want to talk to Nathaniel right now.

'It's hard for your loved ones to understand why you have to leave them. Why you have to do certain things. That's something I've learned.'

'Things are fine.' She found the right button. The phone retracted.

'You didn't tell him about the deal?'

Violet looked down at the contract. It gave ExxonMobil full use of her software, plus her services to activate it. It gave Violet, if her product worked, just under three million dollars. 'It's nothing to do with him. This is mine.'

'All right,' Nathaniel said, and returned to his journal.

It was raining in London. Violet cupped her hands and peered out the windows, but all she could see through the tint and fog were gray silhouettes of low buildings. She reached for the control to wind them down, but Nathaniel's hand closed over hers. 'Sorry. Not possible.'

'Why not?'

'I don't want to be seen. You can do the tourist thing after you've hit Shell.'

'When's that?'

He looked at his watch. 'Three hours.'

'Oh.' She felt her gut tighten.

'Everything will work out,' Nathaniel said. 'Just you wait and see.'

'*You* don't have to go in there.'

'Neither do you. Do you want to back out of the contract?'

Violet looked away. She didn't like Nathaniel very much. 'No.'

Violet was the only tech in the group. She'd been briefed on the server they'd gain access to, but even so, she was no Solaris expert. If she got lost in the operating system, all she had to rely on was a headset and some guys in the London ExMo headquarters. Violet thought it should be the other way around: ExMo techs going in while she sat in an air-conditioned building with a radio.

But this was how Nathaniel wanted it: Violet plus twelve members of the Police – who were soldiers, really, with uniforms and guns and belts with plenty of stuff on them. They rode to Shell in the back of a UPS van. Violet watched to see if they looked competent. She wasn't used to working in a team. She was starting to freak out a little.

'Two minutes,' the leader said. The Police began pulling on balaclavas and slapping weapons together. 'Ma'am, we'll be between you and them at all times. Just go where we push you.'

'You'll look after me, right? You won't lose me?'

'No, ma'am.' She looked for his name tag. It said only: ONE. 'Trust me.'

The van slowed and everyone inside shut up. Then it moved on, then finally stopped. This was the cue everyone except Violet knew: Police soldiers jumped up and slapped open the doors. She was immediately surrounded. Someone kneed her in the butt; she accidentally headbutted a man's back. Her only view was straight up, of the office tower they were about to enter.

She heard glass smash, then a soldier manhandled her through a broken revolving door. Someone said, 'Down! Down! On the ground!' She caught a glimpse of a white-faced security guard. He didn't look as if he felt like taking on a dozen heavily armed soldiers. Violet thought: *Maybe this is going to be all right.*

A few soldiers stayed in the lobby, but the rest stormed a stairwell. Violet's soldier kept one hand on her back, pushing her all the way up. At first she was resentful, but ten stories later, she was pretty much relying on him. When they exited onto a floor, she could hardly breathe.

Then there was a lot of shouting. The floor was a cubicle farm full of shocked-looking employees. The Police kept breaking out of formation to push someone to the ground, and Violet began to feel more vulnerable. A girl with glasses met her eyes. She looked young and scared. Violet felt bad for her.

The speakers in the ceiling said: 'All personnel, all personnel. We are experiencing a dangerous security situation. Take cover under your desk until further notice. Do not attempt to leave the building. This is not a drill.'

'Down, down, down!' the soldier to Violet's left shouted. He ran to where a man was leaning over a desk, talking on the phone. 'Put that down! Get on the floor!'

'I – I'm just closing a deal,' the man said. Violet froze: she couldn't believe anyone would be so stupid.

The soldier thrust his rifle barrel into the man's face. '*Put it down!*'

'Please, just one more—'

The soldier did something to his gun. It made a *click*.

'—minute, please—'

The soldier jumped, twisted, and fell on top of him.

Violet didn't know why she never heard the shot. She was left to infer it from the businessman's horrified expression and the blood. There was a young man across the room, a kid in a suit and a bright tie. He was holding a pistol.

A soldier tackled Violet hard, throwing her to the ground, and then there was a lot of gunfire; she heard *that*. 'Get off!' Violet shouted, but he had her pinned. 'Get off me!' She didn't know why she was struggling.

The shooting didn't last long. There was some screaming, and the Police shouted some more, then Violet's soldier hauled her up and pushed her along. 'Wait!' She twisted, trying to see. 'Wait, what happened to—'

The kid with the pistol was gone. On the wall behind where he had been was a red spray.

'Oh, no,' she said. 'No no no—'

'Get a hold of yourself!' the soldier snarled. He sounded strange, so she turned to look. He was carrying the wounded soldier over his shoulder, who was trying to hold his neck in. Blood ran between his fingers.

She screamed, recoiled against the man in front of her, tripped, and fell.

'Get up!' the soldier yelled. Hands were on her, pulling at her hair and clothes. 'Get up, get up!'

'*No! No!*' She kicked at them. Someone reached a hand toward her and she bit it.

'*Ahh!* Goddamn it—'

'Carry her!' someone ordered, and they did. A soldier picked Violet up and slung her over his shoulders. She slapped wildly at his head. She felt terribly exposed: she could see employee eyes peeking at her around desks and through potted plants.

The soldiers broke open some glass doors. This was the computer room, so busted doors were really going to fuck with the temperature control, Violet knew. Featureless computer servers stood about, spaced evenly across the floor. The soldier dropped her to the ground.

'You! We're here! Do your stuff!'

169

'No—'

'Do it!'

'I can't!'

He slapped her so hard she fell to her knees. It was so surprising and absurd that Violet started laughing.

A Police soldier pulled her so close that she couldn't see anything except his eyes, surrounded by the balaclava. It was enough for her to recognize him: it was the leader, ONE. His hand gripped her neck. 'Do your job or I'll kill you here.'

His words were funny, but his eyes were hard and suggested to Violet that ONE was not the kind of guy to kid around. She struggled for air. 'Wait – wait – I need a terminal. Not the actual computer. A terminal.'

'What the fuck's a terminal?'

'They're in the—' In his grip, she tried to peer around. There was a small, glass-walled room to one side. Three techs stood inside, looking out nervously. 'I need to get in there.'

'Move!' ONE said, and dropped her. She rubbed her throat while the soldiers kicked in the door and hauled the techs out. Violet followed them in and walked between the rows of terminals until she found one that said:

```
[root@sphinx /usr] %
```

ONE was right behind her. 'Is this what you need? *Is this it?*'

'Yes,' she said, and began to work.

45 EXECUTION

In John's opinion, if you'd seen one stock exchange, you'd seen them all: giant screens, paper-strewn floors, and too many sweaty people in close proximity to each other. John hadn't been on the trading floor before, but all that added to the experience was strangers shouting mumbo jumbo in his ear. The only words he understood coming out of these people's mouths were 'gimme' and 'fucking.'

The Shell Liaison was tall, thin, and jumpy. His eyes roved around the boards, and he kept losing concentration while John was talking to him. Between him and the Pepsi kid, John was less than impressed with the quality of US Alliance personnel engaged here.

The takeover had been announced at nine-thirty: Shell was offering $58 for every common share of ExxonMobil sold before the close of trading. 'Is that a lot?' John asked, and the Shell Liaison said, 'It's *double* the opening!' which John took to mean yes.

Since then there had been a lot of excited brokers and the Shell Liaison biting his nails, and John was getting bored. 'What are we doing here?' he asked the Pepsi kid.

'You're talking to me again?' the kid said. He had collected some ripped paper stubs from the floor and seemed to be trying to stick them together. 'We're here for defense. If T.A. tries to storm the exchange, we coordinate with the NRA to repel them.'

'They think Team Advantage will attack the *exchange*?'

'Those NRA dudes aren't for show, man.'

John had assumed they were part of normal security. He began to feel vulnerable. He hadn't replaced the pistol Hack's girlfriend had stolen from him yet. 'Do you have a gun?'

The Pepsi kid patted his jacket. 'Always.'

'Great,' John said. 'Just great.'

'You're unarmed?'

'No one told me people were going to be shooting at me.'

'Aw, nothing's probably going to happen. We caught T.A. off guard, and we've got like fifty guys here.'

'Hmm.' He noticed a commotion spreading through the floor. The brokers were getting even more agitated. 'What's going on?'

The kid was squinting at his torn dockets. 'Dunno. Ask Stretch.'

John saw the Shell Liaison shouting into his cellphone. The cords in his neck were bulging. 'This doesn't look good.'

'Maybe T.A. *are* coming.' The kid sniggered.

A groan rippled through the hall. One of the big boards flashed up: ROYAL DUTCH/SHELL (RDS) BID FOR EXXONMOBIL (XXN) – SUSPENDED.

John walked to the Shell Liaison and took his arm. 'What's happening?'

He covered the mouthpiece. 'We've lost our integrated trading systems. We can't verify buy orders until it comes back up. We're trying to—'

'Is it temporary?'

'I'll let you know. Okay?'

John went back to the Pepsi kid. 'So?' the kid said.

'Some computer problem.'

The kid blew air through his teeth. 'Eggheads, man. You can never rely on 'em.' He smirked. 'If we were being attacked, I would have given you my gun, you know.'

'Sure you would have,' John said.

An hour later, the BID SUSPENDED sign was still up and brokers were getting increasingly pissed off. John was restless: he was here to make sure the buyout went smoothly, and it had come to a grinding halt. This was not looking like a good career move.

'What's taking them so long?' the Pepsi kid said. 'Don't their computers have backups?'

John spotted the Shell Liaison in conversation with a floor trader. 'Let's find out.' He stood behind the man until he turned. 'Are we doing business here or what?'

The Shell Liaison whispered, 'The entire Shell net has been toasted. They don't think they can bring it back up today.'

'Son of a bitch!' the Pepsi kid said. 'What happened down there?'

'An armed group entered the Shell building and disabled our I.T.'

'T.A. *attacked* us?'

'Those fuckers!' the kid said.

'We don't know for sure it's Team Advantage. There's no way we can identify particular—'

'Of course it's them,' John said. 'It's ExxonMobil, it's T.A. What's our counteraction?'

The Shell Liaison rubbed his forehead. 'We need to prepare an announcement for the floor . . . we'll extend the bid until tomorrow, maybe the day after—'

'No,' John said. 'Your competitor just invaded your building. What's our counteraction?'

'There's nothing we can do.'

'Bullshit.' Some people couldn't salvage anything from a defeat, John thought. Well, he wasn't one of them. He was prepared to seize opportunities. 'How many men do we have here?'

'Whoa, whoa,' the Liaison said. 'Nobody's going to—'

'I'm with John,' the kid said. 'Let's kick some ass!'

'We'll refer the incident to the Government, and they will—'

'The *Government?* The enemy kicks you in the balls and you want

173

to fill out a complaint form? You think the Government's even on our side?'

'T.A. are dissing us,' the Pepsi kid said. 'Listen to John-boy.'

'But what are you going to do?'

'I'm going to take these NRA guys and go tell ExxonMobil they made a mistake.'

'Let me talk to the Shell CEO first. Just – John, wait!'

'Too late,' John said.

'You,' he said. 'I need your men to come with me for a counteroffensive against ExxonMobil.'

The NRA soldier looked him up and down. According to his lapel, he was a Lieutenant, but John didn't know how high that was. 'And who are you?'

He flashed his ID. 'Nike Liaison.'

'Sir, I have no authority to initiate offensives. My orders are to hold this position.'

'Do you have orders to protect the safety of Liaisons?'

'Yes.'

'Then you better follow me,' John said, 'because I'm about to go shoot some people.' He didn't wait to see if he was being obeyed. The Pepsi kid was at his side, like a puppy. 'Give me your keys.'

'What?'

'Your keys,' John said. 'I'm driving.'

The kid was right: the Barchetta was an animal. They blew through downtown London while the kid scrambled for his seat belt and shouted, 'Ohhhhh fuck!' when they got too close to other cars.

'Are they following?'

The kid craned his neck. 'There's an NRA truck about three blocks back! But you're losing them!'

The lights ahead turned red, and John gunned the engine. It was a typical narrow London street, just a single lane of cars in each direction, so he jumped the curb, scraped between a pylon and a storefront, and bounced back onto the road. The street ahead was clear. He put his foot down.

'*John!* This car has no clearance! You can't drive on the sidewalk, man!'

'How much further?'

The kid had gotten directions from his cellphone; it was an AT&T service. 'Right there! Eight-ninety-nine!'

He saw the logo. It was a tall, cream-color building with a lobby encased in plate glass. That suited John nicely.

'NRA still with us?'

'They're pretty far back, man. Better wait or they'll miss us.'

'They won't miss us. Hang on.'

'Oh, no, no—'

John dropped the handbrake long enough to spin the car ninety degrees, then nudged the accelerator. The Ferrari leapt towards the ExxonMobil entrance.

'*Ahhhhhh!*' the kid yelled.

The car hit the curb and bounced, so they were slightly airborne when they plowed into the plate glass. The kid was right again: they had no clearance at all. He caught a glimpse of people running and diving, then they hit something large and unmovable and he was drowning in an airbag.

He couldn't see, but he got a hand onto the kid's chest and found his gun. He unlatched the door and tumbled out.

'Are you all right?' a woman said. 'Mister?'

'I'm fine,' John said, and pointed the gun at her. She screamed.

175

It echoed in the lobby. 'Where are the top executives in this building? Which floor?'

He heard the passenger door open and the kid get out, coughing.

'The thirty-eighth, they're all on the thirty-eighth!'

'Thank you.' He walked to the elevators. The kid trailed him silently. John had finally found a way to shut him up. He pushed for an elevator and waited.

The Ferrari was embedded in a huge reception desk, so far in it was hard to tell where one stopped and the other one began. John wondered if anyone had been sitting there.

NRA soldiers entered the lobby, picking their way through the glass. John spotted the Lieutenant he'd spoken to earlier. 'Hey!' he called. 'Security cameras!'

'What?'

'Go find where they operate the security cameras. I don't want to leave evidence.'

'Yes, sir!' the Lieutenant said. He was giving John some respect now, all right. The elevator arrived and John entered it. As they rose toward floor thirty-eight, the car tinkled Muzak at them.

The kid held out for another few seconds. 'You just *assumed* there was a passenger-side airbag.'

'Too much planning gets in the way of execution,' John said.

'It could have been *my* execution.'

'You're fine.'

'*And* you took my gun.'

'You said you'd loan it to me.'

'Yeah, well,' the kid muttered.

John said, 'You know what makes a successful executive?'

'Dude, I *am* a successful executive.'

'Decisiveness,' he said. The doors slid open. A man in a briefcase was standing there; he raised his eyebrows. John pointed the gun at the man's leg and squeezed the trigger. It was louder than he'd expected.

'Holy *shit*!' the kid said.

'Also implementation skills,' John said, and left the elevator.

The board room was directly ahead, guarded by a single P.A. at a desk. She rose as John and the Pepsi kid approached. 'What was that? Was that a shot?'

John pointed the gun at her. 'Sit down.'

She sat. The Pepsi kid took the initiative and pushed open the board room doors. Inside, amongst muted lighting and tasteful paintings, were five men and a girl. They were in such enormous, bloated chairs that it was like they were waiting for John to plug them.

'All right,' he said. 'Who's the big cheese here?'

Silence.

'Speak up!' the kid shouted.

'Okay,' John said, and cocked his gun at the girl. She screamed and crammed her fist into her mouth. There was something familiar about her, something that tugged at his memory. 'Do I know you?'

'No! No.'

He thought she was probably lying, but didn't have time to pursue it. 'Who's the CEO?'

'I am,' a man said. 'I'm Nathaniel ExxonMobil. Let's talk about compensation.'

'I thought you might be in town, Mr. CEO. I had a feeling.'

'Why don't you let these people go? You and I, we'll discuss it like businessmen.'

'Here's a question for you,' John said. 'Did you or did you not commission an assault on the computer network of Shell, a US Alliance company?'

Nathaniel's eyes didn't waver. 'Yes.'

John shot him. The force rolled Nathaniel and his executive chair back two feet, like a display. The girl started crying.

'Okay,' John said. 'Now you fuckers will cease hostile action toward US Alliance. You will acknowledge that your company and your Team Advantage has no ability and no right to compete with us. This is the new economy, and in it you can't hope to fuck with us and get away with it. Do you shitheads understand that?'

One of the men closed his eyes and began mouthing a prayer. John almost clocked him just for that.

'Good,' he said. The Pepsi kid held the door open for him.

46 RESUMPTION

Jennifer slipped out of Buy's bed at five, trying to sneak out. When she came out of the bathroom, his eyes were peeking over a pillow, reflecting the light.

'Jennifer?'

'Hey.' She sat on the bed. 'I gotta go.'

'Oh.'

He looked cute: all disheveled and disoriented. On impulse, she stroked his hair. 'So you want to see me again, or what?'

'Hmm . . .' he said. 'You know, I think I do.'

'You sure?'

'You want me to prove it?' He threw back the covers.

She looked at her watch. She looked at Buy.

'You know you want to,' he said, and she couldn't argue with that.

*

The house was spotless when she returned, and the baby-sitter was curled up on the sofa. She really was good value, Jennifer thought. She would have to start tipping her more.

She tiptoed down the hall and peeked in Kate's bedroom. Kate was asleep, snuggled up to a giant frog. Jennifer crouched down and kissed her. 'Morning, sweetheart.'

Kate's eyes opened, then squeezed closed. 'I'm tired . . .'

'It's time to get ready for school.'

'I don't want to.'

'And yet,' she said.

Kate screwed up her face. 'Mommy, I hate it when you say, "And yet."'

'Come on, sleepy. Today's the big day, remember? We hit the kennels tonight.'

Kate's eyes opened. 'Really?'

'Yep. I promised, didn't I?' She kissed her cheek.

At work, she spent half an hour trying to find someone to talk to in the L.A. office before she checked her e-mail and found a message. It read:

> From: georgia-saints@mktg.nike.com.au
>
> To: jennifer.fieldagent@melb-au.government.com
>
> John. London. Don't know where.

She hit the top of her desk, then kicked the table. That didn't help, so she grabbed the monitor and shook it.

'Whoa,' Calvin said, entering. 'Bad time?'

'He's gone to London!'

'Who? John?' He sat beside her and read the e-mail. 'Ah, crap.'

'How are we going to get to London?'

'I don't know. I wonder . . .' He looked at his watch. 'The brass called a briefing this morning. Something happened in the British Territories, some kind of corporate dispute. Maybe it's related.'

'A dispute?'

'Let's walk and talk. Oh, and I called you in to attend this, okay? That's why you're here, not because you're too pigheaded to stay home.'

'Mmm,' Jennifer said. 'Okay.'

They entered the canteen, which was already full of agents, and took a couple of seats at the back. Elise was up front with more top management than Jennifer had ever seen in one place. Their uniforms gleamed.

'Maybe John *was* involved,' she said. 'Maybe he got hurt.'

'I have to say, you're looking much perkier,' Calvin said. 'One day of rest, you're a new woman.'

'I guess you were right about me needing time off,' she said. 'I guess you really nailed the source of all my problems.'

He looked at her.

'*Or*,' Jennifer said, 'maybe I got lucky.'

His eyebrows shot up. 'Jen! Good *work*. Anyone I know?'

Elise said, 'Let's get this moving, please. First, let me introduce our guests from Head Office . . .'

'A lady never tells,' she said. 'But it was Buy Mitsui.'

'Well *done*.'

Elise said, 'If we can have *everyone's* attention.'

People turned to look at them. 'Sorry,' Calvin said.

A man had taken the podium; he had slides. 'Thank you. The thing we want to get across here is that this was a measured, blatant violation of law. They knew what they were doing, both T.A. and

US Alliance. They decided they could get away with it. We're going to prove them wrong.

'Team Advantage has already admitted it sent a strike team into Shell. They say it was ordered by Nathaniel ExxonMobil, who is now deceased, without the company's knowledge or approval. The Government doesn't consider this explanation acceptable.

'US Alliance, for its part, denies any involvement in the subsequent death of Nathaniel ExxonMobil. The Government also considers this unsatisfactory.

'We are now going to exact compensation. We're going to demand unheard-of penalties. Our most senior people, including the President, are now en route to London to conduct a negotiation.'

London! Jennifer raised her hand. The man pointed to her. 'Yes?' 'The corporates won't roll over just because we tell them to. I hope you guys have a better plan than asking nicely.'

Elise whispered in his ear; another woman touched his shoulder. He convened with them, then nodded. 'Jennifer? You're right. If we can't hit these guys with anything more than harsh words, they'll continue to break the law when it suits them.

'Therefore, the Government is reassigning twenty thousand agents, effective immediately. In two days, we will conduct simultaneous raids against every company involved. We'll arrest every executive we can. We will, if necessary, incarcerate every member of senior management, pending trial, until they concede to our demands.'

Agents were murmuring. 'Holy shit,' Calvin said. 'Is that even legal?'

Jennifer kept her hand up. 'Who gets to do the raids? Excuse me? Who gets to go?'

Some of the agents around her snickered. 'The raiding parties will be comprised of every field agent we can spare in London. And we'll be flying in agents who have particular expertise.'

'I have particular expertise,' she said. 'Even before the Nike Town killings, I—'

'Yes, Jennifer,' he said. 'We know. You're going to London. Tonight.'

PART FOUR

47 NRA (NZ)

When Billy woke, there was a man with a chestful of ribbons sitting beside him.

'Ah, good,' the man said. He was short, crisp, and compact, with gray temples and sharp eyes. 'Billy, I'm General Li. Do you mind if we talk?'

'Uh, sure,' Billy said. He tried to sit up and discovered his wrists were tied to the bed. 'What the—'

'Good! Then let's start with this. Can you tell me what it is?'

The evening sun was streaming through the window, and Billy had to squint. The General was holding his cigarette packet, his bug. Billy suddenly felt more alert. 'That's . . . hey, that's what that Bill guy had. And, man, I think he was talking into it.'

'Mmm,' General Li said. He pondered. 'Let me put this another way. Billy, I know you're a spy.'

'Oh.' He tugged at the restraints.

'The shame of it is, we killed a good soldier. I understand how it occurred, but it really is a pity. Ironic, how he survived a mission against the Government only to be killed by us. I have to explain that to his family somehow.' General Li was wearing a beret; now

185

he took it off and scratched his skull. 'Such things happen in the friction of war.'

'Now – I never wanted to carry that thing,' Billy said. 'The Government made me. I can explain!'

'Ah,' General Li said. 'Please do.'

Billy started talking. He told his whole sorry tale from Abilene, Texas, to New Zealand and active NRA missions he didn't know anything about to Government espionage. The General seemed vaguely sympathetic.

'Well,' he said finally. 'That is a story. That is a story indeed.'

Billy waited.

'There's some debate about what to do with you. There are officers who believe you should spend the foreseeable future in a military prison. That's the field-book solution.'

'No, you can't put me in prison!' He felt his throat constricting. 'I just wanted to go skiing, that's all I wanted! Please!'

'Other officers, however, would prefer to have you shot.'

'Ag,' Billy said.

'But there's something that interests me, Billy. Before this debacle, you were being recruited by us. You had been selected because you demonstrated exemplary skills.'

Billy blinked.

'Marksmanship,' Li said helpfully.

'Right! Yeah, I can shoot real well. Better than anybody.' He felt his wrists growing slippery with sweat where the restraints held them.

'If that's true, I may have a special need for you.'

'Sure, let me show you—'

'I assume you know what kind of job I have in mind.'

'Sure, sure.' He thought. 'Like, sniper stuff?'

'Would you have a problem with that?'

He contemplated this. Yes, Billy would have a problem with

that, but his most pressing problem was getting shot for treason by NRA soldiers. 'No way! Give me a gun and I'll blow away whoever you—'

'Yes, all right,' General Li said. 'In good time. If things work out, we'll have assignments for you. Away from the Australian Territories and the local Government.'

'And if – if things don't work out . . .'

'I was leaning toward the prison option,' General Li said. 'Probably.' He stood. 'Rest up. Tomorrow morning we'll see what you can do.'

'Thanks, man. Thanks.' Just before the General left, Billy said: 'This place where I'd go – the place where I'll do assignments . . . are there mountains? Snow?'

General Li smiled. 'No.'

48 N/A

'Okay,' Buy said, when Jennifer walked in the door. 'I decided on casserole. I was thinking tuna bake, but that box of bread crumbs of yours expired six months ago.' He looked at her reprovingly.

'Oh,' Jennifer said. 'You're cooking?'

'I got restless.' Buy had arranged to meet at Jennifer's house after work, but when he arrived she was on the way out to pick up Kate. So she let him in and told him to amuse himself. He now had three pots bubbling on the stove top and a dish in the oven. 'I hope you don't mind. I thought . . .'

'What?'

'There's a girl,' Buy said, 'hiding behind your legs.'

She looked down. 'Buy, this is Kate. Kate, meet Buy.'

Buy waved. 'Pleased to meet you.' Kate didn't say anything.

She had dark eyes, like her mother. Buy felt a twinge of nervousness. He didn't have much experience with kids.

Jennifer said, 'Kate, why don't you get changed?'

Kate left wordlessly. There was something going on here, Buy thought. Kate's face looked like a storm; Jennifer's was tired and strained. 'She's cute,' Buy said. He stirred a pot.

'Yeah. She is.' Jennifer looked at him. 'Look, I have something to ask . . . a favor. A big one.'

'Sure.'

'I've been given an assignment in London. I don't know how long it will be. Maybe a week.'

'You're leaving? When?'

'Tonight.'

Buy looked at his casserole. 'Do you have time to eat?'

'No.'

'Oh. Lucky I'm hungry.'

'You can say no . . . but I need someone to look after Kate.' She watched him.

Buy almost laughed. 'You want me to take care of your daughter?'

'You'd only have to pick her up after school or aftercare, feed her—'

'Isn't there anyone else you'd rather do this? Family? Her father?'

'Look,' Jennifer said, 'I'm asking you, okay?'

'Okay.' He hesitated. 'You don't know me very well.'

'Sure I do.'

'Well, okay, then,' Buy said. 'I'd be honored.'

'Thanks. Thank you.' He could see the relief on her face. 'I thought maybe you could stay here, so Kate's not in a new environment. Is that all right?'

'Sure.'

Kate reappeared in the doorway. Jennifer said, 'Honey, Buy will be looking after you while I'm away.'

Kate looked at him.

'All right? He's cooking a nice meal for you.' She waited.

'I'm not hungry.'

'You don't have to eat *now*. It's not ready yet. You can eat later.'

Kate was silent.

'I'm sorry,' Jennifer said. She pressed her hand against her forehead. 'Kate, I'm so sorry. I have to pack.'

She left. Buy and Kate looked at each other.

'Well,' Buy said. 'Looks like you and me are in for a fun time.'

Kate looked at the stove. 'What are you cooking?'

'A casserole. You like it?'

'What is it?'

'You don't know what a casserole is?'

Kate shook her head.

'What do you eat?'

'Spaghetti, mostly.'

'Well, then,' Buy said. 'You're in for quite a treat.'

'You speak funny.'

'That's because I was born in France. I can teach you a few words of my language, if you like. You can impress your friends with your command of *français*.'

'What?'

'*Français*,' Buy said, 'is French for French.'

'What's French for Kate?'

'Kate,' Buy said.

'Oh.'

'Most of the other words are different,' he assured her. 'You will sound very sophisticated.'

'Okay.' She smiled a little. 'I think I am hungry now.'

Kate set the table and over dinner they talked about French cheeses. Kate wouldn't believe that France had five hundred types and she asked Buy to name them. He struggled to get past ten, and anyway she accused him of making up Roquefort.

'It's real,' Jennifer said, coming into the room. 'I've seen it myself.' Kate didn't say anything. Jennifer looked at Buy, and he noticed again how tired she looked. 'Thanks so much for this. I'll call as soon as I can.'

'Sure.'

She squatted beside Kate. Kate stared at her plate. 'You know I don't want to do this. Right? As soon as I get back, you and me will go down to the dog shelter. The minute I get back.'

'Yes, Mommy.'

'I love you. I love you so much.'

Buy said, 'Do you need help with your bags?'

She looked up. 'Thanks, no. My shoulder's a lot better.' She kissed Kate, then him on the cheek. 'I'm sorry, I really have to run.'

'Have a good trip.'

'Thanks.' She dragged her suitcase out the front door.

Buy played with his fork. Kate stared at her empty plate. When Jennifer had invited him over, this was not how Buy had envisioned the evening.

'Okay!' he said. 'Should we see what's in the freezer for dessert?'

Kate sniffed. Buy realized she was crying, or about to. He felt panic.

'Hey . . .' He rose and went over to her, feeling awkward. What did he know about kids? Nothing. 'She'll be back before you know it. I bet.'

Kate's lip was trembling; her eyes were filling. Buy didn't know what to do. Then she reached out for him, and he hugged her. Her tiny arms felt strange around his neck. Strange and nice. He stroked her hair.

'You're a very brave girl.' He held her for a long time, until she stopped trembling. 'Some dessert now?' he said, and felt her nod.

49 THE GAP

Everyone was very worked up when Hack arrived at the parking lot. 'Have you seen the news?' Leisl demanded. Leisl had green hair and heavy makeup; her main beef was with genetically modified food but she was basically willing to stick it to anyone who was making a lot of money.

'What news?' Hack said.

'They *shot* some people. One company went in and shot some people from another company. It's like organized crime. It's like the *mob*.'

'Oh, wow,' Hack said. 'No, I hadn't heard.' He wondered if Nike was involved.

'That's why tonight is so important,' Thomas said. Thomas was the youngest, just a kid, really. He hated inequality, like how only rich people got to ride first-class in airplanes. 'Right, Hack?'

'Right,' Hack said. 'Hi, Claire.'

'Hi.' She smiled. Her breath fogged in the night air. 'You still want to go ahead with this?'

'Hell, yes,' Hack said. 'Bring it on.' He wondered if he should make a little speech.

'Yeah!' Thomas said. Thomas was pretty excited. Hack guessed they all were.

'Well, we're all set,' Leisl said. 'I've secured the guy ropes. Any time you're ready.'

'Okay.' He wasn't totally confident about Leisl, so he checked the ropes himself. It was six stories to the ground. Hack didn't want to find out halfway down that Leisl had used hemp rope or something. 'Then let's do it.'

On the side of the parking lot was an enormous billboard, on which a model advertised stretch pants for The Gap. The model was four stories tall but her arms were like sticks. He and Claire were going to go down and spray-paint a speech bubble that said FEED ME.

They got trussed up and stood together on the ledge. Claire's cheeks were red; from the excitement or the cold, Hack didn't know. She took his hand. 'I can't believe we're doing this.'

'Bombs away,' Hack said, and stepped over the edge. The street, sixty feet down, swung out before him. His head spun. His body screamed out for him to get vertical. *What are you doing? Hack, you don't do things like this!* But Hack was doing it. He started to get the knack of it and pushed off from the side, then swung back. It was kind of fun. Soon he was rappelling down the billboard in great leaps. He stopped when he reached the model's neck and looked up. Claire was still edging down. 'You okay?'

'Yes!'

He blew on his hands to keep them warm. Hack was getting a pretty good view of the Punt Road shopping strip from here. The traffic looked like a metal river. He wondered what the drivers made of him and Claire.

Claire slowly made her way down. 'What are you, some kind of stunt man? Jumping and leaping like an idiot.'

He grinned. 'It's fun.'

She smiled, studying him. 'You know, I'm proud of you.'

'What?'

'I thought you'd be moping around, feeling bad about Violet . . . I'm impressed. You're doing great.'

'Violet and me were never such a great couple.' But Claire was right, of course. The old Hack would be inconsolable about being dumped; bitter about being left behind while Violet enjoyed her new success overseas. But this wasn't the old Hack. This was the New and Improved Hack.

'Good for you.' Claire popped the lid from a spray can and started on the speech bubble. She was concentrating hard, her tongue poking out the side of her mouth. Hack smiled. He opened his mouth and what popped out was, 'I loved you first, you know.'

Claire looked at him, startled. 'What?'

'Um . . .'

'What?' She lowered the spray can. 'Tell me.'

'I was in love with you,' Hack confessed. 'Before Violet.'

'Really?'

'Yeah.'

'But I was sweet on *you*. I kept waiting for you to ask me out. But you never did.'

'I didn't know you were . . .' He felt embarrassed. 'I didn't know you liked me.'

'How could you not know? I made it so obvious. You met my *parents.*'

'Yeah . . .' That was when he'd met Violet, Hack remembered: the dinner with Claire's family. 'I guess I just couldn't believe it.'

Claire smiled and turned back to her spray-painting. 'What's so hard to believe?'

'Well, you know . . . you're so . . . so . . .' He hesitated.

She looked at him. 'I'm so what?'

'Curious,' Hack said.

Claire laughed, and the sound bounced around the parking lot. Hack felt happy. 'You're an idiot.'

'*Was* an idiot.'

'And what does that mean?'

'It means I wished I'd asked you out,' he said. He gave Claire's

193

arm a playful push, but of course she was hanging from a rope and she gasped in surprise and grabbed at him. Hack lost his footing and swung into the wall. He hit it awkwardly and his breath escaped in a gasp. Then Claire crashed into his back and they were both hanging against the freezing concrete. He twisted around and got hold of Claire. 'Oh shit, shit, are you okay?'

'Are you trying to kill us?' Claire said, but she was starting to laugh.

'No, I swear.' Her lips were inches from his, and it was too close, really. There was nothing he could do about that. He kissed her and she kissed him back. It felt like something bursting free. He heard someone whimper and didn't know if it was him or her.

'Hey!' Leisl shouted. 'You guys all right down there?'

He broke the kiss. He and Claire were breathing fast, fogging the air between them. 'Yes!' Hack called. 'Everything's fine!'

50 TEAM ADVANTAGE

Violet wanted two things very much: to go home, and three million dollars. She wasn't sure which of these things she wanted more, but that was a moot point anyway, because there were a lot of ExxonMobil people intent on preventing either one. They were very insistent: at one point they used needles to quieten her down. Now she was locked in an office sick bay with no windows and she was having trouble remembering her own name.

She stared at a pair of brown shoes for a while before she realized they implied a presence. She started. Her arms flailed.

'Shhh. Calm down.'

'Who—'

'Don't start screaming again. Don't make me get the doctor.'

'I wasn't screaming,' Violet said, but maybe she had been.

'You want to get out of here?'

'Yes. Home. Please.'

'You think you can answer some questions?'

She bit her lip hard to help concentrate. She nodded.

'Okay. Don't do anything stupid.' Then some other people filed into the room. One was a woman with green eyes and a light brown bob. A man pulled up a chair for her to sit in.

'Hello, Violet. Do you know who I am?'

Violet shook her head.

'I'm Holly T.A. The CEO of Team Advantage.'

The words didn't mean anything. Violet stared at Holly's eyes. They were very green.

'You've been through quite an experience. How are you feeling?'

'Someone stuck a needle in me.'

'That was to help you relax, honey. We're all on the same side. We just want to help.'

Violet said nothing.

'I want to ask you about last Thursday. In the board room of ExxonMobil. You know what I'm talking about?'

'Yes.'

'There was a man. This is very important. The man seemed to recognize you. Do you know who he is?'

'What man?'

'The—' Holly stopped. 'Honey, two days ago you were in the ExxonMobil board room and a man with a gun came in. Do you remember that?'

'A gun?'

'He shot Nathaniel ExxonMobil. Do you know who that man is?'

'He came in . . .' Violet said, and then there were men holding her down. Holly was on her feet, her eyes wide.

'Violet!' one of the men shouted in her face. 'Violet!'

She snapped her mouth closed. Shapes swam in front of her eyes, so she shut them, too.

'Maybe this is a bad time,' someone said. 'What's she on?'

'Ativan. I didn't know anyone wanted to interview her. You said you wanted her quiet.'

'Enough,' Holly said. Violet felt a hand on her forehead. She opened her eyes. Holly was sitting beside her, her green eyes filled with concern. Violet felt a rush of affection for Holly. 'Do your best, honey. Just do your best.'

'Help me.'

'I will. Just tell me who the man is.'

The fog cleared a little. Violet remembered him standing in her living room, his face dark. *Violet, is that your name? If you do this, you'll regret it. I guarantee it.*

She said, 'His name is John Nike.'

'Ah,' Holly said. She nodded, pleased. 'Good girl.'

They took her off the drugs, and then it was better. By the next morning Violet's mind was almost clear, and when they brought her luggage from the hotel, she could shower and change clothes. The downside was that her memories got bigger and brighter; sometimes she couldn't stop thinking about John Nike. She wanted to get away from London.

She was stuffing her old clothes into her bag when Holly appeared. 'Well, you're looking one hundred percent better.'

'That would be because no one's *injecting* me anymore.'

Holly smiled. 'I'm sorry. They tell me you were uncontrollable.' She sat on the bunk. 'Violet, I need you to do something for me.'

'Well, I need you to give me three million bucks,' Violet said. 'And a ride to the airport would be nice, too.'

Holly blinked. 'Pardon me?'

'Nathaniel ExxonMobil bought my software for two point eight million dollars. I did everything he wanted. Now I want to get paid.'

'Hmm,' Holly said. 'That's really something you have to take up with ExMo. It's not a T.A. matter.'

'I don't care whose matter it is. I have a contract.'

'Well, I'll see what I can do. And in return, you can do a little job for me.'

'No. I'm not doing any little jobs, especially for people who think it's fun to stick me with needles. I'm getting my money and going home.'

'Don't you even want to hear me out?'

Violet zipped her bag. 'No.'

'There's an important meeting today, between T.A., US Alliance, and the Government. I want you to come and tell me if you see this John Nike there.'

She felt the air go out of her. 'No way am I going to do that. No *way.*'

'You have a lot of money at stake.'

'You – you owe me that money whether I help you or not.'

'Be realistic,' Holly said.

'No!' Violet heard her voice tremble. 'I'm not going anywhere near John Nike! You get that?' She slung her bag over her shoulder. A man stepped into the doorway, blocking it. He was wearing a Police soldier uniform. His nametag said: ONE.

'Maybe I made this sound too much like a request,' Holly said, and Violet started to cry.

51 US ALLIANCE

John had twenty minutes to review a bunch of advertising campaigns and get his ass down to Parliament House. The agency had set up a room full of mock-ups for him to consider: there were posters on the walls, TVs blaring, radios chattering. They'd gone to a lot of effort because John was here to decide whether they'd get a piece of US Alliance's global advertising budget. John's career had taken off like a rocket in the last week. It had taken off the moment he put a car through the front window of ExxonMobil.

'What the hell is that meant to be?' he asked, pointing at a TV. To his cellphone: 'No, not you, Georgia.'

'We're very pleased with this one,' the agency man said. 'You see, there are elements of George Orwell's *1984*, which of course already has an established advertising mindset thanks to the Apple—'

'You gotta be kidding me,' John said. 'The Government as all-powerful?'

'Ah, well—'

'Keep going,' he said to Georgia. 'You were explaining to me how Gregory Nike found out I have a Government problem.'

'The Government is asking everyone questions.' Georgia sounded tired: it must be late in Melbourne. 'Ever since the ExxonMobil . . . incident. They want to know where our top executives are.'

'Has Jennifer contacted you?' The agency man stopped in front of a poster. It said: LOOSE LIPS SINK SPONSORSHIPS – OBEY YOUR NDA. John looked at him in disgust.

'No, John.'

He sighed. He really needed John to wake up out of that goddamn coma; John would be able to take care of problems like Jennifer Government. He looked at his watch. 'When I next speak to you, you're going to tell me exactly where she is. All right? I'll take care of the rest.' He was about to end the call, then a thought struck him. 'Georgia, is Hack still working for Nike?'

'Hack?'

'The Merchandising Officer who I used for the . . . Mercurys incident.'

'Um, let me check . . . yes, he is, John.'

'Huh.' Details had a way of getting away from you when you were dealing with the big picture, John realized. 'Fire him, will you?' He pocketed his phone. The agency man raised his eyebrows. 'We'll do the *Uncle Sam Wants Your Property* series, the Nelson Mandela *Freedom* series, I want to hold everything that's anti-T.A. to use later, and . . . what was the other one I liked?'

'*Where Would You Be Without Corporations?*'

'Yes. I like the people in caves.'

'Excellent choices!' the agency man said. 'I'm really looking forward to working with you on this, John.'

'I'm sure you are,' he said. The limo was waiting out front.

Traffic was banked up for half a mile around Parliament. Every second car was a limousine; they lined entire streets. John drummed his fingers on the seat. 'You do realize I have to be there in three minutes?'

'Not with this traffic, buddy,' the driver said.

'Fine.' He opened the door. Some people would break the rules to get things done and some wouldn't; it was as simple as that. John didn't have much use for the latter.

He started toward Parliament at a brisk walk. It peeked at him between office buildings, looking vaguely familiar. Maybe he'd seen it in a movie once. It was a sprawling, ornate thing, but John bet it was cold as fuck inside. Governments always built for form instead of function.

'Hey!' someone yelled. The Pepsi kid was leaning out of a limo. 'John! Wait up!'

He tapped his watch and kept walking. The Pepsi kid knew when he was riding a winner: he'd stuck to John like a burr since the stock exchange. John was getting irritated. The kid was leeching off his credibility.

John trotted up Parliament steps. The lobby was packed with suits and a wave of body heat washed over him. He wrinkled his nose.

'Man, you could have waited,' the Pepsi kid said, panting. 'You trashed my Ferrari, the least you could do is wait up.'

There were two main doors from the lobby: one labeled GOVERNMENT and the other US ALLIANCE/TEAM ADVANTAGE COMPANIES. John blew air through his teeth. They should never have let the Government dictate the venue.

'The rental company went nuts, man. I tried to tell them it was good publicity, because you could see their bumper sticker on the news, but some guys are so short-term. They wouldn't even give me a replacement.'

'What do you want me to do? Call them up, tell them it was official US Alliance business?' He forged a path toward the corporate doorway.

'Would you?' the kid said. 'Man, that'd be great.'

'I'm not calling any fucking rental company,' John said.

'Oh.'

The doorway opened into a long corridor. It was less crowded here, and he spotted Gregory Nike. He sighed. He didn't have much use for Gregory these days, either. But Gregory was already beckoning him. John smiled and made his way over.

'John, we were about to go in. You know everyone here?'

Gregory was talking to a couple of big US Alliance cheeses, including Alfonse, the CEO. 'Of course. Nice to see you again, Alfonse.'

Alfonse nodded. Alfonse and John had had several interesting conversations over the last two days. Alfonse had taken a personal interest in him.

The lights dimmed. 'We'd better get in there,' Gregory said. 'All the best, gentlemen.' He put his hand on John's arm.

'John comes with us,' Alfonse said.

'Yes, I'm sitting with Alfonse,' John said. He looked down at Gregory's hand.

Gregory released it. 'I see.'

'It's really quite an honor. For Nike, I mean.'

Gregory said nothing. Then he leaned in close. 'You have a bad habit, John, of forgetting where your loyalties lie.'

'Mmm,' John said. 'That is something to think about. Excuse me.'

The Pepsi kid attached himself to John's elbow. 'We're sitting with the big boys?'

'I'm sitting with the big boys.'

'What about me?'

'Don't you have friends at Pepsi to play with?'

'I thought we were a team, man,' he said, wounded.

'So now you know otherwise,' John said.

They entered the main hall, the quaintly named House of Commons, and it was like walking into a thunderstorm. There were five hundred people seated, maybe more, plus camera crews and clusters of computers. The room was a huge **U**, with chandeliers and balconies and a thickset table in the center. No one was seated there yet: it sat bare as an empty stage.

Most of the US Alliance contingent took outer seats, leaving just

Alfonse, a woman, and John to approach the central table. As the mass recognized them, the noise level rose even higher. John sat and poured himself a glass of water. His hand trembled.

'Alfonse,' someone said. John looked up. Another contingent had arrived: a woman and two flunkies. 'I'm Holly T.A.'

The table was too wide to shake hands across. Alfonse rose a fraction from his chair, nodded, and settled back down. 'Good morning, Holly.'

She smiled. Holly T.A. had sharp green eyes, John noticed. She said, 'Thank you, Alfonse.'

Holly sat, but one of the flunkies, a girl, stayed rooted to the floor. She was staring at John. She made a strange sound in her throat, like a whimper.

'Violet, sit,' Holly said. The girl sat. She turned her head away from him.

It was the girl at ExxonMobil, John realized, who had seen him shoot Nathaniel. But she had been familiar even then . . . 'Ah.' He felt like an idiot. It had been dark, of course, and on the other side of the world, but even so. He never should have forgotten this face. 'Now I remember. Hello again, Violet.' He cocked a finger and thumb at her.

She jumped in her chair, which was amusing, and the other flunky had to restrain her. Holly whispered to both of them.

John relaxed. Now he didn't feel nervous at all. He felt ready to do his job.

At first, he thought the trail of people entering the House were common spectators, or maybe journalists. He should have realized: cheap suits and outdated ties were practically Government signatures. There were maybe fifteen people marching toward the table, and John shook his head. Typical Government, using so many people to do a job the private sector could do with three.

He didn't know which was the President, but a man emerged from the group and strode forward to shake Holly's hand. He was weathered and kind of rough-looking, like an old cop. Holly rose and clasped his hands.

There was applause from the gallery, and a barrage of flash photography. John almost snorted. If they wanted an image to capture the spirit of this meeting, shaking hands wasn't it.

The President spoke a few words to Holly, then rounded the table and shook with Alfonse. More clapping and flashbulbs. 'Thank you for coming, Alfonse,' the President said. 'I look forward to resolving this awkward situation.'

'As do I,' Alfonse said. 'As do I.'

John thought, *What a load of shit.*

The President took his seat at the head of the table. US Alliance and T.A. were facing each other across the sides, which John wasn't happy about. This whole event suited the Government. But that was okay. John was expecting the balance to tip soon.

There were a few minutes of techs running around to mike everybody up, then the President stood. The crowd quieted, and John supposed this whole sorry mess had begun.

52 GENERAL MOTORS

Jennifer had been hoping for some free time after landing in London, enough time to, say, track down John Nike and bust his chops. But it was such a long flight from Australia that she and Calvin were among the last agents to arrive, and they were ferried straight to a warehouse the Government was using as a staging area. She stood in a long line for the communal bathroom, showered, and met with Calvin to report in.

'Ah, Jennifer,' the administrator said. 'You're a squad leader, yes?'

'Really?' she said.

'Sounds like some kind of mix-up,' Calvin said. 'A squad leader? With your people skills?'

'Jennifer, receive your riot gear from dispensary, and meet your team in Area D-21.'

She found the dispensary, which had a longer queue than the bathroom, and received more equipment than she'd seen in five years. There was a flak jacket, a helmet, a nightstick, even a shield.

'You need any help getting into all that, gorgeous?' the man behind the counter said.

'Kiss my ass,' she said, which was her tried and tested response to overenthusiastic Government types. Then she noticed the TV behind him. It was broadcasting live from the Government-corporate conference: the picture showed the three US Alliance members. 'Shit! It's John!'

'What?' Calvin said.

She pointed. 'John Nike!' She turned to the dispensary man. 'Where's this happening?'

'The conference? Parliament.'

'Calvin,' Jennifer said, 'I feel a sudden urge to modify my mission parameters.'

'Jen, we have a job to do.'

'But he's right *there*.'

'If John's part of the US Alliance delegation, he'll be there all day. We'll grab him when we've finished the raids. Everybody goes home happy.'

She stared at the TV. 'Look at him. He's so *smug*.'

'We'll fix that,' Calvin said. 'After the raids.'

*

She met her team: there were five of them and the oldest looked about twenty-three. As the van bumped along a London street they sat quietly and snuck glances at her tattoo. Jennifer wished she had something inspirational to say. She had nothing. She wished Calvin was in her team.

The van halted and the driver banged on the partition. Jennifer opened her mouth and what came out was: 'Let's go!'

They emerged onto a parking lot in front of a gleaming, fifteen-story building. A sign marked it as GENERAL MOTORS. There was even a flag and a wide, green lawn. The sky drizzled light rain. They jogged toward the lobby.

In a way, Jennifer felt bad, busting into such a nice place in full riot gear and scaring the crap out of everybody. But in another, more accurate way, she enjoyed it a lot. She collared a scared-looking receptionist and read out her list of target executives. 'Where are they?'

'They're – different floors. Four, eight, and nine.'

'Three teams!' Jennifer said. 'I'll take level nine. Meet back here.'

'You can't go up there!' the receptionist said, horrified. 'This is private property! You can't!'

'And yet,' Jennifer said. She hit the stairs. She found her target by striding down the corridor and barking out his name: when a man popped his head out of an office, she cuffed him. It was much easier than she'd expected.

'This is ridiculous! I'm a financial controller! I don't even deal with US Alliance! You can't *arrest* me!'

She marched him down the stairs. The rest of her team were already gathered in the lobby, holding executives. Then she saw that a dozen NRA soldiers were pointing semiautomatic rifles at them, and everything stopped being so much fun.

'You! Put down your weapon!'

'We're the Government,' she said, just in case there had been some misunderstanding. 'We are arresting three people on suspicion of murder.'

'No, ma'am. You are on General Motors property and you will comply with GM orders.'

'Team,' she said levelly, 'close your helmets and draw your weapons.'

'Do not draw your weapons!' the NRA man barked. They tensed. There were now a lot of guns looking at her.

'Do it,' Jennifer said, and heard them obey: helmets snapping down, holsters being unfastened.

'Put down your weapons or we will fire on you!'

'You don't want to shoot six Government agents, slick,' she said. 'You really don't.'

'I won't ask you again!'

'Team, follow me out the door. Fire only if fired upon. Do not release the suspects.'

'You think I'm kidding, lady? My orders are very fucking clear! If you leave with our people, we will take you down!' He pushed the barrel of the rifle into her forehead. It felt hard and very cold. 'This is not an exercise.'

Someone whimpered. Jennifer wanted to believe it was one of the NRA, but didn't think it was. The soldier's eyes were locked on hers.

She said quietly, 'You'd better be very sure your employer can protect you from the Government.'

'I'm very sure.'

She felt her heart twist. To her people, she said, 'Let them go.'

The NRA watched them all the way to the van.

'*What is going on?*' she screamed.

'It's the same everywhere,' Calvin said on the radio. 'Roaming

NRA squads, responding within six minutes to calls for help, faster in central London. T.A. are less defended; we're doing better. Jen, don't do anything stupid. We've already got two agents in the hospital.'

'This was meant to be a show of force!'

'What can I say? Try to hit your next building in under six minutes.'

But her next building was the NRA: only an administrative headquarters, but still, she didn't like her chances. She had the van park two blocks away and they squatted against the hedge, checking their equipment as the rain soaked through their clothes.

'Helmets down the whole time. Don't stop for anything. If we run into armed security, abort immediately. You're not authorized to fire your weapon except in self-defense. Is that clear?'

'Yes, ma'am!'

'Go!' she said, and they ran, hunched over, for the NRA building. The lobby was crowded but soldier-free; when they burst in, people scattered. She was looking for security guards first and anyone who looked like they could locate her target executives second, but someone else caught her eye: a young man with a sports bag over his shoulder. He was pushing his way out the revolving doors.

'Ma'am! I have the receptionist!'

'One second,' Jennifer said. The man with the bag escaped the doors and sprinted across the grass. She was hoping he would look back at the road, and he did. It was Billy NRA. 'Shit!'

'Ma'am?' an agent said. 'Our time limit?'

'You're in charge. I'll catch up with you later.'

'What?' he said, but Jennifer was already out the door.

53 NRA/GROUND

Billy sprinted, sucking cold London air into his lungs. Jennifer shouted, 'Billy! Stop, you little prick!' and that encouraged him to run even faster. He crossed the road without looking. A truck's horn blared and he felt a whoosh of air buffet him. A mall was just up the block, and he pounded the sidewalk. At the entrance he crashed through a group of shoppers, spraying their bags and stumbling to his knees. Then he was up and inside.

He spied an exit across the mall and forged through the crowd toward it. The place was crammed, but he was making such a commotion that Jennifer would spot him as soon as she came in. He had to make the exit. He shoved a woman out of the way and hurdled a child.

'Ow! Watch it!'

'Out of the way!' he screamed. 'Coming through!'

'Freeze! Government agent, don't move!'

Billy stopped. The door was right in front of him. He turned around. Jennifer was at the entrance, a hundred feet away, pointing a handgun at him. He couldn't believe it. She hadn't been kidding when she said he couldn't escape her.

'On your knees!'

He almost did it. Then it occurred to him that there were a lot of people between him and Jennifer, and a hundred-foot shot from a pistol was a big call even for a skilled marksman. Billy sucked in his breath, then broke for the door.

He was positive she was going to fire. He hit the door and rolled through, screaming in anticipation. No shot! He scrambled to his feet. There were alleys twisting off in four directions, lined with crates and garbage. He ran down one at random.

Fifteen minutes later, when he was sure he was safe, he sank to his knees and gasped for breath. He checked his bag. Everything was still there. Thank God.

When he was ready, he stepped out onto the street and hailed a cab.

'Parliament,' he said. 'Please hurry.'

Billy just about died: no one had told him Parliament would be crawling with Government. Worse, half the agents were scurrying around in that blue armored getup he'd seen Jennifer in, so he kept thinking he saw her out of the corner of his eye. He felt himself break into fresh sweat. Billy was no longer smelling so good.

General Li was waiting at the top of the steps. 'Good timing, Private. Five minutes early.'

It was probably best not to mention the Jennifer Government incident to General Li, Billy decided. 'Yes, sir.'

Li started walking, and Billy fell into step. He wiped at his forehead. The General would protect him, he thought. No one was giving the General any grief. They entered the great lobby, which was packed, then a corridor, then a side room. There were a half-dozen suits lounging around, smoking and eating lunch from a buffet.

The General stopped beside three men and waited. No one acknowledged him, which Billy thought was kind of rude.

'I *told* you they'd try this,' one of the men said. 'If I hadn't taken steps, half our goddamn staff would be in Government lockup right now.'

'John is right,' an older, shorter man said.

'You're overreacting,' the third man said. 'So they're trying to muscle us. That doesn't mean it's time to – to do what you're suggesting. We can't take that step. It's illegal, and more importantly it's bad business.'

'You idiot,' John said. 'You want to wait until they come for you?

When they raid your house at four in the morning? Things have already gone too far.'

The old man nodded. 'John Nike is now in charge of our operation.'

'Alfonse!' the third man said, shocked, but they were already turning their backs on him.

John seemed to notice the General for the first time. 'Who are you?'

'General Li NRA, sir. We've spoken on the phone.'

'Right, right,' John said. 'Excuse me, Alfonse. I have a few housekeeping matters to take care of.'

Alfonse nodded and moved off. John put one arm around Li's shoulders and one around Billy's. His face was inches from Billy's, which creeped him out a little. Billy suddenly realized: this might be the John Nike that Jennifer wanted him to collect information on. 'So, Li, this is . . .'

'The man you requested.'

This was one of those situations that required a lot of 'sir's,' Billy realized. 'Private Billy NRA, Special Ops, reporting, sir!'

John looked amused. 'Billy, you might get to earn your keep today.'

'Yes, sir!'

'If things don't go our way in there, then during my speech I'm going to point at someone. I assume you know what to do then.'

'Yes, sir!'

'But not inside the House. You mark them, you wait until they leave, you do them on the steps. If you try anything in this building, there'll be twenty Government suits on you before you can twitch. And if the Government gets hold of you, I'll make damn sure you never get to talk to them. You understand me?'

'Yes, sir!'

'I like this kid, Li,' John said. 'He's a quick learner. Okay, Billy, piss off. Me and the General have to talk.'

'Yes, sir!' Billy said. He went out to wait in the corridor.

After a while, the lights dimmed, then brightened. Billy thought there must be some kind of electrical fault, but people started filing into the main hall, so he straightened to attention. John and the General came out together, with Alfonse and a bunch of other suits. Billy waited a few minutes, then made his own way into the main room. He fought his way to a seat in the back few rows. On the way he jabbed someone with his bag.

'Hey, watch it. What've you got in there, steel rods?'

'Sorry.' He found a seat and put his bag between his feet. There was a lot of messing around at the table, then people seemed to get organized and a man stood up and started talking. It took Billy a while, but he realized this was the Government President. He didn't recognize the third group, the one with two chicks in it, but if the Government and US Alliance were here, he guessed they were from Team Advantage. Billy hadn't known so many big enchiladas were getting together in one place.

The President started saying something about freedom and justice, and Billy tuned out. Then there was some arguing, one suit after another jabbering away, and Billy started thinking about mountains. London wasn't so far away from some really good skiing countries. Maybe he could skip over there when all this was over. Then John got to his feet, straightening his cuffs, and Billy sat up.

'We came here in good faith, to talk about solutions.' John's voice was piped through the hall, so it sounded like he were right in front of you. 'But the Government didn't. This morning, it conducted raids against us. It targeted our companies, only because we've been successful at providing products people want to buy. It trespassed on our private property and assaulted some of our executives.'

He paused. The hall was so quiet Billy could hear his own stomach.

'This is intolerable.' He stared at the President. Billy was sure he was going to point at him. But he turned back to the crowd. 'By this action, the Government has proved that so long as it exists, none of us are truly free. Government and freedom are mutually exclusive. So if we value freedom, there's only one conclusion. It's time to get rid of this leftover relic we call Government.'

People started to talk; a few rose to their feet in front of Billy. He craned his neck. John was looking at the young woman from Team Advantage. Billy's hands tightened on the bag.

'US Alliance has had enough of being persecuted for the crime of making money. From this moment, we no longer recognize them as an authority. It's time for a brave new age. I hereby declare the end of Government. And you, sir, are out of a job.'

He pointed at the Government President. The crowd erupted. Billy felt no surprise. He picked up his bag and began to fight his way out of the hall.

He jogged across the road, through the square, and into a restaurant that looked like a boardinghouse. A girl was cleaning glasses at the bar. 'What's upstairs?' Billy asked. 'Rooms?'

'Sure. They start at ninety dollars.'

'I want something that faces Parliament,' he said. 'Um, for the view.'

She collected a key from underneath the counter. 'A lot going on today, hey?'

'You said it,' Billy said.

*

The room was on the second floor, small with thick drapes, which was perfect. He set his bag on the bed and unzipped it. He took out the barrel and cleaned it thoroughly, keeping one foot against the wall to hold the curtain open a fraction so he could watch Parliament House. When the flow of human traffic down the steps increased, he snapped the scope and magazine into place and dragged a chair over to the window. He raised the window and squinted against the icy air that blew in.

People were gushing out of the building, most in suits. Billy worried that he wouldn't be able to spot the President. Then came another thought: maybe he *would* spot the President. That would mean Billy was meant to raise the gun and line a man up in the sights. He felt fresh sweat run down his back. Billy hadn't believed he would ever reach this moment, not truly. The moment when he would have to decide if he would kill a man to escape the NRA. He chewed his lip.

The President emerged, surrounded by a dozen Government agents. Even in the crowd, that stood out. He looked like the center of a bull's-eye.

The rifle lay in Billy's lap. Some snipers – amateurs – raised their guns too early, used the scope to see what was going on. That was risky, the NRA had taught him, because he could be spotted. A good sniper became visible only at the last moment. Billy waited. Then he raised the rifle and fitted the butt into his shoulder.

He rested his elbow on the sill and the barrel against the window frame. There were thirty or so steps up to the House of Commons, so he had plenty of time to line him up. When he saw the man behind the crosshairs, his stomach lurched. His hands shook minutely. There was a variable wind, and Billy thought: *Maybe I'll miss. Maybe I'll do my best but I'll miss.*

The wind eased.

Skiing, Billy thought. *I'm just skiing.*

The President looked up. It was as if he knew it was coming.

54 GOVERNMENT

'*Shit!*' Jennifer screamed. Shoppers hurried away from her. She ran toward the exit Billy had escaped through, but with her helmet and body armor, it was like wading through a river. By the time she got to the door, she couldn't even hear Billy's footsteps.

She grabbed her radio. 'Team one-nine-six, what's your status?'

'We're back at the van. NRA soldiers turned up ninety seconds after you left, lots of them. We never had a chance.'

'Fine. We're aborting. Let's do something useful.'

'Ma'am? Our orders—'

'Shh,' she said.

In normal circumstances, she would put out an A.P.B. on Billy, but today there were twenty thousand agents tied up in raids and no one had spare time to look for young, muscular men with canvas bags. But there was, she thought, really only one place a sniper could be headed. Maybe she could kill two birds with one stone. She sat in the back of the Government van and ignored the glances her team exchanged.

'Traffic's slowing,' the driver called.

'Stop,' Jennifer said. She assembled her team by the side of the road. Parliament House was a five-minute run away, and she felt like a bit of a dick, jogging up the sidewalk with five armored agents. But you had to do what you had to do.

There weren't many people outside Parliament, which was

good: it meant the session hadn't finished yet. 'Teams of two,' she said. 'Look for the bag. Gray with dark red straps.'

She left them to trot up the steps. A young agent with a goatee tried to stop her entering the main floor: Jennifer flashed her ID and kept walking. He didn't chase her. This wasn't security. It was a joke.

There were a lot of people inside, and many of them were shouting at each other. She saw John Nike standing with his arms folded across his chest, smiling. The temptation to run across the floor, slam him face-first into the table, and cuff him was very strong. Maybe that Government shrink had had a point.

She made her way to the Government's private guard. John didn't see her. Jennifer felt glad to have a weapon.

She took a guess at which agent was in charge. These guys had earpieces, sunglasses, the whole works; they looked ridiculous. 'Excuse me.'

'Shh,' the agent said without turning.

'We're done,' John Nike announced to the floor. 'There's nothing more to discuss.'

'We are not done!' the President said. Jennifer could see a vein throbbing at his temple, which probably wasn't a good sign for the negotiations. 'Nobody's leaving until we arrive at a resolution!'

'Hey!' Jennifer said to the agent. He didn't react, so she prodded his ribs. 'Hello?'

'Don't poke me, Agent.'

'I believe a sharpshooter may be about to take a shot at the President.'

He glanced at her, then back at the crowd. 'From where?'

'I don't know. But—'

'Agent, we always assume somebody, somewhere is about to take a shot at the President. That's why we're here. Please step away.'

215

The noise was rising at the table. 'That's it,' John Nike said. 'You people don't know when you're finished.' He turned and walked away. The US Alliance contingent rose and followed him.

'Wait!' the President said, but it was all over: even Jennifer could see that. She looked at John Nike's back.

'Look, I have to go. Just take the President out the back way, okay?'

'We have twenty agents between here and his car. We're not letting them put pictures of him running out the back door on the news.'

'*What?*' There was so much movement in the crowd, she was starting to see Billys everywhere. John was about to reach the corporate exit. 'Mr. President!' Jennifer called.

The agent took her arm and twisted. Her sore shoulder screamed. Her vision flared. She didn't realize he was pushing her against the wall until she hit it with her forehead. 'Don't interfere with our protection of the President, Agent. Do you understand?'

'Let me—' Over her shoulder, she saw agents box the President and begin to lead him from the hall. '*Jesus!*'

The agent spoke into his mike. 'I am occupied with a two-twenty in the main hall, please proceed to—'

She got her legs together and tried to sweep his feet out. How this normally turned out was with them on the floor and Jennifer standing over them with a superior expression, but this guy was well trained and she succeeded only in jolting him. She felt his face brush her hair and threw her head backward. Something soft and probably nasal cracked against her skull. The agent went down, groaning. Jennifer yelled, 'That was my *sore shoulder*!'

The President was already gone, which raised an interesting dilemma: should she save his life or arrest John Nike? But it would be crazy to try to protect the President, Jennifer realized: she'd only distract his guards. She would have to put her faith in the men with sunglasses and earpieces. She ran for the corporate corridor.

It was stuffed with excited suits, talking and gesturing. She pushed her way through. There were too many people who looked like him; she kept grabbing people with similar haircuts. People stared at her. A man said: 'Jennifer Maher?' and she heard others pick up on it: 'Look, that's Jennifer Maher.'

She saw John. He was fifteen feet away, side-on to her, holding court to a dozen other suits. She slipped her hand into her pocket and found her gun.

Her radio said, 'Jen? We spotted your boy.'

Jennifer froze. 'What?'

'The building across the road from here? Your guy just went in. Canvas bag, red straps?'

A woman to her left sprayed laughter. A suit said, '—but then of course they *increased* their equity—'

'Jen?'

She felt sick. 'I'll meet you there.'

She burst through the doors, gun drawn. It was dimly lit, and she had to crouch there a moment, waiting for her eyes to adjust. Her team followed her in. Jennifer felt stupid: this was a pretty good way to let an ambush kill a lot of temporarily blind Government agents. She was rushing, not thinking.

The restaurant was empty except for a girl behind a bar. 'Man came in here a few minutes ago, with a bag,' Jennifer said. 'Where is he?'

'Oh, he took a room.'

'Which one?'

'I dunno if I should tell you that.'

She pointed her .45 at the girl. 'Tell.'

'Twenty-eight.'

They hit the stairs, then jogged down the hallway, peering at door numbers in the gloom. Twenty-eight was the final door. She listened at it for a moment. Nothing. She took a step back and kicked it.

The door popped open. It made a strange sound, like a combination of a crunch and a crack. Then she saw Billy NRA by the window and the thin smoke curling from his gun, and realized she was wrong. It hadn't been a single noise. It had been two.

'Don't move! Put the gun down right now!'

'Shit!' Billy said. 'Shit, shit, shit!' He looked from her to the window and back.

'Drop it!'

'Look what you made me do,' he moaned. 'Oh, shit, look what you made me do.'

The gun shook in her hand. 'Billy, if you've just shot the President, you're leaving this room via the window.' She crossed the room and dragged the rifle from his hand. Outside the window, there were people milling and a man lying bleeding on the steps. A group of agents were hustling the President into a car.

'Who did you shoot?'

'I was trying to miss! You startled me! *I didn't mean to!*'

'You shot someone by *accident*?'

'Don't hurt me! Please?'

'You should have thought of that before,' she said.

55 US ALLIANCE

John walked out of Parliament, trying hard to suppress his exultation. He was preparing to register shock and outrage, because there were TV cameras everywhere and no doubt some were already swinging onto him. He'd barely stepped into daylight when a man grabbed his arm.

'Sir, someone's been shot! You shouldn't be out here!'

'Someone's been shot?' John said. *Shock, outrage.* He hurried to the top of the stairs. Halfway down, medics were attending to a man in a dark suit. He was white-faced, had a thick pad strapped to his chest, and was definitely not the Government President.

John's vision washed red. It was a few moments before he realized the media had clustered around him. 'John! John Nike! Is this attack a surprise to you? Do you know this man! What's your reaction?'

He had to swallow twice before he could speak. Then he caught sight of Billy NRA being led toward a black Government car. On one side of Billy was an agent John had never seen before. On the other side was Jennifer Government.

'I am shocked and outraged,' he said. The words trembled.

He jumped into the first US Alliance limousine he reached, which was General Li's. That was fortuitous: John had a little something to say to General Li. He waited until the General was settled, the doors closed, and the car far enough away from Parliament so that the chance of Jennifer Government pulling it over and sticking a gun in his face was increasingly small. Then he punched the window and put his heel into the TV monitor.

'I understand you're upset,' General Li said.

'I ask for *one* sniper to do a single job! And he manages to not only get himself arrested, but shoot the wrong guy! How does that *happen?*'

'Billy is an excellent marksman. I really don't know.'

'Maybe you think this is some kind of exercise. This is no drill, Li. The Government is *after my ass.* And now Jennifer—'

The phone beside him rang. He was tempted to rip it out and toss it out the window, but that could be a mistake. There were some people he could yell at and some people he couldn't, and there was a good chance this would be the latter. He pushed for speaker. 'Yes?'

'Ah, John.' It was Alfonse. 'That was some speech.'

'I'm glad you liked it.'

'I didn't say that.'

'Well, Alfonse,' John said. 'You asked me to express our indignation. Okay, in the heat of the moment, maybe I got a little—'

'You announced that US Alliance is a criminal organization.'

'Criminal,' he said. 'What is that, anyway? Just someone the Government doesn't agree with.'

'Don't play games with me, John. Our organization exists to gain market share from Team Advantage. The Government is peripheral.'

'How can we fight Team Advantage with the Government as referee? The Government is the major obstacle to our goals. We can't ignore them, Alfonse. They're coming after us. We had to send them a message.'

'Because I partially believe that,' Alfonse said, 'you still have a job. But consider yourself on notice.'

'Thank you, sir!' he said, but Alfonse was already gone. He exhaled shakily.

General Li said carefully, 'Perhaps it's just as well our sniper failed.'

John looked at him. 'You can hit the President before he gets to the airport. Or you can hit him in the air. Do you people have jets?'

Li cleared his throat. 'Forgive me, but . . . I gained the impression Alfonse is not in favor of a direct attack on the Government.'

'Did you?' John said. 'How strange.'

'Perhaps I'm mistaken . . . but was Alfonse unaware of our operation involving Private Billy?'

'I think you are mistaken, Li,' John said. 'US Alliance is totally unified on this one. The Government has to be stopped. They'll come for you, too, unless we hit them first.'

Li said nothing.

John leaned forward. 'If we go to war, which company becomes more important than any other? Which company becomes the most powerful on the planet? It's not McDonald's. It's not Nike.'

Li looked at him for a while. Then he said: 'We have jets.'

'Good,' John said. He began to feel a little better.

He had half an hour in his hotel room before the post-conference meeting. He loosened his tie, poured a scotch from the bar, and walked out to the balcony. It was dark and cold, with a light wind sliding past, but the view was glorious. He sipped his drink and stared at the curve of London Bridge, the light from Parliament House bouncing off the Thames. When he felt calm enough, he flipped open his cellphone and dialed.

'Georgia Saints-Nike, hello?'

'Guess who I saw today?'

'Oh, John . . .' She sounded cautious. 'Um . . .'

'I'll give you a hint: it starts with Jennifer and ends with me in jail.'

'Oh! I'm so sorry, John, I did everything you asked.'

You couldn't rely on anyone, he thought. *You had to do everything yourself.* 'Georgia, you've been talking behind my back, haven't you?'

'No, John!'

'Always asking where I was. And suddenly Jennifer pops up. You told her how to find me.'

Silence. Then: 'I tried to tell you not to do that Mercury campaign, John, I told you it was—'

'You're fired. And let me give you some advice: vanish. Because if I find you, I will take you apart.'

'John!'

He killed the call, disgusted. Georgia Saints-Nike. He should have known. She'd never been the same since she took up volunteer work.

He went back inside and fired up his e-mail. He sent one to terminate Georgia's employment, and another to get security to throw her out of the building. It was a pity he couldn't arrange for John to ensure she never made it home, too. He sighed. He needed a new P.A.

He had an e-mail from Hack Nike. He read it, growing amazed at Hack's arrogance. He tapped out a reply, then checked his watch. It was time to go.

US Alliance had commandeered the hotel ballroom for its post-conference meeting, and the place was already full of suits. People looked around as he entered. Conversations faltered. He took a seat near the front. The Pepsi kid dropped in beside him. 'Kick-ass speech, John. You really told the Feds where to shove it.'

John dropped his voice. 'What do the other Liaisons think?'

'Some think you're a genius. Others think you're nuts and the Government's going to lock us all up.'

'Well,' he said, 'let's just see what the Government is capable of, after tonight.'

The Pepsi kid's eyes widened. 'You've got something planned! What's happening?'

'Shh.' Alfonse was opening the meeting, talking about the new competitive environment. But John couldn't stop thinking about Jennifer Government. He would never be safe while she was after him, that was clear. He needed to get her off his back, no matter what it took.

'Hey,' the Pepsi kid whispered. 'What's so funny?'

'Nothing,' John said. 'I just – had an idea.'

'Something good?'

'Very good.' Kate: that was her name. Jennifer's daughter. John couldn't imagine why he'd never thought of using her before.

56 NRA/AIR

Some pilots didn't like flying on moonless nights. They wouldn't admit it, of course, but night flying was very different to cutting open a blue sky with the world spread out below. On black nights, visibility outside the cockpit was reduced to your own helmet looking back and down at you, illuminated by the glowing instruments. Any good pilot could fly blind without raising a sweat, but there was something fundamentally different about pushing a metal can through five hundred miles per hour when you couldn't see.

Jackpot had been in the air for two and a half hours. Eight hundred feet to his right, according to his instruments, another F/A-18 hung alongside him. They'd been scrambled too early and spent ninety minutes circling, waiting for the target. Both were approaching their fuel limit. 'Jackpot to ground control, request variation of mission parameters.'

'Go ahead, Jackpot.'

'Target is moving very slowly, request permission to approach early.'

'Negative, Jackpot. Wait until they're over sea.'

He chewed on that. 'Then we'll need to land somewhere closer than Luton, base.'

'Roger that, Jackpot. We will advise new runway. Out.'

They hung there, he and his twin, while twelve miles ahead a Boeing 737 trawled westward.

They crossed the coast twenty minutes later, then the two-mile exclusion zone. The fighters pushed forward. Pretty soon the 737 would see them on scope, but Jackpot didn't think it would matter. There wasn't much an airliner could do in the way of evasive action.

He covered the instrument lights with his arm and peered forward. He could see the Boeing's running lights dancing in the night.

'Jackpot to Liontamer, do you have visual contact?'

'Roger that, Jackpot.'

'Launch, launch,' he said, and flipped the switch. He barely felt the uncoupling, but the instruments let him know all about it, bleeping and squealing. 'Missile away.'

'Missile away.'

The two wing-tipped Falcons took eight seconds to eat up the distance, then they caught the Boeing and broke it open. The sky flared momentarily yellow, and Jackpot saw the airplane lose a wing, begin to pitch. Then the F/A-18s shot past it.

They came around in time to see it hit the ocean. They circled until even the flaming debris had sunk, then opened up the engines and headed home.

When they crossed back into England, Jackpot said: 'You ever done anything like that before, Liontamer?'

There was a pause. 'Negative, Jackpot,' Liontamer said. He sounded emotionless and professional. Jackpot took his cue and shut his mouth.

PART FIVE

57 HACK

Hack started varying the way he drove to work, to pass billboards. It was partly for practical reasons: the sooner he knew a company had replaced one, the sooner he could hit it again. But it was also pride. He liked to admire his own work.

The Gap billboard they'd done a week ago was still tagged, which was amazing because it was the biggest of them all, a four-storey monster. Then there was a Nike poster on the freeway that used to say: I CAN SHOOT THE MOON; now it said: I CAN SHOOT 14 KIDS. Beneath it was the line: NIKE KILLS ITS CUSTOMERS. Hack wasn't so pleased with that. The kid, Thomas, had added it. It was too blatant, in Hack's opinion.

He passed a medical insurer that now boasted: WE CARE ABOUT YOUR WALLET. On the corner of Springvale Road, Coke told people to ENJOY STOMACH CANCER. A tire retailer advertised: 25% MORE CARBON MONOXIDE, and CARS = DEATH! Thomas again! Hack was going to have to speak to him.

He parked and went into the Nike building, nodding to the receptionist. He felt more energetic these days, much more confident. He was friendly to people he previously hadn't had the nerve to talk to. The funny thing was that his boss thought Hack had

227

become dynamic and effective, when Hack was doing less work than ever before. In fact, he was hardly working at all.

At his desk, he powered on his computer and started going through his mail. There was a thick, personally addressed letter from Human Resources. He tore it open as the phone rang. 'Hack Nike, Merchandise Distribution Officer.'

Claire said, 'Hi! It's me.'

'Hi!' He flipped open the letter. 'How are you?'

'Good. I missed you.'

'Aw.'

'Are you coming straight home tonight? I thought maybe we could go out somewhere. You know, for dinner.'

'Sure, that would be—' Hack read the first line in the letter. Then he read it again. 'Uh . . .'

'What?'

'I think I've just been fired.'

'*What?*'

'Nike's fired me.' His eyes scanned the page. '"Annual Headcount Consolidation"! What bullshit!'

'Hack, are you okay?'

'No,' he said. 'I have to go.'

He went to Human Resources and asked to speak to Lillian, who had signed his letter.

'I'm Lillian,' a woman said. She looked crotchety to Hack. Everyone who worked in HR looked crotchety.

'I'm Hack, Merchandise Distribution Officer. Did you write this?'

'Let me see it.' She studied the paper for much longer than Hack could believe was necessary. 'I issued this, yes.'

'Why?'

'When departments reduce headcount, we handle the formalities.'

'So who actually fired me?'

'You should already know. The correct procedure is for the manager to discuss the transition with the employee before we draw up the documents.'

'Well, that didn't happen.'

Lillian sighed. 'He really should have discussed this with you first. It's not our job to break bad news.'

'*Who?*' Hack said. He was having trouble remaining dynamic and effective.

Lillian eyeballed him, but Hack was pretty worked up and she didn't do it for long. 'John, Liaison.'

'Thank you,' he said. He returned to his desk and started typing.

> Dear John,
>
> Apparently you've decided to fire me. This is a BIG MISTAKE since I know all about you and the Nike Town BUSINESS. Maybe you think I'm going to keep my mouth shut but you should think AGAIN because I'll tell the Government and the MEDIA everything I know. So don't try to push me around anymore!!
>
> Hack.

He spent the rest of the day browsing the web for new billboard targets. There were six good webcams around the city that were ideal for planning purposes. One, he noticed, showed a new poster being pasted up, patch by patch. It featured a scowling, pointing Uncle Sam, and the copy read: UNCLE SAM WANTS YOUR PROPERTY. Hack blew air between his teeth. That one was *definitely* getting it.

At five o'clock, an e-mail arrived from John. Hack clicked on it, pleased by the quick reply. Even John was taking him seriously now.

The e-mail said:

Fuck off. John.

Then Hack started to get really mad.

58 JOHN

John arrived at US Alliance twenty minutes early and rode to the twenty-ninth floor. He was expecting to be shown straight through to Alfonse, but a young woman with a black bob and natty glasses made him sit out in the corridor. He felt like a naughty boy summoned to the principal's office. After a while, he walked back to the woman's desk. 'I am John Nike,' he said. 'Did I mention that?'

'Yes, sir. You're to wait out here.'

He returned to his seat. He *had* been sent to the principal's office. But then, he supposed he had been very naughty. After the NRA whacked the Government jet, every high-ranking US Alliance suit – including John – had scrambled to get the hell out of London, most heading here to the headquarters in L.A. Nobody had wanted to hang around in a city with twenty thousand pissed-off Government agents.

Twenty minutes later, the woman said, 'You may go in now, John.'

He stood, brushed down his suit, and tugged open the oak doors. The room was a piece of sky with furniture. Forty or fifty suits were arranged along tables that looked as if they'd been carved from thousand-foot trees: there were gold desk plates that read MCDONALD'S and MONSANTO and IBM. John had never been around so many good pairs of shoes.

'Wow,' he said. 'It's like the United Nations in here.'

Alfonse said, 'Have a seat, John.'

He looked around for a NIKE plate. Alfonse cleared his throat and gestured to a plastic chair that was sitting against a glass wall, facing the tables. 'There?'

'Yes.'

He sat with as much dignity as he could manage, which wasn't much. The plastic chair squeaked. He glanced over his shoulder. He at least got a great view of downtown Los Angeles from here.

For a moment, nobody spoke. It was unnerving: John had never been to a meeting that wasn't a fight for conversation space. He spotted the Pepsi kid toward the back. John couldn't work out what was odd about him, until he realized it was the first time he'd seen the kid in a suit. 'Okay, so everyone's a little surprised about the jet thing.'

Snorts of outrage. The McDonald's Liaison looked like she wanted to leap across the desk and slap him.

Alfonse said, 'John, in case you haven't already gathered, we're here to vote on your expulsion from US Alliance. If this vote carries, UA and its member companies will disown any responsibility for your actions. We will deliver you to the Government and negotiate compensation for the damage you've caused.'

'So I was right,' John said. 'It *is* the United Nations.'

'He doesn't think he's done anything wrong,' the IBM Liaison snapped. He was an older man with white hair and a dark blue suit; John had never met him. 'Look at him. He's turned the world's most distinguished corporations into criminals and he's *smirking.*'

'You're right. I don't think I've done anything wrong.'

'Then let me help you out, you moron. First, the Government is

231

going to arrest us. All of us. Second, if they don't, the public is going to annihilate us. You want to see a marketplace backlash? We just assassinated the Government President. Let's see how that affects sales, shall we? Third, you killed people. I don't know if that's a problem for you, John, or for Nike, but it's a big goddamn problem for IBM, for me, and for everybody else here. Does that help? Does that clarify the situation for you?'

Silence. 'Okay, then.' His career depended on his answer, John realized. It was time to pull out all the stops. 'Three points. Okay.'

He rubbed his palms on his pants. 'One. The Government is not going to arrest us. They tried in London, and failed. Now, you can bet they weren't going to pack up their toys and go home. They were going to try again, and again and again, until they'd gotten us. But now, thanks to me, they've lost half their executives. They've lost their ability to coordinate, at least for a while. The Government is not going to arrest us because the Government is no longer able to.'

A wall of stony faces looked back at him. He spotted the NRA plaque, off to the left, but there was an empty chair behind it. He guessed that meant the NRA were in the shit, too. 'Two. There will not be a consumer boycott. The public will not suddenly start buying Whoppers instead of Big Macs or Apples instead of IBMs. Trust me, I'm from Nike. Nobody actually swaps brands because they heard the company did something bad. They keep on buying their favorite product at their favorite price. Yes, there is going to be a media backlash. But there is not going to be a consumer backlash.

'Three.' This was the tough one. John got to his feet. Mercifully, the chair didn't squeak. The room was dead quiet. 'Yes, some people died. But let's not pretend these are the first people to die in the interests of commerce. Let's not pretend there's a company in this room that hasn't had to put profit above human life at some point. We make cars we know some people will die in. We make medicine that carries a chance of a fatal reaction. We make guns. I mean, you want to expel someone here for murder, let's start with the Philip Morris Liaison. We have all, at some time, put a price tag on a human life and decided we can afford it. No one in this room has the right to sit here and pretend my actions came out of the blue.'

He took a risk and paused for effect. If the IBM Liaison was going to preach at him, now was his chance. But he didn't. He just sat there. *Pussy*, John thought.

'Look, I am not designing next year's ad campaign here. I'm getting rid of the Government, the greatest impediment to business in history. You don't do that without a downside. Yes, some people die. But look at the gain! Run a cost-benefit analysis! Maybe some of you have forgotten what companies really do. So let me remind you: they make as much money as possible. If they don't, investors go elsewhere. It's that simple. We're all cogs in wealth-creation machines. That's all.

'I've given you a world without Government interference. There is now no advertising campaign, no intercompany deal, no promotion, no action you can't take. You want to pay kids to get the swoosh tattooed on their foreheads? Who's going to stop you? You want to make computers that need repair after three months? Who's going to stop you? You want to reward consumers who complain about your competitors in the media? You want to pay them for recruiting their little brothers and sisters to your brand of cigarettes? You want the NRA to help you eliminate your competition? Then do it. Just do it.'

Their faces; ah, their faces. They hadn't seen this coming at all, John realized. He was opening the door to a brave new commercial world and they were transfixed by the pure, golden light of profit spilling from it.

'I'm a businessman. That's all. I just want to do business.'

He spread his palms. For a long time, nobody spoke. It was a much better silence than before. John enjoyed every moment of it.

Alfonse said, 'We will need to consider—'

'Fuck that!' the Pepsi kid said. 'Let's vote now!'

The room was full of nodding heads. 'Very well. All those in favor of expelling John Nike from US Alliance?'

Four hands went up – no, five. John felt warmth steal up his body.

'It seems you stay with us, John.'

'I am pleased and humbled,' he said. He couldn't control his smile.

The meeting raged for three hours. The Liaisons were electrified by the possibilities; it was so cute. They threw around outrageous marketing plans, deals for customer referral, for market leverage, segmentation. By the end of it, even John was sick of talk about money.

When it was over he escaped to the lobby, took cover behind a bronze statue of John D. Rockefeller, and flipped open his cellphone.

'General Li NRA.'

'It's me.'

'Ah, John . . . I don't think we should be talking—'

'Forget about that. It's taken care of.'

'If you say so.'

John was beginning to respect General Li. He was straight-talking, no big ego, a results man. 'You'll get verification soon enough. Meantime, I have another job for you.'

A hand fell on his shoulder: Alfonse. 'John. You continue to surprise me.'

'You're too kind.'

'One thing,' Alfonse said. 'It crosses my mind that you may be tempted to press your present advantage. You may think that because you have gotten away with one unsanctioned action, you may do it again.'

'No, Alfonse, of course not.'

'Nothing happens without the approval of the member companies. Do you understand that, John?'

'Totally.'

Alfonse nodded. 'Then I will leave you to your call.'

John watched him exit. 'Still there, Li?'

'Yes.'

'How much muscle can you get to the major cities in three days?'

'You mean—'

'You know what I mean.'

'Well,' Li said. 'A lot.'

'Do it,' John said. 'I've got competitors to take care of.'

59 BUY

Buy got lost on the way to Kate's school, and the traffic was *terrible*, murderous. He tapped the steering wheel, anxious. 'I thought you said it was a ten-minute drive.'

'It *is*, usually.'

'So what—' Then, up ahead, he saw the Highpoint mall was plastered with a gigantic billboard: UP TO 50% OFF TO U.S. ALLIANCE CARDHOLDERS TODAY! Cars were banked up in four lanes trying to get into the parking lot. 'There are sales on?'

'Don't you watch TV?' Kate said.

'Uh,' Buy said. 'Not enough, clearly.' A gap opened in the

adjoining lane: he stamped on the gas. A car behind him tooted its
horn. Buy flipped him the bird. He realized Kate was looking at him.

'That's rude.'

'I know,' he said, shamed. 'I'm sorry.'

'It's okay. There's my school.'

'Don't eat that cake before lunchtime. You remember what we
agreed?'

'Yes, Buy.'

He smiled at her. 'You are a terrific girl.'

She looked away shyly. He couldn't resist kissing her cheek.
'Now off you go.'

Kate jumped out of the Jeep, waved, and started walking
toward the school gate. Buy was watching her instead of the traffic,
and another car tooted him.

'Yeah, yeah,' he said. He didn't feel irritated at all.

When he came back from lunch, the red voice-mail light on his
phone was flashing. He blinked in surprise. Buy hadn't had a voice-
mail message in almost a week. He picked up the handset.

'Buy! It is Kato Mitsui, Liaison, leaving a message. Please call
me back at your conveniences.'

He put down the phone. Kato obviously wanted to know what
bizarre marketing schemes Buy had dreamed up: well, the answer
was none. He decided to call Kato back anyway. He had had
enough of sitting at his desk doing nothing.

He was switched through three secretaries, all of whom spoke
American better than Buy, then connected to Kato. Kato was in his
car, or maybe a plane; Buy heard a rush of air in motion. 'Buy! It
is most pleasing to speak with you again.'

'And with you, Kato. Although I don't have much to report.
Marketing isn't really my—'

'Ah, that is not why I called. I have a more urgent task for you.'

'Oh.'

Kato laughed. 'I am no doubt filling your In Tray to overflowing. Tell me, have you heard of the amazing exploits of John Nike, Liaison?'

'John Nike? No.'

'I must confess great surprise, for he has splashed across the news,' Kato said. 'He is a leading role in US Alliance strategies. And he is from the Australian territories, like yourself. I thought to myself, Buy, what tremendous good fortune it is for you to share so many coincidences with John. So I wish you to form a contact, and make yourself of usefulness to him.'

Buy blinked. 'How, exactly?'

'I do not mind how, Buy. I simply wish to get into bed with him. You will ingratiate the corporation of Mitsui to John Nike through your helpfulness. Sometime later, of course, John Nike will repay Mitsui.'

'Or repay Kato,' Buy said.

Kato's laugh was loud enough to hurt his ear. 'Sometimes my colleagues accuse me of learning too much from America. You are also a quick study, I can tell. Together we make a most excellent team.'

Buy didn't know what to say. 'Thanks.'

'Call me when you have entwined yourself with John,' Kato said.

He called Nike's Melbourne office and reached John's personal assistant. She sounded flustered and upset: she told him she'd only started the job yesterday. Buy suspected his message was one of a great many she had taken. He said, 'Tell him it's from the guy who sent you a bunch of flowers.'

'Pardon me?'

'You sound like you're up to your neck in it,' Buy said, 'so I'm sending you a big bunch of flowers. I hope you don't mind.'

'Are you serious?'

'Yes.'

'That's . . . Buy Mitsui? I'll make sure he gets your message.'

'Thank you,' he said, and hung up, pleased. He didn't have anything to do until John called back, so he decided to go pick out the flowers himself. He grabbed his jacket and caught the elevator down.

In the lobby, he bumped into Cameron. Cameron looked tired and stressed, and Buy wondered if something had happened. Or maybe everyone in brokerage looked like this, but he hadn't noticed before. 'Hi, Cameron.'

'Buy? Where are you going?'

'To get some flowers.'

'Flowers? What do you need flowers for?'

'To send to a secretary.'

'You listen to me,' Cameron said. 'I didn't twist arms to get you this assistant Liaison job so you could hide out on the eighth floor. I've given you as much support as I can. It's time for you to find some goddamn motivation.'

'Cameron, wait,' Buy said. 'I'm—'

'Everyone else is breaking their backs for this company, Buy. Maybe you don't care about that. But we won't carry you forever. Unless you start producing, we will replace you. So if you need something to care about, care about that.'

'I have something to care about,' Buy said. 'Really.' He glanced at his watch. Kate was out of school in a couple of hours. He had promised to pick her up.

60 JENNIFER

First they told her to board the Government jet with Billy NRA and accompany the President back to Washington, D.C. When she questioned the wisdom of putting Billy on the same aircraft as the man he was trying to kill, they told her to stay in London and wait for a later plane. Then two-thirds of the Government's upper echelon nosedived into the Atlantic, and everything turned to shit.

Her transport got postponed, or canceled: nobody told her which. There were agents twenty deep for the phones, and after standing in line for two hours, she got five minutes to talk to Kate before a departmental officer commandeered the line. Then she walked back to her secured barracks to discover a bunch of Government agents from Japan were moving in. 'You're meant to be gone,' they said.

'But my transport isn't here yet.'

'Not my problem, sunshine,' the Japanese agent said, and Jennifer went looking for someone who could sort this out.

'Some Japanese guys are trying to take over my barracks,' she told the Staff Chief.

'Aren't you meant to be in Washington?'

'Yes. I don't have a transport.'

'Well, those barracks are meant to be free.'

'But they're not.'

'Look,' he said. 'Jennifer? Let me be clear. I don't know who my boss is anymore. I have a campus filled with agents who don't know what they should be doing. I have bigger problems than sorting out your accommodation.'

'Then am I authorized to use my initiative to find a solution?'

'What a terrific idea,' the Staff Chief said.

239

'Thank you, sir!' Jennifer said. She walked out quickly. That was just fine.

'I'm sorry,' the US Alliance man said. 'John isn't here anymore. Most top management flew back to L.A. yesterday. Which news-paper did you say you were from?'

'To L.A.? You're sure?'

'I'm positive. I can try to arrange a phone interview, if you like.'

'That's okay,' Jennifer said. 'I'll set something up myself.'

'Wake up,' she said, flicking on the light. 'We're leaving.'

Billy NRA raised his head from the bunk, dazed. 'Leaving? Where?'

'We have a plane to catch.'

'You can't take me outside! The NRA will kill me!'

'Don't worry. I'm very good at this.'

They met Calvin at the airport. He'd been sent to a different Government campus, and he turned up twenty minutes late. 'I'm sorry, I'm sorry. The roads *curve*. They go in circles. I nearly ended back where I started.'

'Can we go inside, please?' Billy said. 'I really think we should go in.'

'What's with him?'

'He thinks US Alliance is going to try to kill him.'

'Are they?'

'I guess,' she said.

At the counter, the American Airways clerk said, 'I'm sorry, ma'am, you can't board this flight. As of noon today, we're not permitted to offer flights to the Government.'

'Excuse me?'

'Our flights are for US Alliance cardholders only.'

'I have a US Alliance card,' Calvin said, feeling his pockets.

'What's your name, sir?'

'Calvin . . . McDonald's.'

'Can I see some ID, please?'

'Uh,' Calvin said. 'No.'

'I'm sorry, sir. I can't book Government.'

They walked away from the counter. Billy said, 'What's going on?'

'Billy, get three tickets, will you?' Jennifer said.

'By *myself*?'

'I presume you have a US Alliance card,' she said. 'You probably get assassin stars.'

'Man, the NRA is going to pop me. You call this an escort?'

'I'm sure they won't pop you,' Jennifer said. 'Go, go.'

Billy threw her a look of betrayal and walked up to the counter. For a moment she thought he was going to approach the same ticket girl. Then he veered off. She watched the people around him, looking for a head coming up, for hands reaching into pockets.

'We can't even catch a flight, now,' Calvin said. 'What's going on?'

'I don't know.'

'And how come the Government wants us in L.A.? I thought we were going to Washington.'

'They told me to use my initiative.'

Calvin looked at her. 'What?'

'John's gone to L.A.'

'*Jen,*' he said. 'We're meant to go to Washington.'

'Yes, yes,' Jennifer said. 'After.'

'So one jet goes down,' she said, tucking the pillow behind her back, 'and the Government is paralyzed. How did we get that

241

centralized? We're not meant to be about individuals. We're meant to be for the masses.'

'They used to fly the top people in different planes,' Calvin said.

'Well, why did that stop?'

'Budget, I suppose.'

'You know, this all started when they got rid of tax. That's when everyone started buying out of society. When we had tax, we had a *community*.'

'Dudes,' Billy said. 'Do you have to yak? I'm really tired.'

'Shut up,' she said.

'At least sit next to each other. Come on, I'm getting this in stereo.'

'Shh,' Calvin said. 'What, you want to reintroduce tax? How do you do that?'

'I don't know,' she muttered. 'But somewhere along the line, this freedom stuff got way out of control.'

'You'll feel better once we arrest John Nike,' Calvin said.

'Yeah,' she said. 'You're right about that.' She closed her eyes.

61 HACK

McDonald's had taken a long time to get a foothold in the Melbourne Central mall. Until then, the only place to get greaseburgers was at a little shop named Aussie Burgers, which, Hack had read somewhere, fought hard to keep the Golden Arches out. But then one day he stopped by and Aussie Burgers was gone. Facing its empty shell was the biggest McDonald's Hack had ever seen, spanning three levels and four shop frontages. It was packed with customers.

Hack had never eaten at Aussie Burgers, but now that it was

gone he wished he had. He was glad to be making it up to them now. He tightened his grip on his duffel bag and walked into McDonald's.

It was crammed with suits, mothers with toddlers, and truant school students. Hack scanned the crowd for Claire, and found her on the other side of the store, leaning against the counter. She met his eyes and smiled. Hack smiled back.

'Hack! Hey!'

He turned. It was Thomas, the kid who spray-painted over-obvious slogans on Hack's billboard jams.

'Man, this is cool. Are you ready?'

'Where's Leisl?' Hack said.

Thomas's face fell. 'I don't think she's coming.'

'What?'

'I don't think this is her kind of thing, man. She doesn't want to get into trouble.'

'Oh,' Hack said. Well, that was okay: three would do. He looked over at Claire and nodded. She began climbing onto the counter.

She was very nimble: she had those long legs up while Hack was still grabbing at the cash register for leverage. Thomas clambered up too close behind and nearly knocked him off.

'What – what are you doing?' a McDonald's clerk said.

'Don't worry,' Hack said, looking down at him. 'No one's going to get hurt.' He opened his bag, pulled on thick gloves, and turned to the crowd. 'McDonald's rapes the environment! It pillages Third World countries for their natural resources to serve us greasy, unhealthy food! McDonald's is a member of US Alliance, which killed people in London! It invades our neighborhoods and forces out small business! It advertises to children!'

'Baby killers!' Thomas yelled, and kicked the cash register. Hack resisted a sigh.

The customers were looking at him, smirking. Claire said,

'McDonald's poisons our lives for profit! So we are going to poison McDonald's!'

Hack withdrew a large tin from his duffel bag and jumped down behind the register. The clerk cringed away from him. 'Excuse me,' Hack said.

'Everybody out!' Claire shouted. 'We're releasing dangerous chemicals! Get out and never come back! It'll never be safe to eat here again!'

They began fitting their gas masks, and that broke the crowd. Hack guessed you didn't want to see people snapping those things on while you sat there with your burger and shake, vulnerable. They stampeded toward the exit. The screaming hurt his ears.

Hack turned toward the kitchen. The staff were strangely frozen, even as he popped open the tin. He shouted, 'Get out of here!' His words were muffled by the mask. 'Dangerous!' He dipped into the tin and drew out a gloveful of green powder.

They ran. Hack tossed the powder around, hitting the frying dishes, the benches, the roof, everything. It sizzled and blistered where it touched the hot plate, throwing off a thick, noxious, green smoke. He watched it, fascinated. It really looked like the most toxic thing he'd ever seen.

Someone grabbed his shoulder. He could barely see Claire's eyes through the mask. She tapped her wrist. He nodded and heaved the remaining powder, dropped the tin, and scrambled back over the counter. They held hands as they ran for the exit.

Customers were gathered thirty feet outside the store, but as the three burst out, they scattered again. Hack's spirits lifted further. No security guard would catch them in this confusion.

He pulled off the gas mask and stuffed it into his bag. They clattered down three levels of concrete stairs, followed a long maintenance corridor, then stepped out onto bustling Bourke Street.

'Wow!' Thomas said. 'That was cool! That was *so cool*!'

'I can't believe how it burned,' Claire said. 'That's just flour?'

'Flour and food dye.'

'No way are people gonna eat there again. No way!'

'You were really good,' Hack said to Claire. He kissed her. 'Your speech, I liked that a lot.'

'Thanks.' She looked embarrassed.

'Man!' Thomas said. 'How are we going to top that?'

'I know how,' Hack said. He'd been waiting for this. 'We hit Nike.'

62 VIOLET

Holly T.A. talked into her cellphone nonstop from Parliament. Violet sat opposite her, their knees almost touching. The limousine's third occupant was the soldier called ONE, and he sat beside Violet, not moving.

'It means we ramp everything up, right now,' Holly said. 'Maybe US Alliance is obsessed with the Government; I'm not. I want directives by the morning.' She snapped her phone closed and looked at Violet. 'Oh, come on. That wasn't so bad, was it?'

Violet said nothing.

'You were useful to me today. I appreciate that. You helped identify an important opponent.'

'He's . . . he's evil.' The way John had cocked his fingers at her . . . Violet shivered.

'All our competitors are evil,' Holly said. She smiled. Violet couldn't tell if she was joking.

'I want to go home now.'

'If that's what you want.'

'I do. I want to get paid and go home.'

'As I recall,' Holly said, flipping open her cellphone again, 'I said your pay was an ExxonMobil matter.'

'No, you—'

'Sweetie, it's nothing to do with me.' She pushed buttons.

'Wait a second!' Violet reached out and took Holly's wrist. Then ONE had his hand around Violet's throat and was pushing her head into the seat. She choked and clawed at him.

'What a funny girl you are, Violet,' Holly said. She looked amused. 'You've got a lot to learn about how the world works.'

Tramp, Violet tried to say, but she had no air. Holly knocked on the window and the limousine pulled over. ONE opened the door and shoved. Violet banged her knees on the sidewalk. She scrambled to her feet. The limousine was already moving again. 'Bitch!' she shouted after it. 'You – you bitch!'

She was on a bridge, with traffic roaring past in both directions. It was already dark. The air was thick with fog. After a while, she started walking.

The return ticket she'd received from ExxonMobil was still valid, and Violet got a flight for Melbourne the same day. Twenty hours later, she was stepping out of a cab at Claire's house. It was eight in the morning but felt like ten P.M. She felt out of sync with the world.

Hack would probably have moved back to their apartment by now, but that was okay: Violet could freshen up before seeing him. She had been short with Hack, she realized now: she had said some things he might have taken the wrong way. Hack could be sensitive. She would need to be careful if she wanted him to help her get her three million dollars.

She still had a key, so she unlocked the front door and went inside. 'Hello?' There was no answer, but she heard the shower running. And talking – Claire singing, maybe. Violet knocked on the bathroom door. 'Hello?'

Silence. 'Violet?'

'Yeah.' She rested her head against the door and closed her eyes. 'I'm home.'

'Oh, ah – how'd it go?' The water shut off.

'Not so hot.' She felt abruptly close to tears. 'Not so great at all.'

'What's wrong?'

'Can I come in?'

'Uh – just a second!'

'I really need to talk,' Violet said, and swung open the door.

Claire was wearing a towel. Hack wasn't wearing anything. She stared at them. It was like a hallucination.

Claire said, 'Violet, before you say anything—'

'What the *fuck*?' she screamed.

'Violet, please, let me explain—'

'How could you? How could you do this to me?'

'Violet,' Hack said. 'You left. You went away and said you didn't want to see me again.'

'That was an *argument*! I can't – I can't believe you're having an affair!'

'An *affair*?' Hack yelled. Hack was being surprisingly assertive for a man with no clothes on. Hack was being surprisingly assertive for Hack. 'We're not together!'

'How dare you say that! We are so!'

'You dumped me!'

'Everybody thinks they can *screw* me!' Violet shouted. She felt tears prick her eyes. 'Everyone thinks they can fuck me over!'

Claire said, 'Violet, I'm really sorry—'

Violet slammed the door. The cab was still in sight, but only just.

She ran after it, waving her hands. Its brake lights flashed. Violet hurried up to it. The cabdriver said, 'Nobody home?'

'No,' Violet said.

The apartment was much cleaner than she remembered. There was no sign of her fight with John in the kitchen, and the crumpet toaster was gone. It made her feel like she was dreaming. She couldn't help wonder if all this had really happened. Maybe if she went back to Claire's house, Hack wouldn't be . . . No, that was stupid. Violet pressed her hands against her face.

Suddenly, shockingly, she started to cry. Great, wracking sobs burst out of her. She couldn't believe it. She sank to the kitchen tiles and wrapped her arms around herself. She shook uncontrollably. She didn't know if she was crying for Hack or for her lost three million dollars or out of jet lag or maybe all of it combined, but she couldn't stop. It was a torrent. It seemed to drag out everything she had left.

She cried and hated herself. This wasn't meant to be her, this small, beaten girl. She was meant to succeed. Other people had taken it all away from her.

She stood up and scrubbed at her eyes. She went into the living room and picked up the phone. Holly T.A. had said Violet had a lot to learn about how the world worked; well, she'd see about that. She'd see how fast she could learn.

It took a long time to get someone, and then the someone sounded as if she weren't taking Violet seriously. 'Tell him it's Violet,' she said. 'Tell him it's the person who watched him kill a man in London. You got that?'

'Wait a second,' the woman said. 'Did you say—'

'Yes,' Violet said.

'I'll make sure John gets your message,' the woman said, and

Violet hung up. She bit her nails. She was doing the right thing. She knew she was.

63 JOHN

John had requisitioned a big table and spread a map of Los Angeles across it. It was covered with red ink, with words like '1ˢᵗ Inf,' and '3ʳᵈ Arm.' He was beginning to wish he'd used pencil; the thing was getting pretty confusing.

'You are *so* the man,' the Pepsi kid said, circling. 'I cannot tell you how cool this is.'

'Tell me about the Liaisons.'

'Most are full steam ahead. The campaigns these guys are rolling out, it blows your mind.' He peered at the map. 'Is this artillery? Are you going to hit the Reebok office with *artillery*?'

'*Most* of them?'

'Aw, IBM still doesn't like it, you know. And a McDonald's store got attacked this morning in the Australian Territories. People are saying it's a grass-roots protest.'

'A protest? About what?'

The Pepsi kid shrugged. 'Consumerism, I guess.'

'Consumerism? Since when did eating a burger become a crime?'

'I dunno, man.'

'Find out who's behind it. I don't want IBM or McDonald's or anyone else to have a reason to start bitching about market backlash.' His intercom buzzed, startling him. 'Quick,' he said. 'Hide the map.'

'John? General Li NRA to see you.'

'Ah.' He relaxed. 'Send him in.'

249

The Pepsi kid smoothed out the map: he had creased it down the 110. 'Can I stick around? I can give you good strategy.'

'No,' John said. General Li stepped into the office.

'Aw, come *on*.'

General Li looked at the Pepsi kid. John said, 'General Li, this is . . .' He realized he didn't know the kid's name. 'The PepsiCo Liaison.'

'A pleasure to meet you,' General Li said.

The kid shook Li's hand with enthusiasm. 'Same, man. I love all this war shit.'

'All right, now piss off,' John said.

'I'll be real quiet.'

'Go!'

'All right, all right.' The kid threw John a sour look. He closed the door hard behind him.

'Tough day?' General Li said.

John sighed. 'Just a couple of Liaisons making trouble. Things were much simpler when I didn't have to listen to other people, Li. Democracy is a pain in the ass.'

Li sat. 'In the military, we have always had a healthy disrespect for democracy.'

'I can see why,' John said. 'All right. Now let's talk about tanks.'

'Before we begin,' the General said, 'I should bring a matter to your attention. You remember our failed assassin, Billy NRA?'

'Is he dead yet?'

'I'm afraid not. Billy was held on a Government base for several days. We've only just reacquired his location. He's on a United Airlines flight to L.A.'

'Well, you take that little prick out,' John said, then stopped. 'L.A.? Why is he coming here?'

'I don't know.'

'If the Government was taking him anywhere, it'd be Washington . . .' He snapped his fingers. 'Billy got away. He escaped!'

Li cleared his throat. 'I believe not. According to United, he's traveling with Jennifer and Calvin NRA. We're sure those are false names.'

For a second he couldn't speak. 'Jennifer's coming *here?*'

'Excuse me?'

'Leave me,' John said. 'I need to think.'

Li looked at the map. 'Sir, if you want to coordinate a military campaign, we need to—'

'*Out!*'

General Li withdrew. John pressed his fingers against his temples. How could she still be after him? The Government took months to organize a bake sale; with their top executives making an unscheduled splashdown in the Atlantic, they should be in chaos. How did they get two agents from London to L.A.?

But he knew: it was Jennifer. He'd been kidding himself, thinking he'd done enough to protect himself. Jennifer would chase him to the end of the earth.

There was a piece of paper on his desk, with a person's number. He found it and studied it. 'Violet ExxonMobil,' he said softly. 'What do you want with me?' He thought it might be worth finding out.

He didn't get out of the office until eleven, and then he was so wired he stopped in at the hotel bar to unwind. He was staring into his scotch when someone sat beside him, brushing his arm. He looked up in annoyance. It was a thin girl in a light dress. She smiled awkwardly. 'You're John, right? John Nike.'

'Who are you?'

She hesitated, then stuck out her hand. 'Vanessa FashionWarehouse.com. I hope I'm not bothering you.'

He was tempted to tell her to get lost, but she was young and nervous and there was a possibility she might be about to offer to sleep with him. 'Not at all.'

'I suppose – you probably haven't heard of FashionWarehouse.com. We're a content provider and on-seller for several major labels.' She searched his eyes.

'Uh-huh.'

'I – we applied to US Alliance a few months ago, but they rejected us. They said they only took companies with revenues of a hundred million plus. But we're new, and high-growth, and I was hoping you could . . . make an exception.'

John felt amused. There was no way Fashion.com or whatever pissant company this girl ran out of her bedroom was going to be accepted into US Alliance. 'You'd have to make a pretty good case.'

Her smile stretched. It was almost painful to watch. 'I might be able to do that.' Awkwardly, she pressed her body against his arm; he felt a small breast on his shoulder.

'Sir? Excuse me?' the barman said. 'Phone call for you.'

John blinked. 'Why are my calls coming down here?'

'Reception noticed you were visiting the bar, sir.'

'Oh.' The Sofitel was big on customer service; sometimes it could get a little creepy. 'Who is it?'

'Violet ExxonMobil.'

'I'll take it in my room.' He stood.

Vanessa said, 'Are you coming back? After your call?'

He looked at her. 'Sorry. I'm busy.'

'But—'

'Sorry,' he said, and walked away. He felt cheated. Jennifer was ruining his accomplishments, souring his victories. What was the point of success, if he didn't have the time to screw a girl like that? He stared at himself in the elevator mirror. 'What am I becoming?' he said, and his reflection looked back at him.

*

'Violet.'

'John.'

'Let's get something clear.' He pulled the phone to the window, so he could see the illuminated Hollywood sign. Columbia had bought it a few years ago and now there was a gigantic Pegasus above it; it was a big improvement, in John's opinion. 'If you're hoping to blackmail me over one dead ExxonMobil CEO, save your breath.'

'That's not why I'm calling.'

'Then maybe you want to apologize for sticking a gun in my face and putting my friend into a coma. Is that it, Violet?'

'I knew I was right to call you.' She sounded excited, so either had a screw loose or was one of those people who didn't know when to quit; either way, John was interested. He had uses for people like that. 'We have a common enemy. Holly T.A. We can help each other.'

'Last I saw you, you were sitting next to Holly T.A.'

'She – she—' Her voice tightened. 'She owes me a lot of money. She owes me a *lot.*'

Uh-huh, he thought. He was tempted to ask Violet if she was nuts, but that was a dangerous question, and besides, he thought he already knew the answer. 'You want me to collect your debts?'

'I can give you information on Holly, I can tell you—'

'Screw that. I don't need help with Holly, I need help with Jennifer Government.' His life was filled with domineering women, he realized: if it wasn't Jennifer, it was Holly.

'Who?'

'Don't bullshit me, Violet, it would be very bad for our relationship. If your little friend Hack hasn't spoken to Jennifer, I'm Ralph Nader. Ask him about her. Then get her daughter.'

Pause. 'You want me to kidnap someone?'

'You got it first time. You get me that kid and we're in business.'

'I didn't . . . that's not . . . I thought I could just give you information—'

'How much does Holly owe you?'

'Three million. She owes me three million dollars.'

'Well, that's a lot of money,' John said. He made himself hesitate, as if he was really thinking about it. 'Okay. Get me the kid, I'll get your money.'

'And – and when you get it, you'll tell Holly it's from me? Can you do that?'

'Sure,' John said. 'I'll really rub it in.'

'Okay,' Violet said, excited again. 'Okay, I could probably do that. I don't have to hurt the girl or anything, right?'

'Uh, right,' John said. Yep: deluded. 'Of course not.' He checked his watch. 'One more thing. Don't even think about betraying me.' He didn't know why he bothered; they were probably each intending to betray the other and it was just a question of who would get in first. 'You've got my number.' He hung up.

No doubt, Violet was flaky, very flaky. But sometimes that was the kind of person who got results. Even an unsuccessful attempt to grab Jennifer's kid would send a message, and maybe that would be enough. If he bought enough time, it wouldn't matter how dogged Jennifer was. Li and the NRA would put her out of a job.

64 BUY

Two days and no reply from John Nike. Buy called the P.A. again. 'Oh!' she said. 'The flowers are lovely, thank you so much! Has John been in touch?'

'No, he hasn't.'

'Oh, damn. Look, um, I shouldn't do this . . . but do you want his cellphone number?'

'That would be great,' Buy said, and wrote it down. 'Thank you again.'

He dialed John's number. While he waited, he surfed the internet for Virtual Animalz. He didn't know what these were, exactly, except that Kate was in love with them. She wanted downloads.

'Hello?'

'John Nike? This is Buy Mitsui, Assistant Liaison. I don't know if you got my message, but—'

'How the fuck did you get this number?'

'Your P.A. gave it to me.'

'That bitch!' John said.

'Anyway,' Buy said. He had the feeling he wasn't going to like John Nike. 'I'm calling because Kato Mitsui, Liaison, has asked me to make myself of use to you.'

Pause. 'You want what?'

'No, no,' Buy said. 'I'm here to help you.'

'Help how?'

'I don't know. Whatever you want done.'

'Oh,' John said. 'Well, um . . . where are you, anyway?'

'Melbourne, the Australian Territories.'

There was a pause. 'Okay, sure. Sure. Get in touch with the local McDonald's office, find out who's been throwing toxic sludge around their stores.'

'You want me to help McDonald's?' This was getting complicated.

'We're all one big happy family in US Alliance, haven't you heard?'

'Of course,' Buy said.

'But no, I don't want you to help McDonald's. I want you to tell me if they're playing straight. Find out who's behind the attack: I want names, their plans, everything. I wouldn't put it past those McAssholes to stage the whole thing.'

'Okay.' He thought: *Paranoid, too.*

'And never call me at this time again. It's five in the fucking morning.'

'Oh, I'm sorry—' Buy started, but John had already killed the call.

Buy set up a three-o'clock to see Lucia McDonald's, Marketing Director, which would let him pick up Kate from school afterward. McDonald's main offices were in Sydney, but Lucia was in Melbourne for crisis management. She wanted to meet him at the store that had been attacked, so Buy wandered up Swanston Street and rode the escalator. The McDonald's store was no longer under plastic: to his amazement, there were people eating in it. He entered, looking for Lucia.

'Buy Mitsui?'

He turned. A woman he'd mistaken for a customer was smiling at him, covering a cellphone with one hand. In front of her was a half-eaten cheeseburger and fries. 'I'm Lucia. Have a seat. I'll be one moment.'

Buy sat and eyed Lucia's cheeseburger. He hoped she wasn't going to ask him to eat. He'd seen the news: they were hosing green stuff off the hot plates. Buy would sooner eat his briefcase.

'All the food is cooked off-site,' Lucia said, catching him. She folded up her cellphone. 'We're positive there was no contamination, but it's a good way to reassure our customers. We're running hot delivery vans up and down Swanston Street.'

'No contamination?'

'It was a mixture of flour and food dye. Just a prank.'

'Oh, I didn't realize,' Buy said. He still didn't want a cheeseburger.

'You and the whole general public. We've got a hell of a PR job. I've got half my staff down here to gorge themselves on Happy Meals.'

Buy looked around. Now that Lucia mentioned it, there was a certain uniformity about all the customers. Most had cellphones pressed to their ears. A few had notebook computers. 'Do you know who attacked the store?'

'As of this morning, yes. Security cameras saw them come out of the store and exit onto the street. We got cooperation from a couple of stores along Bourke Street, ran their security tapes, and saw which parking lot they went into. One of them paid with a Visa card. Since Visa's in US Alliance, voilà, one billing address for a Mr. Hack Nike.'

Buy blinked. He wondered if it was a coincidence that the attacker worked for Nike, like John. There was probably more going on here than Buy was aware of. 'Have you reported this to the Government?'

Lucia smiled. 'We don't work that way, Buy. Too public. We'll talk to this Hack Nike instead.'

'By "talk" you mean—'

She leaned forward. 'I mean we'll mount a very persuasive case as to why he should never try anything like that again.'

'I . . . see,' Buy said. 'I'd like to talk to him first, if you don't mind. John Nike wants to know what these people are about.'

'Yes, *John*,' Lucia said. Her eyes shone. 'I must say, it's very flattering that he's taken a personal interest. How do you know him?'

'It's complicated.'

'I hope you'll tell him how grateful I am for his assistance. If he's ever in town, I'd love to take him to dinner.'

'I will tell him,' Buy promised. 'So can I—'

'Let me write down the details for you.'

*

257

On the Bechtel Eastern Freeway, en route to Kate's school, Buy dialed the number Lucia had given him.

A young woman answered. 'Hello?'

'Hello,' Buy said. 'Can I speak to Hack Nike, please?'

'He's not here,' she said, a little aggressively, Buy thought. 'He doesn't live here anymore. Okay?'

'Oh. Do you know where—'

'Try Claire Sears, Sales Assistant. Why don't you look her up? I'm sure you'll find Hack *there*.'

'Uh,' Buy said. 'Thank you.' He hung up. That was strange.

He called directory information and got a number for Claire Sears. Claire had an answering machine. Buy told it, 'Hi, my name is Buy Mitsui . . . I've heard about your group, about what you do, and . . . I'd like to be part of it. Please call me back as soon as you can.'

He ended the call. He felt kind of bad, laying a trap like that. Before he'd left McDonald's, Lucia had showed him the tape of the attack, and Buy was surprised by how amateurish it all was. On the news, it had sounded like a strategic chemical weapons attack. 'They're kids,' he'd said to Lucia. 'Just kids.'

'They cost us twenty million in brand damage,' Lucia had said. 'Don't feel too sorry for them.'

Buy was early, so he parked the Jeep and ducked inside, hoping to see Kate's classroom. There were pictures of Barbie dolls and Hot Wheels cars plastered everywhere. This was a Mattel school, Buy realized. He suddenly understood why Kate had a Barbie lunchbox.

A security guard stepped in front of him. 'Help you, sir?'

'Oh,' Buy said, startled. 'I'm just picking up my kid.'

'Students can be collected from the gate, sir,' the guard said. 'Please wait outside.'

'Uh, sure.' He turned and walked back. That was a pity. But he supposed the precautions were necessary. You never knew when some lunatic would try to snatch a kid.

Kate was one of the first out the gates. She ran toward him, her schoolbag bouncing on her back. 'Buy! Did you get my Virtual Animalz?'

He opened the door for her. 'I think you need to explain this whole concept to me again.'

'*Buy*. It's *simple*.'

He started the engine. 'To a smart girl like you, maybe.'

'A man came to talk to us today,' Kate said. 'He said some companies are bad. Do you work for a bad company?'

'What?'

'He said the bad companies ganged up on the good companies and they were going to fight.'

'US Alliance and Team Advantage?'

'Yes!'

'This is what they teach you?'

'The good companies are . . . I forget.'

'Me too,' Buy said.

'I know Mattel is a good one.'

'There aren't really good companies and bad companies, Kate. It's not that simple.'

'But Mattel look after kids in schools. There was this sick kid, they gave him a heap of toys. The other companies are mean and greedy.'

'In a way, all companies are greedy. That's why they make things for us. It's how the system works.'

'Can I get a treat? Since you didn't download any Animalz?'

Buy smiled. 'What kind of treat?'

'A Bouncing Beanie Baby.'

'I'm surprised you can't buy them at school,' Buy said. 'I'm surprised they're not mandatory.'

'Mattel don't make Bouncing Beanie Babies. But I like them.'

'You're a rebel.'

'Can I?'

'Sure, I suppose.'

'Thanks! The Chadstone mall is on the way home.'

'Let's go somewhere else.'

'But you said—'

'Just not at Chadstone,' Buy said. 'Please. I don't want to go to Chadstone.'

'Oh,' she said. 'Okay.'

They drove in silence for a while. Then Kate said, 'Do you think Mommy will call again?'

Buy looked at her. 'I'm sure she will. The second she can.'

'It sounded bad. Where she was. Noisy.'

'She'll be fine. I'm sure.'

'I hope she calls again,' Kate said. She bit her fingernail and inspected it. 'What about Sears? They sell them there. Can we get a Bouncing Beanie Baby at Sears?'

'Yes,' Buy said. 'We can go to Sears.'

65 BILLY

Billy woke to Jennifer's elbow in his ribs. 'Hey. Tryin' to sleep here.'

'We've landed.'

'Oh.' He followed Calvin into the aisle and stretched, cracking his knuckles.

'Don't do that,' Calvin said.

'Sorry.' Calvin looked tired and cranky, which was good, because that meant he wouldn't chase Billy so fast. Billy was pretty sure there would be some chasing, because as soon as he got a chance, he was going to run like fuck. He'd had a lot of time to think about this, and decided it was definitely better than the alternative, which was sitting around and waiting for the NRA to pop him. That John Nike had been pretty convincing.

Jennifer and Calvin escorted him off the plane, keeping between him and the other passengers. A neon sign said: WELCOME TO LOS ANGELES – HOME OF US ALLIANCE! 'Man, it feels good to be home,' Billy said, inhaling. 'Smell that air, wow.'

'It's air-conditioning,' Jennifer said.

He spotted a sign. 'Hey, bathroom. I gotta piss.'

'Wait until the hotel.'

'Come on, I just woke up. I really have to go.'

Jennifer looked at Calvin. Calvin said, 'Come on, then.'

'Good deal,' Billy said.

Jennifer put her hand on his arm. 'The NRA may know we're here. Be careful.'

'Wow, okay, sure.' He tried to look solemn. If Jennifer thought Billy's chances were better hanging around a couple of jet-lagged Government agents, she was nuts.

He followed Calvin into the restroom. Calvin checked the stalls, which allowed Billy to get a head start. By the time Calvin unzipped, Billy was shaking off. 'So, you worked with Jen a long time?'

'About a year.'

'Man, how do you put up with it? That chick drives me nuts after five minutes.' He zipped.

'She has redeeming qualities,' Calvin said, and Billy slammed his face into the wall. It made a loud *clunk* and Calvin bounced back onto the tiles. Billy ran for the exit. Jennifer saw him emerge. Her mouth dropped. She looked so surprised and outraged that Billy got the giggles. She was forty feet away. He took off in the other direction.

'Stop! Billy!'

He leapt a row of potted plants and sprinted past counters for rental cars. The main exit was ahead, and there were cabs waiting patiently on the street. He was halfway into one when a man in a black Airport Transport uniform caught his shoulder. 'Get you a cab, sir?'

'Yeah, yeah!'

The man looked at his clipboard. Then he looked up. 'Billy NRA?'

Billy stopped. 'Yeah, who are you?'

'Hold this, will you?' The man handed him the clipboard. Billy looked at it, confused. It had a photograph of himself tucked in the top-right corner. He didn't understand why this man would have his photo, or why he wanted Billy to look at it. Then the man pulled a gun from his pocket, and everything became much clearer.

'No!' He tripped over the curb and sprawled on the concrete. '*No, please!*'

'Sorry,' the man said. Billy could see his eye above the barrel. He could see his fingers squeezing the trigger.

There were two shots, sharp and loud. He felt his body explode, felt blood erupt from him. He couldn't believe it was happening. All he'd wanted to do was go skiing, and he was being shot to death in an L.A. airport. He screamed and screamed.

'Come on,' Jennifer said. 'Get up.'

He opened his eyes. There was a dead man slumped against the cab. He looked down. 'I'm hit! The blood – the blood!'

'It's not yours. Hurry up.'

He touched his belly, then his legs.

'See?' she said. 'Now move your ass. Let's not assume there's only one of them.'

262

She hauled him to his feet and followed him into the cab. Calvin opened the other door. Calvin had a bruise above his right eye, like an egg was trying to push its way out of his skull.

'I think you owe someone an apology,' Jennifer said.

'Uh . . . sorry, Calvin,' Billy said.

Calvin said nothing. Billy thought he might have reached the end of Calvin Government's goodwill.

'And . . . thanks for shooting that guy, Jen.'

'Try that again,' she said, 'and next time I'll shoot you.'

'I won't try it again,' Billy said. But that was a lie, of course.

66 JENNIFER

She wasn't thrilled about leaving a dead guy on the sidewalk, but it was either that or stick around and exchange words with however many other NRA operatives were hanging around. The cabdriver kept his mouth shut all the way to their hotel in Santa Monica, which she figured was understandable given what he'd just seen. She should probably tip him pretty well.

'Look at all these people,' Calvin said, peering out the window. 'Is every shop in this city having a sale?'

'Check out that US Alliance billboard,' Billy said. '"GO HOME, CARPETBAGGERS." Man, that's funny. Where's Team Advantage from?'

'New York,' Jennifer said.

'Huh,' Billy said. 'Figures.'

The cab dropped them outside the hotel. It was a sunny, clear morning, and she thought she could smell the ocean. She couldn't deny it: some part of her was excited to be here. It had been a long time since she was last in L.A.

She fought off men who very much wanted to carry her bag and made her way to the reception desk. A man in a demeaning uniform asked, 'Are you US Alliance members?'

'Billy,' she ordered. Billy produced his card.

'Are you a member, ma'am?'

'I intend to sign up,' Jennifer said. 'Real soon.'

He slid two clipboards across the counter. 'You'll need to do that before you check in. It's an excellent program. You can earn—'

'Jennifer?' someone said. 'Holy shit, Jennifer *Maher*?'

She turned. A suit with brown hair and shiny shoes was staring at her. She searched her memory for a name. 'Max?'

'I thought you dropped off the end of the earth, Barbie doll. What are you doing back in town?'

'I'm . . . here on business.' She felt Calvin's eyes on her. 'Do your forms,' she told him.

'Are you still in advertising?'

'I freelance.'

'Whoa, hey,' Max said. 'If you want work, let's talk.' He pressed a business card into her hand. It said: MAX SYNERGY, CEO, SYN-ERGY CAMPAIGNS. 'I have my own agency these days. We do work for US Alliance. Have you seen it? I would *love* to have you on board, Malibu. People in the industry still remember you.'

'That's . . . nice. But I'm not looking for work.'

'Oh. Well, keep me in mind. Hey, do you want to catch up later? We could—'

'How about I call you?'

'Okay!' Max said. 'Wow, it was great to run into you. Really great.'

Calvin didn't say anything until they were in the elevator. Then it was too quiet: she couldn't handle the waiting. 'Go on. Say it.'

'Say what?'

She looked at him.

'You used to work in L.A.?'

'Maher is based here.'

'Huh,' Calvin said. 'So this is like a homecoming for you.'

'No, it isn't.' But Calvin was right. She could feel it in her bones.

She called Kate, and it was wonderful. Kate was full of stories of what she and Buy had been doing, and listening to her voice, Jennifer started to feel much less like she'd spent the entire last week in an economy-class plane seat and more like a human being. 'I miss you so much,' she said, and Calvin and Billy glanced at her.

After that, she pulled out the phone book and did her journalist routine: call up US Alliance, pretend to be from MSNBC, and say she wanted to interview John Nike. She was transferred to an assistant who said John was in an important meeting and anyway he didn't do interviews with non-US Alliance media. 'Thanks anyway,' Jennifer said, and hung up. Now she had confirmation he was here.

There was a problem with Billy: he didn't want to be left handcuffed to the towel rail. 'We'll only be a few hours,' she said. 'What's the big deal?'

'What if the NRA come in here?'

'Now you want our protection? I thought you were better off on your own.'

'Well, um, now I see you were right about that,' Billy said.

'I'll cuff you to the mini bar instead,' she said. 'You can snack. How about that?'

'Aw, man,' Billy said.

They left him, hoping a cleaner wouldn't stumble onto him. The cab took forty minutes to reach the US Alliance building on

Main and Central because downtown was jammed with people. 'What's going on?' she asked the driver. 'Some kind of riot?'

'Yeah, some kind, all right. It's the Sales.'

'What sales?'

'Are you kidding me? US Alliance and Team Advantage. If you haven't signed up yet, lady, now's the time. You can get some amazing bargains.'

'Mmm,' Jennifer said. She saw two men fighting over a VCR in the window of a Sears; store security were trying to break them up. Across the doors of a K-Mart were spray-painted the words: T.A. – NOT IN L.A. 'Can you let us out here?'

They walked the remaining two blocks to the US Alliance tower, squeezing through the throng of shoppers. 'Wow, Jen,' Calvin said. 'These are some good deals right here.' He stopped in front of a window. 'Wide-screen TVs for two hundred bucks! Can that be right?'

She kept walking. After a minute, Calvin caught up with her.

'Okay, sure, all this is terrible, really. But since we're here . . . you could pick up something nice.'

Jennifer stopped. Across the road, the US Alliance building was ringed with NRA soldiers. She saw helmets, assault rifles, shields.

'What?' Calvin said, then saw. 'Oh, crap.'

'You think that's to stop us, or Team Advantage?'

'Maybe both.' She frowned.

'So what do we do now?'

'I think I call Max,' she said.

67 HACK

Hack was asleep when the phone rang. It was amazing how much more sleep he got now that he was unemployed. He was starting to feel bad for all the people who had to drag themselves into their drone factories by nine. They didn't know what they were missing.

Claire was at Sears. He stumbled out into the kitchen. 'Hello?'

'Hi. It's Thomas.'

'Oh, hi.'

'Look, Hack . . . I've been thinking . . . I don't want to do the Nike Town with you.'

'What?'

'It's just, after McDonald's, it seems like we should lay low for a while. You know?'

McDonald's had been in the news, big time. For two days the TV had been full of shots of guys in moonsuits walking through the store, the shopfront itself wrapped in plastic like something out of a science-fiction movie. Since then it was mostly serious-looking company spokespeople assuring the public that all precautions were being taken, that there was *no risk, none at all.*

'Oh,' Hack said. 'You don't want to get in trouble?'

'Right.'

He felt mad. There was no point in stopping after McDonald's; the point of the whole exercise was Nike. 'Gee, I'm sorry. I thought we were doing this because it was *right.* I thought we were standing up to corporations like McDonald's because someone has to. I didn't know we were doing it out of self-interest.'

'Uh,' Thomas said. 'It's just that—'

'Hey, I've got an idea! Why don't we put advertising on our uniforms? We could get sponsors, and funding—'

'That's not what I'm—'

'—and we'd only attack our sponsors' competitors, and we could charge a lot of money and design a logo and advertise and we'd be *just like them*!'

There was a long pause. Then Thomas said, 'I'm sorry, Hack.'

'Then get lost, you corporate sympathizer.' He hung up.

First Leisl, now Thomas. Hack was losing footsoldiers. It was amazing, he thought, how everyone bitched about corporations but no one was willing to risk pissing them off. Hack was disappointed at the level of motivation among this society's counterculture.

He picked a note off the table. It was the message that man had left, Buy Mitsui. Hack hadn't been going to return his call, but with Thomas pulling out . . . he could do with the extra help. This was Nike, after all. Hack didn't want to make anymore big mistakes.

He met Claire downtown for lunch, and they sat on the same side of a booth in a Johnny Rockets. Sears only gave Claire twenty minutes for lunch, so these meetings were always a bit rushed. Given Hack's financial situation since losing his job, they were an extravagance. But it was worth it to see Claire. Apart from sticking it to Nike, seeing Claire was the only thing Hack wanted to do.

'Thomas pulled out. Can you believe that?'

Claire didn't say anything.

'What?'

'Don't get upset . . .'

'About what?'

'Maybe we shouldn't do the Nike Town.'

He felt stunned. Claire, too? 'No. Claire, no, we're doing it. It's important to me.'

She was quiet. Hack sucked at his milkshake. 'Hack, I don't think this is making you a good person.'

He was bewildered. 'What do you mean?'

'You used to be . . . nicer. More generous.'

'When I was nicer, everyone *screwed* me,' he said, and even he recognized the echo of Violet in his words. He reached for Claire's hands. 'Look, the Nike Town is the end of it. But I have to do Nike.'

She nodded.

'I promise,' Hack said. 'Claire, I promise.'

She smiled a little, and he felt better. 'I have to go.'

'Okay.' He stood to let her exit. 'It was nice to see you.'

Claire left. Hack sat back in the booth and picked at his food. What did she mean, he wasn't a good person? Hack was taking charge of his life. He was dynamic and effective. Hack was a *great* person.

He walked to the bus stop. The bench was plastered with an advertisement for Nike Plutoniums: they were the latest product line, due out in three years' time. Hack snorted. The day before, he had seen Nike Mercurys selling for $99.95 in a bargain bin.

The bus arrived and he climbed onboard. 'Eighty-five cents, buddy,' the driver said.

Hack dug in his pockets. The result was not promising. He shouldn't have had that sundae, he realized. 'I've only got fifty cents.'

'We take cards.'

'They charge me transaction fees,' Hack said. 'Come on, it's only thirty-five cents' difference.'

'You pay the fare or you catch a different bus,' the driver said. 'What's the matter, don't you have a job?'

'Fine.' Hack handed over his card. He sat at the back of the bus and stewed. Transportation was a basic necessity: it should be free.

Maybe at the Nike Town, Hack could swipe some shoes. That wouldn't be stealing, because Nike had underpaid him for years. They owed him a lot more than a few pairs of sneakers. Yes, he thought. He would do that.

*

The phone was ringing as he opened the door. 'Hello?'

'Don't hang up.'

'Violet?'

'I have a question. I need to know where the Government took you when they arrested you.'

'Why do you want to know that?'

'It's very important, Hack. Where does Jennifer Government work?'

'It was downtown. On Spring Street. How come?'

'Thanks,' Violet said, and something in her voice scared Hack a little. 'I won't keep you from Claire. Goodbye.'

'Wait,' he said. 'How do you know Jennifer Government?' But the line was dead. She was already gone.

68 VIOLET

Violet's nose was running and she didn't have a tissue. She wiped it on her sleeve, but it kept dripping. The Government receptionist looked up, and Violet tried to smile at him. It came out feeling too manic, too desperate. She had to stay cool.

'Jennifer Government isn't available,' the receptionist said. He was wearing a yellow tie. A security guard was sitting beside him. Violet could see his holster. 'But you can leave the package here. I'll see she gets it.'

'No can do,' she said. 'Only Jennifer can sign for it.'

'She's out of the country.'

'Oh,' Violet said, and wiped her nose. She was wearing a thick, furry jacket with a SPEEDY COURIERS patch, and it was inflaming her allergies. 'Then I should deliver this to her home. What's the address?'

'I can't give you a home address.'

'But . . .' She wiped her nose. 'Is there someone in Human Resources I can talk to about it?'

'I can get someone for you. But they won't give you a home address.'

Violet felt her right hand start to shake. She shoved it into her pocket. 'I really have to deliver this package.'

'O–kay,' the receptionist said. He called someone, and after a few minutes a woman in a blue cardigan entered. 'Courier?'

'Here,' Violet said. 'I have to talk to you. In private.'

'Ah, all right. Follow me.' She led Violet down a long, dilapidated corridor and into an office. Violet couldn't believe this place; it looked like the set for an old TV cop show. 'Have a seat.'

'Thanks. I have a package to deliver to Jennifer Government and I need her home address.'

'I'm sorry, I can't give out that information.'

'Are you sure?' Violet said. The woman's computer was right there; it was very frustrating. 'It's a really important package.'

'I'm sure.'

Violet glanced at the woman's nameplate. It said: *Wendy, Human Resources.* 'Well, okay. Mind if I use the bathroom before I go?'

'Sure. Last door on your right before reception.'

She found it and pushed open the bathroom door. Inside, she removed her jacket, turned it inside out, and put it back on. Then she went back out and knocked on a random office door.

'Come in.'

She entered. A man with bushy eyebrows was sitting behind a crowded desk. His office had a poster of a rainforest on the wall and no window. 'Hi, I'm with I.T. I'm here about your computer.'

'The e-mail problem?'

'N – yes.'

'At last. I've been complaining for weeks.'

'Sorry, we've been really backed up.' He stood and Violet took his seat. She felt her nerves calm in front of the screen, its radiation like a warm bath. It took her five seconds to determine that this man wasn't in Human Resources, and another ten to find Wendy's computer on the network. She pulled a disk out of her pocket and pushed it into the drive slot.

'What's that?'

'New drivers,' Violet said. It was a six hundred thousand word dictionary, and it cracked Wendy's password (*humanitarian*) in about two seconds. She pulled up the HR database and typed in: JENNIFER.

'That's not even my e-mail. The problem is when I—'

'Hmm,' she said, standing. 'I'm going to need to reload the operating system. I'll be back with a CD.'

'You didn't even look at my e-mail. You didn't see the problem!'

'I'll be two minutes,' Violet said, and left. She walked back to reception, forcing herself to keep looking straight ahead. She had one hand on the door when the receptionist said: 'Hey.'

She stopped.

'Why is your jacket inside out?'

'It was itching me,' Violet said. She pushed her way outside. Jennifer's address was burned into her brain.

Back at the apartment, she dumped the jacket and went into the kitchen. Her laptop was already set up on the bench. Now for the easy part. If Jennifer Government was overseas, her daughter might not be staying at home. But she'd be at school, and Violet could find out where. Some people took care to not let their personal details leak onto the net, but not Government people: they didn't believe in privacy. She sniffed for **JENNIFER + GOVERNMENT + KATE + NORTH MELBOURNE + SCHOOL** and got eight hundred hits.

Almost all were schools: class projects, promotional sites, class lists. She cut the list to two based on geography, then clicked on the first. It was titled, 'Mattel Primary School (North Melbourne, Australian Territories): Class 3A,' and offered a group photograph, class plans and achievements for the year, plus links to each kid's individual page. Violet didn't understand why schools still did this. It was like an invitation to pedophiles.

She scanned the list. There was a Kate Mattel (Starbucks–General Motors) and a Kate Mattel (Government). Violet clicked.

Kate had done a lot of work. There was a long story, a couple of scanned drawings, and a little animation of a running dog. Violet was impressed. At the bottom, Kate had written: 'I am Kate Mattel and I live in North Melbourne with my mom, Jennifer. She is a Government agent. I don't have any brothers or sisters. When I grow up I want to be a vet.'

Violet wrote down the school's address and shut down her notebook. She checked her watch. It might not be too late to get to Mattel Primary School before they finished for the day. She bit her fingernails, thinking.

She took her fingers out of her mouth and looked at them. The nails were broken and ragged. There was blood and torn skin under them. She leaned over and spat, but the taste wouldn't get out of her mouth. She didn't know why that courier girl had put up such a fight. Violet had only wanted her stupid jacket. People always had to make things difficult for Violet. They always had to screw her over.

She spat again and again. When she was done there was a sticky, red pool on the kitchen floor. Violet stared at it. Now she would have to clean that up.

69 BUY

Hack called Buy a few minutes before three. Hack was surprisingly trusting: Buy didn't have to use any of the cover stories he'd invented. 'Just turn up at the Chadstone Nike Town this Friday at six,' Hack said. 'You can help me with the cans.'

'Okay,' Buy said. 'Will do.' He hung up and looked at his notepad. *Nike Town.* He felt nauseous even looking at the words.

It would be better to get it over with. He checked the time and called John Nike in L.A., whose phone diverted to an assistant. 'John asked me to get some information for him,' Buy said, and recited the details. 'It's important. Please make sure he gets it.'

'I will do that, sir,' the assistant said. Buy hung up. Next he called Kato Mitsui. Kato was very pleased to hear from him.

'But this is most *wonderful*, Buy. You have done work of great quality. I will proceed to make contact with John Nike immediately! This is a path to happiness.'

'Well, I hope so,' Buy said.

'I foresee great things for you, my friend. I will be in touch.'

'Thanks,' he said. He put down the phone, feeling pleased. He hadn't had a workday this good since the incident.

He waited in his Jeep until children began streaming out of the gates. Kate ran over and climbed into the passenger seat. 'Hi there,' Buy said.

'Buy! Guess what happened in school today?'

'You learned about quadratic equations?' He pulled away from the curb. 'Or was it a new Barbie?'

'There *is* a new Barbie! How did you know that? But that's not the thing. They're having a Parent Day.'

'A what?'

'Your mom or dad talks to the class about what they do. It's next . . . week, I think. I have a note.'

'Hopefully your mom will be back by then. I'm sure she will.'

'Yeah,' Kate said. 'I hope so. If she's not, will you go?'

He looked at her, surprised. 'What?'

'You can . . . you know, go for me. Is that all right?'

'Of course,' Buy said. He felt his throat tighten. 'I would love to.'

They were sitting down to dinner when the phone rang. Kate leapt up; Buy winced. She had answered too many calls that weren't from Jennifer. 'Hurry back,' he told her. He spread a napkin on his lap and picked up his fork.

'Mommy!' Kate said. 'Mommy, Mommy!'

He started. Kate was in the kitchen, the phone pressed to her ear, her smile enormous. Relief drenched him. *Thank God*, Buy thought.

He put down his fork and listened to Kate talk about things people had said, movies she had seen, meals Buy had cooked. When she was done, she skipped into the dining room and handed him the phone. 'It's Mom!'

'Thank you,' he said. 'You are an excellent girl. Now eat your dinner.' He raised the phone. 'Hello?'

'Hiya.' Her voice was surprisingly clear; it was as if she were right next to him. 'How's my baby-sitter?'

He felt a big, stupid smile break across his face. 'I'm so pleased to hear from you. I was worried.'

'Oh, right, the shitfight in London. I just got into L.A.'

275

'L.A.? Why?'

'I'm arresting a perp tomorrow. Someone I've been after for a long time. Almost there, Buy. Then I'm coming home. How are you?'

'I'm . . .' he said, and realized the answer was: *happy*. 'Things are good. Everything is good.'

'How's work?'

'Interesting. Suddenly I'm working with bigwigs from all these different companies . . . I think I like it.'

'Great, Buy! That's really great.'

'Yeah,' he said. 'I can't wait to see you, though.'

'Yeah,' Jennifer said, and he got the impression there was someone else in the room with her. 'Ditto.'

'So you'll be home soon?'

'Before you know it.'

'Excellent,' he said. 'That is excellent.'

'I gotta go,' Jennifer said. He could hear her smiling. 'I'll talk to you soon, okay?'

'Okay. Miss you.'

'Same here,' she said. He put down the phone.

'That was Mommy!' Kate said.

'Yes,' Buy said. They were both grinning like idiots. 'It was.'

They were early the next morning, so Buy parked and walked Kate to the school gate. A notice was posted about the upcoming Parent Day, and Buy paused to read it. A young woman, a girl, really, stood by the gate. She smiled at him. Buy smiled back. 'Hi,' she said. 'Going to Parent Day?'

'Ah, yes, I think so.'

'Me, too.' Buy was surprised. She didn't look old enough to have a kid in school. 'I'm a veterinarian.'

'Oh!' Kate said. 'I want to be a vet!'

'No kidding!' the girl said. She squatted to Kate's level. 'How about that!'

'Do you give the animals special medicine?'

'I sure do. I make everything better.'

'Off you go, Kate,' Buy told her. 'Straight to class.'

'Aw,' Kate said. They watched her go.

'Cute,' the girl said. Her eyes were still on Kate. 'She's, what, seven?'

'Eight.'

'Such a great age,' the girl said. 'I wish we could all stay like that. So we wouldn't have to find out what assholes people are.'

'Uh . . . yeah,' Buy said.

'I used to think I was cynical about people. But then I realized you can't be too cynical. People will do anything to get ahead. They'll do terrible things.'

He looked at her. 'That is true.' He stuck out his hand. 'I'm Buy.'

She smiled. 'Violet.' They shook hands. 'I guess we have a bit in common.'

'I guess we do,' Buy said, and laughed.

70 JOHN

John woke to a dark hotel room. It was five A.M. and the phone was ringing. He fumbled for it in the darkness. If this was that asshole stockbroker from Australia again, John was going to kill him. 'John Nike.'

'Hello, John.'

'Who is this?'

'Don't be coy, John. You know who I am.'

No wonder it took him a few moments: the man sounded as if he were talking through a mouthful of gravel. But then, what had he expected? It was a miracle he was alive at all.

'John?' he said. 'Is that you, buddy?'

By the time he got to work, John was feeling pretty goddamn good, and there wasn't anything a woman in an ankle-length skirt and brown glasses could do about it. He walked deliberately fast, forcing her to hurry alongside him. As he crossed the lobby, he saw people's heads turning. *Look, it's John! There's John Nike!*

'If you'll just look at the report,' the Johnson & Johnson Liaison said. 'Please, John, look at it. Public opinion is against any aggressive move. Firmly against it.'

They reached the elevator. He pushed for up. 'That's because our advertising hasn't kicked in yet.'

'No, John, it's not. People don't want us to use military force against either the Government or our competitors. They say we must not attack.'

'Who said I was going to attack anybody?' John said, thinking: *The Pepsi kid!*

A young woman with long legs and a US Alliance nametag ran up and asked him to sign her arm. He did, flashing her a grin. Her face lit up with adoration. The woman with brown glasses followed him into the elevator. She was unstoppable.

'John, if you continue down this path, there will be resignations. Nobody wants this to turn into a military conflict.'

'You know what?' John said. The doors opened on his floor. 'It's too late. Let them resign. I have the NRA and I'm going to use it however I damn well see fit.'

'But—'

'All right,' he said. 'This is the part where I go into my office and you fuck off.' He closed the glass door. His P.A. handed him a sheaf of messages.

'I'll be taking this up with Alfonse!' the woman shouted. He could hardly hear her through the glass.

'Good morning, John,' the P.A. said.

'Yes,' he said. 'It is, isn't it?' He read the messages on his way to his desk. The top one was from someone called Buy Mitsui. John had a vague recollection of some junior executive calling to offer help, but that described about twenty people John had dealt with recently. Ever since his career-saving speech, every shiny-shoed Liaison in the Alliance had fallen over themselves to build favor with him.

He read the message. Suddenly he remembered: Buy was the asshole stockbroker. John had asked him to check out who was behind the McDonald's attack. He saw the words: HACK NIKE.

John roared with laughter. His P.A. glanced at him, then away. John laughed until his stomach hurt.

He made some calls to set wheels in motion – important wheels, very important wheels – before his appointment with General Li. Li was the first in a long line of daily meetings for John; after him was the Liaison from News Corporation. There had been a few articles in the newspapers lately that weren't as pro-NRA as John would have liked.

'Good morning.'

'Christ!' Li had a way of sneaking up on you. To the phone, he said: 'Be there at six.' He hung up. 'Good work on security, Li. How many guys do you have out there?'

'Out front? Fifteen.'

'The escort last night was terrific, too. Three cars, right?'

279

'Four. Plus a chopper.'

'I almost *want* the Government to try to arrest me.'

'I'm glad you're pleased,' Li said. 'Because there is another, less pleasant matter I must bring to your attention. I'm afraid you won't want to hear it.'

'Oh?'

'On your instructions, we attempted to acquire Billy NRA upon his arrival at LAX. Unfortunately, given the time pressure, we were unable to—'

'He got away.'

'Yes.'

'Did you plug any agents?'

Li blinked. 'Any Government – no.'

'Hmm,' he said. 'A pity. You're lucky, Li, I'm in a good mood today.'

'I'm pleased to hear that, sir.'

'And I've taken a few precautions of my own. You just keep the Government out of this building, and we'll stay friends.'

'Understood, sir.'

The intercom buzzed. 'John? You have an eleven o'clock to review some advertising?'

'I'm with Li. Tell them I can't make it.'

'Ah . . . you skipped the last one, remember? You said they approved the worst campaign you'd seen since AOL. You told me to never let you—'

'Right, right,' John said. 'Fine, I'll go.'

Li said, 'What about our military buildup? We haven't yet finalized our rules of engagement.'

He put his hands on Li's shoulders. 'You know what I want. You've got the firepower. Go nuts.'

'John, T.A. may be militarizing faster than we anticipated. If they move against us, I need to know if I'm authorized to—'

'Li,' John said. 'You're a smart guy. Use your own judgment. Okay?'

Li straightened. 'Understood, sir.'

'Good man.' John bounced out of the room. Everything was coming together.

71 JENNIFER

Max *had* done well for himself since Maher. The Synergy building was large and well-located, even close enough to the media companies to share the same restaurants. The lobby was large and modern. Jennifer said, 'Hi, I'm—'

'I know who you are,' the receptionist said, smiling.

'Oh,' she said.

Max was in the lobby and kissing her cheeks within a minute and a half. 'Barbie doll, it's super to see you again. I cannot tell you how happy I am you called.' His grin was huge. He held on to both her hands.

'Well, you can take the girl out of advertising . . .' she said, and they laughed. She got her hands back.

'The US Alliance briefing is at eleven. I don't want to pressure you, but it would be unbelievable if you could come along.'

'I'd love to.'

'You're fantastic,' he said. 'I could kiss you.'

'Let's not get carried away,' she said. They laughed again.

'Wait until our clients see you. They will *flip.*'

'They might,' Jennifer said.

'Our campaign plays up the local angle on US Alliance,' Max said in the cab. 'As you might have noticed. I don't like to brag, but US

Alliance has a higher share of subscribers in L.A. than any other major market.'

'Wow,' she said.

'I know,' he said. 'I know.'

'So who's going to be at this meeting?'

'A few US Alliance people, a couple of Liaisons.' The cab pulled over. The windows darkened with NRA bodies. 'The main guy is John Nike; you must have heard of him.'

The cab doors popped open. 'IDs,' a soldier said, and another said, 'Please spread your arms and legs.'

'Morning, fellas,' Max said. 'We have an eleven o'clock. We've been cleared.'

Jennifer's ID was fresh from printing; it said: JENNIFER SYN-ERGY. An NRA man eyed it and her with equal impassivity. Another soldier began patting her down, his hands fast and professional. 'Hey,' she said. 'Watch it.'

'Gun!' he shouted. Suddenly there were a lot of NRA rifles pointed at her. There had been far too many NRA rifles pointed at Jennifer lately.

'Hey, whoa!' Max said. 'Jen, US Alliance are very twitchy on security. Give them your gun.'

'Oh, sure. No problem.' She handed it over. The NRA guys didn't look happy, but they stopped aiming guns at her. Max took her arm as they entered the lobby.

'I should have mentioned that earlier,' Max said. 'I didn't know you carried a gun.'

'Doesn't everybody?'

'Not to business meetings, Malibu.' He laughed. 'You know?'

'Right,' she said. 'I guess I just forgot about it.'

*

An assistant escorted them to a meeting room and Max spent ten minutes fiddling with his laptop computer, trying to set up a slide show. Then US Alliance people began wandering in and Jennifer had to make conversation about audience hits and reach figures. It was surprisingly easy: almost everyone had heard of her, or at least her campaigns. She felt a little surreal. She felt as if she'd never left advertising.

'The '96 Pepsi, right!' a woman said, her eyes wide with awe. 'That was a totally groundbreaking campaign. I can't believe you did that!'

'Only the best talent for my clients,' Max said.

One of the suits was studying her silently. She knew what was coming before he opened his mouth. 'You must know John Nike, then. He worked at Maher around the same time.'

Everybody looked at her. 'John,' she said. 'Yeah, we worked together.'

'Wow, he'll just die when he sees you,' the woman said. She looked at her watch. 'He should be along any minute.'

'We can talk about old times,' she said. Everybody laughed except Max. Max was looking not so happy.

'Jennifer . . . could I get your assistance here a second?'

'Sure.'

He waited until she was hovering over the computer with him. 'I didn't realize that. I never worked with him. John Nike is John Maher?'

'Uh-huh.'

'But . . . but isn't John . . .'

'My ex?' she said. 'Yep. He is.'

'Okay,' a voice said from the doorway. 'Let's see how much money you clowns have managed to waste this week.'

She turned. He looked the same as nine years ago; she suspected he'd flirted with surgery. His eyes swept the room, then jerked back to her. His mouth dropped.

'Hi, honey,' she said.

PART SIX

72 DISINTEGRATION

Billy was starting to suspect that whatever Jennifer and Calvin were doing with him, it wasn't official. He'd had plenty of time to think about it, stuck in the hotel room, and the longer he sat there, the more convinced he was that it wasn't Government protocol to handcuff suspects to refrigerators.

Jennifer had left early that morning, dressed up in a suit and heels and looking very much unlike a Government agent. Billy had no idea what that was about. Calvin hung around until nine, then went out for a newspaper. 'Come on, dude,' Billy said. 'Please, not the mini bar. Take me with you.'

Calvin got out the handcuffs. 'Hands on the white goods.'

When he was gone, Billy kicked it in frustration. Then he made an interesting discovery: it wasn't fastened to anything. It was heavy, sure, but he managed to get to his feet and stagger around the hotel room with it. The bottles of liquor inside knocked and crashed against each other. He put the mini bar down and started to unload it, then changed his mind. He might want those later.

He arranged his jacket as best he could and checked himself in the mirror. He still looked like a man trying to hide a small refrigerator. Well, he would just have to do his best. Billy lurched out the door and toward the elevators.

Thinking carefully, he rode all the way to the car park. No way would he make it out through the lobby like this. He was congratulating himself on his ingenuity when he saw the driveway attendant. Billy stopped, unsure what to do. The attendant saw him. He picked up a walkie-talkie and spoke into it. Billy broke into a lumbering run.

Two hotel security guys caught him before he'd made half a block. Billy was drenched with sweat. His legs were like rubber. His breath was coming in great gasps. The security guys stared at him. One said, 'I thought George musta been kidding.'

'I've seen people steal a lot of stuff,' the other said. 'But this takes the cake.'

'I'm handcuffed to it,' Billy said. Then he realized he should just shut his mouth. They made him sit in the lobby and wait for Calvin to come back. Billy had a feeling that Calvin wasn't going to be happy with him. He was right about that, at least.

'You know,' Calvin said, 'being cuffed to the mini bar is a privilege. I could have left you in the bathroom.'

'I know,' Billy said. 'I'm sorry.'

'They're ejecting us from the hotel. Did you hear that?' Calvin sat on the bed and stared at him.

'I'm really sorry.'

'Now I'm going to have to take you with me.'

'Yeah? Where are we going?'

Calvin didn't say anything. Billy didn't take that as a good sign. He was starting to think he should have stayed in his room.

*

They caught a cab downtown and got out at a large, open shopping plaza. It was directly opposite a big US Alliance tower, and out front a lot of NRA soldiers with helmets and automatic weapons were hanging around. 'Uh, Calvin,' Billy said. 'This isn't such a good idea.'

'So stick close,' Calvin said. He led Billy to a plastic table surrounded by fast food joints, including a McDonald's on one side and a Burger King on the other. 'You want some lunch?'

'Yeah, sure. How about—'

'I can see you gentlemen are in need of some refreshment!' a man said. 'Would you like some coupons for McDonald's? Buy one, get one free!'

'Okay,' Billy said.

'Wait, wait a second,' someone else said. Billy saw a girl, also bristling with coupon books. 'You don't want to eat at McDonald's; they rape the environment, didn't you know? Here, have a coupon for Burger King.'

'Sure. Thanks.' He smiled at the girl.

'I don't want to spread rumors,' the man said, 'but I've seen that Burger King kitchen and it's filthy. I wouldn't want to eat there.'

'That's a crock of shit,' the girl said. 'At least Burger King doesn't have traces of *dog* in its quote-all-beef-patties-unquote.'

'That was *one* store! In New *York*!'

'Look, we've got your coupons,' Calvin said. 'Now go away, the both of you.'

The man and the girl left. 'Aw,' Billy said. 'She was cute.'

'I can't answer my phone at night without some telemarketer trying to sell me something,' Calvin said. 'Now I can't sit down to lunch?'

'They were just giving away coupons.'

'Fine,' Calvin said. 'So go get some McDonald's.'

Billy looked at the Burger King girl. She was handing a coupon to an elderly couple. She saw him and winked. 'How about BK?'

'I have a US Alliance card. I can get points from McDonald's.'

'Dude,' Billy said, 'I thought you Government people were trying to stop that shit.'

'All right, then!' Calvin said. 'Get Burger King!'

'Keep your pants on.' He held out his hand. Calvin dug into his pockets. 'So Jen was wearing some outfit this morning. I never knew she had such legs. What's she up to?'

'None of your business,' Calvin said, but he glanced at the US Alliance building and that told Billy plenty. 'Go get some food. I'll be watching you.'

Billy trotted over to the line for Burger King and waited. The coupon girl was circling the square. Billy hoped she saw him here.

'What's this?' a voice said. Five or six teenage boys were approaching the store, all baggy clothes and tattoos. 'What's the matter, you people don't know where you are? This is an Alliance town. We don't need no T.A. companies.'

Nobody spoke. Billy saw that their tattoos weren't ordinary designs: they were logos. He saw a lot of Nike swooshes and NRA designs. The leader had a US Alliance logo on his shaved head.

'Go on, get lost! Go spend your money on a good company, not these foreigners!'

'Hey, hey,' the coupon girl said. She walked up to the skinhead. 'Take it somewhere else, okay? Trying to earn a living here.'

'Earn it somewhere else, carpetbagger,' the kid said, and pushed her.

She stumbled into Billy. He caught and steadied her, which was pretty good luck for Billy, really. He lifted his head to tell the skin-head something appropriate (*You wanna push somebody, push me;* something like that), but the kid was already in his face.

'You got something to say to me, dickhead?' the kid said. The other punks were gathering around. Customers quietly left the line. 'You better be opening your mouth to tell me you're a UA man.'

'Just keep your hands off her.'

'Which is it? Who you with, man, Mickey Dees or BKs? It's gotta be one or the other, who you with?'

'I'm just buying some burgers,' Billy said. 'Come on, man, you don't need to—'

'US Alliance sucks dick!' the coupon girl said, and everything fell apart from there.

73 VANTAGE

Violet walked away from the school gate until Buy had driven away. Then she turned and walked back. Kate was already a long way up the path, about to enter a building. 'Hey! Kate!' Violet shouted. But Kate didn't turn. 'Shit,' Violet said.

She entered the school. The other children looked at her curiously. She smiled back at them.

The guard caught her as she stepped into the building. 'Ma'am? I'm going to have to ask you to leave the school grounds.'

'Oh,' Violet said, startled. 'Hi. I'm just—' She craned her neck. She could see Kate through the glass of one of the classrooms. 'My daughter forgot her lunch money.'

'I'm sorry, ma'am, you can't be on these grounds.'

'But she's right there. I'll just give her the money and go.' The guard was much taller than her. She smiled and tried to look harmless.

'Well, be quick now,' the guard said, and Violet hurried past him.

In the classroom, Kate was unpacking her bag, alone. She looked up as Violet entered.

'Hi, Kate.'

'Hi.'

'I need you to come with me now. It's very important. Okay?'

'Where?'

'To . . . the vet hospital. You want to come help some sick animals with me?'

'Um,' Kate said. 'No thanks.'

'Sure you do,' Violet said. 'You like vets, right? So let's go.'

'I want to stay here.'

'Yeah, well,' she said. 'You're coming.' She put her hand on Kate's arm.

'Let go of me!'

Violet tugged her. Kate screamed. Violet tried to cover her mouth. Kate bit her fingers. '*Owww!*' Violet yelled. She snatched back her hand and slapped Kate across the face. Kate fell out of the desk and started crawling across the floor. Violet snared her ankles and pulled her back. 'Come here!'

She heard the door open: the guard. 'What's going on?'

'She's – having a seizure!' Violet said. 'Help, quick!'

The guard kneeled beside her. Kate was twisting and shrieking like a wild cat. 'Why is she bleeding?' the guard said, and Violet pulled out her gun – well, John's gun, really – and pressed it to his head.

'Okay,' she said. 'Now you lie down and don't move for a while.' She looked at Kate. 'Are you ready to be a good girl for me?'

Kate nodded. Her teeth were chattering. That was weird. It was about eighty degrees in here.

'Good. Because if you try to run, I'll have to hurt you. Okay?'

Kate whimpered.

'I'll take that as a yes,' Violet said. She pulled Kate out of the classroom. The guard didn't make a sound. Violet felt relieved. That was the hard part done. Now she just had to collect her money. She had a good feeling about this.

*

They caught a cab back to Violet's apartment and she led Kate into the kitchen. 'You hungry? You want something to eat?' The phone was ringing; she picked it up. 'Hello?'

'Is that Violet?'

'John!' she said, pleased. 'I was just going to call you.'

'Do you have Kate?'

'I do! Want to talk to her?'

'I – no, that's not necessary.'

'Okay,' Violet said.

'You'll be pleased to know I've kept my end of the deal. I have your money.'

Her heart leapt. 'Already? How? What did you do to Holly?'

'I was very persuasive,' John said. Violet's heart thrilled. She wanted details; she wanted to hear all about it. 'Got a pen and paper? I'm going to tell you where to make the swap.'

She wrote down the address. 'A Nike Town store?'

'It's nice and public. Makes sure there won't be any funny business.'

'Oh, okay. Good idea.'

'Christ!' John said, but she thought he might be talking to someone else. 'Be there at six.'

The phone clicked. Violet put down the handset, exalted. She had done it! She felt dazzled by her victory. She thought about Holly T.A. in the limousine, telling her *You've got a lot to learn about how the world works.* Well, that just showed how much Holly knew. People were always underestimating Violet. She reached for the phone. She was going to gloat a little.

Holly would be in New York, of course. Violet got the T.A. number from directory assistance. She didn't know what time it was there, but someone answered the phone and switched her through to someone else. 'Holly T.A.'s office, can I help you?'

'It's Violet ExxonMobil. I want to speak to Holly.'

'Just a second, ma'am.'

Violet waited, trembling. This was so exciting!

'I'm afraid Holly isn't available. I can take a message, if you like.'

She blinked. 'Did you tell her it was me?'

'Ah, I'm afraid Holly doesn't recall you, ma'am.'

'*What?*'

'Ms. Holly deals with many people, ma'am. Please don't be offended—'

'You get that bitch on the phone,' Violet said. 'I sat next to her at the London conference. I just got three million dollars out of her, you get her on the phone!'

'Please stay calm, ma'am.'

'I am calm!' she shouted. 'For me, this is very fucking calm!'

'I'll . . . just a second, please.'

There was a click, then Violet was listening to muzak. Holly must be pretending, surely. She must be too stung to talk.

The phone clicked again. 'Okay,' Holly said. 'What's up?'

'Ha,' Violet said. 'It's me.'

'Yes, yes, Violet of the three-million-dollar invoice. What about it?'

This wasn't going how she expected. 'I got it. I got paid.'

'Did you now?' Holly said. 'Well, good for you.'

Violet opened her mouth to say: *I got it from you.* But that wasn't true, was it? Holly wasn't playing with her. Holly hadn't been approached by John Nike at all. Violet put down the phone.

Kate was still sniffling. She kept looking at Violet, then away.

'Something fishy is going on,' Violet said slowly. 'Someone's trying to screw me.'

Maybe John was going to pay her three million out of his own pocket. That was possible. But it was also possible he was planning a nasty surprise for her at the Nike Town. That was very possible.

She checked her pocket. She still had the gun. 'Funny business,' Violet muttered; there would be some funny business, all right. She took hold of Kate's arm. It was time to go shopping.

74 ASSAULT

Hack hadn't been to the Chadstone Wal-Mart mall for years, and it seemed to have grown in his absence, sprouting additional shops and food courts. The parking lot was jammed, and the bus took a long time to fight its way through. He looked at his watch, impatient. Claire would be waiting.

The bus wheezed to a halt and Hack disembarked into a mass of people, shouting and pushing and clutching bags of merchandise. Hack hadn't seen anything like it since the January sales.

He forged his way to the mall's entrance and found a map, which said Nike Town was on level four. Hack walked to the escalators, past a raffle for a BMW convertible, and rode up. His bag was much heavier than it had been for McDonald's. He took the opportunity to rest it a second.

Claire was outside the Borders store, wearing Jackie O sunglasses. She smiled when she saw him. Hack touched her hands. 'How are you?'

'Last one, Hack.'

'Yes,' he said. 'Last one.' They entered the store.

Rows of carefully lit shoes adorned the walls. There was a row of chairs in the center, rock music pumping out of the speakers, and a counter at the back. Hack put his bag down on one of the seats and began unzipping it.

'Can I help you?' a clerk said.

'Yes,' Claire said. She pulled a pistol from her coat and pointed it at him. They had planned fake guns, but it turned out to be easier to get real ones and not load them. 'You can run.'

'Everybody out of the store!' Hack shouted. 'Nike's going down, you don't want to be here!' He pulled a paint tin from his bag and pried off the lid with a screwdriver. The smell was awful.

'Nike kills children!' Claire said. Hack had written her speech; he was pretty pleased with it. 'They pay substandard wages in non-USA countries and sell shoes at inflated prices! One of their factories in China burned down and killed fifty-eight workers! They make huge profits but screw over their own employees in perform-ance evaluations! Their Mercurys campaign killed fourteen children, including one girl right here in this store!'

But the customers just stood there, like at the McDonald's. People were stupid, Hack realized. You couldn't make anything too simple for them.

So he heaved. His tins were filled with blood and offal, courtesy of a visit to a butcher's this morning. The mess burst against the wall. It was almost too authentic. The light bulb above a pair of sneakers blew, spraying sparks.

'People before profits!' Hack shouted. The clerk had split, but customers were still standing around. 'What's the matter with you people?'

'Is this, like, a promotion?' a kid said.

'No!' Hack said. 'It's a protest! Nike is a murderer!' He grabbed another tin from his bag, but it slipped out of his hands and hit the floor. The lid popped off. Offal spattered his pants. 'Aw, crap!'

'Are you gonna be giving away shoes?'

'It must be a new product line,' another kid said. His eyes widened. 'Is it, like, "Nike Murderers"? Is that it?'

'Oh, that would be so cool,' the other kid said.

'No!' Hack said, outraged. 'This isn't a promotion!'

'Throw some more blood, dude,' the kid said.

'Am I wearing a Nike sweatsuit?' Hack demanded. 'Do you see any logos on me?'

'Hey, he's right, man,' the other kid said. 'He ain't wearing logos.' They looked at Hack nervously.

'Out!' Hack yelled, and they ran. One grabbed a pair of sneakers on his way out. Hack felt disgusted before remembering he was planning to do that himself.

'Let me help you with those tins,' Claire said. 'Let's get this done and get out.'

'Okay,' he said. Their hands touched as they reached for the same can of blood. They smiled at each other.

'Hey,' someone said. 'What's going on?'

'Jesus,' Hack breathed. Some people were really slow learners. He turned. But it wasn't one of the kids. '*Violet?*'

'Hack! What are you doing here?'

'I'm—' She was leading a kid by the arm, a girl of about eight or nine. 'What are *you* doing?'

'Are you doing the swap?'

'Swap? Violet, if you're following me around—'

'Hold it,' she said. 'Are you John Nike's contact or not?'

Hack opened his mouth to reply. A man entered the store behind Violet. His face was distorted, like a melted wax sculpture. A line of thick black stitches marched from one ear to the middle of his forehead. His hair was gone. But Hack recognized him anyway.

'No,' the John said. 'I am.'

75 THREAT

'Gark,' John Nike said, or something similar.

'Hey, now,' Jennifer said. 'You don't seem pleased to see me at all.'

He turned and fled. She took off after him. Max Synergy and the US Alliance suits just stood there. This, she discovered, was a common thread to the next four and a half minutes: office workers standing around gaping while she and John zipped past them. John was screaming for the NRA or security or anyone with a gun, *please*, but there was not a lot of action from the suits and skirts at US Alliance. Companies claimed to be highly responsive, Jennifer thought, but you only had to chase a screaming man through their offices to realize it wasn't true.

John tried to catch an elevator, but she was closing on him so he ran up the stairs instead. He gained a little ground by pushing a woman with a stack of files into her path, but only a little, and the more floors they climbed, the more her regular gym workouts and John's regular big lunches became evident. He was gasping and wheezing at the twenty-ninth and her fingers closed on his jacket. He wriggled free and burst out of the stairwell. She followed and found herself in an enormous board room. Two walls were glass. The view over L.A. was incredible. John was flat against a pane as if he were trying to squeeze through it. It was, she realized, a lot like the room in which she'd told John about her pregnancy, eight years ago, when they'd both worked for Maher. She hoped he noticed the symmetry.

'Get away from me! You stay back!'

'Sorry, chum,' she said. 'Can't do that.'

'*Where's the fucking NRA?*' he screamed, and that she couldn't answer. 'Wait. Wait a second!'

'Uh-uh.'

'Stop! Or Kate will regret it!'

Jennifer stopped. 'What?'

'Talked to your daughter recently?'

'John,' she said. 'You don't want to give me any extra reasons to be pissed at you. You really don't.'

'You'd better call home. Your daughter's been missing since this morning.'

'You lying piece of shit.' Her voice trembled. 'How dare you say something like that?'

'You think I'm kidding?' He sprayed spittle. 'You think I'd wait for you to come for me without taking steps to protect myself? You think I'd believe you'd *give up*? You think I'd be *unprepared*?'

She hesitated.

He saw, and his eyes brightened. 'You know me, Jen. Am I the sort of guy to take half-measures?' There was a phone on the counter. 'Go on, call home. Find out for yourself.'

She took a deep, steadying breath. 'If you're lying, I'm going to beat the shit out of you.'

'Do I look worried?'

She walked over to the phone and dialed Buy's cellphone. 'And if you're not lying, I'm going to kill you.'

His smile flickered.

It only rang once. She heard Buy's voice. It was anxious and strained. 'H – hello?'

'It's me.'

'Oh Jen. Jen. I'm so sorry.'

She put down the handset.

'So,' John said. 'Now we understand each other.'

She started walking toward him.

'Ah-ah! Not a good idea, Jen. Not smart. You want to hold it right there.'

Jennifer stopped. Her hands were shaking. 'She is your *daughter.*'

'Oh, please,' John said. 'I made this very goddamn clear eight years ago. I never wanted a kid. *You* wanted it, and I couldn't stop you. I couldn't do a goddamn thing to stop you. So, fine, you had a kid. But don't think you can turn me into a *father.*'

The elevator dinged behind her.

'At last!' John said. 'What took you assholes so long?'

She felt rough hands seize her arms. 'Sorry, sir! There's a disturbance out front. We responded as soon as—'

'Not good enough. I'll be speaking to Li.'

'Sir, what would you like us to do with . . . ?'

'Take her somewhere,' John said, 'and shoot her in the head.'

The soldier said nothing.

'You have a problem with that?'

'Sir, I'm not sure you can authorize me to do that.'

'I fucking can!' John shouted. 'Don't make me take this to Li!'

'Yes, sir,' the soldier said. Jennifer could barely see him. She was starting to cry. She let herself be dragged.

The two NRA soldiers took her down the stairwell. She felt as if she were shaking apart. She wanted to catch the first flight back to Melbourne, and hunt down John and kill him, both at once. But she couldn't do both. She couldn't do either.

Halfway down, one of the soldier's radios said something, and he spoke into it. Then he looked at his companion. 'They want us out front. It's getting worse.'

'What about her?'

'I dunno.'

Nobody said anything for a moment. Jennifer waited for them to decide whether they were going to kill her.

'I mean, if they want us out front, that's an NRA order. That takes precedence over what Nike wants.'

'Does it?'

'Shit, I dunno,' the soldier said. 'But I'll tell you right now, I don't want to shoot this woman in the head. That's just wrong.'

Suddenly, Jennifer's cellphone rang. Her nerves were so frayed that she jumped.

'What's that?'

'It's my phone,' she said.

'Uh . . . well, you get that,' the soldier said. 'We need to discuss this situation.'

She answered her phone. It was Buy. She could hear the pain in his voice. They spoke briefly but usefully. Then Buy had to go. She closed her phone and looked at the soldiers.

'Okay,' the first one said. 'We're going to reinforce the front entrance. You're coming with us. Then what you do is up to you.'

'Thank you,' she said. Her voice broke.

'Don't thank us yet,' he said. 'You don't know what's going on out there.'

76 DIVESTITURE

Buy left Mitsui late, but the traffic was light and he arrived at Mattel Primary School on time. Normally he had to double-park or leave his car around the block, but today the street was almost empty. That was weird: children should have been dribbling out the gates, parents jamming the street. He got out and walked down the school path.

In the administration building, six people were conferring on the other side of the counter. He saw Government IDs. 'Help you?' a woman said.

'I'm here to pick up Kate,' Buy said. 'What's going on?'

The woman's hand rose to her mouth. Suddenly everybody was looking at him.

'What?' Buy said.

'Sir,' an agent said. 'Would you like to take a seat?'

'Where's Kate?'

'Our security didn't slip up,' the woman said. 'I want you to know that. A guard did try to stop her. There's nothing wrong with our security.'

'Stop who?' Buy said, but he already knew: the answer was thickening in the air.

'Sir, there's been a kidnapping.'

'But . . . who was kidnapped?' Then a loud rushing sound filled his head and fluorescent lights like blurry comets passed through his field of vision.

They made him coffee, but his hands wouldn't stop trembling. The agents spoke on their phones and asked him questions. With each one, Buy felt himself forced into a new reality, where Kate was missing and it was all his fault.

'You're already under investigation,' one of the agents told him, covering his cellphone. 'The Nike Town shootings? You were interviewed by Field Agents Jennifer and Calvin.'

'I . . . was at the mall that night,' Buy said. 'That's all. I tried to help the girl who was shot. Hayley McDonald's.'

The agents exchanged a glance. 'She was a relation of yours? A friend?'

'I just tried to help her. Why is this important?'

'Now another girl you're associated with is missing,' an agent said.

'So . . . what?'

'Sir, can you tell us your movements this morning?'

'I dropped Kate, I drove to work.'

'Is there anyone who can confirm you left the school grounds?'

'But why – you think *I* took her?'

'Settle down, Mr. Mitsui,' an agent said. 'Is there anyone who can confirm you left the school grounds?'

'I – yes! I spoke to another parent, she would have seen me leave. Her name was . . . Violet. I didn't get her surname, but she works as a veterinarian.'

'Can you describe this woman for me?'

'Young, short brown hair . . . she was wearing a green parka.'

The agents exchanged a glance. 'Sir, that fits the description of the kidnapper.'

'What? How is that—'

'We're going to need you to accompany us to the station.'

'No,' he said, rising. 'I have to look for her!'

'Sit down. Now.' Everyone was looking at him.

'You must have been pretty angry with the Government after they let that girl die at Chadstone,' the other agent said. 'Maybe you thought you'd get even by snatching a Government kid.'

'No!'

'But you admit you had prior contact with the kidnapper.'

His cellphone rang. Everyone stopped.

'Answer it,' an agent said. 'Maybe it's your little friend.'

Buy pulled it free. The display was no number he recognized. 'Hello?'

'It's me,' Jennifer said.

'Oh Jen.' He didn't know what to say. 'Jen, I'm so sorry.' He heard his voice break.

'Is that Jen Government?' the agent said. 'Give me that.' He took the phone out of Buy's hands. 'Hello? Hello?' He looked at Buy accusingly. 'There's no one here.'

'She was – you must have pushed something.'

'I didn't push anything.'

'Call that number back,' the other agent said.

'Good idea.' The agent pushed buttons. Then his expression changed. He handed the phone back to Buy.

'What?' Buy said. He put it to his ear. 'Jennifer?'

The phone said: 'Sir? US Alliance switchboard, can I help you?'

'But – that makes no sense.'

'Jennifer Government, my ass,' the agent said. He detached his cuffs and reached for Buy's wrists. 'Don't make this difficult.'

Buy made no conscious decision to run: it just happened. He turned and took three steps and only then did he realize: *I am fleeing the Government*. The office door was mostly glass and *then* he made a decision: Buy had had an accident with his younger sister when they were kids, so he knew how this worked. He flung the door closed behind him and heard an agent go through it. By the time they were clearing the school grounds, Buy was inside his Jeep.

'Stop!' they shouted. Buy saw guns. He didn't think Government agents were allowed to shoot him just to stop him fleeing, but they looked pretty pissed off so he floored the accelerator and swung out into traffic. Then there were horns and screaming tires. A sedan passed by his door so closely he couldn't believe they didn't collide. Then he was roaring away from Kate's school.

He found a leafy side street and parked. He had Jennifer's cellphone number. It rang forever. Then she picked up. 'It's me.'

'How did this happen?' Her voice broke his heart. She sounded destroyed.

'I don't know. I'm sorry, I just . . . don't know.'

'Listen to me. It all depends on you now. I can't touch John Nike while he has Kate. I need you now.'

'Wait,' he said. 'John Nike?'

'John Nike is the criminal I'm chasing. But that's not important. What's important is—'

'No,' he croaked. 'I . . . I'm working for John.'

'What?'

'He's – a Liaison in US Alliance. And . . . I'm an assistant Liaison.'

'Oh, shit,' she said. 'Oh, shit, what have you done for him?'

'He asked me to find some people in Melbourne. Some protestors.'

'Who?'

'Um . . . Hack Nike . . . a girl, I think her name—'

'Hack, yes! It's him!'

'I saw the kidnapper. It was a girl. Violet.'

'That's Hack's girlfriend! I can find out where Hack lives—'

'No, that's okay.' He felt light-headed. He felt sick. 'I know where Hack is.'

77 EMANCIPATION

'Hey, wow,' Violet said. 'You're okay, I'm so pleased.'

'You left me on your kitchen floor,' John said. There was some kind of emotion on his face, but it was hard for Violet to tell what it was. 'You left me looking like *this.*'

'You look great to me, I don't know what you're talking about,' Violet said. She backed away, dragging Kate, until her heels hit the wall.

John reached out and wrapped a hand around her neck. It was becoming clear to Violet that John was not here to deliver her three million dollars. 'Payback's a bitch, isn't it?'

'Hey!' Claire said. Claire had herself a gun, Violet saw, and was pointing it at John. She had never felt so relieved. Although this didn't seem like the Claire she knew. Everyone had been changing in Violet's absence. 'That's enough!'

'Shoot him!' Violet said. 'Do it, Claire!'

John's eyes didn't leave Violet. 'Why don't you take a hike?'

'All right,' Hack said. He took Claire's hand.

'Not you, asshole,' John said. 'You I have business with.'

'We are leaving this store,' Claire said. Her voice shook; so did the gun in her hand. 'And Violet's coming with us.'

John said, 'Little lady, you've got a lot—'

For the first time, his eyes flicked away. Violet took the opportunity to plant her right knee in his nuts. John dropped to the ground as if she'd shot him.

'Ha! Take that!' She went to kick him and he grabbed at her pants. Violet screamed: it was just like back at the apartment. She flailed and tore at him. John's grip gave way and she was free, running toward Hack. She was leaving Kate behind, but that was too bad: Kate was no longer Violet's top concern. There was a door at the rear marked STAFF ONLY and she yanked it open. 'Hack, come on!'

Hack ran, pulling Claire with him. Violet slammed the door as soon as they were through it. It was pitch black inside. She groped for something resembling a door lock.

'What's going on?' Hack said.

'Hold the door handle.'

'What?'

'Hold the door handle, I can't find the lock!'

'Oh, shit,' Hack said, and John hit the door from the other side. Someone screamed, and it might have been her. 'Where's the lock?'

'I don't know, I can't see!'

The door rattled. 'I'm losing it, I'm losing it, find the lock!'

'Lock the fucking door!' Claire shouted.

306

Violet found a bolt and slid it across. John hit the door again. She sagged in relief.

'You did it.' Hack's voice sounded warm. 'Thank God.'

'Yeah,' she said. She suddenly thought: was Hack hitting on her? Yes, she thought, he was. Hack had dallied with Claire, with shy, quiet Claire, but Claire wasn't enough for him. Hack needed someone like Violet, who could take charge of him. She'd told him that a thousand times. 'Isn't it funny, how we should meet again? It's like fate.'

'Where's the light switch?' Claire said.

'Uh,' Hack said. 'I guess, yeah.'

She found his arm in the darkness and squeezed. 'We should go somewhere and catch up.'

The light flicked on. Claire was standing next to a switch. The room was filled with shelves and boxes.

'Hey,' Violet said. 'Well done, beanpole.'

'Violet?' John said through the door. 'Can you hear me? I think we got all mixed up. I'm here to do the trade. I've got your money. I'll leave it on the desk, all right?'

She bit her lip. 'I wonder if he really has my money.'

Hack said, 'Violet, this guy's not here to do you any favors.'

'Hmm,' she said. 'You're right. Let's get out of here.' There was an exit at the rear, leading to a dark stairwell.

Halfway down, Hack said, 'Violet?'

'Yeah?'

'Who was that little girl with you?'

'Oh!' she said. 'No one.'

They exited on the ground floor, between a Disney store and a Starbucks. The mall was so packed with shoppers that the air felt hot and humid. It was hard to breathe. Violet's mind was racing.

This was some good luck, reuniting with Hack. She wanted to capitalize on it. 'Let's go back up.' She tugged her gun from her pocket. 'Let's get John.'

'Uh,' Hack said, 'Violet, I think we should just get out of here.'

'I should have shot him through the door,' she said. She felt like an idiot. 'Why didn't I shoot him through the door?'

Hack and Claire were staring at her.

'What?'

'Are you *nuts*?'

'Hey,' Violet said, stung. 'You don't know what I've been through. I'm just trying to get what's mine. If I have to shoot someone, I'll do it.' But Hack was looking at her as if he'd never seen her before. Claire was standing there, letting it all happen, and Violet realized she'd gone too far. She decided to tear up. 'Hack . . . it's been so hard.' She clutched at his shirt. 'I only wanted to get ahead, but everyone kept screwing me. I'm sorry I hurt people. Forgive me?'

'Don't touch me! You need help! Seriously!'

'Why, you little shit,' she started, but that was as far as she got. There was a man in the crowd, and his eyes were locked onto hers. He looked familiar. When his face darkened and he began to move toward her, she remembered. She'd met him this morning, at Kate's school. His name was Buy. 'Oh-oh,' she said.

78 HUBRIS

When the NRA took Jennifer away, John sank to the carpet. He closed his eyes and pressed his face against the glass. Then he started laughing. At first it was a snigger, then it ballooned out of control. He screamed with laughter. He felt tears streaming down his face.

The funny thing was Jennifer's face. She'd thought she had him. She'd thought she was about to exact righteous vengeance. Then, BAM! He had her. It was classic. It was why people like John got ahead in life and people like Jennifer took Government jobs.

He stayed there for too long. Then the glass against his cheek trembled. He sat up, startled. The entire building vibrated. Then it stopped. John waited. There was a booming, rolling *crump*. The building shook again, harder.

John bit his lip. He had a feeling that he knew what that might have been. That might have been General Li using his own judgment.

The elevator doors dinged. 'John?' He turned. It was the Pepsi kid, looking somber. 'John, you need to come with me. It's important.'

'Did you just feel that?'

'Come on. This is serious.'

'Are we being attacked? Is it Team Advantage? I need to see General Li.'

They entered the elevator. 'That's where I'm taking you.'

'You're a good kid,' John said. 'You've stuck with me from the beginning. I won't forget that.'

'Yeah, thanks,' the kid said. 'You have, what, some kind of disturbance up here?'

'A domestic dispute.' He grinned. Then he saw where the elevator was headed. 'Where are we going? That's Alfonse's floor.'

'That's where Li is.'

'Wait,' John said, panicked. 'What's going on? What did—'

The doors opened. The area was packed with Liaisons. Heads turned. Conversation died. Alfonse was standing in the middle of the room. General Li was with him, his beret in his hands.

'What the hell?' John said.

'John,' Alfonse said. 'Are you aware of what's going on outside?'

'What's happening?'

Alfonse looked at Li.

Li said, 'John explicitly authorized me to use any and all resources at my disposal to respond to enemy assaults.'

'What the fuck is *happening*?'

'You have done precisely what I forbade you to do,' Alfonse said. 'You have involved us in further military action. This must end. Immediately. It is not a profitable environment for business.'

'Okay, wait.' This was going to require another speech, John realized. 'Yes, okay, a few people will get killed. Change is always messy. But let me be clear, we are going to be the winners in this new world. Without the Government, we can eliminate Team Advantage. Without Team Advantage, we have no competition. That's worth a little conflict. This is all just aggressive competition within a free market.' He looked around. There didn't seem to be many nodding heads.

'This isn't freedom, John. It's anarchy.'

'Well,' John said, 'if you're going to split hairs—'

'There has been a vote.'

He froze. 'Excuse me?'

'The member companies have decided that an unregulated market does not serve our interests. We have already begun a dialog with the Government.'

'Who? Which companies? Because, fine, let them go. We don't need those pussies.'

'Most of them.'

'Oh.' He swallowed. 'I see.'

Alfonse said, 'We will, of course, be disavowing any responsibility for damage caused by your actions.'

'Of course.' He could feel the hysteria rising in his throat. 'Sure, go ahead, paint *me* as the bad guy.'

'Security will escort you out of the building.'

'I have a right to be here! I'm the Nike Liaison!'

'No, John, you're not.'

He turned. Gregory Nike was against the wall. John hadn't seen him. 'Well,' John said. 'Isn't this sweet.' He turned to the Liaisons. 'Who's with me? Who wants to keep up the fight? We can start our own loyalty program! We can finish what we started! *Who's with me?*' Suddenly a lot of Liaisons were frowning at the floor and studying the paintings. 'You cheap fucks,' he said.

An NRA soldier took his arm. It was one of the same guys who had thrown Jennifer out; of course it was. 'Let's go.'

'Li! Don't let them do this!' But Li said nothing. Li knew where his budget was coming from. The soldier began pushing him toward the elevator. As they reached the stairwell, John caught sight of the Pepsi kid. 'And *you!*' John clung to the door frame. The soldier tugged at his arms. 'You little shit! You always were a spine-less parasite, you Pepsi asshole!'

'Don't make this difficult,' the soldier said. John lost his grip on the frame. The door banged shut. Then it opened. The Pepsi kid appeared at the top of the stairs.

'Hey, John,' he said. 'My name is Theo.'

'What?'

'My name is Theodore.'

'What makes you think I give a shit?'

'No reason,' the kid said. Then the soldier dragged John down another flight of stairs and he lost sight of him.

'Okay, wait, wait,' he said. 'You don't need to take me straight out. At least let me get some things from my office. Let me make a couple of calls.'

'My orders are clear, sir.'

'That Government agent – you shot her, right? She's not still around, is she?'

The soldier glanced at him. 'It was decided to eject her from the building.'

'You *asshole*! You talk about orders, what about my goddamn orders?' The soldier said nothing. 'Okay, wait. I'm sorry. You're just trying to do your job. I appreciate that. But you don't have to take me out the front door. Let me leave through the parking lot.'

'I'm taking you out the front door.'

'I'm very close friends with General Li! Very close! You don't want to piss me off!'

'I'll take that risk, sir.'

'I have two hundred dollars,' John said. 'Right here in my pocket. Go on, take it.' They entered the lobby: the glass revolving doors loomed. He tried to dig in his heels, but his business shoes slipped on the polished floor.

'Please, sir,' the soldier said. The lobby doors slid apart, and then there was sunshine, and people. 'You're demeaning not only yourself, but the entire US Alliance organization.'

'Oh, shut the fuck up,' John said.

79 LOSS

The NRA soldiers marched Jennifer out onto the street. She was so numb from the news of Kate's kidnapping that at first she didn't realize what was happening around her. Then the NRA soldier nudged her and said, 'Ma'am? You should go now.'

She looked up and shook her head, trying to clear it. She felt slow and stupid. She felt beaten.

'Ma'am? Please.'

'Right,' she said. There was a mall across the road, with a McDonald's on one side and a Burger King on the other. In between the two was a riot. A bunch of kids in baggy clothes were looting the Burger King: pulling down posters, smashing cash registers. She caught a glimpse of Calvin trying to separate a fight, then lost him.

She stepped onto the road. A horn blared somewhere, but by the time she realized she should turn her head, it had stopped and the driver was yelling at her. Jennifer kept walking. When she reached the other side, two black vans jumped the curb and flung open their doors. Police officers spilled out, jostling past her. They ran toward the rioters.

'*Jen!*'

She saw Calvin again and tried to head for him. Calvin would help her.

'Move away from the store!' one of the Police shouted, and then somebody fired a gun, either the looters or the Police, either the US Alliance people or the Team Advantage people; she didn't know which and it didn't matter anyway. A lot of people hit the deck, which made it easier for her to spot Calvin. She wound her way toward him between red and yellow plastic tables and chairs.

'For fuck's sake,' Calvin said when she reached him. 'Get your ass down!' He pulled her into the doorway of a stationery store. It had a sign on the door which said PROUDLY INDEPENDENT, and another below that that said GOING OUT OF BUSINESS SALE! 'What's the matter with you?'

'He took Kate.'

'What?'

There was another, longer rattle of gunfire. The Police had formed a cordon around the Burger King. The looters were retreating to the McDonald's. NRA soldiers were reinforcing them, taking positions behind the counter and cash registers. There was a lot of shouting going on. Then someone fired again, and a bullet ricocheted off a Burger King cash register with a *clang*.

'Kate,' she said. 'He took my daughter.'

Calvin stared. 'Kate's here?'

She shook her head. 'In Melbourne. He says he'll kill her unless I let him go.'

'Oh, Jen.'

'Calvin, I don't know what to do.'

'Okay,' he said. 'It's okay, Jen, we – we'll arrest him. We'll make him let her go. We can——' His words were lost in one of the loudest sounds Jennifer had ever heard. The Police had mounted a machine gun on the Burger King counter and it was chewing up the McDonald's store. Shreds of red and yellow plastic spiraled into the air like confetti.

'I'm going back in.'

'Jen, you can't! Get down! We'll work something out!'

'I should have shot him,' she said. 'When I had the chance.'

'Jen, wait! Did you see Billy?'

'What? Billy's here?'

'I had to bring him. Then I lost him. For Christ's sake, get *down*!'

'I have to go,' she said, and stood.

She'd taken ten steps when she heard it: a spitting sound, like air hissing out of a tire. She noticed a puff of white smoke at the top of the US Alliance tower, like the world's smallest cloud. Then something sleek and metallic drew a white line from the cloud to the Burger King and an invisible fist hit Jennifer in the chest and she was deaf.

She wasn't sure if she passed out. She became aware that Calvin was above her, shouting. She read *missile* from his lips. The Burger King was on fire. Everything was drenched in black smoke. She looked around. She could barely see the base of the US Alliance building. She could barely see the glass lobby doors open. She could barely see John Nike come out of them.

'Calvin?' she said. 'Can I have your gun, please?'

314

His lips said: *What?*

'Just—' she said, and through the smoke John saw her.

She tore Calvin's gun from his holster and started running. She leapt over bits of ex–Burger King and dodged stunned Police officers. The smoke curled and drifted, hiding John from view and revealing him again.

John stepped onto the road and held up his hands. She thought he was surrendering. *Too late for that,* she thought. Then she saw the cab. John flung open the door and jumped inside. He must have said something highly motivational, because the cab took off, its tires smoking. She was too far away to stop it. She was much too far.

'No!' she screamed. '*No! No!*' Then she just screamed.

80 RECIPROCITY

Billy and the coupon girl were cowering in a doorway a few shops down from the McDonald's. This wasn't so bad, since he got to snuggle right up close to her, but there were also a lot of bullets flying around. Billy wasn't so comfortable with that.

'This kind of shit never happens in Colorado,' the coupon girl said. '*Never.*'

'It doesn't happen so often in Texas, either.' There were about thirty feet between them and the road, with the US Alliance building rising beyond that. Billy weighed their chances of making that distance without intercepting a bullet. So far he wasn't confident. The Police were strafing this whole side of the mall with a machine gun, and he didn't think the coupon girl's employment history would make any difference.

'This city,' the coupon girl said. 'I swear.'

'You know, this is all your fault. Why couldn't you just say McDonald's had better burgers?'

She glared at him. 'Why should I let them intimidate me? You let people push you around, you spend your life trying to keep everybody happy.'

'Yeah, I guess,' Billy said. 'Yeah, you're right! That's what's been happening to me for *weeks*.'

'I don't believe anyone could push *you* around,' the coupon girl said, and her lips curved. Billy smiled back. Then a line of bullets scored the wall a few feet above their heads and the storefront window imploded. Billy shielded the coupon girl from the falling glass. 'Thanks,' she said.

He looked up. 'We really have to get out of here.'

'No shit,' she said, and then there was a whooshing and the Burger King across the mall exploded. It felt like an earthquake.

'Now!' Billy said. He hauled the coupon girl to her feet. '*Come on!*'

He took her hand and they ran blindly through the black smoke. The coupon girl stumbled over a piece of rubble and Billy caught her from falling: it was just like a movie. They cleared the smoke and there were NRA soldiers everywhere, but no one was paying any special attention to Billy. Then someone familiar came out of the US Alliance building. Billy stopped in surprise. It was John Nike, the dude who'd ordered him to shoot the Government President in London.

For a second he was tempted to walk up to the guy and slug him. But Billy had other priorities, like getting the hell away, so he started running again. John pulled over a cab and got inside.

He heard a scream, and turned. For a second he didn't know who the figure stumbling out of the smoke was. Then he realized. It was Jennifer Government.

'*Billy! Stop him!*'

He looked after John's cab. It was a bit late for that, he thought. He looked back at Jennifer.

'*Please!*'

'Aw, shit . . .' He looked around. 'I need a gun.'

'Um . . . okay.' The coupon girl bent over and picked up a piece of rubble from the gutter. 'Here, use this.'

'No, a *gun*. Something to shoot with.' But the coupon girl was already hurrying to an NRA soldier. Billy looked at the chunk of rubble. It didn't offer any clues to him.

The coupon girl grabbed the soldier's shoulders and screamed into his face. '*Help me, help me!*'

'Hey! Calm down! Miss!'

'Please, please!' She tugged him in a half-circle, so his back was to Billy.

'Oh,' Billy said, understanding. He stepped forward and hit the soldier on the head with the rock. The soldier yelled and clutched his head. Billy grabbed his rifle.

'Geez,' the coupon girl said. 'I thought you were never going to get it.'

'Shh,' he said. He spread his feet, balancing himself, and lined up the retreating cab. It was a ridiculous shot, really: the car was already a block and a half away and there were about a million people running in and out of the way. 'Just . . . be quiet.'

She fell silent. Billy inhaled. You had to fire during a slow, controlled exhale: it was when your body was steadiest. You had to squeeze the trigger between your own heartbeats. The world dropped away. He fired.

'Holy *shit*!' the coupon girl said.

The tire blew: he saw the spray of rubber. The cab veered ninety degrees, was clipped by a delivery van, and rammed into a storefront. Billy lowered the rifle. The girl was staring at him.

'How good are *you*?'

He looked back for Jennifer, but the smoke had obscured her again. 'Let's get out of here.'

'Yeah, good idea.' She took his hand. 'Where to?'

He smiled. 'You like skiing?'

'Are you kidding?'

'Why?'

'I live in Aspen,' she said. 'Aspen, Colorado. In the winter I work as a ski instructor.' She shifted. 'What? It's not so weird.'

He found his voice. 'I . . .'

'You like skiing?'

'Yes,' Billy said. 'I really do.'

'Cool,' she said. 'Let's split.'

81 FORTITUDE

Today is a great day, Buy thought.

The funny part was that only a month or two ago he'd been ready to kill himself. He was still walking around only because he didn't know enough about guns to locate the safety on a Colt .45. Everything since then, you could argue, was borrowed time.

I am a great person.

His legs were shaking as he entered the Chadstone Wal-Mart mall, and he felt like he might throw up soon. That was funny, too. He wasn't scared of dying, not even a little, but the idea of taking the escalator up to level four terrified him. He couldn't believe that when he got there he wouldn't see a girl sprawled on the floor in a spreading pool of blood.

'Hey. Are you okay?'

He realized he'd swayed; almost fallen. A girl was looking at him with big, concerned eyes.

Buy turned away. 'I'm . . . fine.'

'You sure?'

'Yes,' he said, and it was a gasp. He couldn't breathe. He felt her eyes on his back as he pushed through the crowd. The elevators rose before him, a fusion of steel and shopper.

Every obstacle is an opportunity.

He wasn't expecting to see Violet on this level, and so he stared at her for entire seconds before he realized who he was looking at. Then he started toward her.

She saw him. 'Oh-oh,' she said. She produced a gun. Buy almost laughed. 'Okay, you just stop there.'

'Gun!' somebody shouted. The shoppers around him scattered. Buy kept walking.

'Hey! I'm not kidding. Look, I'm sorry about your kid and all – hey! Stop! You want me to shoot you?'

'Where is Kate?'

'*Stop!*' she screamed, and he saw her finger tightening on the trigger. The realization swept through him: if he died, he couldn't save Kate. He stopped. The gun was two feet away from his chest.

'Violet?' said a young man beside her. Buy thought that was probably Hack Nike. 'Come on, put the gun down.'

'Shut up! You don't care about me!'

'Where's Kate?' Buy said again.

'She's upstairs,' Hack said. 'John's got her. On level four, in the Ni—'

'*Shut up!*' Violet yelled.

'Violet,' Hack said carefully. 'Mall security is probably on the way. Don't make this worse.'

'I know what you're all doing. Everyone's going to get what they want except me! I'm getting screwed over!'

'Nobody's getting screwed.'

'Please,' Buy said. 'I need to find Kate.'

'What's in it for me?' Violet said.

'Please.'

'I just wanted to be an entrepreneur. I just wanted to sell my software and make a little money. Is that so wrong?'

'Violet, you're holding a *gun*!' Hack said. 'You kidnapped a child! You want to know why things haven't worked out for you, start there!'

There was a long pause. Then Violet said, 'There is no justice.' Buy realized her intent a second before she did it. He started to twist out of the way. Then the bullet kicked him and he was lying on his back, looking at the mall's fluorescent lights.

There was some screaming, and people's feet thudding by his head. It seemed like a good idea to lie still, so Buy did that. His bicep was throbbing. He touched it gingerly, and looked at his fingers. They seemed to confirm that he'd been shot.

Hack's face appeared above him. 'Oh, shit, are you all right?'

'I . . . don't know,' Buy said.

'Um . . . I don't think you are. You better not move. It's okay, Violet's gone.'

Buy sat up. It didn't hurt as much as he'd thought. Maybe he was in shock. 'My name is Buy Mitsui. I need you to help me find Kate. She's Jennifer Government's daughter.'

'Oh, man . . .' Hack glanced at Claire. 'Look, we really need to get out of here. We're kind of wanted. I'm sorry.'

'Oh,' Buy said. 'Okay.' He tried to get to his feet. Hack helped him.

'I'm really sorry,' Hack said. 'It's just, if Nike catches me . . .'

Buy's vision glazed white, but he could see the elevators. He began to walk toward them. His arm was starting to hurt.

He reached the second level before Hack and Claire came back. 'Okay,' Hack said. 'I'll help.'

'Thank you.'

'What do you want us to do?'

'Distract him,' Buy said.

320

82 ANCESTRY

Jennifer was running in one direction and about ten thousand people were running in the other, streaming out of a strip mall. She guessed there was nothing to clear an area like a missile strike.

When she got inside, the place was almost drained of shoppers. She was struck by familiarity: the layout was the same as the Chadstone Wal-Mart mall. There were even two sports cars being raffled. But then, these places were probably all built to the same plan. They were standardized.

She spotted John just as he reached two NRA soldiers. He gasped to them, 'Help me! I'm a US Alliance Liaison, there's a woman with a gun after me!' He pointed at her.

They drew their weapons. 'Hold it there, ma'am.'

Jennifer dropped to a walk. She pointed her gun skywards.

'Shoot her!' John shouted.

'Ma'am, you need to drop the weapon, right now.'

She kept walking.

'Ma'am—'

'She's not going to stop, you dumb fucks! Shoot the bitch!' John began to edge away.

'We're not kidding! This is your last chance!'

'All right,' she said. She holstered her pistol. A soldier reached for her. She took his arm and twisted. He gasped in surprise, and she rammed his head into the second soldier's face. They fell to the floor and she kicked their weapons away.

'*You morons!*' John screamed. He ran for the escalators. He was surprisingly fleet: he didn't appear to have been injured in the cab crash. She took careful aim.

The bullet clanged off the escalator's steel sides. John stopped

321

running. He leaned over the railing. 'Are you *stupid*?' In the empty mall, his voice echoed. 'Do you want me to hurt Kate?'

She corrected her aim, but this time he read her intent and ducked. She missed everything. She jogged toward the escalators.

'If my man doesn't hear from me, he'll kill her!' John shouted. But Jennifer didn't believe that. There was a note of rising panic in his voice, and besides, John wasn't the sort to make plans in the event of his own death. She caught a glimpse of him scrambling from one escalator to the next. 'You better back off, right now!'

He tried to give her the slip on level five, but she saw him reflected in a store window, trying to hide behind a pillar. He was doing something with his hands. She raised her gun and carefully moved toward him.

John heard her coming. 'Jen! Don't do anything stupid!'

'Come out, John.'

'I'm on the phone!' he yelled. 'I'm on the fucking phone, do you want me to kill her?'

She stopped.

'That's right, Jen, I have a live connection here. You better think very clearly.' He stepped out into the open. His cellphone was pressed to his left ear. There was a sheen of sweat on his forehead. His business shirt was soaked through. 'Put down the gun.'

'I can't do that.'

'You want me to make him hurt her? I can do that!'

Jennifer looked at her gun. It seemed a pity.

'*Do it!*'

She put the gun on the floor. 'Hang up.'

'Kick your gun over here first.'

'You hang up, I'll give you the gun.'

'Not your place to bargain, Jen. It's really not.'

Jennifer considered. It would be a bad move for her to give

322

John her gun; very bad. She was pretty sure he'd just shoot her. She put her foot on the gun.

'Careful, Jen. Nice and slow.'

'I don't suppose you ever saw any of the kids you had killed,' she said. 'I did. It was in a mall like this one.'

'Oh, *please*,' John said. 'Don't start *moralizing*. I've had about as much of that as I can take. Give me the gun.'

She pushed it with her foot. It spun across the floor, the barrel describing lazy ellipses, until it disappeared off the edge of the level. She heard it hit one of the cars on the ground floor with a bang.

John's eyes bulged. 'Was I not *clear*?'

'Hang up the phone.'

'You couldn't let me go, could you? You had to chase me across half the world. It's pathetic, Jen. You're *obsessed*. You think you changed when you left Maher? You think you grew a conscience when you got pregnant? Bullshit. You were a corporate bitch at Maher and you haven't changed, same as that tattoo. You're not doing your job. You don't give a shit about those Nike teenagers. You're after me for what I wouldn't give you eight years ago. This is *personal*.'

Jennifer didn't think that was a fair characterization. She was going to debate it. But then her cellphone rang.

83 REDEMPTION

A lot of people were hurrying out of the mall, courtesy of Violet discharging a firearm. The Nike Town was just up ahead, and Buy saw a man poke his head out and look at the people scurrying past. As a head, it was nothing to boast about. It looked like Buy felt.

From behind, Hack yelled, 'Hey! Asshole!'

The man's face whipped around. Hack and Claire were by the escalators, waving their arms.

'John, you ugly prick! Hey!'

John stepped out of the store. He was dragging Kate with him. Buy's heart leapt. Kate's face was streaked with dried tears. *Just another minute, honey,* he thought.

'What?' John called. 'I can't hear you!' His free hand slipped inside his jacket pocket.

Buy staggered up to him. His arm was bleeding profusely. 'Excuse me.'

'Hey.' John's face wrinkled. 'What the hell do you want?'

'Forgiveness,' Buy said, and wrapped his arms around him. 'Kate, run!'

'What the *fuck?*' John said. Kate stared at him, frozen. Then she ran. Buy had never seen anything more beautiful than her retreating back and bouncing hair. 'Get off me!'

'Sorry,' Buy gasped. 'No can do.'

'Let – me – go!' John slammed Buy against the Nike Town door, and he lost all his air in a rush. John pulled back for another attempt. Buy suddenly realized that the Nike Town door handles were long metal swooshes, tapered to fine points. That was kind of dangerous, he thought. Someone could get hurt on those.

John slammed him backwards again. Buy heaved himself to the left and swung John around. John hit the door, and Buy lost his grip. He fell to the floor and coughed.

He almost expected to start feeling John's business shoes connecting with his ribs. But not really. It had been a good swing: a very good swing.

'Buy?'

'Every obstacle is an opportunity,' Buy said. He tried to laugh, but it came out as a hacking cough.

Blurry faces appeared above him. 'Somebody call an ambulance! Call nine-one-one!'

'Use my American Express card,' Buy said. He was full of witticisms; he couldn't stop.

'Buy, just stay still.'

'Kate. Where is—'

'I don't know if you want Kate to see this,' Hack said. 'John is . . . he's on the swoosh.'

'Please, I must see her.' Hack started to leave. Buy grabbed him with his good hand. 'Hack. Thank you.'

Hack looked embarrassed. 'No problem.'

Buy closed his eyes. He was going to faint soon, and that wasn't good. There was something he had to do first. He had to hold out.

'Buy! Buy!'

He opened his eyes. Everything was hazy: he couldn't see Kate properly. Then something wet fell on his face and he realized she was crying.

'Hey. I will be fine. Really.'

'Are you sure?'

'I'm really sure.'

'Okay.'

'Now, Kate . . .' Someone started wrapping something around Buy's arm. He felt dimly grateful, but it was starting to hurt a lot. 'There's something I need you to do. It's very important. You have to do it straight away. All right?'

'What?'

'Call your mother,' he said, and passed out.

Jennifer looked down at her pocket. Her cellphone trilled again.

'Don't answer that,' John said. 'Just — just slide it over here. Come on.'

She pulled out her phone.

'I'm serious! Drop the phone!' He was spraying spittle. 'Don't fuck with me, Jen. I'll do it!'

She considered. Then she flipped open her phone. 'Hello?'

'Mommy?'

A surge of emotion rocked her. She couldn't speak. She looked at John. 'Hi, sweetie.'

John dropped his phone and backed away, his palms raised. 'Okay, now, Jen, let's not do anything rash.' His eyes flicked from side to side. 'I think there may have been some kind of miscommunication . . .'

She started walking toward him.

'Jen — Jen! Listen to me. Let's not make any snap decisions! Let's not make any value judgments!'

He broke and ran. Jennifer leapt and caught his jacket at the neck, swinging him into the guardrail. His breath whooshed out of him and then she had him bent over the railing, staring down at the cars below. She forced his arm up his back.

'I wasn't going to hurt her! I swear!'

She whispered, 'She'll be better off without a father like you.'

'*No! Jen, please!*'

'Like the view? Want to see what I saw in a mall like this one, when you killed a schoolgirl?'

'*No!*'

'You were wrong about me,' she said. She took her arm off his neck. It felt better than she had imagined. It was surprisingly satisfying. 'John Nike, you are under arrest for the murder of Hayley McDonald's and up to fourteen other people.'

'What? *What?*'

'You will be held by the Government until the victim's families can commence prosecution against you.' She hauled him up and marched him toward the escalators. He was a pain to move. His legs kept slipping out from under him, as if he was drunk.

'You're *arresting* me? Are you serious? I don't belong in *jail*!'

'And yet,' she said.

85 COMPLETION

By the end of the flight, Jennifer felt ready to murder someone. She shifted and fidgeted; she glared at the flight attendants.

'Shhh,' Calvin said. 'Settle.'

'A stopover in *Auckland*,' she said. 'It's unbelievable.'

'Read the magazine,' Calvin said. 'Or watch the movie. They have computer games; why don't you play one of those?'

'I want to get home.'

'You want me to ask if you can go up and meet the captain, look at the controls?'

She looked at him.

'Thirty-five more minutes,' he said.

'All right,' she said. 'All *right*.' Calvin flicked through a few pages of his magazine. After a while, she said, 'By the way . . .'

He looked up. 'Hmm?'

'It's Malibu Barbie. My tattoo. It's the product code for a Malibu Barbie.'

Calvin blinked. 'Really?'

'I was the Mattel account manager. Plus I lived in Malibu. So I got the tattoo.'

'Oh. Huh.'

'You think it's stupid.'

'No, no. Not at all.'

'It was very hip at the time.'

'I'm sure it was.'

Jennifer eyed him. 'You won't tell anyone this, right? It's a little embarrassing.'

'Sure thing,' he said. 'Your secret is safe with me, Barbie doll.'

'Please don't call me Barbie doll,' she said.

Jennifer deplaned feeling like she'd been beaten, and walked down a long white corridor where sliding doors opened onto a mass of people. For a second all she could see was a jumble of color. Then Kate was running toward her. Her legs weakened.

'Mom!'

She dropped to her knees and Kate cannoned into her. She felt tiny arms around her neck. 'Oh, Kate!'

'I missed you.'

'I missed you, too, sweetheart.' She closed her eyes. 'I love you so much.'

'I love you, too.'

'Watch Mommy's shoulder,' she said. 'Let me look at you. Wow! Buy must have taken good care of you.' She looked up, and there he was. He looked awkward. He smiled as if he were trying to stop himself.

'Hi.'

'Come here,' she said.

'Down there?'

'Yep.'

Buy crouched and she hugged him, too. 'Ow,' he said. 'Watch Buy's arm.'

'Oh! Sorry.'

'It's okay.'

She touched his face. He looked like he wanted to kiss her, so she leaned forward and they kissed. 'Thank you so much,' she whispered. 'Thank you—'

'It's okay.' He looked embarrassed. 'I'm . . . happy to have you home.'

'Me, too.' Her voice was a whisper. She hugged them both as tightly as she could. Kate's small hand wrapped around her own. Jennifer's face pressed against Kate's hair, and its familiar smell suddenly squeezed a sob out of her. She cried for a while, and nobody moved.

'Hello?'

'Jim GE?'

'Who is this?'

'It's Jennifer Government.'

'Oh—'

'Jim, I'm calling to tell you the Government has identified and located the perpetrators in your case. I'll be sending you my case file in the next few days. You should choose a legal firm so you can prosecute.'

'You know . . . you know who killed Hayley?'

'Yes.'

'Oh, God. Thank you – thank you so much—'

'You're welcome. Goodbye, Jim.' She put down the phone.

Buy was looking at her. 'All done?'

'Yes,' she said.

EPILOGUE

86 REHABILITATION

The woman flicked the pages of John's CV back and forward, back and forward. He forced himself to wait. He was not going to lose his cool with this interviewer, no matter how much of a condescending, tight-haired, natty-glasses-wearing bitch she was.

She looked up. 'You were a Nike Liaison?'

'Yep.' He drummed his fingers on his thigh.

'Wasn't there some trouble . . . wasn't Nike one of the main instigators in the—'

'Aw, that was such a beat-up.' John smiled. 'Okay, yes, some people got a little gung ho, but the rest of us were far more cautious.'

'But you did work for US Alliance?'

'Not on *that* side of things,' John said. 'I was more into customer promotions and the like.'

'I see,' she said. 'And this was . . . twelve years ago?'

He held the smile. 'That's right.'

'And since then you've been . . .'

'Working on special projects.'

'I see . . .' She stood and offered him her hand. 'Well, thanks for your time, John. We'll be in touch.'

'That's it?'

'Yes.'

He made himself say: 'Thank you for the opportunity. I really appreciate it.'

She smiled. On his way out, she said, 'Have a nice day, now.' His hand tightened on the handle. His vision flared white. He closed the door carefully and walked away.

For a city devoted to the automobile, Los Angeles wasn't offering John much in the way of cabs. In fact, it wasn't offering him much, period. He regretted coming back here. He remembered this place as being much cooler.

He walked along Wilshire for a block and a half before gaining a cab's attention. As he walked toward it, a guy in a snappy suit emerged from a restaurant and strode forward.

'Hey!' John said. 'Asshole! My cab!'

The suit turned. It was the Pepsi kid.

'Holy shit,' John said.

The Pepsi kid – not a kid anymore, of course; he was as old as John had been – grabbed his hand and shook. 'John! I almost didn't recognize you! What are you doing here? Man, how long has it been?'

'Hey, wow,' John said, thinking: *What was his name again?*

'Geez, sorry, I didn't mean to steal your cab.'

'No . . .' He waved the apology away. This was an opportunity, bumping into the Pepsi kid: a huge opportunity. 'How've you been?'

'Great, just great. I'm V.P. Sales at PepsiCo now, did you hear?'

'No.'

'Man, I'm so jazzed to see you out of jail. No place for a guy like you. When did they let you out?'

'Two weeks ago.'

'What a gyp,' the kid said. 'I still can't believe Nike wouldn't front for your defense. I mean, I know why, but . . .'

334

'Those assholes—' He stopped himself. 'Anyway, I'm looking for a job.'

'Hey! If you're in need, Pepsi will take you in a second. I mean it.'

'Really?'

'You're the man, John. Just say the word.'

John felt a rush of genuine gratitude. The Pepsi kid had been a good friend, except for the end, and that could be forgiven, couldn't it? Under the circumstances. 'Pal, I'll take anything with "marketing executive" in the title. I'm getting crucified out here.'

The kid's face fell. 'Well, John, we couldn't put you in marketing.'

'What?'

'It'd be a bad idea to put you at a customer interface. After . . . you know.'

'So what kind of job are you talking about?'

'We've got an opening in Credit, and I think something in Order Processing—'

'*Credit?* You think I'm going to work in *Accounts?*'

'I'm trying to help you out, buddy.'

'Hey!' the cabby called. 'Someone getting in here or what?'

John jabbed at the kid's chest. 'I'm an *executive.* I was *this close* to executing the greatest goddamn business coup in history!'

'Yeah, well,' the Pepsi kid said, 'no offense, but close doesn't get the cigar, you know?'

'You little fuck,' John said.

'I have to go. If you want a job, give me a call.'

'One day, we're going to finish what we started!' John shouted. 'Nothing's changed, you know! One day, we're going to try this again, and *win!*'

'Maybe,' the kid said, getting into the cab. 'But not with you, John.'

ACKNOWLEDGMENTS

Most of the time, being a writer means sitting in front of a computer and fighting against the urge to play Minesweeper. It's like that for a couple of years and then you get published and everyone wants to talk to you at once. But some people are there from the beginning, and these are the ones you can't do without.

Kassy Humphreys, Gregory Lister, and Roxanne Jones read an early draft and provided excellent, much-needed feedback. So did Wil Anderson and Charles Thiesen, in amazing and profoundly helpful detail that took far too much of their time. Geoff Wong vetted some chapters for wild claims about computer viruses. Carolyn Carlson convinced me to cut a major character, which was painful and difficult and a really good idea. Todd Keithley, my ex-literary agent, provided enormous support throughout the writing of the book, and when he quit his job left me devastated and convinced I'd never be published again. Luke Janklow, my rockin' new agent, made sure I *was* published again. He also landed me with an editor more insightful and assiduous than I could have hoped for in Bill Thomas, who somehow managed to write a five-page edit letter I totally agreed with. Finally, Jen, my brilliant and beautiful wife, kept me happy when the words weren't coming, got excited with me when they were, and continues to make my life hilarious.